MW01130516

CRUCIFIXION

Shirley Giebel

Copyright © 2015 Shirley Giebel
All rights reserved
First Edition

PAGE PUBLISHING, INC.
New York, NY

First originally published by Page Publishing, Inc. 2015

ISBN 978-1-68213-413-9 (pbk)
ISBN 978-1-68213-414-6 (digital)

Printed in the United States of America

Dedication

For my daughter, Gina

Acknowledgements

Crucifixion, is tightly framed around Holy Week in a fictional locale in northern New Mexico. But in the actual towns and villages even today, tensions run high as curiosity seekers hope to observe the religious rites of *Los Hermanos Penitentes.*

Doing final research, I was permitted inside a Penitente *morada* (meeting house) after my description and car were confirmed and a camera strictly denied. I attended a Catholic Maundy Thursday service in one of the remote villages where young Penitente men participated, and was told the priest attends some of their rites "not as a priest, but a Penitente." This unprecedented access helped me understand this unique brotherhood's devoutness and sacrifice, and lent a richer, more even-handed perspective to these beliefs and rituals as they play out in the novel.

There are many to thank. First, thanks to my friends and family who read the manuscript, and commented. Thanks for the time extended by New Mexican county sheriff's personnel, and a newspaper editor. Major thanks to Charles MacKay, formerly General Director of Opera Theatre of Saint Louis, and now General Director of Santa Fe Opera Theatre, who kept me from the worst errors in opera references. To you all, any mistakes are my own. Names, characters, incidents, places and certain locales are the product of my imagination, or are used only as the backdrop of fictitious events.

Chapter One

Ojo Tres Mineral Springs, New Mexico
First week of April 2001

The man removed the black hood and rubbed his hands over his hair several times. His body was wet with sweat under a long, priest-like robe. Shedding it quickly, he rolled the garments into a tight ball and stowed them in a canvas bag. Hopefully there wouldn't be many more occasions to wear them.

Without turning on lights, he eased into the shower stall and felt blindly for the water faucets. The water spit hard, its cleansing heat unknotting muscles. He wanted to linger, but didn't want to risk being heard and maybe questioned. The faucet squeaked as he shut if off. He stood scarcely breathing to see if it had raised an alarm.

There was urgency in his movements as he dressed and slipped out into the night. The mountain air settling to the desert floor was so dry, cold and clear it seemed to pinch his nostrils as he pulled it into his lungs. He zipped his jacket to the chin and pulled on a pair of leather gloves.

Straining his ears for the sound of a car, he waited before approaching the bridge, but heard only the roiling water passing underneath. He trotted across, veering off the road on the other side. The moon gave stingy light, and he came up hard against the fence that marked the Ojo Tres property line. Cursing to himself, he climbed over, careful not to catch on the top strand of barbed wire. On the ground again, he set course along a dry wash dense with rabbit brush, taking care to avoid prickly mats of cactus lying in ambush.

The ground began to slope upward sharply. As he gained the top of the rise he stood for a moment to get his bearings. In his path, not far ahead, he made out the bulky shadow of a house and what appeared to be an adjacent mobile home. He cursed himself for not having checked out the area more closely. He thought he'd have a clear path all the way to the highway.

Sharp staccato barking cracked the still night. From the sound, it was a big dog and close by. The man froze. A light came on in the trailer silhouetting a figure in the doorway. A sleepy voice commanded loudly to the dog, "Go get it or shut the fuck up."

The man swung around and raced back down the wash, running low to the ground. The barking stopped. Hoping he was far enough away from the house, the man once again emerged at the top of the wash, the roadside gas station less than twenty yards away. Relief flooded over him

He waited, catching his breath. The light in the trailer blinked off.

Suddenly his eye caught a flash of white. Trotting fast, nose to the ground, he saw the dog working the trail he had just come. It tracked with the deliberateness of a wolf, driven by faithfulness to protect its master and his property. He could hear its labored breathing.

The man scrambled up the bank to the back of the building. In the thin yellow glow of the night yard light, he saw the dog lift its wide head, small pointed ears focusing like radar, hackles raised, slobber in ropy strings swinging from its jowls. As it came closer he saw the dog was fluffy and sweet-faced, too fat.

He looked for something to throw and came up only with handfuls of loose rocks. "Go on, get out of here, go home." The man kept his voice low but heavy with threat as he pelted the dog with stones.

It backed off a few feet, a deep growl growing in intensity as the dog gathered itself low to the ground. It charged fast, snarling, ears flat to the head, bared sharp-crowned teeth snapping the air. The man barely had time to brace himself against the wall and draw his jacket sleeve down over his gloved fist.

Long-ago, training kicked in. Take out the dog! Right down the gullet. As the dog lunged, jaws open, the man drove his knotted fist with all the force of his body down the open throat.

He pulled up sharply, swinging the animal's feet off the ground, clutching the dog's neck, with his free arm pulling its head to his chest. The dog gagging against the trapped fist twisted its body clawing for purchase against the man's torso, fighting to break from his grip. Its back paws caught in the man's belt, nails clawing into tender belly flesh, giving the dog a momentary toehold that kept its neck from being snapped.

The man, crying out with pain, used his greater height and weight to twist away and slam the dog to the ground, throwing his body on top of it. Pinned, the dog snarled and snapped as the man's arm was jerked from its throat, both of them fighting for more air.

In that instant of release he felt the dog's powerful muscles drawing up under him, memories of his master's command still alive. Fear welled up in the man. He grabbed the animal's neck, fighting to get a chokehold around the thick cushioning ruff of hair that neutralized the pressure of his fingers.

"You son-of-bitch, die." The man, breathing hard, spit dirt and gravel from his own mouth, felt himself tiring even as the animal seemed to be gaining renewed strength, a determined light in its soft brown eyes. "Die! Die!" With all his might, the man hammered his elbow into the soft exposed hollow of the dog's neck, crushing down with all his weight on its throat, pinching shut the cold leathery nose, until he felt the animal's body go slack and still.

Dead, the dog looked like it might be asleep on its favorite rug. He sat beside it sucking in air, his head in his hands waiting for his heartbeat to steady. Muscles twitched with the sudden ebb of adrenaline.

Aware he'd lost too much time, he rose and, keeping out of the light, slid around the edge of the wall. He looked up and down the highway. Satisfied that no one was coming, he grabbed the dog by its collar and dragged it into the road. Hopefully someone would hit it before daylight and make it look like a road kill. If not, he didn't think anyone would connect the dots.

He fed quarters into the pay phone and punched in the numbers, watching for passersby. He counted off a dozen rings. He clicked off and said each number aloud as he punched them in again. The phone was picked up before the ring completed.

"Hello?" There was irritation in the voice.

"It's me," the man said.

"Was that you just called? Why'd you hang up? How many times do I have to tell you ten rings is only a minute?"

"Shut up. We've got a problem, Houston." He grinned at his own attempt at humor. He was feeling upbeat, anticipating the effect his news would bring at the other end of the line.

"That kid I told you about," he started.

"What *kid*? This person got a name?"

The questioning irritated the man. This asshole always carried on conversations like doing an Abbott and Costello routine. Precise names. Precise details. Slowing down the real point of the conversation.

"Justin something. I don't know his last name." He explained as patiently as he could, "He's the new kid who works down at the

Springs cleaning the bathhouse pools and taking people out on trail rides. He's the one who's screwing around with old Martinéz' niece."

"That kid. Okay, so what's up that's urgent enough to call me at this hour?" And then with a hard edge to his voice, he added, "I take it you had enough sense not to call from the hotel."

The man considered telling him about the dog and what this effort to telephone had cost him. He said only, "You know I did. Now shut up, please, before I run out of change."

He took a deep breath, regaining some of the thrill he'd felt. "I followed this Justin kid, okay?" He spoke rapidly to avoid interruption. "He knows. He went straight to the right shaft at the old mines. I don't know how he found out, but I wouldn't put it past him to try to rip off some of the stuff."

No need to tell you I was careless and the little shit-heel swiped the map and coordinates off my desk.

"You followed him?" It was like a delayed reaction. "I hope to God he didn't see you. He didn't, did he?"

The man had expected the question and was ready with an answer. "Yes, as a matter of fact, I *wanted* him to see me. It scared the hell out of him too."

He held the receiver away from his ear waiting for the explosion at other end of the line and wasn't disappointed.

"What do you mean? You actually let him see you?" The shouting turned to curses and finally into a whining tirade. "You're making me sorry I ever listened to you or got involved in this. We just need until Easter, you goddamn fool. It means money, big money, unless you screw it up."

He sucked in breath and kept on ranting. "Some people get cheated; they deserve to get cheated. You're one of them. You're too damn dumb or too cocky, I don't know which."

What he said struck a nerve, and the man at the other end of the line responded angrily, kicking his shoe heel into the hard gravel of the parking lot. "You son-of-a-bitch, you're only in this for the money. My father settled for being cheated, but by God I'm not. I intend to settle this score. And I'm doing it my way, with you or without you."

"Okay, okay, okay. So this kid saw you. Tell me how that's a plus?"

"He saw what he thinks is a Penitente. He didn't see me, my face or anything that would identify me."

"Okay?" He drew out the word as if waiting for the punch line.

"There's only a handful of us staying at the Springs right now. Mostly curiosity seekers who check in every Holy Week season to hunt Penitentes, trying to get a look at what these guys do. They were sitting around bullshitting about how the Brothers beat themselves bloody and crucify and, how one of them, dressed in a robe and hood, cuts a deep cross in your back with a razor-sharp rock if he catches you spying on them. This Justin was hanging on every word. These guys had him going pretty good about how Penitentes go after strangers for new blood. He was scared as hell." The man stopped to push more change in the phone.

"So you think dressing up in a robe and hood like one of the Brotherhood scared this Justin kid off?" Scorn seeped through every word.

The phone shook in the man's hand. What did this butt-wipe know about anything? He wasn't there when, near death, his father unfurled the black robe, pressed it and the hooded cowl into his hands.

"Wear this mantle like an avenging angel." Then the old man, confused and lost in time, lapsed into the *alabados* of his youth, the ritual hymns of the Penitentes. But his meaning was clear. It was up to him now to take back his birthright and extract vengeance for the injustice done to his father.

He thought of the dead dog and felt a moment of regret. It too had been on a mission. It deserved better than it got. And he deserved better than this pisser's scorn.

He came back to the moment and said icily, "We may need a more permanent solution for Justin."

"You watch yourself, buddy. No violence. That's our deal. And don't you forget it."

"Yeah, that's easy for you to say. But I'm on the ground here. You're not. This kid needs watching. I need you to send someone to help keep an eye on him. I can only do so much without blowing my cover."

"I'll do what I can, somehow. No violence! You've got to promise."

The man stared at the highway watching a tumbleweed driven by the wind bounce across the asphalt and brush against the dead dog

"I'm not the violent type," he said reassuringly. He smiled to himself. *Unless pressed.*

Chapter Two

St. Louis, Missouri
First week of April 2001

She flipped open her phone on the third ring, her father speaking before she had a chance to answer. "Sunny, I know it's early. I'm sorry to wake you, but I needed to catch you before you got off to convention hall. I have to talk to you."

She wasn't asleep. She was sitting in her car in a church parking lot, her eyes on the house across the street.

The better part of the night had been spent imagining Doug, in the bedroom she'd shared with him for more than a year, spooned around Ms. Knockers, his hands cupping her oversize assets.

She couldn't decide whether to ring the bell and confront them, or find a way to do them in. She wanted what? Hurt for hurt? Revenge... if she could get away with it scot-free? Not sure of her answer, she was beginning to scare herself.

In the near dawn darkness her father's unexpected call shook her back to reality.

"Something's gone wrong with the project," she said, expecting the worst, her stomach churning.

"No. Calm down. Doesn't a wall full of awards count for anything? Why do you go to pieces every year when you put this thing on? Everything's fine. I need to talk to you about another matter entirely."

Despite his assurances, she still had doubts about her creation, putting a girl in a larger-than-human-size-bird-suit as a love interest for St. Louis Cardinal's mascot, Fredbird. Today would wrap up months of work to capture the duo pursuing and wooing each other in ads and commercials showcasing the city's attractions and business community for the sake of charity.

"Then this call had better be damn important. You know I've got a lot going on today." She felt resistance gather like a ball in her chest. Much as Sumner Bay, Jr. adored her namesake and business partner, Sumner Sr., was a master at getting his way. She didn't need him to dump anything more on her plate.

He was saying, "Meet me for breakfast. I can't do this over the phone." He rattled off the place, a hotel coffee shop downtown off Convention Plaza, near where she was headed anyway.

Before agreeing to meet, she flushed out a hint of what he wanted. They had a new client with a project in New Mexico and he desperately needed her help with a problem with her mother.

It didn't make sense. Their public relations firm had all the business they could handle right here in St. Louis. And from where she sat, her parents' life was perfect. *Unlike my life, which sucks like a draining toilet clog!*

If she used a couple of shortcuts she could get to her home in the city's Central West End, shower, dress and race downtown by seven. She signed off with Sumner and hung a right onto Forest Park Parkway.

"You'll have to go to New Mexico… Santa Fe and a little place called Ojo Tres. A week or so tops. I'm counting on you, Sunny."

She'd known something was up ever since she'd watched him work his way to the booth she'd staked out in the busy coffee shop. There was a subtle look of defeat about his shoulders even as he acknowledged greetings, shook hands, stopped to talk to a group of young women at a center table. Mr. St. Louis Public Relations in action.

She'd noted the way the girls' eyes followed him, proof that even at 63, he could still turn pretty heads. Had he ever been unfaithful to her mother? Resentment at Doug blazed up in her for making her doubt every man alive.

"Why are you looking at me like that? Whatever it is I didn't do it." He smiled his irresistible George Clooney grin, sliding his large frame into the booth and signaling the waitress, placing their order.

"I know my timing is bad. I'm sorry," he said. "But things need to move fast for this client. It's someone I go way back with. Someone I can't afford to—" His jaw tightened, working in and out.

Not his usual upbeat response to new business, Sunny noted.

Then in a eureka moment, she pointed her finger at him. "You're about to tell me this is some big fat freebie for a friend, aren't you? Pass on it, Sr., that's my vote. Isn't your line always we can't afford to be like the good-hearted girl who gave away a million bucks worth of sex before she realized it was worth something?"

The waitress brought sweet rolls and coffee. Sumner impatiently jingled change in his pants pocket until she left.

"Not this time, Sunny. We'll be paid handsomely. Whatever time or expense it takes. Cream?"

"No thanks. And it's legal?"

"I hope so." His voice faltered, and he wasn't smiling. "Just hear me out. No interruptions, okay?" He drummed his fingers nervously until she gave a curt nod.

"The client is Kay Waring. She's a major arts patron around town. I'm sure you know who she is."

For a moment Sunny couldn't place her. Then she remembered the statuesque blond with the athletic build holding court from a wheelchair in the lobby of the Loretto Hilton Center when her parents drug her to last year's *La Boheme*. She had one foot in a stacked-heel MaxMara pump, the other encased in a plaster cast to mid-calf.

Her mother nudged her in the ribs whispering with some heat, "That's Kay Waring. She probably tripped running to ground something younger and hotter than hubby. I don't know whether Homer Waring doesn't see or doesn't care. Him," she said with a tip of her head indicating the solemn man with calm brown eyes and thinning hair at his wife's side.

At the time, Sunny had been startled at her mother's uncharacteristic gossip. Now Sunny wondered if there was more behind Molly Bay's invective, and she listened with sharpened senses to catch some betraying nuance in her father's demeanor that he had romantic history with Kay Waring.

But his gray eyes were steady on hers and as innocent as a cherub's as he said, "Our main connection is the Opera board."

Asked and answered. He and Molly had nurtured Opera Theatre of St. Louis since it was only the spark of an idea in a small cadre of opera lovers. A passion she didn't share with her parents.

"So what's the big problem?" she asked.

"Kay's sunk a bundle underwriting a new opera work with an up-and-coming composer she discovered at a New Visions/New Voices symposium in New York a couple of years ago. A young guy from Santa Fe named Raymundo Manzanares.

"Their deal was to have a finished work last month. Kay's worked her tail off and managed to schedule a reading and presentation in a matter of weeks with one of the national art groups that encourage new American works. If they gain that group's approval and endowment, then they've got a real shot at this. Suddenly, for no apparent reason, Manzanares starts dragging his feet, missing deadlines, making excuses. Now he refuses to see Kay or talk to her at all."

"I take it there's no contract," Sunny injected, raising an eyebrow.

"No, but that's beside the point. One of Kay's theories is that Manzanares is afraid, or has been threatened." He held up his hand warding off her questions.

"The opera as it's now written could be construed as a betrayal of sacred traditions and rites of the Penitentes, a secretive brotherhood, which is strong in New Mexico. According to Kay, the Penitentes keep a low profile but wield powerful social and political influence all the way to the New Mexico statehouse."

"The other possibility is he's trying to cut Kay out and peddle this work himself directly to an opera company."

"Can he? It's his work," Sunny said.

"Not likely. Right now Manzanares is just a talented nobody without a clue how difficult it is to get an opera actually produced. The opera world has more politics and intrigue than Washington. Kay knows the ropes. She has influence with the right people. He needs her whether he admits it or not."

Sunny sipped her coffee, picked an almond and some frosting off the top of her roll. "Then surely she can pull the purse strings and bring this guy into line. Let her handle it on her own. Better yet, let her hire a lawyer. That's where this is headed, you know."

"Kay wants to avoid that at all cost. It'll just tie things up so nobody wins. She wants us to find out what Manzanares is up to first."

Sunny threw him a wary look.

Then he dropped his first bombshell about the need for her to go to New Mexico. The second one, it had to happen day after tomorrow.

"You're as crazy as this Kay. Forget it," Sunny blurted. "Suppose, just suppose I get to talk to Manzanares. What makes you think he's going to confide in me if he won't even talk to his benefactor?"

"Kay says she has a foolproof plan. I've set up a meeting for the two of you tomorrow."

"Cancel it. There are a million reasons why I can't—make that won't—leave town right now." She told him briefly about Doug, sparing most of the details, and reminded him Michael was coming home for spring break and she was taking time off to spend with her son. "Get someone else. Better yet, you're the big opera buff. You've made all the promises. You take this on."

"Kay is adamant that a woman stands a better chance dealing with Manzanares. And I don't want anyone else from the firm involved in this."

"Now you're making it sound shady. Don't I have a say?"

He pushed away his untouched coffee, and fiddled a moment smoothing his tie. There was a drawn look around his eyes. "Kay is putting on a lot of pressure. We have to do this," he said. "If we refuse it could hurt us."

He looked at her and something flickered in his gaze too quick for her to read. Shame? Guilt? What?

"Do you want to level with me or do you want me to use my imagination here?"

"All we've got in this business is our reputation, Sunny. Please believe me when I tell you we've got to do this. I've told you everything I can tell you, all I will tell you," he amended, catching his upper lip between his teeth and tapping his closed fist on the table's edge before standing abruptly.

"Where are you going, Sumner? Sit down. What about my mother? You said there's some kind of problem. Is she okay?"

He sat back down, reached over and took her hands in his. "No, Sunny, Molly is not okay. You've been so wrapped up with Doug that you haven't even bothered to call her in weeks."

"I've had a few things of my own. I'm sorry. Tell me."

He gave a bewildered shake of his head. "I don't know. She seems depressed, maybe clinically. She won't talk to me about it, and refuses to see a doctor. She's fixated on an invitation from her old college friend. Remember Ann Martìnez?"

"You mean Tsia, Ann Tsia?"

"Not anymore. Seems she's divorced her Indian artist and taken back her name. The Martìnez family owns a mineral hot springs called Ojo Tres, and run some kind of spa. It's an isolated burg way up in northern New Mexico.

"Ann goes on about the healing waters and the magic of the place. Molly is determined to go. I'm asking you to go look after her."

"Well, now, isn't that just too convenient?" Sunny snapped, pulling her hands away from his. "I can't believe Molly—"

"I didn't orchestrate this, whatever you may think. This business with Kay is just a coincidence. One I thought might work out to give you and your mother some time together."

"And don't forget, make Kay Waring happy."

"This doesn't have to be a Mexican stand-off—" He pushed a slip of paper with Kay's number across the table.

"No. I can't deal with this right now. I'm late as it is," she said, trying not to notice he looked as if the starch had been wrung out of him as he walked away.

With sudden resolve Sunny punched in the number and arranged to meet Kay Waring at four o'clock.

Chapter Three

Kay Waring's slim pumps clicked a staccato beat across the parquet floor, breaking the late afternoon stillness of the nearly deserted Cardwell's at the Plaza where Sunny had chosen a dark little table off the bar.

Unseasonably warm for the end of March, she nevertheless arrived in full-length dyed mink. The fur, with tawny stripes of shading, was a subtly darker golden shade than her hair. A pale lavender skirt peeked from underneath as it swirled around spectacular legs.

Sunny groaned inwardly. Talk about Neiman Marcus meets Banana Republic! She rose to greet her, wishing she'd chosen something less casual than the khaki pantsuit with epaulets and gold buttons. *Please God, when the mink comes off let there be sweat rings on her Armani armpits.*

Kay Waring shook her hand, her eyes falling like a laser on Sunny's cuff. "Did you know you're missing a sleeve button?"

Well, this is off to a good start.

She dropped her coat and handbag in an empty chair, ordered coffee without consulting Sunny and settled herself with a flurry. "I have a dinner engagement. So we need to make this quick."

No argument from me.

"You made the noon TV news, so I feel I know you. Please call me Kay. I understand from your father that you've just been jilted by that vacuous news reader on Channel 10. The one who tries to sound like Tom Brocaw."

Kay continued, oblivious to Sunny's cool silence. "You can do better… while you still can… with those blue eyes and that cute angelic face. What are you, mid-thirties? If you want my advice, concentrate less on Prince Charming and more on King Midas. Rich husbands, my dear Sunny, make the best accessories."

She laughed, petting the mink. "Sumner is well connected, after all. Unless you really like being single, you should take advantage of that."

Sumner's "connections" were responsible for her being here right now. Reminding her won no points. "I'll take it under advisement," she said levelly.

Kay exploded with sudden laughter, startling the waiter pouring coffee, causing him to spill a dollop and rushing red-faced for another cup. "In your place I'd have told me to go to hell by now. You know how to put your emotions in your pocket and be objective. That's good. That's very good, because this job is going to take the ability to handle the unexpected."

"We need to stop right here, Kay. I don't want this job. Swallow some pride, fly to Santa Fe and take care of all this with Senor Manzanares yourself," she said, surprised at her own brusqueness.

Kay gave her an appraising look. "If you must know, I did." Her pale skin suffused deep red with suppressed anger. "I stood outside the house I paid for and banged on the door and begged him. He wouldn't let me in. He won't speak to me. He's walled himself off in that damn studio."

"Try again. He might be ready to listen to reason."

"You don't understand. We're not dealing with logic. Raymundo's shunning me is all emotion and religious hogwash, his way of paying me back because I found out things about him I shouldn't have. Things he'd taken a sacred oath not to tell."

She let the words lie there, repeatedly tucking her hair over one ear while she seemed to consider whether to explain or not. "It may not come as a surprise that Raymundo and I became lovers," she said edging closer. "We didn't intend for it to happen. But one night we'd drunk a bit too much wine—" She lifted her shoulders in a what-can-you-do shrug.

"I'll spare some of the more salacious details, but in the small of his back he has thick ridge-like scars along both sides of his spine, each about five inches long, and in the form of a cross. My God, the first time I felt them it was like finding he had Dr. Spock ears or something!" She gave a throaty laugh.

"Did he explain?" Sunny asked, wondering how this bit of elaboration was pertinent.

"First he tried telling me he got those scars in a Boy Scout initiation." She rolled her eyes. "I told him, 'Honey, I've laid more Boy Scouts than you can count and none of them had anything like this.'" The tip of her tongue slid like a small pink grub between her teeth, then back, breathing faster. "I bided my time, until he was pumping away in the short rows. Then I pulled away and threatened to leave unless he told me. Suddenly he yells '*The Sello! The Sello. La Obligation.*'"

She gave out a little snort that sounded triumphal. "Turns out he was talking about the Penitente seal of obligation. In case you miss the implication here, Manzanares is a practicing Penitente. I hope Sumner told you something about this secret brotherhood?"

Sumner. What was he getting her into? If Kay's revelation was supposed to have an impact on her, it did. Utterly speechless, she barely managed a nod.

"Ray is the genuine article. This seal is serious stuff, a fifteenth century ritual from Spain that requires fasting and making vows of adoration for Christ before the actual cutting of the flesh. The slashes in his back were made with a razor-sharp piece of flint by a *Sangrador* from his village, dressed in a black robe and hood. This is just an ordinary person, understand, not a doctor. No surgical tools and no anesthetic.

"That same night I discovered the seal, Ray nearly dragged me to his studio. He shoved a pair of old work boots into my hands, the leather stiff and cracked. Then he confessed the opera he's written isn't fiction, as he first told me, but the truth about the ritual murder of his father and what happened to his mother in the small Penitente village of woodcarvers where he grew up.

"His father, his mother's lover, was married. She got pregnant. Unfortunately, her lover's father-in-law was the *hermano mayor* of their village, a position of undisputed power within each Penitente community. Raymundo's mother believed with all her heart that it was he who manipulated the choice of her lover to be the *Cristo* for the village's Good Friday rite of crucifixion. The choice is one of honor, so her lover went willingly to be scourged and bound to the Cross with ropes. But they planned all along for him to die.

"The death was unreported. When he was missed, the villagers claimed he just left the village and no one knew where he was. No one in the whole community, not even Ray's mother, dared say otherwise. After his death, his shoes were placed on her doorstep to let the village know of their sin. Otherwise, in such a death, the shoes would have gone to his wife as is the Penitente custom. It's the kind of rough justice that many think is practiced even today in these small remote villages."

She paused, fidgeting with her spoon, her eyes looking as if they were fixed on something happening elsewhere. "Ray only learned the truth from his mother as she lay dying. Believe me, these people are intent on keeping their secrets.

"He wanted revenge, and wrote the opera as his way of getting back at the people of his community who shunned his mother and did nothing about his father's murder. Now I believe he's having second thoughts because he's broken this strict Penitente vow of silence, first to me and then to the world, if he leaves the libretto as it is now."

She took a deep shuddering breath. "I'm not letting him get away with some half-ass absolution for betraying Penitente secrets. I tried to convince him that its time for real scrutiny of these medieval practices. We argued bitterly over this."

"I think you're overdoing the sensationalism for your own purposes," Sunny said firmly. "I'm sorry, but I'm having a hard time—"

"If you doubt me, there's been plenty written by outsiders trying to penetrate the Penitente world for you to confirm the things I've told you are real."

Kay, looking up from under her brows at Sunny, shook a finger warningly. "Emotions run high at this time of the year in New Mexico. I advise you not to tell anyone anything I've told you about the Penitentes. Ordinary people become militant if they think you're sticking your nose in where it doesn't belong."

"If I were going, I seriously doubt, with the exception of Manzanares, that I would be running into any of this sect."

Kay ignored the "if." "It's not a sect. It might be a school teacher, a carpenter, a business owner, anyone, and they might be more or less committed to the beliefs, so don't be so sure. You might be among believers and not even know it."

"Frankly, I see nothing our firm can help you with."

Kay held up her hand entreating Sunny to listen. "Ray's last volley before we stopped talking was a foot-stomping insistence that he would only proceed if I promised the world premiere be at the Santa Fe Opera. From the beginning, we'd been in agreement that our St. Louis opera company is our best shot, when the time is right, because it has a well-deserved reputation for new works. And I have a certain influence—"

She rapped her knuckles against the tabletop with each following word. "Understand neither opera company is committed or involved at all."

"Ray's insistence on Santa Fe is the best indication that he intends to revise the work and go it without me."

She leaned toward Sunny, and with a conspiratorial smile said, "Favorable, early publicity to drum up interest in this new version would be very enticing to Raymundo, if he is trying to peddle the opera himself. A skillful journalist would also be able to reveal his intentions. That's where you come in, Sunny."

"If that's the direction he's taking," Sunny shot back, "you need someone from the local press. Or a stringer from a national publication if there's a legitimate angle. I'm from St. Louis. Why would he talk to me?"

"Because, vain bastard that he is, he didn't turn down an interview with a photojournalist from *People* magazine. He's eagerly expecting you. I can almost hear him laughing his ass off at my expense because he thinks I set this interview up for him before his defection,'" the last word ringing bitterly. "It's all explained here." She took a folded letter from her handbag and handed it to Sunny.

Sunny stared in disbelief. The letterhead of the magazine looked authentic. The credentials introducing her as the assigned photo journalist were phony. So was the signature over 'Assignment Editor'. It was unmistakably Sumner's handwriting.

Sunny shook her head as if she could make this go away. "This isn't ethical. Sumner wouldn't—" She choked, knowing that Sumner already had.

"Ethics," Kay snorted in answer. "This is just harmless subterfuge, a little undercover game, nothing less, nothing more. No one gets hurt."

How could this woman coerce Sr. into doing this? "And if I won't do it?"

"You will, Sunny. In case you haven't guessed, I collect old skeletons from other people's closets. Sumner's not always been a good boy." She actually wagged her finger, and Sunny held herself in her chair watching it circle inches from her face. It wouldn't do to bite it off in the middle of Cardwell's, certainly not with the place filling up with people.

"I think you're bluffing."

"That's of little consequence. Sumner knows I'm not. Try me and you'll both be sorry."

Scenarios raced through Sunny's mind. Is Sumner hiding an infidelity with Kay after all? Or is he hiding something more serious, something illegal, or criminal? Her father couldn't have done anything bad enough to kowtow to Kay Waring. His reputation was sterling. But why couldn't he tell her?

If Molly was as emotionally fragile as he implied, would she be able to handle some revelation of Sumner's infidelity or misdeed? Sunny suddenly felt fiercely protective of them both. She would take the damn assignment in New Mexico. *Only I'll choke before I tell you so!*

Kay picked up the conversation as if they'd just been discussing the weather. "I understand you and Molly might be making a little vacation out of this. Are you really going to stay at Ojo Tres?" she asked, as if whiffing overripe cheese.

Damn you. That's information you could only have from Sumner. Sunny pushed back her chair and stood gathering her things in clumsy haste.

Kay stood too. "It's settled, then. Tickets and instructions are at your office, along with a cell phone with proper 'credentials'." She wiggled quotation marks with her fingers. "Caller I.D., you know. Your flight to Albuquerque leaves day after tomorrow." She reached for the mink and settled it around her shoulders. "This has been lovely."

"Fuck you," Sunny said, and not in a low voice, bringing appreciative notice from the Happy Hour crowd.

Chapter Four

After alerting her indispensable assistant Moira to the outcome of her meeting with Kay, Sunny maneuvered through rush hour traffic mentally doing laundry, packing, pitching perishables, stopping mail and, best of all, dumping client projects on Sumner's desk.

As Sunny entered the office, Moira called, "Sorry to disappoint, but there's no web site for Ojo Tres, just a hyperlink listing hot springs and spas in New Mexico. It gives address, telephone and fax number, but no e-mail."

She swiveled in her chair. "Sunny, Max hunts with an old army buddy all over that northern New Mexico country. He's willing to convince Sumner that two city girls have no business traipsing off— oh my god, you're not going to cry on me, are you?" She thrust a crumpled but clean tissue into Sunny's hand.

Sunny shook her head, unable to speak around the lump in her throat. Moira had married Max Metzger and come to work for Sumner right out of high school, she and Sunny kind of growing up in the business together. Max, a former cop, now ran his own security business. They were pit bulls where Sunny's welfare was concerned.

"You guys are just the best," she managed finally. "But it won't do any good to talk to Sumner. There's something else I want you to do for me Moira." She jotted quick instructions. "Charge it to Kay Waring's tab," she smiled wickedly. "Now go home to that sweet Max."

Chapter Five

Albuquerque and Ojo Tres, New Mexico
Nine days before Easter, 2001

It was already early afternoon before Sunny and Molly were loaded up and ready to roll out of the airport in Albuquerque.

Trying to get the feel of the unfamiliar rental car, Sunny nearly missed their exit off the interstate onto a narrow two-lane highway.

"Ann's explicit directions," Molly said, intonating the importance of something chiseled on a stone tablet instead, as Sunny noted, scrawled in her mother's inimitable hand on the back of a used envelope.

As civilization slipped away, Sunny already hated the miles and miles of gaunt, arid, lonely country that stretched ahead, an alien landscape as far as her eyes could see. They rode in stubborn silence, until Sunny punched on the radio to a lively Mariachi band and Molly punched it off.

Throwing both hands heavenward, she burst out "I don't want you here. You don't want to be here. But here we are." She slapped her thighs, hands curling into tight fists. "You just up and take Sumner's word for it that I'm suffering from depression. Well, young lady, it isn't depression. It's a bad case of Sumneritis!"

She turned toward Sunny, "Did he tell you he asked his mother to sell her house and come live with us? Not asking me if it's all right, he just up and asks her. She's considering it."

Her voice rose as if preparing to man the ramparts. "I'm fed up with saying 'Yes, Honey' to Sumner and doing for everybody else." She thumped a staccato beat mid-chest. "This is my time to do things I want to do. I grabbed at this invitation from Ann. I need a friend right now and a change of scenery. Are you listening?" she demanded.

"I'm not deaf," Sunny snorted, taking her eyes off the road momentarily to meet her mother's blazing blue eyes.

"I know all too well that Sumner has put you in one of his famous binds because he doesn't have Kay Waring's big brass balls. She, incidentally, is off limits totally as a subject of discussion, as is your father, and just about everything I've mentioned. If you can live with that, we may even enjoy ourselves."

Molly settled into the seat, arms akimbo, wearing a satisfied look, her face flushed and almost as red as her hair.

Her parents' rupture was making Sunny's insecurities bloom like teenage zits. Despite her public take-charge competence, deep down there would always live her rudderless eighteen-year-old self, raising a baby alone after a high-school marriage gone sour, no money, little education, or job. Molly and Sumner had stepped in, a solid, dependable unit. She didn't have a clue how to do the same for them. She had never felt so torn.

The prospect for the next few days seemed as inviting to Sunny as eating dirt.

They counted only a handful of cars and trucks and one gas station since leaving Eagle Wing thirty miles back. Sunny was sure they had taken a wrong turn, and pulled over. She got out of the car and tried to call Ann, turning the cell phone first one direction then the other, walking a few feet down the shoulder, across the road, to no avail. "I'm just not getting a signal," she said, climbing back into the car.

"A phone booth is so much more reliable than those cell things," Molly opined, as Sunny pulled back on the highway.

"And, just where in the hell do we find one of those?" Sunny waved her hand at the expanse of brushy desert all around them.

"I told you to stop back in—"

"You turned down every place I suggested," Sunny said, through gritted teeth.

When she spotted a sign for a roadside café ahead, she made up her mind, "Look, we need a pit stop and it's either here or on the side of the road," she countered Molly's "This is just a hole-in-the-wall. I'm not going in there."

Sunny laid Molly's growing disagreeableness to second thoughts about this leap into the middle of nowhere. Who knew what this place they were headed was really like? Or Ann, for that matter? It had been years since Molly had seen her. College chums, the friendship had become for the last several years only an exchange of Christmas letters and occasional telephone calls.

Sunny was losing patience. "For Pete's sake, just use the john while I see if someone here can give better directions to Ojo Tres than what we have."

The only other patron was settling up his check with a large fat man in an apron, who talked like he owned the place.

Molly returned, "I used the last of the paper," she said in a stage whisper, as she slid onto a stool next to Sunny. She pulled a couple of paper napkins out of a metal container on the counter top and slipped them to her, eyebrows moving like butterfly wings.

The man approached with two plastic sleeved menus, which Sunny considered redundant, since the apron over his protruding stomach was incrusted with bits and pieces of what looked to be his entire bill of fare. Several days' worth, in fact.

"Just a couple of bags of potato chips," Sunny said quickly, pointing to a rack behind the counter. "And two of those candy bars. And, uh, two Cokes for here, some—" She spotted bottled water, pointed, "Two of those to go." She gave her most winning smile as she handed him money for the purchases. "I'm hoping you can give us some directions."

"Where you headed?" he said affably.

"Ojo Tres."

"What is this place?" he queried as if perplexed, as he counted out her change.

"Ojo Tres," she repeated. "It's some kind of resort, a spa and hotel… mineral springs. Surely you've heard of it." Are we that far off course, Sunny wondered, with a little edge of panic?

She read the hastily jotted directions Ann had given Molly. "According to our friend, we're supposed to take this highway all the way from Eagle Wing."

He listened without seeming comprehension. "I've only been here a couple of years." He gave a helpless gesture with the open palms of both hands. Then, as if a light dawned, "Ah, maybe you mean that place people around here call the 'Springs.' Calling it a 'resort' threw me. Yeah, the place I'm thinking of is maybe fifteen, twenty miles up the way you're headed." He gestured in a northward direction. "Be prepared, you're going to hit dirt road about five miles from here."

"Thanks for the warning." She gestured a hurry-up-and-get-through to Molly, still sipping at her Coke and munching chips. Sunny headed for the john, calling back "I want to get to Ojo Tres before dark."

The man followed them to the door and stood watching as they got in the car.

Starting the ignition, Sunny noticed her fuel gauge. "Great, we had to rent a gas guzzler with a tank the size of a flea bladder." She leaned out the window and called "Is there a gas station somewhere near here?"

"Eagle Wing is all I know. I'm told there used to be one up the way you're going. They did a little auto repair, fixed tires and things. You might take a chance that they're still in business. Out here you never know, but people up that way got to buy their gas somewhere, no?"

Sunny considered. If they doubled back, they would be looking for Ojo Tres in the dark, or forced to overnight in Eagle Wing. "Thanks. You're right. We'll take our chances."

"Good luck," he called.

The road seemed to disappear into a canyon of startling tent-like rocks, golden in the waning sun, capped at each pinnacle by formations that looked like carved heads, sentinel-like guardians of the narrow road stretching between them. In the distance were rugged snow capped mountains. And from the sound of the motor they were climbing.

As predicted, at exactly five miles, the narrow pavement gave way abruptly to a graded dirt road, and the landscape changed to dark mesas and clumps of nut pine and yucca. Forced to slow down to avoid hard, dry ruts in places, the miles seemed endless. Then inexplicably, the road turned again into a thin ribbon of dust-swirled black top.

Just ahead, Sunny spotted the hoped for gas station. That was the good news. The bad news was the "Closed" sign posted on the door. She had been counting on filling the tank and getting directions. *Now what?*

Molly poked her arm, pointing out a pay phone on the side of the building, a hint of smugness playing over her lips.

"Probably out-of-order," Sunny said sourly.

She fed in some change and punched in Ann's number. She let the phone ring a long time but there was no answer. She rechecked the number and dialed again.

"Molly," she called, "Ann's not home. Maybe we should try the hotel. Give me the number."

The look on Molly's face told the whole story. "I don't believe this!" Sunny stormed, totally exasperated. "And of course there isn't a damn telephone book."

Molly was out of the car, looking close to tears. "You got me off in such a hurry. I just didn't remember to take it with me. So shoot me."

"Just get back in the car while I figure this out." Sunny looked helplessly around. Black rocks, like giant cinders, spilled down to the road amid dry sage-colored plants. A plane, too distant to hear, shone silver in the last rays of sun. The air had sharpened with a creeping chill. In the almost painful silence, she thought she heard voices.

She followed the sounds, peering down the steep slope at the edge of the parking lot. Three children arranged bouquets of dried weeds on a mound of dirt under a stick cross that wouldn't stay upright. They got hurriedly to their feet when Sunny called down to them.

"Station's closed until morning, huh?"

They looked at her without speaking.

Sunny tried again. "That looks like a grave."

The eldest of the trio, a girl of about ten nodded. "Our dog got killed."

"He got ran over," the youngest said, pointing accusatorily toward the highway.

"I'm sorry," Sunny said. She meant it.

"Can you help us? We're trying to find Ojo Tres—the Springs," she added, using the local designation. "Do you know where it is?"

The older girl never took her eyes off Sunny, but pointed back over her shoulder.

Sunny could see only a thick line of trees where the girl pointed and nothing that remotely resembled a building. Further questioning brought no better response.

"Well, thanks anyway. I'm so sorry about your dog."

Less than a mile after leaving the station, they saw a driveway leading to a high fence of thin split cedar poles almost hiding a house and two small sheds behind it.

"Look, there's someone," Molly said, pointing to an elderly man peering around the end of the fence, where two hogs rooted at some dried stalks.

Sunny stepped out of the car, waving and smiling, asking directions.

He shook his head saying something that sounded like Spanish.

Sunny struggled for words. "Uh, *donde esta las Ojo Tres?*"

He stared at her a moment, then pointed back over his shoulder as the girl had done, followed by a stream of rapid words.

"*Gracias.* Thank you." Sunny called, smiling at the man and climbing back into the car.

"Well?" Molly asked.

"I haven't heard Spanish like that since that summer we went to Spain. I didn't understand a damn word. Now I see why New Mexico adds U.S.A. to its license plates," she said, spinning gravel as she backed up the drive. "It sure isn't apparent!"

The gas gauge icon lit up, pinging its near-empty warning. The landscape had changed again, the road bordered by a stretch of tall cottonwoods. Molly lowered the window, sniffing the air. "I think I smell water."

"In the fucking desert?" Sunny did an eye roll to keep her sanity.

Just then the headlights popped on. Molly jabbed her finger excitedly, "The sign. See, there."

The black lettering was faded, but Sunny made out: Ojo Tres, Three Springs Hotel and Mineral Baths. An arrow pointed left.

Easing off the main road onto a gravel lane, they crossed a single-lane bridge over a swift-running stream.

"What did I tell you? Water," Molly said triumphantly.

The hotel nestled in an amphitheater of flat-topped sandstone bluffs where the road came to an end. "Oh. I'm not sure what I expected," Molly said, with an audible exhale, as they pulled to a stop in the parking lot.

Sunny raised her eyebrows as she counted only three other cars. "I, for one, thought there would be more people staying here. The place looks almost deserted."

"Look at that veranda," Molly said, unfazed. "This looks like an old Mexican hacienda. Look how elegant," she said, her hand air tracing the building's curved arches supported by nine thick carved pillars, pointing out glazed tiles inset in thick fortress-like adobe walls.

Sunny made silent note of the peeling paint around window sills, pots holding drooping vestiges of dead flowers and a general rundown look.

"Are you coming?" Wrapping her arms around herself, Sunny signaled with her head for Molly to follow. "There are lights on in the hotel at least."

She pushed open an iron gate entering an adobe-walled court-yard. Broad walkways edged an unfilled swimming pool, where clumps of cottonwood leaves lay in brackish water in the deep end.

"I'm definitely going to spend time in those," Molly said, point-ing to a group of rustic wooden rockers on the veranda.

"Poolside?" Sunny inquired snidely.

She wanted to scream at Molly that this was one big mistake, but seeing the anticipation on her mother's face she settled for, "Ann surely will be here."

Chapter Six

Sunny swung open the lobby door to shouting, angry voices. Before she had time to pull back, a young man burst through the doorway clipping her shoulder and sending her into a sprawling pratfall.

"Holy shit! I'm sorry. Let me help you up." The silver stud in the hollow under his lower lip bobbed up and down with his agitated apology. "You hurt?"

Sunny waved away his help. She guessed him to be about Michael's age and he seemed genuinely sorry. "Nothing's broken, I'm okay," she said, with more assurance than she felt.

He swung his head around as if he thought his adversary would be bursting from the lobby after him. "I'm screwed now for sure."

On the back of his head Sunny was startled to see what looked like a dull bruised circle starting on his neck and continuing up his closely shaved scalp. Even in the bad light, and partially obscured under the battered Stetson he wore, it appeared to be a crudely tattooed snake swallowing its own tail. *No tattoo parlor did that. More like a jailhouse pastime.*

As he turned back to her, she waved him on. He shot her a grateful look and disappeared into the night.

"Well, welcome to the Land of Enchantment," Sunny said, feeling more aggravated by Molly's burst of laughter than her accidental attacker.

"You have to admit it has its funny side," Molly explained, try-ing to draw her face into a sober look.

"Tell that to my thirty-seven-year-old butt bones," she growled, moving gingerly.

Molly held out a hand. "Let me help—" She stopped when she saw Sunny staring straight ahead and turned to see what it was.

A man had stepped from behind the registration desk and was standing poised and motionless watching them from across the lobby.

Sunny had to tear herself away from the slightly simian black eyes that stared like two beams directly into her own before she could take in the rest of the face. More disturbing, he looked vaguely famil-iar, then she realized the tanned, fleshy face looked a lot like Picasso in old age. He had the famous Spanish painter's same virile stocky body and his head was broad and slick bald. Slightly bow-legged, he wore high-laced work boots run over at the outside below a baggy pair of Dockers. His black tee and corduroy shirt seemed youthful, though Sunny guessed from the flat brown spots that covered his forehead that he was older than he looked.

They tried not to stare openly, but found themselves mesmer-ized as he shuffled across the lobby toward them. His legs jerked up as if lifted by an unseen hand, the feet flopping loosely before land-ing flat. The high stepping, foot flapping sequence propelled him forward in a kind of zigzag dance.

"Jake leg, as I live and breathe," Molly said in a stage whisper, glaring Sunny into silence.

The man ignored their ill-concealed curiosity. "I've been expect-ing you," he said, the voice raspy and strong.

You won't catch me taking a shower here, Norman Bates. Sunny rolled to her knees and stood, making a great show of brushing dust from her jeans to cover her reaction to him

Molly moved forward, gushing. "Well, you must be Ann's Uncle Leandro. I'm Molly Bay. I'm so glad to finally meet you. And this is my daughter, Sunny."

He bobbed his head to each in greeting.

"Sunny, Mr. Martínez owns Ojo Tres." Turning back to Leandro, Molly said, "I understand from Ann that this place has been in your family for three generations. She told me prehistoric Indian tribes, then Spanish conquistadors came here."

"Our land was originally part of a Spanish land grant. My grandfather was the first Martínez owner," he said. He moved his hand as if brushing aside further pleasantries.

"I must explain to you about Anna—Ann," he said, correcting himself. "My niece prefers the anglicized name to the one she was given."

Sunny detected a definite note of disapproval.

"She's so sorry not to be here, but she had an emergency with her daughter, María. Her youngest, but you know that. We've got a situation with that punk who ran you down." His voice was venomous as he continued, "María's just sixteen, and he's been sniffing around her. He just got a warning from me. Leave her alone, or else."

A believable menace in his look and tone convinced Sunny that she wouldn't like to be on the wrong side of Uncle Leandro.

He looked suddenly uncomfortable. "I'm sorry, loading you with all our problems." He turned away abruptly, waving them to follow him.

His jerking movements looked painful to Sunny as he made his way across the shag carpet, matted into dreadlocks by wear. Looking around she found the small lobby stark and forbidding, dimly lit by a single overhead fixture. The furniture was overly plain, masculine, consisting of a sofa with cracks in the leather and a couple of matching chairs in front of the unlit stone fireplace. A collection of arrowheads and old pottery, some merely large shards, rested in a glass case. Battered antique crucifixes interspersed with mounted strands of twisted barbed wire hung on the dark wood-paneled wall above it. *What would you call this style? Early Monastery?*

"Ann left you some provisions," he was saying, and Sunny turned her attention to him. "The dining room is already closed and everyone's gone home. Your apartment has a kitchenette. I'll get your key and explain about the water and—" His voice trailed off.

"We're not staying in the hotel?" Sunny asked. "We'd rather—"

"No, no. Ann wants you to have the apartment near the bath-house. It's our best accommodation. Come."

Hoisting the box of groceries in her arms, they followed the beam of his flashlight across the courtyard.

"Be careful where you step," he warned as they skirted the pool.

"Is it broken or just not open yet?" Sunny asked, shifting the heavy box in her arms.

"It's to be repaired," he said over his shoulder. With Leandro's flapping footfall, their procession made a strange rhythmic crunching in the fine gravel that sounded unnaturally loud to Sunny's ears in the palpable silence of the night.

He halted at a small adobe bungalow that set apart from a row of about eight common-wall units in a long, low building. There were no cars in front of any of them.

Sunny's nose wrinkled at an earthy, slightly rotten-egg smell. "What's over there?" she asked, pointing to two large buildings that abutted each other and seemed to be linked by a portico to their unit.

"Those are the bathhouses," he said. "Women's is right there. The other is the men's. There are working mineral water pools in both of them, since you seem interested."

Grabbing the handrail, he hoisted himself up onto the low stone porch of the apartment. "Let me get the lights on." Inside, he snapped the switch, bringing on a harsh overhead in the kitchen and bedside lamps that spread small yellow islands in the dimness of the combination living and sleeping room. The space smelled unused and decidedly musty to Sunny, with an accumulation of faint rusty minerals and gas stove odors.

Using the heel of his hand, the old man pushed open the sash in the kitchen's deep-set windowsill, as if reading her mind.

Sunny eyed the refrigerator. *Wow! Harvest Gold, probably circa 1970.* She opened the door and peered inside. "The lights burned out."

He ignored her, striking a match from a box he dug out of his pocket, the flame igniting the pilot light on the outdated range.

"You'll find the water takes some getting used to. What flows out the tap is perfectly safe to drink, but it's heavy in minerals." He scrubbed his hand over the brown stain in the sink. "Good for what ails you, and let's say it makes an interesting coffee. Ann put a jug of the water we drink around here in your box of supplies. It comes from one of the springs too, but it's a better taste and doesn't smell."

Molly called from the other room. "This is absolutely charming. It's a fireplace," she said pointing to a small egg-shaped opening above a wide extended shelf at floor level that seemed sculpted into the thick whitewashed adobe wall opposite the beds. Molly reached out letting her hand run over the smooth curved surface.

Leandro came around the wall that separated the rooms, moving like a marionette. "That's the traditional fireplace in this country. We'd better get a fire started."

Sunny stuck her head out of the bathroom. "There's no shower or tub, or am I missing something?"

"All baths are taken in the bathhouse. Ann will explain it all to you in the morning."

Ann has a lot of explaining to do.

"These baths, they're supposed to be a miracle cure for whatever ails you?"

"We don't claim any cures. Can't, of course. But our family's seen some miracles through the years from people taking these waters." He hesitated, seeing Sunny's skeptical look, "Except for me, of course. Water doesn't undo this kind of damage."

"Now that you've brought it up, one can't help noticing your walk—"

"I get questioned a lot," he said gruffly, then launched into what seemed to Sunny a well-practiced tale.

"We ran a pharmacy here in the old days. During Prohibition and for some years after, we did a big business selling a medicinal mix called Jamaican Ginger. It came in two ounce bottles, with roughly the same alcohol as a shot of whisky—" he said, pausing a long moment as if he'd lost his train of thought.

When he spoke, his words seemed less rehearsed to Sunny, almost a soliloquy.

"After Repeal, my father let me peddle Jake out in the pueblos. It was cheaper than booze and legal for the Indians. There was money to be made," he said. His next words were forced out as if something heavy was pressing down on his chest, "I was just a kid. What happened wasn't my fault."

Molly and Sunny exchanged glances. Was Leandro having a senior moment?

When he spoke again, he seemed recovered and clearly back in spiel mode. "Our supply was shipped from the east coast. Some profiteer began lacing the Jake with a synthetic chemical that later proved to be a neurotoxin. It turned a harmless patent medicine into a killer and a crippler," he said, fumbling with the short pieces of firewood he was trying to lean upright against one another in the fireplace.

"Tippled too much of my own poison and got the Jake leg. End of story."

"There were songs written about the phenomenon," Molly chimed in. "A musician, who—"

"Yeah, I know," he said, cutting off further comment. He scooped kerosene soaked sawdust from a coffee can sitting on the hearth, and sprinkled it on the wood. He held a twist of lighted newspaper to it until it caught, straightening up as the wood began to blaze, releasing an almost spicy, piney fragrance.

"There's more piñon wood on the back steps," he said, handing Sunny two keys, and moving toward the door.

"I don't see a telephone." She'd expected something with a rotary dial about the size of a breadbox, based on the age of rest of the furnishings.

"We only got a public telephone in the lobby when it's open."

"What happens if there's a medical emergency?"

He looked at her blankly for a moment. "Who would you call? We're pretty remote here, Miss. It's not like the city."

She brought out her cell phone from her jacket pocket. "I suppose this won't work either." She had hoped her inability to reach Ann with her cell was just a fluke.

"You got that right." He backed out the door and closed it behind him.

"Molly, I want some answers," Sunny yelled, kicking off her clogs and padding into the kitchen after her mother.

She was at the sink, her back to Sunny, holding a can of soup. "I don't know about you, but I'm starved," she said.

"Forget the food. Forget the gas. I'm ready to push the car back to Albuquerque. Surely you expected something better." Sunny was unrelenting, listing Ojo Tres' shortcomings, Ann's disappearing act.

Her mother kept her back to her through the whole tirade, her head with its tousled red curls sinking onto her chest.

"Why would you want to come here, to this god-awful run-down stinking water hole? Sumner is going to have a fit when I tell him."

Molly's knuckles turned white as she gripped the sink. She whirled around to face Sunny.

"Don't tell Sumner. Please, please, don't tell Sumner. You're as judgmental as he is, Sunny. Do you realize that about yourself? Instead of being so disappointed, why can't you just see this place as rustic? Treat it like an adventure. I don't ask for much from any of you. Why can't you make it easy for me just once?" she asked bitterly, tears rolling down her cheeks.

Undone by the tears, Sunny busied herself shutting the window, the latch closing reluctantly. "I won't tell Sumner," she promised against her better judgment.

Molly dried her tears with the backs of her hands, and said shakily, "I do agree Leandro Martínez is a bit scary. I think we upset him asking about his condition. Ann talked about it once, but it's been so long ago I don't remember much, except there was more to it. Some young Indian boys died, I think. Maybe that's what he meant by it 'not being his fault.' Maybe it'll come to me."

Switching gears, she asked, "What about our luggage?"

Sunny hesitated, thinking of the dark parking lot.

"Do you want me to come with you?"

"No, just heat up the soup. I'll be fine," she said.

She took a few steps, searching out stars in the velvet black of the night sky, stopping to listen every few seconds for unfamiliar sounds, aware that her heart was beating faster than normal. It was times like this she regretted giving up smoking.

When she reached her car, she was surprised and a little relieved that several more cars had pulled into the parking lot nearest the hotel, illumined by a low-watt light on the corner of the building. All the late arriving cars were nice, upper-end, classy even. Somehow she'd imagined the clientele in K-Mart floppies and bathrobes driving RVs. Maybe she was misjudging this place after all. *But why aren't there more lights on? There's not a light in any of the rooms.*

45

She was just ready to pop the trunk when she heard a suppressed cough nearby, close enough to smell cigar smoke and hear low voices. The sudden red glow on the drawn cigar helped her locate two shadowy figures partially concealed by a large tree.

Should she acknowledge that she saw them? "Sure is cold out here tonight," she decided to call in a cheery conversational tone.

They split apart at the sound of her voice. Without answering, one man headed back toward the hotel at a fast walk. The other passed briefly under the yard light before slipping into the darkness beyond. *What in the hell is that guy wearing? It looks like a long coat and a hood of some kind.* The hairs suddenly stood straight up on the back of her neck.

With Kay Waring's warnings about the Penitentes flooding her mind, she fumbled for the bags, just grabbing the essential gear they'd need tonight and in the morning. *Damn it, the rest can wait.* She sprinted back to the cottage.

Chapter Seven

Eight days before Easter

All but the last car rolled out of the parking lot headed back to Santa Fe. Jimmy Dodson looked up at Leandro Martínez from the pit of his Mercedes coupe letting his hands rest on the steering wheel. It was nearly two in the morning, but he was in no hurry to leave.

Leandro trembled with loathing. First the father, then the son, and now the grandson. He hated Jimmy's sharp-nosed face, a genetic rubber stamp of the father and grandfather. It had the same confident politician's smile, the same flat ruthless eyes that could magically switch on sincerity in campaign photos. He had the same penchant for expensive suits and stylish cars. Only Jimmy wasn't content with the power of Dodson & Dodson and the state legislature, as had his forefathers; he had his eye on Washington D.C.

As long as there is a Dodson alive, Leandro concluded, his past was going to remain a stone around his neck. "What do you want to talk about?" he asked with dread as he leaned down resting his weight against the car.

"I want to thank you for the campaign donation." Jimmy emphasized the words and laughed as if he'd cracked a joke, patting his chest pocket conspiratorially. "It's generous."

Leandro gave a derisive snort.

The high-stakes poker game played in the back room of the hotel provided a gentlemanly conduit for making untraceable payoffs to the Dodson family. No checks, no chits, just cash. *Like internal bleeding,* Leandro thought.

The scheme had been Jimmy, Sr.'s idea, worked out with Leandro's father. It was the price for the lies and perjury that kept Leandro safely out of jail.

"I don't mind the money so much, Jimmy. But I sure as Christ hate looking like such a lousy poker player losing to a wet-behind-the-ears pup like you," he said through a tight smile, resting his hands on the chrome housing of the car's window. "This can't go on forever," he said with quiet challenge.

Jimmy pushed Leandro's hands away and wiped the chrome with his handkerchief, tossing it into a leather trash canister under the dash.

"Murder doesn't go away."

"And just how would you explain your family's overlooking a little issue like murder all these years?"

"I wouldn't have to. Just a word in the right places would do the trick, Leandro. The Indians are better organized now than in your day. You know and I know there are still people in the Pueblo who remember what happened to those five Indian boys."

"It happened to me too."

"Yeah, but you didn't die. You just got the walk." He jerked his shoulder up and down in a pumping motion mocking Leandro. "And you supplied the 'weapon,' shall we say."

"I didn't know—"

"You didn't want to know. You thought you knew more than your old man."

"It's water under the bridge."

"You think so? Some smart Indian lawyer gets access to those old Jake bottles still locked away in Grandpa's trial evidence, what with DNA and all that shit? You're toast, man. I can turn those over anytime I want, Leandro. Anytime I want. It wouldn't even have to be a criminal case. In these politically correct times you could be tried for civil damages." His laugh was mirthless and cruel.

Leandro didn't trust himself to speak

"That Indian, Tómas, got screwed, and you know it. I can't imagine what his tribe might extract in retribution if the truth were to come out. But I suspect your holdings with land and water rights here would be a damn good start. This would make one helluva spot for one of their casinos. And if that weren't enough, I wouldn't sleep too soundly if I were you. Someone just might come after you for revenge."

Jimmy was enjoying himself. *Looks like he's about to take a dump in his pants.*

Leandro pushed his face in close to Jimmy's. "You're bluffing. Without more evidence or a witness, you've got nothing. Time's on my side. And I'm through letting your family bleed me on this. Understand?"

This was the moment Jimmy had been waiting for, the royal flush for real. "Oh, did I forget to tell you? Tómas Acoma has come home after all these years."

The effect on Leandro was better than he expected. The old man stumbled backward, sucking in his breath sharply, as if someone had literally pushed him.

Blood drummed in Leandro's head blotting out Jimmy's laughing face. Tómas Acoma alive? No word for sixty-one years, it had been reasonable to assume Tómas had died, and everything he knew with him.

Recovering, Leandro charged, his hands reaching out as if to grasp Jimmy's neck. "You're making this up, you lying son-of-a-bitch."

Jimmy hit the electric button, the car's window sliding up, leaving only a crack. Jimmy continued his taunts. "His son came to see me last week. His son knows all about what happened back up there on the mesa, Leandro. Tómas came home just to set the record straight with him after all these years."

"His son!"

"You boys were so young. But you know how it is in the Pueblos. Tómas had a girl pregnant. And here's the best part Leandro. Talk about truth being stranger than fiction. This is the real mindblower. Guess who his son turns out to be? *Tony Tsia.* Your Ann's husband, well ex-husband, is Tómas Acoma's son." He let the words fall like hammer blows.

The old man roared with disbelief and shock, then pressed his hands against the glass and spoke through the narrow crack, his voice a hoarse whisper. "Even if this is true, why did Tony come to see you?" he said.

"Tómas remembered the Dodson name from the trial, Leandro."

"You're my lawyer, don't forget that."

"Precisely. Tony knew I'd deliver the message."

"Which is?"

Jimmy lowered the window halfway, keeping a sharp eye on Leandro. "Revenge, plain and simple, old man, to settle the score for Tómas. But I can handle Tony Tsia. All you've got to do is worry about me."

He loved seeing Leandro spluttering like this. "Maybe you'd better reconsider shutting me off." Turning on the ignition, he gunned the engine. "Bye, bye Leandro. See you next week. Oh, and brush up on your poker, for god's sake. I'm in the middle of an expensive campaign."

Chapter Eight

Sunny said nothing to Molly about her encounter with the hooded man in the parking lot. She lay awake, watching the reflection of the firelight dance on the ceiling, not able to convince herself she'd been imagining things.

Sunny pressed the button at the side of her watch, lighting up the dial. *Two-damn-thirty. I need some sleep.*

Her hip was aching from the fall on the veranda. In the bathroom she found her bottle of Tylenol and downed one dry, not wanting to risk the water. She put another log on the fire and wandered into the kitchen, testing the window latch and rechecking the safety chains on both doors. She wished mightily for sturdy deadbolts like she had at home.

Being quiet, she stepped around Molly's bed to the window that faced the hotel and peered outside. The parking lot was almost deserted again. *What's going on? I didn't imagine those cars.* She peered into the shadows, watching for movement, with a growing sense of vulnerability.

She slipped around to her own bed. She felt in her suitcase until she found what she was looking for. A year ago, when she was still green about her inner city neighborhood, she'd opened the door to strangers. They'd knocked her down, tied her up and burglarized the house. When she wasn't hurt further, she felt grateful. Then she couldn't sleep; she was afraid all the time. Then she was angry and decided to take matters into her own hands.

She felt comforted now by the weight of the gun in her hand and was glad, despite Molly's vigorous protest, that she'd gone through the hassle of declaring its presence in her checked luggage. She slid in the clip, slipping the gun into her handbag, close enough to grab in the dark.

Across the way, she watched a light moving in a bobbing motion through the hotel lobby. Leandro, she wondered? A room lit up momentarily, a figure moved across it, then blackness. She continued to watch, eyes feeling like two burnt holes.

Reaching his office in the hotel, Leandro shut the door quickly, standing with his back against it, as if he could shut out Jimmy's revelations.

In the bright light, he shot a disdainful look at the old framed photos of Ojo Tres, his parents and grandparents and brothers that lined the wall, saddling him with the past. He'd pack them away in the morning. It's time for something more than the calendar to change in here… and fast.

His grandfather, who won the hacienda in a poker game, knew nothing about sheep or farming and never bothered to learn. He might have lost Ojo Tres altogether except for the foresight of Leandro's own ambitious father, who took advantage of the 1920's tourist expeditions spawned by the art colonies in Santa Fe and Taos. He turned the place into a thriving hotel and health resort where people flocked to take the waters.

Not a day of Martin Martínez' life went by, including the day he died, that he didn't implore his son to hold on to these Springs. "Never forget, Leandro, there's nothing more precious than water in a dry land." *Too bad he only saw its worth as a watering hole,* Leandro said to himself. *The time is past for people sitting in it or drinking it from little cups, old man.*

Sitting at the desk that had been his father's, he swiveled the chair around and spun the combination on a big steel safe, taking out a thick manila envelope bearing the corporate logo of Arizona and New Mexico Land and Mine Consultants.

Water, water, water, the new oil of the West, the land company said, promising a buyer for Ojo Tres in no time. He thumbed through pages of documents and tables. The possibilities excited him. Bottling the water. Direct flow water rights for irrigation. A thermal energy plant. And the green gold of golf links. He planned to live out his last days as a rich man.

The thought of his father spinning in his grave brought a smile to his face. His brothers, Antonio and Leon, were long dead, and with them their devotion to keeping the Springs basically unchanged as long as there was a Martínez alive. There was no one to stand in his way. Ojo Tres was his, and his alone, to dispose of as he wished.

As to his brothers' heirs, there was only Ann. He had no intention of giving Leon's daughter anything. Antonio had a son, but whatever happened to the child, no one knew.

Little María, once his favorite, was a disappointment. Ann's two elder sons were established in Phoenix. Besides they were too like their father, too Indian, for Leandro to consider seriously as heirs. He owed nothing to any of them.

He threw the land proposal back into the safe and locked it, Jimmy Dodson's threats returning like a kick in the stomach. What if he's telling it straight?

Tony Tsia, Ann's ex, is actually Tomas' son? By God, Tony's a vengeful enough bastard to go after me, and with Tómas' testimony and Jimmy's evidence...

Leandro wadded a piece of paper and hurled it at his father's portrait. "Goddamn you, old man," he cursed at the photo. "If only you hadn't turned our Jake business into a pissing contest, how different all our lives might have been."

He put his hands over his ears, but he couldn't shut out the words shouted at him right here, at this very desk, all those years ago.

"You will obey me, Leandro. Destroy every last goddamn bottle, do you understand?" his father said, waving a letter he held scrunched in his hand.

"Why? Tell me why. I demand to know." Leandro made a grab for the letter, his father blocking his move.

"You demand? You demand?" his father shouted. "I'm in charge here, and you'll obey me."

Leandro's mind raced to the box hidden in the horse barn. Just the one final deal and it would be full enough with bills and coins to get him out of Ojo Tres for good. He wasn't going to let his dreams be ripped from him on his father's whim.

He needed the Jake, but it was only the means to a more lucrative end. When his Jake buyers didn't have money, they paid Leandro in the crafts they had few ways to sell.

On a winding back street in Taos, he'd found a dealer hungry to get and willing to pay hard cash for the pottery, jewelry, carved saints, feathered dolls and rugs. Leandro soon became impatient for more to trade than he could realize from the time-consuming pharmacy business.

He found Tómas and the boys, already accomplished thieves, and struck a deal. He gave them all the Jake they could drink, and just enough money not to arouse suspicion in their pueblos, to supply him with what the dealer wanted. No questions asked.

"I'm not getting rid of the Jake, no matter what you say. This is stupid." Shaking with anger, Leandro pushed his face in open defiance to within inches of his father's.

His father's blow sent him reeling across the room.

The striking of the clock jolted Leandro. It hurt to breathe, as if he was strangling on the old rage. He might hate this office with its bad memories and rebukes, but he found comfort in knowing he'd proven one thing in his life—no one had better get in his way.

Chapter Nine

He'd better not be late. If he still had a job after last night's fight with the old man and knocking that lady down.

He jammed his feet into the gray snakeskin cowboy boots that were his pride and joy, hobbling toward the refrigerator. He popped the top on a can of soda drinking it in gulps. Ripping the paper off a candy bar, he stuffed most of it in his mouth in one bite. Grabbing a clean tee shirt, he pulled it over his head and hurried out the door of his bunkhouse quarters.

He busied himself with cleaning equipment in the bathhouse, but couldn't shake last night's nightmare. DeWayne Garry's rheumy accusing eyes followed him through images of exploding houses, sirens and hiding out in dark woods. "Go away," he said half aloud to the ghost of his friend. "You're dead, blown to damn smithereens. You were a dead man anyway."

The candy bar backed up in his throat, tasting sour. He swallowed hard, not able to stop remembering.

When he'd done what he had to do to his dying friend, he felt sick like he had the day DeWayne made him cut the throat of a wounded deer to put it out of its misery. He sat with his buddy's body as long as he dared, until he couldn't remember anymore of their good times. With dangerous fumes filling the old farmhouse, he stepped around the curtains of fishhooks and mousetraps baited with shotgun shells DeWayne had rigged in case the law came calling. He bagged the money and the stash of clear, chunky crystals, slipped out the door and ran like hell.

The house blew about the time he reached the woods. A girl he knew got him to Joplin. He sold the meth and hitched his way to Santa Fe. As he crossed the New Mexico state line, something his mother always said kept coming back: "Live the low life and trouble always finds you."

He counted that moment as the birth of Justin James, of his new self. He'd carried the name in his head since he'd seen it in a St. Louis cemetery on a tall, carved angel headstone. That Justin James must have been somebody and maybe rich, and now the name was his.

He'd meant to make something of it, but things were going bad again.

Justin let the vacuum disappear into the murky water, watching it crawl along the bottom of the men's bathhouse pool, a little stream of bubbles marking its path.

He stepped outside to take a quick smoke. Heading his way was the woman he'd run into last night. She was waving a water jug at him in a friendly way.

"Which one of these taps has drinkable water?" she called.

"You'd be better off with bottled beer, but you might try that one," he said, pointing out a pipe and faucet coming from the wall of the bathhouse.

"Beer makes lousy coffee." She laughed. "By the way, I'm Sunny Bay."

"Justin James." It always felt funny when he said it aloud. "I'm glad to see you're not on crutches."

"Me too," she agreed.

He took a drag on the cigarette, blowing smoke away from her. "Thanks for not making a big deal last night with the old man. So far, he ain't fired me."

Sunny screwed the top back on the jug after filling it. "No problem." She used her hand to screen the sun from her eyes as she looked at him. "How old are you anyway, if you don't mind me asking?"

"I'll be nineteen in about two weeks. The year I was born fell on an Easter Sunday. My Mom always said I was the best thing the Easter Bunny ever left her." He studied her, his head angled and lowered, looking up through lashes like Prince William with eyes just as blue. Then he blushed and stamped out the cigarette, kicking dirt over the butt. "That was a pretty stupid thing to tell you." He laughed.

"Don't sweat it. I've got a son your age," Sunny said.

"No way. You don't look much older than me."

"Hey now, you're much smarter than my son."

He laughed again, and she thought it made him look vulnerable. He was wiry and pale with that sunken-chest look of kids brought up on bologna and candy bars. By forty he'll have lost most of his teeth and have a consumptive cough. *Listen to me, for Pete's sake.*

"Where you from," Sunny asked. "You don't sound like you're from around here."

"I come from a little crap town in Missouri. Billings? Nobody's never even heard of it."

"As a matter of fact, I know it's down in the southwest part of the state near Springfield. Talk about a small world, I'm from St. Louis."

"No shit. I was in St. Louis once. We went to a big old cemetery with these creepy statues everywhere."

"Sounds like Bellefontaine. It's a pretty neat place, but there are more fun things. Did you ride up in the Gateway Arch or get to the Zoo?"

He shook his head. Sunny read old disappointment in his face and was instantly sorry she'd asked.

"By the way, what was the beef with Mr. Martínez last night?" She thought Justin deserved a chance to tell his side.

"He wants me to leave my mother fucking hands off his niece, María," he explained. "Like she's the Virgin Mary? What about her hands all over me?"

Sunny tried to keep her eyebrows in place and overlook the language. It pained her that she even considered correcting him. He wasn't Michael, after all, and not her responsibility. But something about him managed to push her parental buttons.

"Justin, I don't want to get involved here, but you're nineteen and María is sixteen. She's jailbait. You know the term?"

"It's not like that. We're in love. We've got plans. We know what we want to do with our lives." He hesitated, taking Sunny's measure. "María thinks she's pregnant."

"Oh, jeez, why did you tell me that?" All her life people confided things in her she didn't especially want to know. She would be meeting Ann in a little while, and she really didn't want to know this about María. "You and María don't know for sure?" she found herself asking anyway.

He shook his head.

"Pharmacies sell pregnancy test kits, you know."

"You don't understand. You're talking local girl here. She'd rather go up the road to Opal and let that old woman see if a broom straw turns on her stomach or something."

"Who is she? Or what is she?"

"Around here they call her a *curandera*, a *medica*, a folk healer. Some shit like that. She delivers babies. She's got a house full of hocus-pocus remedies. She does something with the feet that cures tumors or rheumatism or whatever."

"Oh, right. I believe that. Rub your foot and your tumor disappears. Come on, Justin. If María is pregnant the clock is fast ticking off your options, you know?"

Suddenly his face took on a closed, scared look. "Walk beside me," he said, with some urgency, keeping her between him and whatever he was looking at.

Sunny turned in that direction and saw a car slowly circling the driveway. It had a bar of "cherries" across the top and a big star with Santeria County Sheriff painted on the door. If this is Leandro's plan to scare the kid, it's working, she thought. Or is it something else?

"Tell me I'm not aiding and abetting here," she said, turning back to Justin, only to find that he had slipped away and was ducking into the men's bathhouse.

A man leaning in the frame of the doorway, arms akimbo, an ankle crossed resting on the toe, unwound himself and stepped in front of Justin, grabbing him by the arm. He kept looking at Sunny as he talked, Justin shaking his head.

The man let go of the boy and sauntered toward her. "He said he wasn't bothering you. I hope that's the case."

He was tall, with a body that looked like he gave it a lot of attention. His full lips had a slightly mocking lift on the left side corner that made them sexy as hell, Sunny thought. His eyes were a smoldering Latin black, but his hair and brows almost white blond, a startling contrast against the tan. The hair was cut close to the head, but spiked in front. Not a handsome face with the slightly broken look to his nose, but exceedingly masculine. Pleasing somehow, and maybe a little dangerous.

"That kid can be forward," he said, and there seemed to be a question in it.

"He wasn't. I asked him about the water, and we just got to talking. Turns out we are fellow Missourians. He seems a nice young man." She started to add 'about the age of my son' but stopped herself. *Idiot! Try being a woman of mystery for once.*

"I'm Gordon Grantwood, by the way," he said.

With that name and that dimple in his chin, he could step right off the pages of a velvety thighs and throbbing members romance novel. "Gordon Grantwood would make a wonderful stage name," she said brightly.

He colored a bit on his high cheekbones, she noticed.

"I think I'll stick to massage therapy." He pointed to a door behind her where Mexican tiles spelled out Massage over the lintel.

"Oh, you work here," she said feeling flustered. "I'm sorry, I forgot to introduce myself. I'm Sunny Bay. My mother is an old friend of Ann Martínez."

"Yes, I know," he said, rather bemused. "Ann asked me to schedule you for a massage at one o'clock, if you'd like. That should give you plenty of time to get acclimated here and to sample the baths."

"Thank you. I accept."

"Duty calls." He put his hand briefly on her shoulder. "See you."

Sunny looked around her. The Sheriff's cruiser was gone and several cars had pulled into the parking lot. A gaggle of bathers in housecoats and loose sweats were lined up at the bathhouse door. The place looked positively lively in the bright clear sun of the day.

Maybe her imagination had been in overdrive last night.

Chapter Ten

Ann Martínez had morphed from the beautiful young girl of her college days into a truly alluring mature woman whose recent photos didn't do her justice. As she walked toward Sunny, her hair, still worn long and full, caught the light, its natural black sprinkled with only a few gray hairs. It was a style not many women her age could pull off. She wore a dainty print dress. Six small rows of ruffled lace from shoulder to waist revealed a perfectly proportioned hourglass figure. The hollow of her throat was deep, the pulse visible.

Her smile lit up soulful black eyes. "Sunny, ohmigosh. The last time we were together you were something like thirteen." The voice was warm and lilting and seemed to match the lightness of her walk.

It was a big deal, Sunny remembered. Ann and her husband Tony stayed at their house on a visit to St. Louis. Ann was a vague memory; it was her husband who still remained vivid for Sunny. Tony Tsia was a reasonably successful Native American artist who grew up on a pueblo near Ojo Tres. He was in St. Louis to be a quest lecturer at the School of Fine Arts at Washington University. Under pain of death, Molly warned Sunny not to stare or ask questions about Tony. Three of her best friends begged to stay over. None had ever seen a real Indian either. She remembered him as tall and bronze with a way of slowly dropping his head and turning it to look at them, a half smile on narrow sculpted lips and straight black hair pulled into a tight tail at the nape of his neck, long before that was a masculine fashion statement.

"Thirteen, the year of braces and braids. I'd hoped you wouldn't recognize me."

"Only those beautiful eyes, like cornflowers. My daughter, María, looked at the picture of you Molly sent at Christmas time and said you look like Meg Ryan in some movie with Tom Hanks. I hope that's good."

"Way over the top, I assure you," she said. Sunny couldn't see the resemblance, but it was something she heard often.

"Come with me. Molly is already in the grotto pool. Let's join her. Then I've taken the liberty of booking you a massage."

Sunny thanked her, omitting her meeting with Gordon.

As uninhibitedly as a child, Ann Martínez unbuttoned her dress and let it slip to the floor, wrapping her nude body in a towel, placing her clothes in an open bin along the wall. "Wear a bathing suit only if you're modest. It's best to expose your body to the waters as fully as possible."

"When in Rome," Sunny said, glancing around. Other women were walking to showers and entering rooms where she saw tubs filled with steaming water. Some were wrapped like mummies lying on high tables still as corpses. Reddish brown boulders contained a pool of mud where three women in plastic shower caps submerged to the chest looked like chocolate candy figures. She had never seen so many bare bottoms and cellulite at one time. Maybe it was just the postage stamp towels, she thought, trying her best to cover the essentials.

Watching Ann walking with the grace of a runway model, Sunny wondered what had happened to the marriage to handsome Tony. He had been the reason Ann left St. Louis University where she and Molly met and became friends. According to Molly, the couple kept their attraction for each other secret throughout high school. Ann's parents shipped her off to St. Louis and Tony entered the University of New Mexico.

They lasted a semester apart. Molly flew to Reno, Nevada, to witness the marriage at one of the chapels where couples went forward one after the other to say their vows. Their union, as Molly told it, was a lot like Romeo and Juliet. Both families opposed the marriage. In their respective communities, it caused almost as much stir as the scandal in Taos sometime in the 1920s when Mabel Dodge married Tony Luhan. Unfortunately, Molly said, Ann and her Tony weren't wealthy like Mabel Dodge, and no one had to accept them. According to Molly, Ann's father Leon supported Uncle Leandro's move to make it legally impossible for her or any children of the marriage to inherit any part of Ojo Tres as long as she was married to Tony. Sunny wondered if that had changed now that she and Tony were divorced.

Ann opened sliding glass doors to the pool. Mist rose from the water toward skylights in the roof, turning into droplets that ran along the heavy wooden beams and fell back into the water in musical cadence.

Molly's fair skin looked like a boiled lobster, standing shoulder deep in the pool, steam rising around her. "Look. This is better than a WonderBra," Molly chortled, her sagging bosom floating high and perky in the water.

Sunny stayed in the shallower water near the stairs, where bright sunlight fell from the skylight. Something about the vaporous shadows in the back of the grotto, where Ann and her mother floated, gave Sunny the creeps.

All she could think of was the pottery bowl designed by Tony and gifted to Molly and Sumner as thank you for staying at their house. At the bowl's bottom was a plumed serpent, a mini Lock Ness monster. It didn't take much of a leap for her to imagine it lying in wait under this murky water.

She closed her eyes and let the drops of water falling from the ceiling cool her upturned face, the timelessness of the place seeping into her until a sudden sucking sound broke the silence. She opened her eyes to see Ann and Molly getting out of the pool.

"Water comes in at 143 degrees Fahrenheit. Thirty minutes is the limit," Ann said. Sunny took a couple of swimming steps through the water and joined them.

"Oh no, I'm claustrophobic," Sunny said, not joking, as the bathhouse attendant finished wrapping her in a steaming hot flannel sheet pulled from a nearby vat.

The girl patted her hand on a high padded table giving Sunny a no-nonsense "Up here."

Over Sunny's protests she pulled a heavy blanket over her sheeted body, tugging and tucking the ends in so tightly there was no possibility of movement. Wrapping Sunny's head with a bath towel that left only a small circle of open space for breathing, the girl murmured reassuringly that she would check on her.

Sunny tried to move her arms to no avail. Rivulets of sweat tickled all along the length of her body, and she wriggled inside the cocoon, longing to scratch. Her heart was running at open throttle, knocking like a car that continues to run after the ignition is shut off.

"How much longer—Rosita?" she asked, spotting the attendant's name tag as she came back to mop sweat off her face with an aromatic towel.

"You've only been wrapped five minutes," was the unsympathetic reply.

"I can't breathe." Sunny panted, sucking in air, her tongue suddenly feeling like a bolt of flannel in her mouth.

"Twenty more minutes. Don't worry. Sweating does you good after the pool." The rhythms of Spanish softened her English, but not her intention.

"Ann," she appealed.

Molly answered. "Don't be such a whiner, Sunny.

"Just relax, relax," Ann said, barely breaking stride in her conversation with Molly, despite being wrapped like mummies.

"Relaxing is sprawling out with one of those chilled things with a little umbrella in it," Sunny said, glumly aware Ann and her mother were no longer listening.

They were arranged on tables in a kind of spoke formation with their heads close enough together that she couldn't avoid hearing Molly and Ann's conversation. She tried ignoring them, but her ear's pricked up at the mention of Justin's name.

"He's a bad influence on María." Ann sounded worried. "These days it isn't like the crushes we had at sixteen, Molly." She let her voice drop so low Sunny had to strain her ears to hear. "I'm sick with worry that she might be pregnant," she finished, the words barely whispered.

Sunny felt decidedly uncomfortable knowing what Justin had revealed about María. Should she say something? *Keep out of this, Miss Butinski.*

"It's not just a pregnancy I'm worried about. You don't know my uncle, Molly. I don't know what he might do to Justin. Or have done to him. Or to María, for that matter." Her breath came as fast as if she'd run up a long hill. "Shame on me. How can you relax and hear all this trouble?"

"Ann," Molly assured her, "I'm your friend. I want to help, even if that means just listening."

There was a catch in Ann's voice, "You don't know what that means to me."

"What about Tony, can't he do something?" Molly asked.

"Tony's back living in the Pueblo, did I tell you that? He grudgingly agreed to let María stay with him. But she tried to run away after two days. That's where I was when you arrived. Tony and María, those two are so alike and so angry with each other." She made a growling sound in her throat. "They had another big fight. María detests the Pueblo and its ways."

For a long moment neither made a comment.

Then Molly said, "What about your boys? Could they help you with María?"

Sunny had been wondering the same thing. Molly had explained once, "Maria is Ann's change-of-life baby. Ann's grown twin sons born the first year Ann and Tony were married are corporate types, both married, no children, living in Phoenix, doing well."

"They have their own lives," Ann said flatly.

A bell chimed in the sweat room and Rosita appeared as if by magic. Ann, changing into her happy voice in front of the young attendant, said, "Let poor Sunny up first. We have a few minutes wait for our turn in the bathtubs. More hot water to come, girls, but you'll survive. Is anyone in the hair salon?"

Ann led them like a procession of postulants wrapped in their long sheets to a side room with a row of hair dryers along one wall and comfortable wicker chairs and ottomans next to tables with magazines. It was cheery and bright after the cavelike pool and sweat tables. Rosita brought pitchers of ice water and paper cups and insisted they drink.

"Ann, I'm just flabbergasted about you and Tony. You were more in love than any two people I ever met."

"I thought we were." Her voice sounded rueful. "It's just that everything about us is so complicated by our cultures. I know you always thought of Tony as a regular guy who just happened to be an American Indian. But here it isn't that simple."

She swallowed some water.

"For indigenous people, there's always this balance between who you are and who you have to pretend to be to get ahead in an Anglo world. He's always been uneasy within himself. He even came to see his art as selling out his native culture."

"I still don't get it. It was so sudden. There must be some better explanation," Molly said gently.

"All I know is that one night two men came from the Pueblo. Tony left with them. When he came back..." She didn't speak for some moments, her voice quavering when she did. "He told me he never wanted to look at my face again. Then he disappeared for several days. He returned to tell me he'd seen a lawyer and that he was divorcing me. He looked crazy and said violent things about getting revenge on the whole Martínez clan."

"Why, Ann? Why?"

"I was too afraid to ask. And so hurt, I couldn't think straight. He pushed a paper in front of me, and I signed it. There wasn't much else to the divorce."

"Well, you obviously have legal grounds, Ann. You weren't represented," Molly spluttered.

"Molly, a mixed marriage? I didn't think I'd have a much better time of it in the courts. Besides, I didn't have the money for a fight. As long as he wasn't trying to take María from me, I just wanted out without making things worse."

Sunny burned with questions. "Couldn't your Uncle Leandro have done something to help you, like loan you the money?"

There was more than a little bitterness in her answer. "My uncle considers me and my children tainted, because of my marriage to Tony. Do you have any idea how hard it was to crawl back here just to ask him for a job and a place to live? I'm sixty-three-years-old with a sixteen-year-old to raise, and I haven't anyplace else to go. Believe me I don't rock the boat."

Sunny wondered if Ann held on to some hope that she would inherit the Springs if she hung around?

Ann looked up before Sunny could think of some tactful way to ask that question. Rosita stood in the doorway, fists clenched, angry tears pooled in her eyes.

"What's wrong?" Ann was on her feet, taking charge.

The girl nodded in Sunny's direction. "His Highness says I mixed up the appointment tickets. He sent me to tell you he needs your friend for her massage right now, or the whole schedule is going to be messed up."

"You wouldn't be crying like this if that was all of it. What's Gordon been up to now?" Ann asked with exasperation.

"He went tattling to Mr. Martínez about the two new girls being lazy. Mr. Martínez takes his word without even asking us and fires them. Now we're short handed, and Gordon says I'm going to do their work too. It's not fair!"

"I can't undo Leandro's decision, Rosita," she said, her fine brows knitted together in consternation, as she slipped into a robe. "But I can talk to Gordon about Sunny's appointment." It was obvious she was working up courage for a confrontation.

"Wait," Sunny said. "Let me skip the tub and grab a quick shower. Rosita, tell him I'm on my way. Okay, Ann?"

"Sunny, I'm sorry… but thank you." Then she added, "Please hurry." Her shoulders slumped with defeat.

Chapter Eleven

The wind blew the screen door to the massage room out of her hand before Sunny could catch it, its spent spring creaking, the wooden frame slamming forcefully against the wall.

Gordon Grantwood's face was suddenly pasted against the glass, frowning until he saw who it was. He dropped the gathered pleats of the privacy curtain, clicked off the lock and opened the door. He was holding a half-eaten sandwich and a bottle of juice in his free hand. "Come on in. I'm just grabbing a bite."

She wanted to say something about the sprout hanging from the corner of his mouth, but didn't. He'd barely given her time to shower and stuff herself into a sweat suit, and now he was going to make her wait while he ate his lunch? She was annoyed enough to cancel the appointment, but thought better of it for Ann's sake.

"Take your time." She managed not to make it sound sarcastic and ran her fingers through her wet hair to let off tension.

"I was surprised Ann didn't book your mother for a massage. Do you know why?" he asked, wiping his mouth with a napkin and taking care of the sprout problem.

"I don't know. We're kind of leaving things up to Ann."

"I don't want to speak out of turn, but Ann likes to send people to Opal. Leandro forbids it absolutely, but I know she does it. Just a friendly word to the wise, don't."

He pointed to his registration with the New Mexico Board of Massage Therapy and waved his hand in the direction of a wall of framed diplomas and certificates of natural healing in everything from aromatherapy to yoga. "That woman is not certified in anything."

"Who is she?" She had Justin's take on Opal, but she was interested in Gordon's view.

He snorted dismissively. "No one seems to know. She calls herself Opal, The Healer—not even a last name. She dabbles in massage therapy, herbal remedies, witchcraft for all anyone knows."

"Well, be assured my mother doesn't think much of traditional medicine, let alone seeing some quack." She hoped she had implied present company included, but it seemed to have gone over his head.

"Good. That relieves my mind. I hate to see unsuspecting people get taken in."

What is there about me, Sunny thought, that makes everyone dump unsolicited confidences in my lap like we're old buddies? First there was Justin and his frank revelations about Ann's daughter. She thought even Leandro let a lot of things slip out about María and Justin when they hadn't anymore than walked in—well, fallen through the door. Now Gordon is accusing Ann of what? Taking business away from the Springs? Being disloyal, or at least ignoring her uncle's wishes?

Gordon was rearranging his sandwich to keep the lettuce from sliding out. He'd replaced the green wool shirt he'd worn earlier with a black tee, stretched tightly across his chest, the hard muscles under it etched clearly against the material. She drew her eyes away. Her first impression was right. This was a man who could wheedle a girl out of her drawers without half trying. He seemed totally out of place with the room's soft yellow walls and cloying New Age music, heavy on flutes and harp.

"I'd prefer no music," Sunny said, "unless you've got a little Miles Davis or Charlie Parker hidden over there."

He laughed and turned off the music. "Okay by me. I inherited this junk."

"So you're new?"

"There was another massage therapist when I came. But she didn't last long." He put the last of his sandwich into his mouth and chewed, watching her. He picked up a tangerine, peeling it with slow intensity.

Down to its pink and trembling nudity, flashed in Sunny's mind watching him 'undress' the fruit. She turned away, feeling his eyes follow her, as she wandered around the room.

He made discreet sucking sounds as he ate. The spicy citrus smell mingled with emanations of essential oils and lotions arranged for sale next to a fishbowl for tips, half full of green bills.

She was intrigued by a mound of smooth white marble stones of varying sizes, the oval kind thin enough to skip across water. They rested in an insulated tub of crushed ice set on a wide work shelf. A foot away, thin clouds of steam rose off black stones.

"What do you do with these?" She picked up one of the heated stones. "Wow, that's hotter than I thought." She shuffled it like a hot potato till it cooled enough to hold in her hand.

"Heated stone therapy is one of the latest gimmicks in our industry." He came to stand beside her, pitching the peels and napkin in a bright straw basket, using a wet wipe to clean his fingers.

"Let me show you." He popped a video tape into a portable combination television/VHS player.

From the first frame, Sunny saw that Gordon was obviously producer, director, star and cameraman of a grainy, amateur video of the stone massage technique.

"Sorry, I really need an equipment upgrade, but—" He turned off the machine

"That's okay. I get the idea, but it's not for me."

He didn't seem offended as he looked down at her smiling, standing close enough that his bare arm brushed hers.

She stepped away, putting the stone she held back in the water. She turned her head, giving him full-headlight baby blues that took him in head to toe.

"What brought you here?"

"I've knocked around a little of everywhere. One place is as good as another, but I like it here."

He washed his hands vigorously in the sink next to the cooking stones. "This place has potential as a real curative spa. It could be again what it was in its heyday." He dried his hands on a paper towel, wiping between each finger.

"I have to warn you, Gordon, I'm not a true believer when it comes to all this alternate therapy stuff. Give me a pill to pop any day."

"Maybe I can change your mind." His eyes slid away from Sunny's, and she found the little Mona Lisa smile that played around his lips unreadable.

He had moved closer to her and all she could think about was the heat in his nearness. If he put his arms around her, would she let him? *I'm pathetic! Damn you, Doug.* The thought was a dash of mental ice water, and Sunny stepped away from Gordon. This time he acted rebuffed.

He turned abruptly and pulled a folded sheet off a stack, holding it out to her. "Has Ann said anything to you and your mother about Leandro selling this place? Or maybe you're here because you're interested in buying it?"

"Excuse me? My mother's here to visit Ann. Period. I have business in Santa Fe. Believe me, if I had money, this place is the last pit I'd throw it down. You'll pardon me if I don't quite see the magic." *Jesus, what next?*

"We keep hearing rumors that Leandro is going to sell Ojo Tres," he pressed. "We're all worried about our jobs. The uncertainty is getting to us. Forgive me, but we're a little suspicious of everyone who could be a buyer."

"If you don't mind me saying so, Gordon, a new owner might improve this place."

"You think so?" He pressed his lips together, the skin around them turning white. "I just thought, being close to the family, maybe you knew something." He looked at her quizzically.

"Well, I'm not the person to ask, Gordon." Possibilities ran through her mind. Maybe he already knows Leandro's plans and is angling to see if anyone else knows? Or he hopes to stir up trouble if the conversation is repeated to Ann.

"Maybe you and Ann should have a talk, then both of you speak to Leandro. Common sense argues he can't live forever, and Ann is going to need dedicated people to run this place. You know, you and Ann might make good allies if you give each other a chance."

He colored, red spreading across his face like spilled wine on a white tablecloth. "Ann is inheriting Ojo Tres?"

Sunny drew back, his anger palpable. "I can see that I spoke without thinking. I know nothing of the sort. I just made a logical assumption. Ann is his niece, and she is already involved in managing here."

"Ann is incompetent," he said coldly.

"But she's a Martínez," she snapped back.

"Yes, she is a Martínez… again, at least for now."

"Don't try to put me in the middle of your office fight, Gordon." She snatched the sheet out of his hands. "If it wouldn't cause uproar for Ann, I'd walk out of here right now. Ann is our friend."

This exasperating man. She had been looking forward to a massage to wring out some of the tension of the trip. Now she felt not only stressed but also bullied. She needed to get back in control here.

74

"Gordon, why don't we start over? You step outside while I put this on." She bounced the sheet she'd folded over her arm. "I'll rap on the glass when I'm ready. Then just give me a straight old-fashioned massage. No stones, no talking, no New Age bullshit, thirty minutes tops."

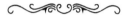

"You've got an unbelievable amount of tension, some mild muscle spasm. "I'll take credit for this one, and this one." He laughed. She relaxed a little and laughed with him, their tiff temporarily forgotten.

From the corner of her eye she watched him measure oil into a glass beaker and warm it over a candle. "It's a carrier oil made from almonds," he answered her question, and added six drops of a pale yellow-green liquid, rocking the beaker vigorously back and forth.

Sunny's nose wrinkled at the sweet, nutlike odor, so pervasive it was almost heady. "What did you add?"

"Clary sage, to which I'm now adding a couple of drops of lavender, both called essential oils, and very therapeutic."

He stood over her, "I undrape you one part at a time. Are you comfortable with that?"

When she nodded, she felt the sheet move and a small stream of warm oil pour from thigh to foot. She couldn't control a tremble.

After kneading pressure points in her feet, he worked up to her ankles, then smoothed the long muscles of each leg. In turn, he worked her shoulders, the backs of her arms and her back muscles—all melting under his touch.

She hadn't realized how truly exhausted she felt by everything that had happened in the last few weeks, let alone the morning's enervating mineral pool and table sweat.

His moves were perfectly professional, but so sensual Sunny couldn't help but speculate what it might be like to make love with a man who knew so much about touch.

"Don't be startled," he said in a low voice, his lips almost against her ear. "Please turn over on your back." He helped her, carefully maneuvering the sheet to keep her covered.

His fingers massaged her scalp and neck and she heard tiny popping sounds. Sunny stiffened. "Don't crack my neck. I forgot to tell you that."

He gave her a reassuring shake of his head. "I don't do that ever."

He poured more oil into his palms, slipping both hands down her arms, thumbs pressing deeply into muscles, as if stripping them, creating pain mixed with a sense of pleasure.

Somewhere in the room a clock ticked off the minutes. In spite of a certain wariness, she felt her eyes closing, her muscles giving in to his hands.

She came alert suddenly, feeling the passage of time. Had she fallen asleep? She heard a swishing sound above her body, felt currents of air passing over her. Peeking through her lashes, she saw Gordon's hands cross rapidly back and forth in slow sweeping movements as if getting rid of some evil essence. His eyes were closed and his head was thrown back. She expected him to break into a mantra or to suddenly levitate. *Oh my god, is that an erection?*

Before she could tell for sure, he walked around to the head of the table. She jumped when he laid his hands on her shoulders.

"Don't tense. Just relax." His hands slid under her shoulders and down under her back. Her whole body lifted slightly as he pulled his hands slowly up the muscles of her back.

When he repeated the movement, a groan of pleasure escaped her lips. She felt herself falling under his spell again as he massaged her shoulders. Then, with slow downward pressure, his hands glided down her chest, moving onto her breasts, lingering a too long moment, on the way to her abdomen.

Before Sunny could react, he took the edge of the sheet folded at her pelvis and flipped it up quickly to cover her chest, telling her to stay as long as she liked, before excusing himself.

Sunny heard the door close and struggled to sit up. Had he just hit on her? *Don't tell me my breasts are so damn small he couldn't see them.* Or had she just imagined it? Like the erection? *No, damn it, he was definitely aroused, and titty rubbing is titty rubbing. That wasn't massage.*

She got off the table and pulled on her clothes as fast as she could, feeling angry and violated, sick at her stomach that she had thought about him *that way* for even an instant. As she slammed out the door, she saw his little tip jar. *As far as I'm concerned, buddy, you've had your tip.*

Chapter Twelve

Infuriated with Gordon, needing to blow off steam, Sunny stopped at the apartment to change clothes and throw her billfold and sunglasses into her camera bag. A note from Molly invited her to a late lunch. She strode to the hotel to beg off with the Golden Girls. But first, she had to call Moira.

"About time we heard from you," Moira complained good naturedly.

She explained, "No cell signal here. I'm in one of those old-fashioned pay phone booths in the hotel lobby. It's the only phone available, can you believe it?" She spent the next several minutes filling Moira in on no showers in the rooms, the tortures of the mineral baths, Uncle Leandro, Ann, the tattooed teenager and especially feely-finger Gordon.

"I'm surprised you didn't karate chop the erection!" Moira howled, clearly enjoying the episode.

"It all happened so fast," Sunny said feeling better for the laugh. "He thinks Molly and I are here to buy the place. Maybe he thought I'd be so pissed he'd scare me off."

"He obviously doesn't know you."

"Anything new on the Manzanares meeting, like maybe it's been cancelled?" Sunny said, fingers crossed.

"Sorry." Moira let out a whoop. "Oh shoot, I almost forgot. KW left you a note. She said I had to tell you, or forfeit my first born—" Sunny could hear her shuffling papers on the desk. "Yeah, here it is.

"She reminds you that your Friday meeting is Good Friday. She said you'll never make the appointment on time unless you stay clear of Chimayó." Moira spelled it and gave her road numbers and instructions. "She said unless you do that you'll get trapped in some kind of religious pilgrimage. Apparently thousands of people walk and drive to some little mission church, and it's on your way to Santa Fe."

Sunny dug out a note pad and pen, copied down the information and read it back to confirm.

"Moira, I really don't know if I can last here until next Friday," she said, unable to mask her dread.

"What aren't you telling me Sunny?"

She confessed her fear about the two men she'd seen in the parking lot after dark last night. And about the fancy cars that came in and then left in the wee hours of the morning. She told her about loading the gun and keeping it handy.

"I don't like the sound of this one bit. I'm putting Max on standby, hear?"

"There are just so many cross currents and conflicts between everyone I've encountered. I feel... so alone." A wave of homesickness engulfed Sunny.

"Aw, kiddo—"

"I miss you and Sumner and work. I miss St. Louis. I miss civilization. I miss Michael, I miss Doug so much. I don't suppose he's called?" She wanted to hear and she didn't want to.

"He called the morning you left. He really wanted to talk with you, so I gave him the number and the address where you're staying."

"I knew it! I'll call him."

"I wouldn't, Sunny. He and Ms. Knockers are still together. I'm sorry."

"Well, I asked. Then why did he call?" Sunny whispered, feeling numb.

"He wouldn't say." Moira said.

"Ms. Knockers? Were you able to find out who she is?"

"Her name is Penny Cregan. She and Doug worked together in Baltimore. She was named as the other woman in his divorce. They split up when he took the anchor job in St. Louis. Now, she's landed the investigative reporter assignment at Doug's station."

"That bastard. He lied to me about his divorce too."

"Then maybe you'd like to know there's already delicious gossip about Penny and Harry Landon. This came straight from Tilley Tooley at Channel 10."

"Tilley had better be careful telling tales on Landon," Sunny said, papering over her feelings, trying to keep it light, knowing Moira was trying to be upbeat for her sake.

"Not to worry. Ever since Tilley won her age-discrimination suit against the station, she claims she'd have to piss on Harry's leg in public before he'd consider firing her."

Tilley's coup was popular with coworkers. Harry Landon got to be station manager the old fashioned way; he ate his young.

"So," Moira continued, "Tilly walks into Harry's office, and Penny was apparently making a case to move up to an anchor position, her big bosom resting halfway across Landon's desk. Old Harry's eyes were practically crossed leering at them. Tilly says the office pool is up to around three grand on who will be the next anchor."

"Maybe she'll get Doug's job."

"My hubby says that would be poetic justice."

Chapter Thirteen

Sunny found Molly and Ann in the spacious hotel dining room, with it's collection of wooden pedestal tables, lace curtains and antique sideboard.

"Ann was telling me about all kinds of interesting things. There's abandoned mines, Indian ruins, riding trails on the mesa. The little town of Ojo Tres, where Ann lives, is just a mile or so up the road from where we forked off to come here. You can buy gas there. Now aren't you relieved?" Molly said breathlessly, before Sunny could tell her she wasn't joining them for lunch, and was taking a hike instead.

"You're going to miss out," Molly said with disappointment.

Sunny wasn't worried. She knew she could count on Molly for an encore presentation of the conversation later.

She was out of the dining room and half way across the lobby when Ann caught up to her. She handed Sunny a sandwich wrapped in a cloth napkin, insisting she eat something. Ann put her hand on her arm, seeming uncomfortable.

"Sunny, Molly is exaggerating a bit about what I told her. The mines, the ruins, the mesa are really not much to see." She dropped her eyes, locked fingertips pulling and fidgeting. "How can I say this? All the way through Easter, many people in this area participate in sacred rituals. Outsiders are resented." She pointed at Sunny's camera. "Should you snap a picture it could be very unpleasant. I can't vouch for your safety."

"I'm guessing you mean the Penitente brotherhood, Ann," Sunny said. She ignored the flash of anger in Ann's dark eyes. "Do you know anyone who is a Penitente? Anyone I could talk to? My interest is not casual. It's important for my meeting in Santa Fe."

"No one," she said, looking levelly into Sunny's eyes. "I don't know who you've been talking to, but I think you've been misinformed." She turned stiffly, leaving Sunny standing alone.

Chapter Fourteen

Sunny reached the top of the long hill leading to the little town of Ojo Tres, breathing hard from the unaccustomed altitude. Behind her she had a good view of the Springs, and the rocky, piñon-dotted mesa. It looked deserted, making Ann's warning seem lame. She wondered if she had other reasons for not wanting her exploring and taking pictures.

The town proved to be only a small settlement. Adobe houses, with their turquoise blue doors and window frames, squatted in meandering lines down the few narrow side streets, many sadly in need of repair. Everywhere Sunny noticed crude wooden crosses nailed to fences and trees, their numbers making them seem more warning than devotion.

An American flag fluttered outside a tiny post office tucked under a portico at the side of the town's general store. A single gas pump stood in the store's driveway, a couple of pickup trucks and a car angled in near its entrance.

Along with wanted posters tacked on a wooden bulletin board at the post office, Sunny spotted a cardboard sign warning about *Hantavirus* in the area. Hand-pasted photos of rodents accompanied gruesome details of hemorrhagic fever neatly printed in Magic Marker, with underlined notice not to inhale dust where rodents hung out.

This is like a Third World country. She watched people come and go at the store, no one ringing up more than a couple of gallons of gas at a time, or carrying away more than just a few items of groceries. Yet, listening to people call friendly greetings in a mix of Spanish and English, no one seemed beaten up by how run down and poor things were. Life can't be easy here, but it's proud and full of community, she concluded, feeling a little ashamed of her superior attitude.

Sunny wandered up the street, absorbing the sunshine. A small motel, a camp ground with a Laundromat, and a storefront café with living quarters in back completed the town's business district.

She noticed buds swelling on early-blooming fruit trees and breathed in the scent of new-turned earth, a garden spot anticipating spring. In a nearby yard she watched a woman bend over to pull a loaf of bread from an igloo-shaped adobe oven with a long-handled wooden paddle.

It was her photographer's eye that sighted the church with its hand-shaped walls glowing golden in the sunlight. Snapping fast while the light was right, she kept her eye pressed to the viewfinder, moving in on shadows cast by gates of ancient wood, catching reflections off the bell in the alcove of the adobe belfry. She had already clicked on a pair of shoes and black pants, dusty almost to the knees, before she was aware of the man who had stepped into her lens view.

"I'm sorry. Should I have asked permission to photograph?"

He wore a plain black shirt and clerical collar. There was no visible cross. He was spectrally thin, tall and narrow-shouldered. His sparse black hair lay as if plastered to his skull. Maybe it was the small round glasses or the way his upper and lower teeth met and pressed together as he smiled, but he made her think of those solemn pinch-nosed priests on the tribunals of the Spanish Inquisition.

His smile, though, was friendly and welcoming. "I'm Father Emilio. The church is beautiful, no? I can understand you wanting photos of it. We're always pleased to have visitors." He slung the hooded black windbreaker that he was carrying over his shoulder. "May I show you around, Miss—?"

Sunny introduced herself and told him she was from St. Louis when he inquired.

"Ah, yes. I know St. Louis and the good Jesuit brothers at St. Louis University. I did research for three months in their fine library."

She realized as he talked that he was much younger than she first thought, mid-fifties probably.

He grasped large iron pulls to open the tall double doors. Sunny entered after him. Ambient light swimming with dust motes rode along slants of sunlight from high narrow windows to light the sanctuary. Above her came the cooing of mourning doves sitting in the rafters.

Along the whitewashed walls were long wooden slabs marking the Stations of the Cross. Painted on them were primitive saints with faces so real they seemed to look at her. A huge wooden cross with the crucified Christ, as thin and elongated as Father Emilio himself, hung above the altar. Raised streaks of painted blood splashed bright red down the arms and chest.

The Christ and some statues on pedestals were shrouded in purple hoods in preparation for Easter. The warm smell of burning candles reminded her she hadn't been to church in a long time. For some reason tears threatened, and before she could wipe them away they suddenly cascaded down her cheeks.

"I'll be in my office, when you have a moment." She nodded as Father Emilio withdrew and walked toward a side room.

The first thing she noticed was the blinking cursor on his computer.

"My God… oh, forgive me," she apologized, flustered. "You're on the internet!" Her eyes catalogued his equipment from scanner to fax to printer, deciding it wasn't state of the art, but pretty good for way out here.

"Satellite," Father Emilio explained. "Reception is spotty. Not a lot of our parishioners can afford these services, so the church is getting into this, or at least I'm trying to convince them to. This is a pilot project. Many in our community have family in the service or away at school. Some of the men work in Albuquerque and Santa Fe and don't get home often. Phone calls are too expensive. So they can chat by email here. I dream of being wired into the Archdiocese in Santa Fe and other parishes. We could save lots of time on church business. A network like this could help us spread our message."

He turned in his chair and hit a key, bringing up a screen saver that said 'God Bless You' in moving colors. "What brings you to Ojo Tres?"

She explained about Ann Martínez and Molly, and they talked a little more about St. Louis University. It had been twenty years since he'd been in St. Louis, and Sunny tried to catch him up on all the changes. He listened sympathetically when she confessed about falling away from the church shortly after her divorce. She told him about Michael and her work. He shared his need for an assistant. It was obvious that he welcomed the unexpected company.

Sunny shifted in her chair, remembering her assignment from Sumner and Kay Waring. She wanted to know more about the Penitentes before her meeting in Santa Fe. What better time than now?

"I'm also here to do some research. Maybe you can help me. What do you know about a secret brotherhood known as the *Los Hermanos Penitentes*?"

86

It was as if a veil suddenly dropped over his face. His exaggerated shrug and the compression of his lips spoke more than words. It was reminiscent of Ann's denial.

"Are you indicating you don't know anything, or you won't tell me anything? I was told they operate outside the Church, but are practicing Catholics."

He sighed. The intense eyes fixed on her face, blinking as he gathered his thoughts. "What is there to tell?"

Sunny stared at him, waiting for him to fill the silence. He was obviously uncomfortable. His body pulled back in his chair as if trying to create space between them. He spoke, choosing his words carefully.

"*La Fraternidad Piadosa de Nuestro Padre Jesús Nazareno*, the Brotherhood you speak of, is a lay religious society. They're devout, but they've been forced to become secretive, fraternal, to protect themselves. They're misunderstood by outsiders. Like yourself." He wiggled an index finger, but she ignored the admonishment.

"Then you're saying none of this bloody stuff goes on? Beating themselves with whips, imitating the crucifixion using real people, cutting signs in their flesh, wearing black hoods, dragging crosses and all the rest?" It flashed in Sunny's mind, that if it weren't true, then Manzanares would have no real reason to be afraid.

"You're Catholic, Miss Bay. You know that penance has a long history in the Church."

"Come on, Father Emilio, it's the twenty-first not the fifteen century."

"In this time maybe we need penance, real penance, more than ever!" He appeared agitated and stopped speaking.

She was afraid he was on the verge of asking her to leave, but she'd gone this far. "I'm asking you if it's true. Are these rituals done now, right here in New Mexico? In Ojo Tres even?"

"Look." He dropped the flat of his palms against the desk edge. "The Church does not condone, shall we say *excessive* practices or abuses. Nor does it seek excommunication of the Order. The Church is ambivalent because members of La Hermandad are sincere in their faith. As a tenet of membership in the organization, they must do charitable acts and good deeds. To be frank, Miss Bay, this group has never been such a problem that the Church felt compelled to attempt to confront or dissolve it. Can we just leave it at that?"

It had seemed a good idea to ask a local priest. She had expected a sympathetic, knowledgeable source. Instead she had the distinct feeling she was being stonewalled, and if so, the answer to her question was probably yes. The rites continued.

"Would you let your own parishioners belong to the Brotherhood? Do you know if some of them do belong?"

He spoke stiffly, as if trying to remember the party line word for word. "In the past there have been archdiocesan statements refusing Sacraments to known Pentitentes. Denying legitimacy to their children. It's my opinion, Miss Bay, that *anonymity* suits their situation best, as well as the Church." He let the stressed word sink in. "As to this church and this priest, I choose to recognize the piety of all the members of the church without question."

Talk about parsing one's words. She sat forward, a thought occurring to her.

"What would happen to a priest, say like yourself, who tried to intervene in their rituals?" She held her breath, hoping for but not expecting an answer. Yet she sensed his engagement. This was clearly a man of letters, and perhaps he fancied he was sparring with the devil.

"Every priest knows well the legend of good Father Avel who did just that over in the parish at Mora." His face reflected something unpleasant. "Supposedly the Brotherhood poisoned the altar wine and he died."

She felt a shiver as if legions of Penitentes lurked in the gathering shadows of the room. Or maybe that was the point. He hoped to scare her off.

He stood abruptly and pointed his finger at her. "You should see your face. That's just the kind of tale people want to believe. These are decent people, Miss Bay. They do good works. They deserve religious freedom, free from the desecration of curiosity.

"And just let me warn you as politely as I can. These are deeply held beliefs and traditions. I wouldn't go around asking anyone else about them if I were you." His voice dropped. "The only people who know about the Penitentes aren't likely to give you answers anyway. And that…"—he pointed to the camera hanging around her neck— "could put you in real danger."

He stepped from behind his desk, a sign of polite dismissal. "Remember, I know something about St. Louis. In many ways some of its communities are as closed and ethnic as we are here. So tell me, Miss Bay, would you venture into a South St. Louis neighborhood bar asking nosy questions and snapping photos of the locals? Hmmm?"

She decided he definitely had a point.

"But if you're interested in the piety of the Penitentes," he said, following her back through the church, "Los Hermanos from the local *morada* will be giving the Rosary here at this church on Holy Thursday. You, but not your camera, are certainly welcome."

She couldn't believe what the priest had just admitted. So there were Penitentes here. Maybe everyone in the town belongs. Maybe even Ann and Leandro and María. And *Los Penitentes* are welcome in this church.

Chapter Fifteen

Where had the day gone? Outside, the blue sky had given way to a horizon streaked with banners of fiery gold and red. A penetrating chill filled the air as twilight dimmed the landscape.

Sunny cut a diagonal across the street, relieved to see the small general store still open. She gravitated to the warmth of a pot-bellied stove in the middle of the store's one room, wooden floorboards worn silky smooth with age creaking under her feet. Every available space was stuffed with groceries, hardware, feed and sundries, smelling of apples and grain and spices.

Chili suddenly sounded wonderful. A man behind the meat case offered a friendly greeting and exchanged pleasantries as he packaged a pound of ground beef for her. Pushing a small cart, she found canned tomatoes, onion and a packaged spice mix. She picked out apples, cereal, powdered milk and a box of Pop Tarts and rolled up to the checkout, where she spied a peck box of fresh chili peppers.

She asked the young woman behind the counter, "Are these hot?"

The clerk lowered the magazine she was reading, nodded and pretended to fan her mouth, "Hot, yes. *Muy picante.*"

Sunny added a handful of them to the growing collection of purchases.

"Magazines?"

The woman pointed to a rack almost hidden behind a stack of motor oil. Sunny quickly selected a paperback novel for herself and an *Enquirer* for Molly, Sumner not here to frown at it.

"Boy, I got more than I intended. And I'm walking. I'm staying down at the Springs."

"That's a good ways. Better let me triple bag that stuff." The young woman's accent lent charm to her friendly words.

With bags in both hands, Sunny said cheerfully, "Well here goes."

"Gonna be dark before you get down to the Springs," the young woman said with a note of concern, as she held the door open for Sunny. "It's not a good idea to be walking around here at night by yourself. These teenagers around here race down that road, all wild and crazy or hopped up. If they see a pretty girl some of them get other ideas too, if you know what I mean."

Without landmarks to guide her, Sunny had no idea how far she'd come or how far she had to go. She walked faster, the sound of her steps loud in her ears, her arms feeling ready to come out of their socket. Why had she bought all this stuff? Sweat trickled down her back and under her arms from exertion.

She whirled around as a pair of high beams lit up the road less than half-a-mile behind her. Something about the bend in the road had muffled the sound until too late.

Panicked, she plunged into the brushy ditch, tough twigs tearing at the bags. Her feet slipped on the graveled incline, pain shooting through her leg, as her ankle twisted. Crouching low, balanced on her good leg, she watched a pickup truck roll past, then stop, back up. The door had a creak as it opened.

"You hurt?"

The voice didn't sound like a drugged-out teen, and he didn't say 'Gotcha, baby' or something worse. She knew he could see her plainly, while she had to shield her eyes from the glare of the head-lights to look at him. He was heading down into the ditch. When he was within a few feet of her, he sat on his haunches, taking off the Stetson he wore, running the brim in his fingers.

"Now I don't know what you're doing down in this ditch, but I've got an idea you're scared. I'm one of the good guys. See, I've got a white… well at least a tan hat." He waved it slowly back and forth. "I'm headed down to the Springs to take the waters. I'll be more than glad to give you a lift the rest of the way."

He seemed to be waiting for her to say something. She took in the full effect of his easy, open attitude and the charming smile. *They say Ted Bundy was charming.*

"Okay. Okay. I'll make a deal with you. You get in your truck. I'll ride in the bed. If you try to go anywhere but Ojo Tres, I'm jump-ing out."

"That's a deal."

She didn't appreciate the chuckle. But he got in the truck as directed. She felt around for her spilled groceries, gathering every-thing but a few apples, deciding she didn't need every frigging last one if rodents with *Hantavirus* might be involved. He didn't offer to help as she struggled, limping up the embankment hauling one bag at a time, camera gear around her neck.

She bounced up and down in the back of the truck until her teeth chattered. The ankle hurt like hell, but she was pretty sure it was just a minor strain. Tears of frustration streamed down her face as she remembered there was no shower or tub in their room; nothing to lie down in and soak away the pain.

As they neared the Springs, she banged on the rear window, pointing wildly which direction he was to turn. He drove her straight to her door. Before coming around to the back of the truck, he stood on the running board for a moment seeking her permission. "If you want, I can lift you down. I must say you're a sorry sight."

"Yeah, I can only imagine. Thanks for the ride. The girl at the store scared me out of my wits about the danger of being alone out here. Talk about letting your imagination run away with you. I feel absolutely stupid."

He lifted her easily. He walked with her a few steps before letting go, making sure that the ankle wasn't sprained after all. "Sure I can't take those inside?"

She shook her head. He shrugged and set her groceries and camera bag at the door. Then he climbed back in the truck.

He leaned out for just a moment, his face obscured by the hat. "Don't feel too stupid for being suspicious of me. You don't know me from Adam. It never hurts to be careful."

Was he teasing or warning her? She hurt in too many places to care.

She expected the truck to swing into the parking lot. Instead, he continued past the hotel. Was there even a road there? She watched, seeing his headlights seem to climb the side of the bluff. She lost sight of them for a moment, hearing only the growl of the four-wheel drive. Then the lights flashed into sight again as the truck disappeared over the top of the mesa.

Why had he lied about staying at the Springs? What was he going to do on the mesa?

Chapter Sixteen

Her mother smiled at her from the room's one easy chair. She was dressed for bed, and doing her nails. She listened while Sunny poured out her tale of the mysterious cowboy and about falling in the ditch. Molly unwound her long legs and padded out to the kitchen.

"You bought me an *Enquirer*. Blessed child, what would Sumner say?" She patted Sunny's face, smiling gleefully.

"Yeah, well, just don't share about the ten-year-old giving birth to the alien baby."

"Ooh, I missed that," Molly said with mock excitement, flipping the pages of the magazine.

She had forgotten how much fun her mother could be, how close they used to be.

"Tell you what, hon. I'll whip up the chili and you take a bath so you aren't sore in the morning."

"Don't be cruel." Sunny groaned. "We don't have a bathtub."

Smiling, Molly took a key from her robe pocket and shook it enticingly. "Surprise. Ann said we can use the bathhouse after hours. How about that?"

Sunny didn't need a second invitation. She grabbed a set of fresh sweats, her pool shoes and shampoo.

Molly walked her to the door. "Go to the back corner of the building. There's a door marked "Private." Molly fished a flashlight from her handbag. "Better take this."

Not locating the right light switch, Sunny played the beam of the flashlight in the cavernous darkness, until she spotted the door to the tub room.

Inside, she pulled back the curtain on the first of eight cubicles, grabbing the pull chain light above the gleaming white tub. In its soft light, everything was clean, cozy and private. She helped herself to towels, anticipating the healing soak in the steaming hot water cascading into the tub.

The bathhouse became deadly still when she shut off the water. She hesitated a moment, listening. Satisfied that no one was there, she undressed and eased into the tub, tense muscles and aches melting away.

She lathered her hair, creating an upswept style that kept shampoo from getting in her eyes, while she soaped and scrubbed the rest of her.

Something scraped loudly, like a door dragging on the floor in the direction of the grotto pool. Bracing her arms, Sunny slipped up the back of the tub, swinging her legs over the edge, and pulled off the light.

Shivering, she wrapped the towels around her head and shoulders, and cracked open the door. She heard excited whispering and low laughter, a female voice. The other, speaking in a low tone, was definitely male. The hallway light came on, steps coming her way.

Sunny tugged on her sweats over her wet body, trying to make no sound. If they opened the door she'd dash shampoo in their eyes and make a run for it.

"Stop it." The male voice. "We haven't got time for that. Over here. Are you sure it'll fit your backpack?"

Justin. She put her eye to the crack in the door. No one had to tell her his companion was María Martínez Tsia. She was a younger carbon copy of her mother, except the girl wore a sullen look that pulled her lips into a near pout, today's usual teenage moue.

"I told you it would fit." She pushed a bulky package wrapped in newspaper and secured in duct tape into the bag. "Jimmy's starting to ask questions. I wish we didn't have to use him at all." She gave a little squeal and did a jumping dance around Justin. "Just a few more days. Feel," she demanded, putting his hands on what, to Sunny, looked like a perfectly flat belly. "I don't care who knows then."

Was María pregnant or conning Justin? What was in the package? Who's Jimmy? What were they planning? Nothing good, she was sure. What should she do about it? Ann intimated Uncle Leandro would do something violent. Maybe she should talk to Justin. Let him know what she'd seen, and threaten to tell Ann. *Tomorrow, Scarlet, think about that tomorrow.*

To Sunny's dismay, the girl tossed her head, saying, "We've got time now." The light was switched off. The unmistakable sounds of teenage fumbling, moans and heavy breathing, reached Sunny from the dark hallway.

She waited, her scalp tingling and itching from the cold congealed shampoo, every muscle knotted back into its original tension.

Chapter Seventeen

After making sure the lovebirds left the building, Sunny cleaned the tub and hit the shower, rinsed away the caked shampoo, and hurried back to the apartment. She was certain of one thing, she wasn't telling Molly what she'd just seen.

Luckily Molly was ready to dish in more ways than one. Sunny tucked into the chili and hot peppers her mother had waiting for her. Never one to spare a captive audience, Molly unloaded the news of her day.

"You won't believe what Ann told me. Her Grandpa Martínez signed Ojo Tres and everything here over to Leandro, while her dad and Uncle Antonio were overseas in World War II. Isn't that simply awful, them off serving their country and all?

"Antonio was the eldest of the three boys. When he found out what his father had done, he stayed in the Navy and never returned. Ann's father came back, but according to her, was never much more than a hired hand."

Kind of like Ann is now. Sunny munched an apple. When Molly got started, she didn't require comment.

"Ann's father called his brother one-night-stand Antonio, quite the lady's man." Molly carried Sunny's dishes to the sink, washed and put them away without losing a beat. "He had one night too many, and got a young woman pregnant. Now this is where it gets bizarre.

She was an opera singer and a rising star. Ann doesn't know her name or any details beyond that. She deserted Antonio and the baby, who was named after his father, not long after the child was born.

"Ann says there was some talk about her folks raising the boy, but the uncle wouldn't hear of it, and they lost touch. Her uncle passed away a couple of years ago, according to some notice from the military… I think she said. Ann feels so bad knowing she has a first cousin somewhere who doesn't know he has family here."

Sunny stopped brushing her teeth, Molly having followed her into the bathroom, and spoke through a mouthful of toothpaste, "Has she tried the internet?"

"Antonio Martìnez? Ann says that's like looking for Joe Smith."

Sunny didn't agree, but didn't argue. Maybe Ann didn't want to find him, just one more possible heir.

Molly kept up a line of chatter and speculation after lights were out. The last thing Sunny heard before she pulled her pillow over her head was "An opera singer? Who could that be?"

Chapter Eighteen

Palm Sunday

Her feet hit the tile floor hard, and she sat for just a moment on the edge of the bed trying to remember where she was. She only knew where she'd almost been. She and Doug were at climax, leaving her a hard ache in her pubes, reminding her that guys weren't the only ones to suffer from uncompleted sex. Even dream sex.

Oh my god. My mother's here. No privacy. Shit.

She reached for her watch knocking the apple she'd left on the bedside table to the floor. Force of habit. She and Doug always kept an apple ready, an old French custom, to freshen the breath in case they awoke in the night to make love. It made her sad.

Molly roused, asking sleepily. "You were groaning. Does your ankle hurt?"

"It's only five-thirty," Sunny said crankily. "My ankle's fine. I'm going for a run. Go back to sleep." She pulled on her clothes, already hearing her mother's soft snoring.

Without bothering to warm up, Sunny took off at a fast trot in the pale first light, not sure where she was headed until she passed the last row of bungalows beyond the hotel, and began searching for the road the cowboy took the night before.

She didn't know what she had expected, but she found the road little more than a dry wash with deep eroded cuts and boulders that dropped off into an arroyo on the outer side. She could just make out a narrow track that hugged close to the crusty pink sandstone bluff and some recently crushed vegetation here and there with a partial tire track where rock had turned to sand. *Cowboy, you had to be plumb nuts to drive this in the dark.*

It was steep going as she neared the top of the mesa, and breathing hard, she used her hands and arms like an extra set of legs to propel herself over the edge.

She didn't see the cowboy until she stood. About thirty feet away he was scattering hot rocks and coals, kicking out the remains of a fire. He didn't seem surprised. She supposed he had heard her huffing and puffing the last fifty feet.

"Well, well." He smiled. "Look who's here."

Bent over, resting her hands on her thighs and still fighting for oxygen, she managed an imitation of her favorite *Casablanca* line. "Of all the cheap mesas in all the world, you've got to pick this one."

He stepped toward her, not looking amused. The wind had come up chilly and gusting, whipping her pants legs. She stood her ground.

"What are you doing here?" There was gruffness in his voice.

"Back at you, buddy. Why did you come up here last night when you said you were going to the hotel?"

"I don't think I said that," he said, turning away and tossing some of his gear into his truck. "But given your frazzled condition last night, I won't argue. Why do you think I came up here?" He looked at her levelly. "And why do you care?" He laughed.

That made her furious. "I don't like being lied to. You said you were going to the Springs to take the waters."

"Aha. You see, I didn't say I was going to the hotel."

"Oh, for god's sake, if you didn't outright lie, you certainly misled," she said, stomping her foot.

"Did you just stomp your foot? Well, now that the social niceties are out of the way, turn around."

"What did you say?"

"Turn around, dammit, or you'll miss it. There," he pointed behind her.

She turned. As if on cue, the desert floor began to glow at the horizon. Shapes in dark silhouette took form in glowing steaks of yellow, orange and a dozen shades of red, the sun's golden touch bathing canyon walls and lending gilt edges to night clouds. Beyond, the river in the valley separated into braids of small interlacing streams turned now to molten gold.

She was transfixed until the sun lifted above the horizon, and she felt him nudging her arm. He had poured each of them coffee from a thermos, and held out a plastic cup.

"Peace offering." He laughed. "It's not poisoned," he said, as she reluctantly lifted the cup to her lips.

"And you made this when?" she asked, making a face at the strong bitter barely lukewarm brew.

"Make hair grow on your chest," he said toasting her and taking a long sip.

"Every girl's dream."

She studied him as he finished his coffee. He was probably around her age, even though the close-cropped curly hair was gray, as were his eyes, a startling, slightly wolf-like combination. Tension lived in the weathered lines of his face. Though outwardly relaxed, the hollows of his cheeks moved as if he was biting down hard. He seemed tightly coiled, she thought, emptying her cup into the sand.

"The name's Robson Steele. Rob."

"Unusual name."

SHIRLEY GIEBEL

"Family surname on my mother's side," he responded.

"Sumner Bay, Junior. I'm named after my father. But I go by the more user friendly Sunny."

"Well, nice to meet you, Sunny Bay."

"You too." The silence that followed was awkward. She found herself asking, "Do you know what those mountains way over there are called?"

"Those tall peaks? Those are the Sangre de Christo, means the blood of Christ." He tapped her shoulder, pointing for her to turn, "And off there, those folded hills that look almost purple, are the Jemez." A little grin played across his face. "Anymore questions?"

"No." She felt herself flushing with embarrassment.

She wanted to ask him about himself, but he seemed suddenly no longer able to contain his restless energy. Taking off his hat and beating the dust off it against his leg, he said, "I need to be going."

"Yeah, me too. There are supposed to be old mines around here. I thought I'd take a look."

"Oh, and just where are these mines?" he asked.

"I don't know exactly," she said, waving at a line of piñon trees and rocks. "Back there I imagine."

"Back there is a lot of lonely territory. You don't look prepared to hike. Not even any water. And other than me, who knows you're here, if you get lost?" His gray eyes seemed locked on her.

She felt a little edge of fear, that Ted Bundy doubt thing again.

The mines seemed suddenly a lot less interesting, but she wasn't going to let him know. "I'll find them." She stepped off briskly, picking her way around cactus and rocks, turning to give him a little wave.

A moment later his truck pulled up beside her. "Careful you don't twist an ankle in a snake hole," he called.

102

He accelerated, sandy gravel spraying from under his tires. Without a backward glance, he picked up a trail road and disappeared over a hill, leaving her alone on the mesa.

Robson Steele pulled over, grabbed his binoculars and raced up an escarpment less than a mile from where he'd left Sunny, climbing over a tumble of boulders to the topmost spot. He focused in, bringing her image close, and waited.

He had to give it to her—she kept coming at a steady determined gait. He watched as she trudged through a dry wash, sinking to her ankles in sand.

A grin spread across his face as she came out of the wash and stopped. She had her hands cupped to make a sun shade, walking gingerly around an area, not taking her eyes off it. He bet she'd seen something she thought to be a snake hole. That was inspired, he told himself, when she took off in full retreat to the Springs, running like a deer.

Round one, he said wearily to himself, deciding she wasn't going to make it easy for him to do what he had to do.

Chapter Nineteen

A note from Molly was taped to the door.

> We both forgot today's Palm Sunday. Ann's
> invited us to church (11 a.m.) and to her
> house for dinner afterward. See you there!

Sunny dumped sand from her shoes, still irritated by her dust-up with Robson Steele. Inside, she pulled a jug of cold water from the refrigerator and drank deeply, surprised that she was getting used to the mineral taste, wondering what to wear.

The bell began to toll thunderously. Sunny made a dash for the church, sprinting the equivalent of half a city-block and up the steps.

She nearly bumped into Leandro Martínez waiting with a group of men just inside the vestibule. Two of the burliest of them supported a heavy oak cross. Could there be any doubt these were men of the Brotherhood? No wonder Ann was so uncomfortable, she thought, Leandro is a Penitente.

Sunny slipped around them, dipping holy water from a stone fount and hastily signing the cross. The church was full. She spotted

Molly, Ann, and look-alike daughter, María, bunched together in a pew. Sunny took her place with other latecomers, standing in the back of the sanctuary.

At the first hymn a woman nudged her softly, offering to share a dog-eared hymnal. There was no piano or organ, but Father Emilio's clear, strong, melodious voice carried the congregation. Leandro was helped down the aisle to stand in front of the altar, the processional of cross bearers joining him.

The service, like most conversations she'd overhead, mixed English and Spanish. Father Emilio, much taken in his homily with "the Rooster," told of the cock's crowing and Peter's denial of Christ. In its telling, he became less the intellectual she encountered and more the simple padre.

The service ran long, her stomach growling loudly by the time she joined Molly and Ann. They were enthusiastically loading a box of cinnamon rolls, cookies and half-a-dozen slices of different cakes from two long tables of homemade baked goods to raise funds to aid a family in need.

María barely acknowledged the introduction to Sunny as the four of them piled into Ann's Bronco. "You can have your friends to dinner. But I can't have my friends. It isn't fair." Molly and Ann rolled their eyes at each other, and no one cared when María slammed her door and refused to eat with them.

The day was so warm Ann set the table outside in the small enclosed patio under an apple tree just starting to bloom. She served a lamb, corn and tomato stew she had left simmering on the stove while at church with homemade whole-wheat dumplings, accompanied by a green salad, wild sage bread and hot pepper jelly. They groaned as she brought out apricot rice pudding and piñon nut cookies for dessert.

Molly and Ann lingered over coffee while Sunny cleared the table, but insisted they would do the dishes. She was just starting to doze off in the sun when she heard María yelling, "I'll go see Justin if I want to, and you can't stop me!"

"María." Ann's voice was controlled, reasoning. "You'll only get Justin in trouble. They were able to replace the motor on the swimming pool filter yesterday. He has to clean and fill the pool today. Stay here, for God's sake. We don't need more trouble with your Uncle Leandro."

Sunny opened one eye as María flounced out to the patio.

"I won't have to put up with her shit much longer, or Uncle Flippers," she said, throwing herself into a chair. She stared at Sunny, the black eyes narrowed and calculating. "I know who you are. Justin says you seem okay. Can you keep a secret?"

Oh, please, don't tell me something I don't want to hear.

"Justin is going to take me away from this place. I'm pregnant. We're getting married."

Well, there it is. The whole damn package dumped in my lap.

"Justin doesn't have a pot to piss in. You haven't had a pregnancy test. You'll need your parents' consent to marry at sixteen, which I give as much chance as a snowball in hell."

"Justin has a plan. We'll have plenty of money. I don't need some stupid test. I know I'm pregnant," she countered.

"How pregnant? How many months are you?"

"Two. No three," she corrected herself hastily. "Three for sure." She stood up pooching out her stomach and her cheeks at the same time, making her look more the willful child than ever. Even with her best effort her cheeks looked more pregnant than her stomach, which remained unrelentingly flat.

"And I won't need anybody's permission. With more makeup I look eighteen easy. Justin says it's not that hard to get a false ID or whatever. He's going to marry his *chica*," she said proudly, leaning toward Sunny, daring her to top that.

Sunny knew *chica* was roughly equivalent to being Justin's "woman." But it was more hip and centered on María's good looks and pleasing figure.

"Well, wait 'till Justin gets a load of you preggers, okay? See how much of a *chica* he thinks you are then."

"What do you mean?" María asked uncertainly.

She was being hard on the girl, but knew from experience María badly needed a dose of reality. Sunny learned the hard way about teenage boyfriends faced with a surprise pregnancy and a too-early marriage. Looking with disgust at her swollen belly when she was almost due, Stephen had hit the road. She told María her story, frankly spelling out the physical changes of pregnancy.

María seemed uncomfortable, eyes looking down. Sunny noted the deep flush that spread over the high cheekbones. When María lifted her eyes, the tough-as-nails teen had returned. "You're old. Things have changed. Justin is different."

Sunny was certain the girl was inventing her 'pregnancy' to manipulate Justin into marrying and helping her run away from home. But in this case, there might be deadly consequences.

"Just keep lying about this, and you may get Justin killed."

A flicker of something like fear leapt in the girl's eyes. "What do you mean?"

"Your Uncle Leandro threatened to fire Justin and warned him to leave you alone. Your mother thinks he would do far worse than that to him if he gets wind you're pregnant. You know your uncle better than I do. What do you think?"

A faint line of moisture clung to downy hairs above María's upper lip, as she struggled with the information. Then with hands on hips, she said smartly, "We're not afraid of Uncle Leandro. Justin's got a plan. And I don't care what you think, Justin won't let me down."

Sunny itched to ask if this so-called plan had anything to do with the package he'd given her, but decided talking directly to Justin was more likely to throw an effective monkey wrench into the works.

"And just what is this great plan?" she asked, checking absently for hangnails.

"You think I would tell you?"

"Whatever," Sunny shrugged, capturing that precise tone of teenage indifference.

María actually laughed.

Sunny would always wonder if Ann and Molly hadn't chosen that very moment to return to the patio if María might have told her the plan after all. If she had, it might have made all the difference in the world.

Chapter Twenty

"At least keep an open mind," Molly cajoled.

Just the three of them were on their way to see Opal, The Healer—María off to watch movies at her best friend's house.

"I get the impression Opal is some kind of witch." Sunny was only half kidding, weighing the assessments of Opal's treatments by Gordon and Justin.

"Opal a *bruja?*" Ann's laugh was spontaneous and rich. "No, no. She's passed that test many times. Witchcraft is still taken seriously in our community. When Opal first came here, people wore crucifixes when they went to her for herbal remedies and treatments. Some even hid crosses of needles by her door. The belief is that a true *bruja* has such great fear of the symbol she couldn't exit such a door."

Sunny leaned forward from the back seat, the rough road almost causing her teeth to chatter, "Is it true that Leandro forbids you to send people to her?"

Molly and Ann exchanged glances. "That came from that toad-eater Gordon, didn't it?" Ann sounded amused and irritated at the same time. "He keeps tabs on everyone and reports to Leandro. He thinks that gives him job security. Mostly, he's jealous, because people prefer Opal's massage and reflexology to his."

Her voice hardened. "My uncle will never give me a reason about Opal. So I ignore him. There's bad blood between the two, and I don't have a clue what it is."

"Today we're just dropping off the baked goods from the church and picking up some salve Opal makes. My knees are acting up," Molly said. "So you can unpucker your brows."

Ann laughed. "Don't worry, Sunny. I go to Albuquerque for a mammogram. But I come to Opal for a lot of things. Clinics are opening in some of the counties near here, so things are beginning to change a little. But for now, we rely on Opal and other *cuanderas* like her, and my bet is so will the clinics. It is our way, Sunny."

They turned onto a dirt lane and rattled across a cattle guard. Ahead of them was a low tin-roofed house. A band of brown and white speckled hens scratching in the front yard darted in front of the wheels, wings lifted, feathers ruffled, squawking indignation as Ann pulled up.

The wails of a distressed child assailed their ears.

"What are they doing?" Sunny asked, alarmed as two women struggled to restrain a boy of about nine, hosing water over his naked body.

"It burns, it burns, it burns!" Dancing up and down, he cupped his hands over his genitals, trying to hide them from the women. His face balled up manfully to keep from crying. But the tears came anyway.

Ann threw open the van door, Sunny and Molly following in her wake. "Opal, what's happened to Jimmy?"

"He's been burned by something," burst like thunder from the woman Ann addressed as Opal. She shut off the hose. The other woman, almost dwarfed by her large companion, wore her snow-white hair in braids wrapped in a coronet. She was trying unsuccessfully to comfort the boy.

His skin was burned an angry red, blisters forming in a splatter pattern across his chest and arms. They had cut his shirt off to remove it, because pieces of it stuck to the burns.

The sight of the ruined shirt brought fresh tears from the child. "Now I'm really going to get it."

"Hush, Jimmy, I won't punish you. We'll talk about what you did wrong later, so it won't happen again." The tiny woman spoke gently but with authority. She stuffed trembling hands into the pockets of her spotless, starched dress. "You must listen to me now. You've got to be strong. Opal is going to help you, but it's going to hurt." She smiled reassuringly, and he nodded.

Sunny could stand it no longer. "I don't know what caused this. But the child needs a doctor and probably a hospital. Those are at least second degree burns."

The older woman turned to Sunny and spoke as calmly as a schoolmarm tutoring a slow student. "I'm Jimmy's grandmother, Adeline Ruiz. It would be hours getting him to a proper hospital, longer calling in a doctor on a Sunday and a holy day at that. A little first aid here might be the best thing. Jimmy trusts Opal. We all do."

"Do you even know what you're dealing with?" Sunny persisted.

With two fingers, Adeline Ruiz gingerly scooped up a two-liter soda bottle more than half-full of liquid, a foot of plastic tubing like that found in aquariums taped to the container's opening.

"Jimmy was hunting Easter eggs Opal hides for him every year. He found this up by the road. This is what got on him."

She shook the benign looking contents in the bottle. It suddenly bubbled into pinkish-orange foam, oozing from the tubing onto the ground. An acrid odor filled the air.

Sunny knew that smell. She noticed it for weeks coming from the garage across the alley behind her house, wondering what it was, but putting off reporting it to city authorities. She awoke to reflected flames dancing on her windows, heard the deep-throated bawl of fire engines, then a loud boom sent pieces of fiery wood sailing into the air.

Sunny moved quickly and grabbed the bottle from the startled woman's hand. She ran toward an empty area of the yard and hurled the bottle with all her strength toward the road. There was a flash and an explosion as it hit.

"Awesome!" burst from the small boy.

Adeline Ruiz' face went white with shock. She crushed the boy in her arms, tears running down her face. "You could have lost an eye or fingers."

Sunny grimaced with pain, using the tail of her tee shirt to daub at the foam burning into her arm. Patches of bright red were turning to blisters. She raced for the water hose.

She hadn't considered the back splash. She was just thankful she had managed to hurl the bottle far enough that it hadn't exploded near her or the others, but no one had to tell her how dangerous, or how stupid, it had been.

"Don't just stand there," Sunny called to the group, frozen now in a dumbfounded tableau, as she sluiced water over her arm, "you need to call someone in authority."

With big fleshy arms winging out for balance, Opal lumbered toward the house. Her heavy body seemed permanently bent forward at the waist above two legs the size of tree trunks. She moved with surprising speed in a rocking motion, swollen bunions popping through holes cut in the sides of an ancient pair of faded leather huaraches.

They crowded into the small house after her. A bluish-black mynah bird hopped around its cage, its yellow beak lifted in the air screeching hospitably in a perfect mimicry of Opal's voice, "Come in. Come in."

She lost no time putting through a call to the Santeria County Sheriff's Department. Hanging up the telephone, Opal spoke gruffly, directing the others to get out of the way, "Except you Jimmy and you, Miss."

"Me? I'm Sunny. But don't bother about me."

Without ceremony, Opal picked up Sunny's arm and looked at the burns and snorted. "You'd better let me do something now if you don't want a scar."

The burns hurt too bad to argue.

With that settled, Opal lost no time. Removing a pitcher from the refrigerator, she filled two glasses. "You like strawberry Kool-Aid, don't you, Jimmy?" From a small jar, she measured a yellowish powder on the tip of a knife and stirred it into the drinks. "This will keep those burns from hurting so bad while I treat them."

Jimmy downed his drink, leaving little red wings at each side of his mouth that looked like a smile. Not to be outdone, Sunny shrugged and drank hers, making a face at the slightly bitter aftertaste.

She was surprised at how quickly the pain receded, but she was still leery as Opal laid strips of clean gauze in a metal bowl and poured a tea-like solution from a quart fruit jar. With tweezers she lifted the soaked cloths one strip at a time and laid them on Jimmy's burns. She repeated the process on Sunny's arm and asked her to wait while she tended to the boy.

Only too glad for the reprieve, Sunny took in the large room with its deep adobe window sills filled with bright red geraniums and the low ceiling held aloft by round hewn logs. The bedroom at one end of the room had a drop down curtain. She supposed it must serve as a treatment room. That would explain the waiting row of mismatched wooden chairs set against the wall, where Molly and Ann sat, chatting and keeping out of the way.

Above a big wood-burning cook stove, narrow pine shelves held labeled bottles and jars of herbs and remedies side-by-side with familiar cooking spices. Aromatic bundles of drying plants hung from a taut clothesline between the refrigerator and sink, mixing with the redolence of home-cooked fried potatoes and onions and garlic. Dishes were stacked in the sink where a single spigot dripped nosily.

Looking around, Sunny found it curious that there wasn't a book in sight. No family photos. No mementos. No keepsakes. A bank calendar on the wall was the only decoration. One easy chair, a small combination TV/VCR, a record player, some dusty records and a worn plastic radio spoke of a solitary life.

Sunny turned her appraisal on Opal. Her facial features were definitely not Hispanic. She looked more like the Central European immigrants moving into some of St. Louis' old city neighborhoods. A gypsy? Maybe. Where had Opal, The Healer, come from? Unless you were as famous as someone like Cher or Madonna, why the single name? Was she hiding something?

Sunny wandered out to a small enclosed back porch. Mrs. Ruiz was taking down and folding sheets and towels from a clothesline in the yard, trying to keep busy.

"Let me help you," Sunny offered, joining her.

"Opal said my hovering over Jimmy wasn't helping." She gave a shrug, snapping a towel and folding it into a perfect square. "I don't know how to thank you, Miss Bay." The dark eyes were bright with pooled tears. "Since his parents were killed last year, he and I are all we have." A troubled look passed over the serene face.

"Jimmy seems very brave. But burns like this are bad business."

"Opal will fix both of you. You'll see. She's one of those God gives natural talent for healing," she said, as she laid a cool and comforting hand on Sunny's, and motioned for her to take one end of the sheet she was preparing to fold.

Cures for everything around here, but nothing apparently for Opal or Leandro. Sunny spoke aloud, "I'm sorry to be so skeptical, but Opal has serious physical ailments."

"She hasn't always been like she is now. It was only after… When she came here she was beautiful, slim, stylish, educated. I taught school, and we took to each other immediately."

She paused. "Walk your corners to mine," she said, directing the proper folding of the sheet.

The old face came so close to Sunny's own that she could see tiny freckles of yellow in the clouded brown iris of Mrs. Ruiz' eyes, like reflections of remembered images hidden within them. She sighed. "Opal always had a certain sadness about her, but she would sing it away in those days. She sings like a bird. She knows all the great arias. Sometimes she gets in these wistful moods and sings as if she's in another world, but sad and utterly hopeless."

She smoothed the folded sheet, clutching it to her chest. "That's what he did to her with all his lies and promises, and making her into his—" She swallowed something unspoken like a bitter pill. After a moment, she said, "He wore down her spirit. But she fought him. And he almost beat her to death. I know, because I found her battered and bleeding like a stuck pig. He is evil, evil incarnate."

"Who, Mrs. Ruiz? What in God's name are you telling me."

She grabbed Sunny's shoulder. "Leandro Martínez, that's who. I know more, but I can't tell. Only other person who knows is Father Emilio. I thought she was dying. I called him to give her last rites." Her small birdlike hand crawled along Sunny's good arm. "I wasn't supposed to, but I heard her confession to him that night. That's how I know for sure."

She dropped the sheet into the basket. "It all goes back to that bad business with Leandro's father. When Martin Martinez gave Ojo Tres to Leandro, he dropped a rock in a pond that keeps creating waves and never seems to come to rest at bottom. Mark my words, there's more trouble coming. I worry about Ann."

"I don't understand—"

Before Mrs. Ruiz could add anything else, Opal called out loudly from the kitchen door, "I need some help here."

They hurried inside only to see Molly had gone to Opal's side. "Let me help, Mrs. Ruiz. This will be hard for you to watch. I'm guessing you have to get those threads and little pieces of shirt out of the blisters," she said to Opal.

"Yes. I'm not as steady with the needle as I used to be. You break the blisters, and I'll tweeze out the material. Use that brown soap to scrub your hands."

Opal asked Ann to fetch alcohol from under the sink to sterilize kitchen tongs. Using them, she fished out tweezers, scissors, and sewing needles aboil in a makeshift autoclave that had started life as an electric skillet, placing the implements on sterile gauze.

"Adeline, take that bucket of corn by the front step and feed the chickens. I don't need you fainting on me," Opal ordered. "And you." Opal nodded to Sunny. "You could be some help here with Jimmy."

Sunny felt squeamish at the thought of watching Drs. Nip and Tuck at work. "I thought you weren't supposed to break the blisters on burns."

Molly glared her into silence, indicating Jimmy who was looking uncertainly back and forth between the adults.

Sunny tousled his hair and whispered encouragement in his ear.

"You are going to have to be very brave for the next part," Opal said to the boy. "Sunny is going to keep you still so you don't jerk away at the wrong moment. Do you understand?"

With chin held high, his voice clear and firm, he said: "I can take it. I'm a Penitente like my Dad and Grandpa."

Penitentes can be anyone Kay Waring warned—the sheriff, the priest, the storekeeper… but a little boy?

The words were out of her mouth before she could stop herself, "What does it mean to be a Penitente, Jimmy?"

"Being Jesus," he said, with more fervor than she would have imagined from so small a child.

"Like Jesus?" Sunny corrected trying to be sure what he was saying.

He shook his head, persisting, "Being Jesus."

"I don't understand—"

"Now is hardly the time for such questions, Sunny." Ann stood directly behind her, her voice hard with disapproval.

Jimmy clutched Sunny's hand as Molly deftly slid the needle into the first blister. He didn't cry out once as the material pulled from his wounded flesh grew into a small tangled mound.

Opal stepped back at last. Molly wiping her forehead with the back of her hand seemed satisfied. "That's the lot of them."

Opal shook a white powder into odorless oil, rocking the bottle back and forth to mix the elements. "Sulfa," Opal explained to Sunny.

She opened a cloth wrapped package and removed a turkey feather, dipping the soft speckled plumage in the oily mixture and touching it gently to each of the burst blisters on the child's body.

Finally, Opal grated an aromatic root, mixing it into a jar of melted tallow, which smelled to Sunny like nothing more than beef drippings. *Yerba mansa*," she said to Jimmy, who nodded knowingly.

She quickly salved the reddened areas. "Tell Grandmother to use the ointment until the redness leaves and the blisters heal." She wrapped him expertly with fine loose gauze and helped him into a tee shirt that nearly swallowed his small frame shoulder to ankle. "You need to rest when you get home. Your body needs to heal. You promise?"

He nodded solemnly. "Can I watch while you do her?" he asked, jumping off the stool and offering it to Sunny. "Bet you yell. That's a big blister!"

Sunny jerked her arm back from the boy's probing finger. "Hey, look but don't touch." She bared her teeth at him in mock ferociousness, and he gave her back a shy smile.

Opal repeated the steps on Sunny with Molly acting like an expert now. She had just finished bandaging her arm when the mynah bird began squawking his 'Come in' invitation.

"Shush, Tristan," Opal called fondly to the bird.

Perched on a swing, it called back, "Opal loves Tristan," ending with a loud melodic trill.

Jimmy raced to the door. He gasped as he pulled it open.

Chapter Twenty-One

"It's only me, Jimmy. Sergeant Ortega. You remember me coming to your school?" The angle of the late afternoon sun sparkled off metal buttons and badge.

Sunny had forgotten all about the call to the Sheriff's office. She took in the size of the man in his dark brown Stetson hat and shirt and the smartly creased tan trousers that matched the epaulets and pocket-flap trim of the shirt. Her eyes ran over the radio clipped to his shoulder and the heavy looking gun butt that protruded out of his holster. Beefy, linebacker shoulders, seemed to hold his arms out from his sides like he had a piece of cactus under each armpit. It gave him a slightly swaggering look.

Jimmy backed up. "I didn't mean to cause trouble. Don't take me to jail. Please."

The officer whipped off his hat, the leather of his sidearm squeaking as he squatted on his haunches so that he was at eye level with the boy.

"Nobody is going to jail, Jimmy. Just tell me what happened here. *Que pasa? Solemente?* You understand?" The English was heavily accented.

Everyone was suddenly talking at once until Mrs. Ruiz' voice commanded silence. "This young woman," she said, pointing to Sunny, "knew Jimmy had picked up something dangerous. If she hadn't grabbed it from me—" Her hand flew to her chest unable to get out more words.

Sunny craned her neck as Sergeant Ortega stood. He had a round face that might have been jovial with his small O-shaped mouth under a mustache trimmed to curve around his upper lip, except for his eyes. Black as coal, they glittered hawk-like under prominent brows that nearly met above a long nose. He certainly didn't strike her as "Officer Friendly."

He pointed to her bandaged arm. "What happened?"

"Jimmy picked up a plastic soda bottle with tubing, full of something acid. It smelled like methamphetamine. Some of the contents got splashed on Jimmy, and some on me."

"How do you know what meth smells like?" It sounded accusatory.

She explained about her neighbor's methamphetamine lab that had blown to kingdom come.

The radio at his shoulder squawked, and he turned his head to answer, then fixed his stare back on Sunny. "You took the bottle from the other lady, then what?"

"I wanted to get it away from everybody. I threw it. It exploded. The backsplash got me."

He spoke sternly. "You could have made everyone go inside to protect them, and then called us. You put all of you in considerable danger. And you destroyed a piece of evidence."

Sunny was speechless.

He slipped a notepad and pen out of his pocket and made a notation. "Jimmy, do you feel up to showing me where you found the bottle?" He turned back to Sunny. "You can come. I'd like the rest of you to stay inside until we finish."

Jimmy jumped around with excitement, running ahead and waving his hands for them to follow.

They came upon pieces of the bottle that blew apart. Sgt. Ortega bagged what he could find. "Not much point in wasting our time on this," he said tersely. "Where were you standing when you threw this?" he asked Sunny.

"About ten yards this way from the Bronco."

"Well, I'll say this, lady, you've got an arm on you."

"I was scared," Sunny said.

"Lead on, Jimmy. Just don't pick up anything," he warned. "If you see something, just point it out and let me handle it."

They walked along the ditch at the side of the road.

"There," Jimmy called, pointing to a weedy patch at the mouth of a round metal culvert that ran beneath the road.

The big man squatted on his haunches again, taking hold of the boy's arm so that they were almost face to face. "*Amigo* Jimmy. This is *muy importante. Si?* You understand?"

The boy looked as if he wanted to draw his arm away, but met the probing dark eyes and nodded.

"Did you find this, or did you see somebody throw it in the ditch?"

Jimmy's eyes wavered, sensing he might be in trouble no matter what he said. At that moment Sgt. Ortega smiled. "Tell me the truth. *La verdad.*"

Jimmy's voice was low, hesitant. "I saw a truck. It went fast. A guy—" He made a broad throwing movement with his arm.

"Driver or passenger?

"Only one guy."

"What kind of truck?"

"Pickup."

"You know most of the trucks around here, don't you?"

Jimmy nodded. "I never seen it before."

Sgt. Ortega seemed satisfied he was telling the truth. "The truck you saw. Can you describe it?"

"Like Uncle Jesus's truck." After several minutes of questioning it was determined that meant too old, beat up and dirty to tell what color or make.

The cowboy's truck flashed into Sunny's mind. *Should I say something?* But she couldn't describe the truck any better than the eight-year-old. *I've apparently caused enough trouble for one day. Let sleeping dogs lie.*

Sgt. Ortega searched and found another bottle under the culvert, photographed it, and after drawing a test sample to take with him, destroyed it without incident.

He came striding back to Jimmy and Sunny. "It's meth paraphernalia alright. They got a problem with it over in Bernalillo County I understand. But we haven't seen much of that stuff around here." He smiled ruefully. "We got enough to do with cocaine and Black Tar heroin. We don't need this."

Sunny didn't know why she was surprised to find there were drugs here. She thought it was just an urban problem. She had assumed Ojo Tres' isolation was protection. It made her sad and apprehensive.

"I just need to get some information for my report, then we'll be done. Picture ID, please?"

Jimmy offered to run inside for Sunny's handbag. When he returned with it, his grandmother was at his side, ready to go home. He grabbed Sunny around the waist and hugged her tightly.

She dropped a kiss on his head. "Hang, tough, *amigo.*"

"Your Spanish accent is terrible," he laughed, avoiding her mock punch to the shoulder, and ran quickly to the waiting car.

Sgt. Ortega cleared his throat impatiently, and Sunny handed over her driver's license for him to copy.

"What brings you here?" he asked, as he wrote with one foot propped up on the bumper of the car.

Her eyes took in the rusting dent on the passenger side and guessed the car was probably a good fifty thousand miles past optimal trade-in time. This might be an impoverished small town department, but Sgt. Ortega seemed smart and no one to fool with.

"My mother and I are here visiting Ann Martínez at the Springs. Then I have some business in Santa Fe for our public relations firm while I'm here."

"Doing what?"

It was conversational. He seemed interested, but she learned from talking to city cops that one question usually led to another and before you knew it, innocent or not, you'd said something they could misconstrue. She didn't want to get into her real reason for being here. *Well, officer, I'm masquerading as a People magazine reporter. Just an innocent little fraud I'm perpetrating on one of your leading citizens.*

She flashed her brightest smile. "It's just a routine, boring project for a client who wants a brochure and photographs."

"Good." He folded his big frame into his car and slipped on his sunglasses, the kind that reflect you back like a mirror. "I'd suggest you stick to that and leave the crime scenes to us."

Chapter Twenty-Two

Holy Monday

Molly insisted on an appointment with Opal, setting a late afternoon time on Monday.

According to Molly, when she'd been helping treat Jimmy, Opal told her she had an aura of resentment so strong that the healer could feel and see it—something about negative thoughts using up her energy and troubling her life. Opal suggested a simple *barrida*.

"A rubbing ceremony," Ann explained in answer to Sunny's what-the-hell-is-that. "Opal will rub a fertile egg over Molly's body. There are prayers and chants. The belief is the offending emotions go into the egg. The egg is then broken and discarded, and wellness results. It is a common practice in our community."

Molly piped up with "I just hope Sumner feels like he's had a great big pin stuck in him."

"I think she's missing the point, don't you Sunny?" Ann laughed, as she drove once again toward Opal's house.

At least Ann was talking to her again. She had largely ignored Sunny during the morning bathhouse rituals, brooding over her questioning little Jimmy Ruiz about the Penitentes, until they had a moment alone. She had her say and obviously expected Sunny to apologize.

"Ann, I'm sorry for speaking without thinking yesterday. It was just that Jimmy's statement was so forthright, it took me by surprise."

"He is a devout little boy. I was afraid you would say something against the Brotherhood to upset him or Mrs. Ruiz."

"I've just been trying so hard to understand."

"I know, and I haven't been very helpful." Ann paused, looking at Sunny a long moment, a bemused look crossing her face. "What you really want to know is, am I one?"

She raised her hand, and laughed. "Though, I'm not very religious, Sunny, like most of the women around here, I belong to the *Auxiliadoras*. We women get together just like any other church or fraternal group. We do things like making our traditional Lenten dishes to take to the *morada*, our meeting hall, on Holy Thursday."

"And the rites of penance? Do women do that too?"

Ann let out a loud sigh. "Long before my time, it is said some did penance using old rituals just like some of the men did then, and some do now. Just last year some girls wore bracelets of cactus and walked with rice in their shoes to the holy Santuario in Chimayó. Maybe they were sincere, but I thought it was a stunt, just like you probably do."

When Ann added her standard, "It's just our way," Sunny chimed in saying it with her and they both laughed, any strain between them disappearing.

Opal's door was unlocked and Ann pushed it open, calling her name. The mynah did its "Come in" and "Opal loves Tristan" routines, but the little feathered talker soon exhausted his vocabulary, and settled for throwing bird seed from the cage.

Ann picked up a note from the kitchen table. Opal might be delayed by an unexpected delivery to yet another Trujillo baby. "Her tenth," Ann said. "All delivered by Opal."

She held out the note to Molly. "She says for us to make ourselves at home. She wants to do the *barrida*, if you can wait."

Sunny pointed to a turquoise-hued saucer on which lay a perfect white egg, a rosary of carved beads beside it. She picked up the egg, cupping it in her hands, rubbing it along her arm. "It's still cold. She hasn't been gone long. She may not be back for—"

"We had such a late lunch, I don't think any of us are ready for dinner. Let's wait," Molly said, brushing aside objections.

"Okay by me," Ann said, turning on a lamp in the gathering dusk. "There's nothing on TV. Since we've got time to kill, I'm sure Opal won't mind if we play some of her records. Pick something, Sunny."

Glad for the diversion, Sunny quickly shuffled through the topmost group of singles and albums—Christmas carols, some country western, an old Perry Como.

Midway in the stack, wrapped in a piece of red velvet, were two records in dust covers. "Oh, wouldn't you know it, opera?" Sunny groaned. "However this is *The Magic Flute*. I tolerate Mozart. This is the quintessence of opera, Ann. It's got it all, attempted rape and conspiracy to murder, revenge and cruelty, comedy and tragedy. You name it, it's got it."

"Trashing opera is just your last vestige of rebellion," Molly said, at her side, holding out her hand for the recording. She squinted, "My contacts aren't that great. What does the label say?"

Sunny held the record up to the light. "The year says 1942, I think. If I make it out right it is a live performance recording at the Met."

"This has got to be a rare and valuable recording. Who's the artist?" Molly asked, sounding excited.

"The name has a scratch through it. I can't make it out."

"Maybe, if you just play it?" Ann suggested helpfully.

Sunny set the record gently on the turntable. The old 78 spun slowly at first, and she lowered the head of the needle-arm, keeping carefully outside the grooves. The introduction began faintly, slightly tinny. Then the ominous spaced chords took hold, and the great familiar music of the opera's overture rose, filling the small room as the first act began.

They listened; each caught in separate emotions until Molly abruptly lifted the player's arm, the platter continuing to spin for a few seconds in the sudden silence, after she turned off the power. "If this artist is who I think she is…" She picked up the second record, set it to play, lowering the needle. She shook her head, lifting the arm again, lowering it this time just at the beginning of the Queen of the Night's aria.

The high demanding notes of the music rang pure and clear. The singer's dazzling coloratura self assured, almost florid, as she reached the summit of the highest notes, her voice strong, effortless, passionate. The interpretation was so electric the recording captured the collective gasp of the Met's audience.

"That voice. My God, that's Garcella Klafsky's debut at the Met!"

Before anyone could say anything, Opal's heavy bent body appeared like an avenging apparition almost filling the doorway.

Looking up, startled, Ann stammered an apology. "We didn't think you'd mind."

Opal closed the door. "I heard the music, and didn't know if it was you or someone else." She hung up her sweater and patted down her hair before turning to them.

"Where in the world did you come by this recording?" Molly asked, her voice almost trilling with excitement. "I can assure you it is a rare treasure."

"Who remembers? It's just some old record bought cheap at a sale, more than likely." She seemed irritated at the questions. "What's so special about it?"

"Garcella Klafsky's tragic story, for one thing," Molly began, clearly in her element. "They called her the Prairie Nightingale. She came to New York from a small Nebraska town, and in Cinderella fashion was plucked from the chorus to debut at the Met when she was only eighteen years old. Her voice was something of an aberration, a mix of soprano coloratura, and the rare soprano *acuto*. That means she could hit the natural E the way Delibus scored it in his 'Bell Song.' Not since Lily Pons... oh, well, really high," she finished, seeing she was losing her audience.

Molly held up one of the recordings. "The opening night, when she sang this, they say a crowd of ten thousand people surrounded the Met, almost a third of them were turned away. Those lucky enough to hear her gave the performance a twenty-minute ovation. Garcella was like a meteor, singing all the major opera houses. Then, in less than three years, she dropped out and disappeared. So you see why this is so valuable," she said, turning to Opal.

The old woman had moved into the kitchen, and was standing pale and silent by the table, when she seemed to sway on her feet. She caught herself and sat heavily in a chair, waving off their help. "I'm suddenly very, very tired. It's been an exhausting day. I'm sorry, I can't do the *barrida*." Her hand swept back.

The bowl with the egg crashed to the floor. She stared at it, then lifted her eyes, searching their faces. "Did anyone touch this?" Her voice was tight with tension, as she pointed down at a bloody mass atop the broken yoke.

"Trouble," she moaned. "Trouble, for one of you."

Chapter Twenty-Three

"Ma, it's me." The man rattled the back screen door and found it hooked. He rapped sharply and waited. He heard her crazy mynah bird setting up a racket. He knocked again, calling louder this time, peering into the darkness of the yard, fearing someone might hear him.

"Antonio?" She unhooked the latch.

He pushed past her into the kitchen. "What took you so long coming to the door? I don't like standing out there."

"I was cleaning up. I had people here. I thought they would never leave."

She was going to tell him who it was and what had happened but decided to let it rest. She still had to sort out in her own mind if any damage had been done with the discovery of the recording. She thought Ann had looked strange when Molly said Garcella Klafsky. If she ever heard the name, would she remember it? What did it matter? No one looking at her now could bring the story full circle.

As she moved across the cold linoleum flooring in her bare feet she remembered gliding in silken shoes across the stage of the Met for curtain calls. The elaborate costume of the Queen designed to show off her shoulders and throat, her high full breasts, her dark glowing beauty. She had her Hungarian grandmother to thank for

129

that. And so does my son. He favors my family, thank God. Not like a Martínez. Not like his father.

Without asking, she began setting out bread and meat and cheese and cold sweet pickles she'd put up last summer. She knew he would slice everything just so, carefully layering each ingredient, two slices of everything one way, two slices the other way. Nothing falls out, he explained to her once, pressing down with his hand to settle the ingredients before halving the sandwich.

She got up, poured him a glass of milk and sat back down to watch him eat, her heart swelling with joy in her chest. *All those wasted years, giving into Leandro's disgusting demands, believing he would help me get you back.* She smiled to release the dark memories. He smiled back at her as he chewed, little crinkles appearing at the sides of his eyes.

When he finished, he unfolded a napkin from the holder in the center of the table and wiped his hands, cleaning each finger, then wadding it up.

"This lawyer, this Jimmy Dodson, I don't know what to think about him. I think he may be playing both sides of the street, me and Leandro."

He reached across, holding her arm tightly in his fist. "I promise you, Ma. We'll both get our revenge on Leandro."

He took cigarettes and a lighter from his shirt pocket and held them up questioningly. She moved across to the sink and opened the window above it. She didn't approve, but she could deny him nothing.

"You can stop worrying about the house," he said, letting out a long stream of smoke. "I had Jimmy Dodson look at the deed. He says there's no doubt. Leandro put it in your name free and clear, no strings attached."

This house was all she had in the world, but memories of Leandro poisoned her pleasure in it. She tried not to let her eyes follow to the edge of the light, where in the shadows she fancied Leandro advancing on her, swinging a piece of firewood like a bat, demanding she shut up, stop threatening to go to the law.

Her tongue slipped automatically to the empty wide spot in her gums. They say you can't remember pain. It's a lie. And she felt again Leandro's first blow, two teeth hanging on her chin by bloody strings of tissue and saliva.

Antonio seemed to be waiting for her to say something.

"I'm relieved about the deed. I have Father Emilio to thank for the house and for you, Antonio."

"You have the internet to thank for finding me, Ma. Father Emilio just knew how to look into it."

He covered the roast beef with tinfoil and put the glass dome back on the cheese keeper. He fished out a pickle and ate it, then screwed the lid on and carried everything to the refrigerator.

"What did that tight-ass priest have to do with getting you the house?"

He was standing at the table now, looking down at her, waiting for an answer. He was taller than his father or her father as she remembered at least. She didn't know where Antonio got his height. From his expression she wished she'd spoken more carefully about Father Emilio.

"That isn't a nice way to talk about a man of the Church. It's disrespectful."

"Okay, I'm sorry. I know you've gotten to be quite the mackerel snapper." He smiled and laid a hand affectionately on her shoulder.

Better she tell him a lie than the truth.

"Leandro decided the house was too big a price for my silence and he reneged. I called his bluff. I went to confession. I worked into my sins everything about Leandro, how he cheated your father and uncle of their birthright, how he wanted now to rob his brother's wife.

"I don't know how Father Emilio managed it, given the sanctity of the confessional, but the issue came to the attention of the *hermano mayor*. Leandro was never a good member of the Brotherhood, like your father. And it wasn't long after that, Father Emilio delivered the deed to me himself. I didn't ask any questions."

He let out a roaring laugh that threatened to tip him over in the chair. "That's a ripper. I would have given anything to have seen old Leandro when the Brothers took after him." He took her hands in his. "Wouldn't have left out a sin or two of your own now, would you, Ma?"

She remembered just the way Father Emilio looked bending over her, his stole brushing against her face, his hands shaking as he prepared for the sacrament of anointing the sick. She remembered he looked scared and unsure as she begged him to hear her confession. He kept his thumbnail pressed against his lips when she told him how she had abandoned her baby son when he was only fourteen days old. She spared herself nothing. When she told him what Leandro had done to her and why, she saw anger spark in the sad dark eyes.

"You know, Ma, I've never been to confession." Antonio's eyes looked straight into hers.

For a terrible moment she thought he had read her mind, until she remembered the lie she had just told him about how she got the house. "Maybe you have nothing to confess, son."

He gave a soft laugh. "You can be sure I have sins to confess if I believed in that stuff."

"I want God to forgive me. But your forgiveness is more important."

He stirred uncomfortably. He didn't want to hear it all again. The handsome sailor who came to the stage door and charmed her into going with him, lying about shipping off to war, getting pregnant on her first time, the quickie wedding that made her an honest woman. He didn't want to hear the excuses about being slapped and bullied, forbidden to sing, his father's machismo. He certainly didn't want to go over how she had held and suckled him, her tiny baby, deserting him for a career and a dream of supporting him that came to nothing.

"Ma. Believe me, I don't hold anything against you. I'm just glad I have you now. You don't know how I hated God when I was a little boy because I prayed for my mother. He never let her come." He tamped down the tobacco in his cigarette and brought it to his lips, spinning the flint of his lighter several times with his thumb before he got it to flame.

He stood abruptly. "It's not too cold outside. Maybe we could sit awhile down under the apple trees." He brought her shawl.

The moon was round and white in the black sky. A subtle perfume rose from the nearly open apple blossoms, and Antonio pulled a laden twig and handed it to Opal.

He braced himself and lowered her into an old wicker chair that leaned against the biggest of the trees. He sat and leaned back against her legs. She pulled the afghan down and around his shoulders, sharing its warmth.

"Sing to me, Ma. Sing to me."

She had promised God that she wouldn't perform again, if only He would restore her son to her. God required atonement, after all. But her voice was also a gift from God and not entirely hers. So she promised Him she would always take care of it, and all these years in secret practice she'd kept her voice alive. God also would understand she couldn't be selfish with her blessed Antonio.

Escaping the old bent body, she became the Druidess Norma in the sacred forest, offering her voice in invocation to the moon. *Chaste Goddess who silvers those holy ancient trees...* She knew as she sang, her son, like the ancient Druids, dreamed of vengeance. As the aria's last note died on her lips, she felt Antonio's hot tears slip down across her hands.

Chapter Twenty-Four

Holy Tuesday

"Don't be an old stick in the mud. Come to Taos with us," Molly coaxed. It was barely seven o'clock, and Sunny sat on the edge of the bed in her Cardinal's baseball shirt, still groggy from sleep and with furry teeth.

"Sounds like fun. But it's already Tuesday, and I need to prep for my meeting in Santa Fe. Remember, I'm here to work and not just play.

"We're getting such an early start, we should be back by mid-afternoon," Ann said. It's a beautiful drive, mountains and twisting roads and little villages on the way."

"Bring me back a souvenir," she said, getting up and hugging Molly goodbye at the door.

She was looking forward to grabbing breakfast at the hotel by herself. She had her fingers crossed that there was a message from Doug. She wanted to find Justin to talk to him about María, and was hoping to run into Gordon Grantwood so she could tell him off. She needed some down time.

Sunny almost sprinted to the bathhouse. She called to Rosita, "Just a shower for me today." The girl seemed to like Sunny, enjoying teasing her about her fear of the sweat table. "But I'd like to ask a favor. I may need a little help getting a bandage on this." Sunny held up her arm.

The girl looked behind her toward the massage room as if Gordon might be lurking, "Opal fix your arm real good, eh?"

Ah. The community drums at work. There are obviously no secrets around here. I wonder if Mr. Fingers knows we went to Opal?

Sunny unwound the bandage, pleased to find the redness nearly gone, and only the largest burn still seeping a bit of clear yellowish fluid.

"That must have hurt so bad. It was awful what happen to Jimmy Ruiz and you. You were brave to handle that stuff. So much crazy now, you know?" She gave a slight "chew" sound to each word beginning with "y." Sunny liked hearing her talk.

"Lot of drugs around here, huh?"

"Yeah. Big money." She rubbed her thumb rapidly across the inner tips of her fingers. "It's worse since the casinos. They bring in the wrong crowd. Lots of strangers. And the locals go too. You'll see. Even Easter Sunday they'll be at the casinos. Drugs. Money. Too many of our people are forgetting our old ways, our customs."

Leaving the bathhouse, Sunny marveled at the clear electric blue of the sky overhead, like standing in a great painted dome. The place was growing on her, she had to admit.

The outdoor pool, repaired and ready, was undisturbed under its blanket of misty steam. But not for long. Two families with children pulled into the parking lot, clamoring to get into the water.

Sunny entered the hotel, nearly bumping into the line at the front desk waiting to buy tickets to the bathhouse and the pool. The cowboy was fourth back behind a man on a walker, two guys that seemed to only have eyes for each other, and a balding father in flowered trunks with three kids hanging to his leg.

Sunny pulled back so she couldn't be seen and watched Robson Steele standing impatiently first on one foot, then the other. He had a towel slung around his neck and didn't look like he'd shaved since she saw him last, but otherwise he was dressed in Western garb as before. No doubt about it, he didn't like to wait.

She had to admit he was kind of cute when he was agitated. *If you like the type. Tall, slender, wide shoulders with a big chip on them.* They definitely didn't hit it off. Was it him? Or had she lost her touch? Or, was she still carrying a torch, hoping Doug would come through the door, sweep her into his arms, beg her forgiveness. That was exactly what she was thinking.

Avoiding the crowded dining room, Sunny chose a stool at a counter that looked directly into the busy kitchen, noisy with the sizzle of frying bacon and the bang of cooking pots and clink of silverware. She drank a cup of coffee while she waited, anticipating *huevos rancheros* with green chili salsa. It came with black beans and buttered rye toast on the side, the eggs runny, just the way she liked them. She tucked into the food like she was splitting rails the rest of the day instead of loafing around.

"How do you stay so skinny?" Robson Steele slid onto the stool beside her.

She reddened and pushed back some of the beans she'd been planning to eat as he looked unabashedly at her nearly empty plate. He was showered and shaved so close the planes of his face appeared shiny and chiseled.

He picked up a menu out of the metal rack, made a selection and ordered. The waiter set down a mug and filled it with coffee.

Sunny felt like the cat had her tongue, unable to think of anything to say except, "That was quick." She added hastily before he could say anything. "I saw you in line. Would you like cream for your coffee?" She shoved the pitcher toward him, annoyed at the smirk on his face.

"Never use it," he said, pouring in a teaspoon of sugar and stirring.

"If you don't mind my saying," she began, her curiosity getting the better of her self-consciousness, "you don't seem the spa type."

"That so?" He seemed to be waiting for her to continue.

"Well, you know what I mean." She smiled, wrinkling her nose, realizing she was sounding pretty silly, even flirty. "You seem more the outdoor type. You looked pretty grungy before you went to the bathhouse. Have you been camping all this time up on the mesa?"

"You checking up on me?" The idea seemed to amuse him.

"Of course not. I hadn't seen you around is all. You show up this morning looking like you hadn't had a shave or a bath in a couple of days." The gray eyes locked onto hers, but he said nothing. "So, were you camping on the mesa? You seemed to think it was too dangerous for me."

"It's different for me. I'm a—" He seemed to suck the gender word back into his mouth.

She gave a nasty little chuckle.

"What happened to your arm?" he asked, changing the subject.

"Oh, this?" She twisted it around like she was admiring a diamond bracelet rather than a hunk of gauze. "You should see the other guy." *What's wrong with me?* She managed to redeem her awkwardness and relate straightforwardly what had happened.

"You and the little boy are both okay?"

"Yeah, it seems so. I don't know what the sheriff's department is going to do about it. They seem pretty overwhelmed." She relayed what Sergeant Ortega told her about drug traffic in the area. "He doesn't think they have a meth problem yet. I'm not so sure when you see paraphernalia being thrown out along the road."

He gave an appraising look, studying her face as he took a bite of toast and sipped his coffee, the sum total of what he'd ordered, she noted. When he swallowed he said, "You could be right. I've got a friend in the DEA over in Albuquerque—" He pushed back his plate, wiped his mouth and moved the stool around a quarter turn toward her. "It seems the Mexican crime families that are running hundreds of methamphetamine laboratories in California may be moving into New Mexico. They finance a network of locals or set up superlabs themselves."

"Interesting," Sunny said, not knowing what else to say on the subject. She drank the last of her coffee. "That where you're from? Albuquerque?"

"I'm from down southeast of here in the old Comanche country. Ever hear of the *Llano Estacado*?" He watched her shake her head. "Nothing but sand, bluestem grass, shinnery oak and *cholla* as far as the eye can see."

"Gee, that sounds touristy. What do you do? Are you a cowboy?"

"Some people call me a cowboy." The enigmatic look was back in the gray eyes, and he seemed to think the remark was funny because he chuckled.

Talking to him is like bouncing a ball off a wall. "I mean do you have some regular job?"

"Yep. Like everybody else in this country, I get in my vehicle and commute."

"Where?"

"To an office in Albuquerque." He suddenly had a wary look in his eyes.

"But I thought you said—"

"You asked if I was from there. I'm not. The job is." *Now why did he have to tell her that?*

"So..." She drew her finger in a circle in the air. We're back around to my question. What do you do, you know, at this office in Albuquerque?" Sunny could feel her irritation rise, but she kept a pleasant smile on her face and her eyes directly on his.

He didn't answer. Instead he was getting up, and he seemed slightly flustered as he prepared to pay his check. *Darn it, you're going to answer me.* Sunny checked her tab, slipped some bills under her coffee mug, and dogged Rob's steps.

"Real estate," he said, sort of looking sideways and twisting his mouth like the words hurt him to say them.

"You're a real estate agent? That's what you do? Why was that so hard?" Sunny thought about Gordon's concern that Leandro was selling out. "So that's why you're up on the mesa. You're checking the property. Are you here to buy the Springs?"

He reached out suddenly, and with the tip of his index finger, tapped up and down on the end of her nose. "You never quit, do you?"

Chapter Twenty-Five

Robson Steele watched Sunny heading for her apartment from the window of his hotel room. He stepped into the hallway, hurried to the telephone booth, and put through a call.

"It's Rob," he said as soon as he heard the receiver pick up. "Can't you get someone else up here to watch this woman? I've got more things to do than baby-sit."

He ignored the soothing pep talk calculated to calm him down. "I know how important it is to you. But, dammit, I want off the assignment." Rob almost shouted. "Because I'm not doing so hot, that's why."

"Why not?" he repeated, hesitating, swinging the telephone book back and forth on its chain, trying to find words to answer the question. "Well, she's got this way about her, like she's not buying anything I tell her. It hurts me to admit, but she surprised me and backed me in a corner on a couple of things."

He didn't appreciate the amused laughter.

There was no amusement, however, in the man's question.

"No, nothing compromising," Rob assured him. "She just lobs these innocent questions at me, then waits for me to put my foot in it."

Wasn't it enough that he felt stupid as hell already without having to go into the details? He choked down his temper. "Okay, she put me on the spot about what I do. I told her I'm a damn real estate agent. And that seems to have opened up another can of worms."

The response at the other end of the line wasn't exactly a reprimand, more a matter of disbelief.

"Yes, I remember. I'm just supposed to be a rancher getting in a little camping and fishing and taking the waters. No, sir, it's not that hard. But I'm kind of stuck with the real estate thing now, and I just thought you should know."

On a positive note, he was able to relay that he'd gotten the information they wanted from Sunny. "She doesn't seem to know anything more about the meth thing than just what happened at this Healer's place. In fact, she didn't even seem very curious about it at all. But she's sure as hell suspicious of me, and I can see that being trouble. Things are definitely heating up. So, damn it, get someone down here to help me."

The slow negative drawl on the other end of the line made him feel like banging the phone against the wall. "Well, maybe this will change your mind." He turned his back to the lobby, tucking the phone close to his mouth and lowering his voice. "We aren't the only ones watching the girl."

Chapter Twenty-Six

How could I not have a spare battery? Sunny dumped her camera bag onto the bed and searched through everything with no luck. She would simply have to find a place to buy one on the way to the Friday interview.

She clung to her old faithful 35mm Nikon, heavy as it was, and still using real film. What was that old saying about the kingdom lost for want of a horse's shoe, she asked herself, dropping the dead battery into her hand. She was feeling a little old fashioned and out of touch.

No time like the present to get familiar with the new digital camera, no bigger than a cigarette pack, she planned to use to set up her shots, viewing them in the camera's LCD monitor, before shooting the 35mm film exposures with the Nikon.

There was also the handheld Global Positioning System Sumner gave her the morning she left St. Louis, that she had totally ignored. She punched its buttons and coordinates popped up on the small screen. She ran through the unfamiliar menu, realizing the unit was a little computer with a memory that could mark a hiking route and return.

Awesome. Now keep me off your old mesa, Robson Steele.

Sunny was almost whistling as she repacked the camera case. There was still prep work for the interview, and she focused for the next hour on a strategy and wrote questions to ask Raymundo Manzanares.

It was just past noon, when Sunny had had enough of being indoors.

She'd begun to worry about not seeing Justin around anywhere. He clearly was afraid of the Sheriff. Leandro had already threatened him. Who knew what kind of trouble he was courting with the package he gave María. Or maybe he'd just quit and gone on down the road, which would take care of telling Ann about María and Justin's plan.

Justin wasn't at the bathhouse or hotel, so she made her way to the laundry, where the desk clerk said he hung out sometimes. Inside the metal building, four girls chatted over the din of washing machines and dryers, snapping and folding sheets unmindful of her. No Justin here either.

Maybe he was at the barn. An old man made soft raking noises with a curry comb, as his hand moved expertly over a roan gelding. "Justin?" he answered her, shaking his head. "Justin no *trabajo* today. *Su casa*. Bunkhouse." He threw his arm out, his finger pointing straight through to the other end of the barn.

At first she didn't see the long adobe building tucked up against the rough sandstone bluff because it was obscured from view by a mass of twisted tree branches and overgrowth of weeds. It had a sloped, rusted-tin roof, and she counted eight doors opening off a long common porch held up by a row of thin rough-hewn pine logs. Big patches of the adobe were worn away all along the roofline, giving a sense that the whole structure was about to collapse back into the earth from which it came.

Before she could decide which, if any, of the doors might be where Justin stayed, she saw a man running along the top of the mesa at the bluff's edge. He jumped over the steep front, hands and feet digging into the rough gravelly surface to break his momentum. Sunny sucked in breath, watching him try to stand, then losing his balance and sliding on his rear end, grabbing at juniper roots to slow his descent. Where the bluff flattened into fat folds about halfway down, he gained his footing and traversed in a zigzag run. When he was above the building, he leapt, suspended in air, dropping onto the roof in a shower of clattering stones and dirt.

Oh my god, that's Justin. She let out the sharp intake of breath. For a moment he seemed dazed, lying quiet and unmoving, face-down. She feared he was seriously injured and started toward him, calling his name. His head came up, and he waved her back, twisting his neck to see the mesa above them, listening intently. She stood still as stone not wanting to draw attention from some unseen threat. Time seemed to stand still. The only sounds seemed normal ones of birds and insects. She heard snatches of conversation floating in the still sun-warmed air like one of those telephone conversations on a crossed line.

Then in an easy movement Justin swung himself over the edge of the porch and dropped to the ground, disappearing into the second doorway.

Just as she started to cross the open area to follow him, she saw them, four men at the top of the bluff. They pranced at its edge like joggers waiting for the light to change. Panicked, she drew back to keep from being seen.

The man in front gave a short chopping motion with his hand. Two of the men spun off in a trot, headed farther down the bluff. The remaining two stepped gingerly over the edge, cautiously following the same route Justin had just taken. They were heavier and less agile than the youth and were forced to go slowly, engrossed in keeping a footing on the steep rocky crust.

Sunny seized the moment to dart across the open courtyard. She hammered on Justin's door. "They're coming!" she called as loudly as she dared. "Two men! They're coming after you! Justin, please let me in."

The door swung open. He had a backpack laced tightly around him. His shirt and hair glistened with sweat, and he was breathing in great hard gulps, but he was grinning with excitement, totally pumped.

"I don't know what you've got yourself into, Justin, but those men will be here any second. And they look like they mean business."

She looked around desperately for someplace to hide. There was only one room. The bathroom was a stool and sink behind a wooden partition with no door.

They heard fists hammering on the first door down the way.

Justin seemed suddenly cool and focused. He lifted off the backpack and shoved it under the bed. He gestured rapidly as he barked orders in a near whisper. "Dig a couple of soda cans out of the trash, put them on the table and set yourself in that chair."

Her presence seemed to crowd the tiny room, and they danced around each other as he stripped off his dirty wet shirt and buried it under a pile of clothes in the corner of the bathroom. He kicked his running shoes under the bed. Reaching up, he pulled a pair of shiny gray snakeskin boots off a shelf and jammed his feet in them.

"Hurry. For God's sake, hurry." Sunny whispered, trying to understand what he was doing. Quickly, he slipped on a dry tee shirt, smoothed back his hair and set the Stetson he'd been wearing the first time they met at a jaunty angle on his head.

"Sit at the table," he hissed, emphasizing the order with fast down motions with his hands. "Get the two empty cans like I told you, dammit." She followed his commands, scarcely daring to breathe.

He pushed a deck of cards on the table toward her. "Deal two hands, five cards each, facedown. Do it," he said as she hesitated, her hands visibly trembling.

The men's banging, loud now, just next door, seemed to shake the whole room. Her eyes widened with surprise and horror, and she started to rise to her feet in protest as Justin flung open the door and stepped back, sitting down in the other chair, crossing his legs in a single fluid motion, looking relaxed and lazy. She sat back down, putting her hands under her thighs to keep them still.

He laughed, pretending to drink from the empty can and picking up an imaginary conversation. "Sunny, poker's not a lady's game."

He seemed to be waiting for her to say something. From the corner of her eye, she could see the men at the door. She hoped they couldn't see her heart beating through her shirt. They just stood there. She pretended to keep her attention on the cards. She had to go along, and she'd better be convincing. "Show me again. Please. I'm such a dunce when it comes to cards, as if you hadn't guessed. I'm sorry it's taking so long for me to catch on." The improvisation sounded silly, but she was surprised at how normal she sounded.

"You're lucky you're better at other things." He laughed, then suddenly acted distracted, looking beyond her as if he'd just noticed the men at the door. She felt a tingle run up her spine. *Be careful, Justin. This is no game.*

"Hello. What can I do for you?" His tone said he wasn't pleased to be bothered at this precise moment.

Think! Do the normal thing. Sunny, almost frozen in position, turned slowly in the chair to see what the interruption was all about. The men had their hands cupped around their eyes, squinting through the screen, taking in the whole room, their expressions skeptical.

"Sunny, could you get me another soda? Mine's empty," he drawled. He crushed the can in his hand and tossed it into the trash basket. "How about you guys? Want a soda?" He was at the door, holding open the screen, Mr. Hospitality himself.

They stepped out of the way of the door, scrutinizing Justin closely. "Did you see someone run by here? Young guy? Some Anglo. Wearing a backpack. Skinny, like you," the taller of the two, who seemed to be the leader, said pointedly. They were waiting for an answer, clearly suspicious, their eyes taking in every detail about Justin, looking for any confirmation he was their man.

Sunny stood awkwardly, pulling soda from the refrigerator, waiting for Justin to take them. Panic returned with a jolt. The seat of his jeans were stained with red dust, pocked with small tears from sliding over rocks. *Don't turn around. My God, don't turn around.* If he turned back into the room to take the soda, they would know it was Justin.

Before he could move, she was beside him, popping the top of the soda can.

"When? Just now?" she asked calmly, taking a sip of the sweet liquid, then handing it to Justin. She let her eyes linger on his face, letting it seem intimate.

"Just now," they said, almost in unison. Up close she felt their eyes all over her body like heat. Sweat running like melted fat down their faces stained the fronts of their shirts with dark wet vees. They leaned into the room, their arms against the doorframe, their odor emanating rancid and overpowering. Sunny forced herself not to recoil.

Frustrated and getting angrier, the shorter of the two kept bouncing up and down on his toes like he was about to spring into the room. "Come on! You see somebody or not?"

Sunny pushed aside strands of blond hair from her forehead. She didn't doubt for a minute that these two had guns tucked in the waistband of their jeans like on TV.

Keep cool, keep cool, keep cool. Don't overplay this, she told herself. "No, we haven't seen anybody all day. But then we haven't exactly been looking." She smiled up at Justin.

Having had their look at her and Justin together, a knowing smirk curled the corners of the mouth of the man closest to them as he took in her meaning. "Sorry to disturb things," he said, managing to make the words sound dirty and intimate. He made a remark to his companion in Spanish, and they laughed and backed away.

Sunny watched them go. She counted to ten, then closed the door and turned the thumb latch, keeping her back braced against it as if she could stop the men breaking through if they came back. The old refrigerator clunked as it cycled off, the silence creating tension as they listened for the men's return.

The cramped space made her feel suddenly claustrophobic, and she was acutely aware that Justin was still standing too close, looking at her. She was suddenly fearful that he might have taken her pretended interest in him seriously. All she needed was a pass from a teenage Lothario.

"Move over," she said, finding her voice. "My God, this place wouldn't make a big closet."

The words broke a spell, and whatever might have been going through his mind was forgotten as he moved to the table. "On the plus side, it's easy to clean," he countered, release of tension in every line of his lean body.

"How would you know?" Sunny pointed out the sink piled high with dirty dishes and pans. "And that? She waved her hand at the overflowing trashcan, smelling of rotting food. "And that?" She zeroed in on the pile of dirty clothes smelling of stale sweat. "Or those sheets." She wrinkled her nose at the dirty-socks-musk of teen-age testosterone. "Or were they gray to start with?"

Justin flopped down on the bed, smiling at her. "You sound like my Ma."

She meant to. The only thing that mattered now was finding out what he had done to bring those men to his door, the ramifications of the risk she'd taken. *This isn't Michael in a jam needing someone to protect him. I don't owe this kid a damn thing. What was I thinking?*

He spoke as if oblivious to the danger he had placed them in. "Man, the way you handled those guys. You're really something, Sunny. If it hadn't been for you, those guys would've been all over me and asked their questions later."

She told him then about his jeans and her fear it would give him away.

He blanched and, without hesitating, kicked off his boots and took off the telltale jeans with the innocence of a child. He stepped into another pair he took off a peg on the wall, which served as a closet for his meager wardrobe.

"Okay," she drew the word out. "We've got our breath. What is this all about? I saw you come down the bluff. I know there were four of them chasing you."

She pointed toward the bed, tipping her head as if to look under it. "What's in the backpack? They mentioned the backpack, remember? You have something they want."

"That's my ace in the hole, my ticket out of here. But you don't want to know, Sunny. You really don't want to know."

The less she knew, the safer she was? Was that what he meant? "Bull! If that pair decides you're their man, they'll assume I know everything, after our little charade. The damage is done. How long do you think it'll be before those men come back to take what you stole from them?"

"They're not going to find me."

"That's the smartest thing you've said yet." She advanced on him, shaking a finger at him. "Look, buddy, let me make something real clear. If you're going, fine. But you better go alone. Leave María out of it."

He looked out from under his eyebrows at her with that Prince William look. Only this time his blue eyes were cold, and something seemed to glitter in their depths.

She inched closer to the door, continuing to have her say, her hands only inches from the knob. "There's something else you need to know right now. María isn't pregnant. Earth to Justin," she said louder when there was no reaction from him. "You aren't going to be a Daddy. You're free as a bird."

"I love her," he said defiantly. "She loves me."

"Well, you can't protect her." She put together the two Mexican bad guys with Robson Steele's conversation about the methamphetamine drug labs, and made a wild leap, hoping to scare him. "Now you've got the Mexican Mafia after you. Those two banditos at the door could have stepped right out of central casting."

"Oh, yeah? I'm shaking in my boots. I've seen those guys doing scut around the casino over at Eagle Wing. It takes more than a couple of stupid beaners to scare me."

His teenage bravado made her want to smack him. "You take all the chances you want with your own life, Justin. I can't stop you. But I'll do everything I can to stop you taking María. What kind of life can you offer her?" She gripped the handle of the door in one hand.

"Stay the fuck out of this. I'll take care of María. I've got it all worked out."

"With a sack full of meth?" Sunny blurted. She closed her hand around the doorknob, yanking it open as he lunged toward her, confusion in his young face.

"Stop! If I scream, I can have those men right back here."

She slammed back the screen door and sprinted across the gravel, zigzagging around the barn and running hard toward the hotel. Reaching the wall around the pool, she nearly cried to hear happy voices and splashing water. People. Lots of people. She slowed, allowing herself to look back. Justin was no where to be seen.

Suddenly she heard her name. "Sunny! There you are." Molly was just getting out of the Bronco and waving broadly to her. Ann came around the front of the vehicle, the two of them looking relaxed and carefree.

"We're here to pick you up. Ann's not taking no for an answer. She's made reservations at Rancho de Chimayó. She says we can't possibly come to New Mexico without going there to eat. It's a pretty good drive, so we need to leave here in about twenty minutes."

"What about María?" Sunny asked, trying hard to put the adrenaline genie back in the bottle. "Let's make it mother- daughter night." She had to try to keep María out of Justin's reach, or God forbid, those two thugs.

"Nice thought. But notice my happy no-teenager-around look?" Ann joked, with an exaggerated grin. "María's gone with her best friend to the Tafóya's family reunion up at Angel Fire. She was waiting for them to pick her up when we left this morning. I've got two whole days."

Relief swept over Sunny. She remembered how happily María had gone to the Tafóya's house on Sunday. María is miles away, safe with her friends. Problem solved. *I'll keep my fingers crossed Justin disappears before María gets back.*

Chapter Twenty-Seven

María watched Jimmy Jaramillo's broad flat face as he drove her over the back roads away from Ojo Tres. She could almost read his thoughts. It disgusted her. Since fifth grade he had been doing favors for her, hoping to get into her pants. She always knew when he was thinking of her that way, because he got a funny smell, sort of like wet sour towels.

"Pull down there in the shade," she ordered. He obeyed, she knew, because she let him believe it was going to be the three of them going away together. It served him right for all his nasty thoughts.

The motor gave off pings and smelled of diesel as he pulled up and stopped. "You sure this thing will get us to Albuquerque?" she asked.

"All the way to California if you want."

She narrowed her eyes. So he had read the notes. Good thing they'd been careful with the packages Justin had Jimmy smuggle to her, wrapped with so many layers of tape he couldn't possibly know what they held or open them without telltale signs.

She brushed at a swarm of tiny flies buzzing in the warm air as she climbed out of the truck. She eyed the monster wheels and wide steer horns mounted on the hood, signs that Jimmy might not be so docile after all. What if he decided to take off? She wasn't taking any chances and asked him to lift her suitcase and the duffle bag from the bed of the truck. She and Justin's future were in that bag.

She'd camouflaged them in big black garbage bags so the neighbor next door wouldn't be suspicious. Now she slipped off the bag around her suitcase, leaving the treasure bag secured, and made the plastic a ground cloth to sit on.

"You sure you know where you're going to pick Justin up?"

"On the lane back of the *morada*." His voice wavered, eyeing her suspiciously.

She knew he thought he was being tricked, that the meeting place was changed, that any moment she would laugh at him.

She smiled sweetly. "That's right. Just checking."

María ignored Jimmy, and tried to get comfortable against the wall of the old barn, dreading the long wait. She couldn't believe her luck getting the invitation from the Tafóyas. The moment Ann left for Taos, she'd called Mrs. Tafóya, pretending to have stomach flu. "I don't want to throw up on everyone in the car."

That was the clincher for Mrs. Tafóya, already harried with packing and shepherding her husband, the four boys, her own teenage daughter, and two family dogs into the van. All she needed was a car full of sick kids. She promised to call Ann that evening to see how María was feeling.

María figured when she got with her sisters, Mrs. Tafóya would be so busy running her mouth she'd forget all about calling Ann. But just in case, she turned off the answering machine. She needed to buy all the time she could before her mother found out she was gone.

María startled awake. She hadn't meant to fall asleep. Long shadows already fell against the dry earth.

Jimmy snored on a blanket under a stunted piñon tree beyond the truck, banished by her contempt and anger for a fumbling attempt to feel her breasts. She was on her feet and prodding the boy's fat rump with the toe of her shoe. "Wake up. You need to get on your way."

"I'm thirsty," he said, coming to, slurring his words as if his tongue was big in his mouth.

"Well, that's too bad. The water's gone."

"I got to a have something to drink."

"Then get your butt out of here. Don't you dare be late to get Justin, Jimmy Jaramillo, or you'll regret it." She made a little fist and waved it in his face.

It was fully dark, and María was in tears pacing back and forth. It had been hours since Jimmy pulled out. She was hungry and thirsty and scared. Something was wrong.

The sound of a motor hummed through the night air. "Well it's about time," she said aloud. She watched the headlights dancing like fireflies as the truck maneuvered the hills and dips in the road. As the truck hit a flat stretch of the road, María froze. The lights weren't high enough in the air to be Jimmy's truck.

Panic gripping her, she tried grabbing the bags, staggering under their weight. Bracing her feet, she pulled and dragged them until she reached the dilapidated building. Feeling her way in the dark, she fell over timbers from the collapsed roof, stifling a cry as a nail ripped her leg. Sitting down, she scooted under the slanting boards, and one by one pulled the bags in after her. Clutching her chest with both hands, she tried to slow her breathing, sure her heart was beating loud enough to be heard in Eagle Wing. Possibilities flooded her brain. Justin hurt. Justin caught. Justin dead. Jimmy. Jimmy ratted to get even with her.

She forced herself to breathe. Think! Get hold of yourself. There's nothing wrong. Jimmy's truck broke down. That's it! Jimmy's truck broke down, and that's why they're late. They borrowed another truck!

There was sudden stillness as the motor cut off. Then truck doors slammed. "María? Where are you?" It was Justin's voice, and she started to call out, but something about it sounded strange.

There were other voices, men's voices, ones she didn't know. They were coming closer. "I told you she'd get tired of waiting," Justin said airily as if talking to chums. "Women? What can I say? Hey, quit shoving," he said angrily.

She heard the motor start up, felt the vibration in the ground under her as it pulled across the entrance to the barn. Peering through a crack in her hiding place, Justin stood illuminated by the blaze of a searchlight circling the interior like a giant eye. Her hand came to her throat. He was cleaned up special for her in his good jeans and Western shirt with the pearl buttons, the gray boots he loved so much, his Stetson. *Just like Clint Eastwood in— Oh, god, why can't I think of that movie?*

She pressed her hands to her cheeks trying to remember, forcing from her mind the tall figure next to Justin in the long dark robe and hood that kept poking him with a big shiny gun, each jab forcing him closer to where she hid. Any minute now there's going to be a commercial, she told herself. But deep down she knew there wouldn't be.

"Don't hurt him. Don't hurt him, please," she pleaded with the unknown gunman as she pushed the bags out in front of her and crawled from under timbers, holding her arms up to shade her eyes from the blinding searchlight.

The man in the robe threw an arm around Justin, half dragging him away from her toward the truck, his boot heels making tracks in the soft dirt floor.

A short fat man approached her and picked up the bags, hoisting the duffel bag into the cab and tossing hers to a man standing up in the bed of the truck. María shivered. They wore black hoods like the man in the robe.

Justin was already in the bed of the truck, and she climbed up beside him when she was told to. The two men taped their hands behind their backs and made them lie down in the truck. As soon as the men jumped down from the truck, María whispered. "What happened? Where's Jimmy?"

"Those two." Justin lifted his head, trying to see if any of the men were close enough to hear. "They followed me from the Springs, and when I got to the *morada,* they jumped me. We hid in the chapel. When Jimmy got there, they made me call him over." Shame welled up in him as he remembered Jimmy with his trusting face walking toward him through the tall dry weeds.

He watched the men close around Jimmy like a pair of clamps. It took them less than a minute to hammer María's whereabouts out of him.

"What did they do to Jimmy?" María choked back a sob.

He couldn't tell her what happened, so he just said, "He shit his pants. They let him go."

She moved her head closer to Justin trying to see his face. "What are they going to do to us?"

He brought his lips against her forehead. "María, listen to me. Do what they say, okay? I made it clear you are just sixteen. I told them Jimmy was too. I think it helped. But don't count on it, or being a girl. That could go either way."

She knew from the catch in his voice that he was afraid they would rape her.

"Bad guys always rape girls in the movies," she said without emotion. In her mind she was seeing herself whirling and kicking, her flashing feet and hands knocking all three men out, a master of the martial arts like *Charlie's Angels.*

"Forget the movies, María," he snapped. "I'm sorry, baby, I'm sorry, but this is real. These are bad guys, no shit. I told them I gave you the duffle for safekeeping. You don't know what's in it. Keep to that story and you may get out of this. No matter what happens to me, you've got to get out of this."

"Who are they? Did Uncle Leandro send them?"

"No, I don't think so. I don't know. The head guy in the robe, he's one of those Penitentes. I seen him once before. This is screwy as hell."

María was dismissive. "He's not a Penitente."

"How can you be so sure? Some men at the hotel said they look for new blood. And I'm new blood."

"That's stupid. Most of them around here go to our church. I know everybody. They wouldn't hurt a fly. He's just trying to look scary," she said bravely.

"Well, he keeps jerking my head around so I can't see him. And he never says anything. The other two I recognize from their voices." They were the men who followed him off the mesa. He gave her a short version of Sunny helping him fool them.

"Wow, I can't believe she did that." Her mind was seeing Sunny in fatigues, a brave Meg Ryan in *Courage Under Fire.* She babbled on, trying to make Justin see it too.

"María, stop that stuff. Get real!" Justin said through clenched teeth.

María wished suddenly that she was in the back of the Tafóya family van, sharing secrets with Lisa about boys and movies.

His words, "get real," jerked her back to a world she was trying to dim. She felt the sweat flowing down her body and the numbness of her hands tied behind her back, the hard metal of the truck bed pressuring her bones, the pain in her bladder as she held in. She sucked on her cheeks trying to make spit enough to swallow. She was so thirsty.

"Justin. I need water. I need to pee." She groaned.

The men had finished searching the barn. Satisfied there were only the two suitcases, they were talking among themselves in a tight circle out of Justin and María's hearing.

Justin hollered, "Hey. The girl needs a drink. Needs to go to the bathroom. What about it?"

María started when a hooded head peered suddenly over the truck's side. "Anybody see a bathroom around here?" There was rough laughter.

"Come on, *chica.*" The man jumped up into the truck bed and María felt herself lifted up, then swinging out into space, before her feet hit hard on the ground. He came right after her, restraining her. The truck's doors were open, the dome light spilling pale light on the man's thick arms and belly and making the eyes glitter behind their mask. He smelled bad and María made a sour face at him.

He cut the tape around her wrists letting her hands free. "Squat," he said unceremoniously.

"Here?" she said with disbelief.

The other men turned to look at her, then turned away. But the man watching her never averted his eyes.

María could feel heat and anger flush her face, but the pain in her bladder was too great to be ignored. Hiding herself as best she could, she pulled down her jeans and, squatting with feet wide apart, pulled aside the crotch of her panties and let go.

She stood and fastened up quickly, stepping around the wet spot. "Water, please."

There was a cooler in the back of the truck. The man fished around the cans of beer and found a soda and handed it to her.

As she reached for it he pulled it back out of her reach. "I need a kiss for this," he said. She danced out of his way. He stepped after her, one foot slipping in the ground she'd just wet.

"Goddamn! Don't think you're getting this now." He wound up, readying to hurl the can when a hand came up behind him, staying his arm in a hard grip. It was the man in the robe. He leaned in close and said something in his ear, then swung him around, looking at him to be sure he understood.

The man handed María the soda without a word and walked away.

Only moments later they were all in the truck, María with hands once again taped and her legs bound to Justin's by a short rope. Doors slammed, the engine revved, and they were on the move.

Chapter Twenty-Eight

The truck slowed a short distance later and stopped, the driver exchanging quick words with two men in a newer pickup truck parked on the side of the road.

Justin caught most of what was said, directions given to take the abandoned mine road on the mesa above the Springs that long ago had been a shortcut between Ojo Tres and the little town of La Placita and the old state road leading into Eagle Wing.

Locals knew it was passable by traversing around a washout that sliced the road in half midway to the top, if you were loco enough to try it. The only advantage was no one was likely to see them either from the town or the Springs.

Justin prepared by pushing tight against María, using his feet to wedge her suitcase between them and the tailgate, bracing his feet against the bag. "Get your fingers around my belt," he said into her ear. "Hold on tight, María. I mean it. Or you could go flying out of here."

The man guarding Justin and María called angrily, "What the hell are you doing?" The pitch of the engine rose, the truck lurching and laboring as it climbed. Suddenly the trail's steep angle gave the sense that the truck might rear up and spin backward on top of them at any moment. The man forgot about them, sinking to his knees, his hands clutching for a firm hold.

Struggling to stand once more, fighting the motion of the truck the man began banging on the truck cab. "This is bullshit! We're going to turn over, you damn fools." The truck lurched again, knocking him off his feet, slamming his head against the edge of the truck bed. He scrambled back on his knees, slapping his open hand on the rear window and screaming.

Justin could tell the driver was inexperienced with this kind of terrain from the way he kept grinding gears, racing the engine and overcompensating his steering as the tires bounced against boulders and slipped into ruts. As the light truck slowed to a crawl, Justin guessed they were nearing the washout. The truck dipped, then eased off the road onto the face of the bluff's steep face and immediately began slipping sideways. The driver worked frantically to keep moving upward, spewing gravel from under the rear wheels.

Cursing, their guard threw one leg over the edge of the truck bed making ready to jump. Justin scooted up, pushing his hands tight against María's mouth. Instantly she understood as he felt her strong teeth gnawing hard at the single loop of tape binding his wrists, quickly making a tear in the edge. He kept the binding taut, hoping she could tear it through.

Afraid to jump, their guard swung both feet back in the truck. With growing desperation, he pulled the beer cooler up, climbed atop, and leaning out around the cab, tried to grab the driver's arm through the open window. He screamed, "You son-of-a-bitch. You listen to me. Stop this thing." Suddenly the box shifted from under him. He fell backward, sliding, his head butting into the tailgate, his body going limp.

Justin pulled his wrists, putting tension on the ruptured tape. Once more María grasped the loosened edge of the tear in her teeth, pulling downward until it ripped open. His hands were free. He jackknifed his body so he could reach the knot on the rope that held his legs. He almost laughed out loud. The jackass had tied a slipknot.

He ripped the tape from around María's wrists just as a shout went up signaling that the lead truck had crested the mesa. Straining to follow after it, the small truck was almost at a standstill. The motor's tappets pounding like a jack hammer were signal enough for Justin to begin coiling his body in readiness. The driver hit the gas, flooring the accelerator. The truck shuddered and stalled, the motor flooded. Brakes creaking ominously with strain, it began slipping backwards, fishtailing as the driver pumped uselessly on the brakes.

Justin and María were over the sides of the truck in an instant. Going back down the road, they would be overtaken easily. He grabbed her hand, and they scrambled past the truck and up onto the mesa, running free before anyone knew they were gone, the darkness their friend.

Chapter Twenty-Nine

They stumbled and slid on loose rock and gravel, feeling their way around the darker shapes that were piñon trees and cactus. Justin knew the mesa's trails like the back of his hand after months of trail rides and forays to the old mines. He also knew there were few places to hide and nowhere safe. Justin steered them toward the steep rocky south face of the mesa where the trucks would be useless and the men would have to follow on foot. There he and María had a chance.

Justin whispered urgently, "Stay as low as you can. When the moon comes out from behind that patch of cloud cover, they've got a better chance of seeing us." Suddenly underfoot the hard packed surface of a dirt-bike trail made running easier, and they sprinted along it as their eyes adjusted to the light from the stars that filled the velvety dome above them.

The path ended abruptly in the soft loose sandy soil of a dry wash. They followed the cut only a few yards before giving it up, their feet sinking in to the ankles with each step, tiring their legs.

"My shoes are full of sand," María whimpered, beginning to limp as she ran, pulling against his grip, her breath labored, as he dragged her along. "We can't stop now," Justin said, trying to keep the panic from his voice as he tightened his hold on her hand. "Come on. Come on. Take deep breaths. Run!" he encouraged, putting an arm around her and letting her lean on him.

His breath quickly turned to fire in his chest, with her added weight, sweat stinging his eyes. Winded, he headed down into another wash, thick with salt brush.

"I can't go on." She sobbed, pulling away from him, her face in her hands, her voice small and desperate. "I want my mother."

Just then the trucks came roaring after them, the searchlight cutting away the distance between them in methodic sweeps across the dark landscape.

Survival fueled Justin as he hid her under some brush, clawing sand over her body. "Hide. I'll get help and come back for you," he promised, giving her hand a quick squeeze.

He sprinted away in a broken-field run bent low to avoid the lights. He made for the edge of the mesa to his left, his feet drumming on the hard earth as he cut diagonally away from María. Even if they saw him now they wouldn't be able to pinpoint her location.

The second truck picked him up in its headlights and crashed through brush and cactus, spinning its wheels and careening after him. He ran blindly, gasping for breath, the truck almost on him. He could smell it and feel it, hear its roar at his heels.

Throwing his hands defensively in front of him, he fought to get out of the truck's path. He sprawled backward, gasping with sudden agony, lanced with a thousand sharp needles. Caught in the thorny embrace of a great antlered buckhorn cactus, he thrashed and struggled, branches broke and clung to his back and sides and front, the barbed spines burrowing deep into his flesh with his every movement.

The truck stopped inches from his body, dust swirling in the air against the lights, its body a great beast spewing fumes and heat. The driver flashed a signal with his lights and, stepping out on the running board, yelled back to the other truck, "We got him. But the girl's not here. Goddamn. Will you look at the bastard shimmy!"

Justin danced as he ripped at his shirt, pulling it away from his body, tearing cactus and thorns moored in his flesh. He staggered blindly with the pain, slamming into the side of the truck. A second man jumped down from the cab, came around the back of the truck and took hold of him, jerking him to a standstill.

"For Christ's sake, help me," Justin pleaded.

The man, who was big and thick bodied, stepped stolidly between Justin and the other man, pulling the hood up off his face and wiping away sweat with his big rough hand. Justin had never seen him before.

He opened a long bladed knife, the kind Justin used to gut deer. "Hold still," he said, grasping the waistband of Justin's jeans. With sure, steady strokes, he cut the jeans apart and pulled them off

The smaller man looked fearfully over his shoulder. "What the hell are you doing? The boss, he tell you to wear that hood. He said this kid don't get sympathy. You trying to get us killed too?"

"Had a cow go loco once from this stuff," the man answered. He flicked one of the spiny antlers of cactus that clung to his sleeve off into the darkness. "No need to make this sorry business you got us into any sorrier than it is." He closed the knife and shoved it back into a denim loop on his jeans.

"I didn't see you turning down the money."

Reluctantly the big man pulled the hood down again. "It's a sacrilege. The boss isn't one of us. You know that."

"All I've got to know is he's got the money. And he's got the gun. You got anything more to say?"

"God have mercy on us, this is murder."

A low keen escaped Justin's lips like the sound of women lamenting their dead. "What are you going to do to me?" He shivered in the wind. Naked except for his briefs and his boots, there was nothing but the blanketing pain that ran like fire along his neurons. He wanted to run, but his brain short-circuited by the thorns' poison coursing through his veins, turning his legs to lead. He dropped to both knees, unable to stand any longer.

There were three sudden sharp horn blasts, an impatient summons.

The big man signed the cross with quick motions and brushed a kiss to the fingertips he pressed momentarily to his lips. For the first time in his life it occurred to him to wonder if God punished the woodcarver who made the cross Christ endured. Would God punish him for using his woodcarving skills to make this cross?

Chapter Thirty

When they came to a stop, the driver left the headlights on and pushed Justin into the circle of light. A man labored with a posthole digger, glistening with sweat, his shirt tied by the arms around his waist, a hood covering his head and face.

He stopped digging, tested the depth, seeming satisfied the hole was deep enough. He leaned down by the light of his lantern and saw Justin staring at him. He grabbed up a pack of cigarettes from the ground, turned his back, and pulled up his hood to smoke.

The hoods! A thought like a tossed lifeline rekindled hope in Justin. *I can only identify them if I'm alive. Otherwise, why would they care? They're just trying to throw a scare in me.*

He pushed his hair across his forehead to cover the movement of his eyes, searching for an opening, a moment to run. They've had their joke. They've got the damn meth back. They probably won't even stop me.

The other truck pulled up, brightening the perimeter just as he coiled to run. The door opened, and the man in the long robe emerged pulling a reluctant María after him. Justin froze, flight forgotten. He realized with a shock that he had forgotten all about María. Her face was streaked with dirt, her hair full of stickers where she had burrowed under the brush, hiding like an animal.

In that instant, seeing her, he knew something else. The hoods were for María's sake, not for his. It was María they were afraid could identify them. He sagged as hope drained away.

María started toward Justin when she saw him, but the robed man grabbed her back, hoisting her roughly onto one of the fenders.

The men gathered around the back of the truck, the robed man signaling directions. On the count of three they lifted together, the truck rocking, relieved of its burden, as the four shouldered a wooden cross and carried it to the digging site.

The timber was almost the length of three men with the traverse arm mortised solidly toward the top. At the sight of it, Justin thought it a human figure at its most elemental.

They dropped the hewn timber into the hole to test the depth, then drew it out and laid it on the ground.

When they stood, the man in the robe, beckoned to them. With the solemnity of a priest offering the Host, he passed each of them short lengths of rope with frayed ends knotted around small stones. He raised his hand and dropped his head in a slow nod.

Wordlessly, the men circled Justin, began a boxer's dance around his body, their feet scuffing against the rough earth, the ropes snapping in the air.

Then, as if with one arm, the lashes fell on his back. Justin dropped and rolled, drawing up his feet and lashing out. Rolling up on his feet again, he whirled like a dervish within their tight circle, his sweating body eluding their whips or their hands until one of them pulled his legs from under him and he fell thudding to the ground. The whips ate fast and hard into his back, and he tucked his head under his arms to escape seeing sprays of his blood paint delicate patterns on their boots and jeans.

The churning dust filled his mouth and clouded his eyes, but for an instant he saw María fighting loose from the robed man. Suddenly, she was in the circle of whips, screaming and clawing, her feet flying off the ground as she swung from the back of one of the men like a small terrier.

From the ground Justin could only see María's feet bounce up into the air, then down, hitting the ground. Suddenly she was crawling toward him on all fours. She looked fearlessly into the hooded faces ringed above them. "Stop this! Stop this, you cowards!"

The robed man charged into the circle, catching hold of her feet, dragging her across the hard ground. Incoherent sounds of rage burst from him more terrifying than words. Flipping her over, pinning her head in the crook of his arm, he stuffed a rough gag in her mouth. She fought, kicking out with her legs, until he grabbed her by the hair and slapped her over and over, subduing her finally by tying her to the truck's bumper.

Justin stared up at the hem of the robe brushing his face. Other hands grabbed him, turning him onto his stomach.

Adrenaline pumping, his heart hammering out of his chest, he could feel the robed man kneeling beside him. He tensed at the man's touch. The hands, smooth and almost soft, massaged the small of his back in ritualistic rhythm, to a whispered chant. In spite of everything, he felt his body relaxing, his heart slowing. Maybe the worst was over. Maybe now they would let him go.

The rubbing slowed and ceased. Something else now, a line being drawn down his back low and close to the spine by something cool and hard as stone. With the first warm spurt of blood, everything around him dimmed and went far off as the pain grabbed him.

Consciousness roared back. Knees and boots and hands pinned his heaving body as the robed man brought his hand down again. Somewhere in his head he counted the gashes, three down, three across.

Justin kicked blindly as the cutting stopped and the hands let go of him. Grabbing dirt in his hands, he threw it into the eyes that stared at him from beneath the hoods. He rolled, feinting and gaining his feet under him, crouching like a sprinter at the starting line. *I can make it! I can make it to the edge of the mesa! I can make it down the trail!*

A hand pushed him hard from behind, the wind knocked out of him as he hit the ground.

Chapter Thirty-One

They wrestled Justin onto the cross, holding both arms down on the crossbeam. They tightened the stiff new rope, knotting and double knotting the coils around his arms from wrist to shoulder, his legs from ankle to thigh. Even before they finished, his limbs began to swell around the bindings, taking on a bluish cast.

No slip knots this time, he said to himself, feeling somehow detached as they jostled his body.

The man who cut Justin's jeans off, took off his own shirt. He secured the shirtsleeves around the back of the cross, the cloth falling like an apron over Justin's near nakedness.

"What in the hell's that for?" his partner scoffed.

"It's more fitting," he said, the language of his big body defying anyone to challenge him. He eased off Justin's boots. "These belong to the girl," he said gently. No one stopped the big man as he approached María and handed her the boots. "It would do the boy more good now if you just stay quiet," he said to her. When she nodded, he pulled out the gag, then turned aside from the plea he saw deep in her eyes. He had done all he dared do.

The robed man moved forward impatiently, orchestrating the men's moves with gestures of his arms and pointing finger. Straining under the added weight of the boy, the cross rose upright, the men twisting the great timber in small side-to-side movements, walking it inch-by-inch to the waiting hole. They let it drop with a jarring thud.

Justin sagged forward from the jolt, the ropes creaking with the strain, his screams echoing unheeded in the night. Working quickly now, the men shoved brace timbers in at the base of the cross, shoveling dirt into the hole around it and packing it solidly. Blood from his wounds made slow pilgrimage down the crude cross, the darkening drops falling on the ground at their feet.

Anxious to be done with this, the men shuffled and looked at each other as the robed man directed them to gather in a tight group at the base, making María stand in front of them. They groused among themselves, "What's he up to now?"

He waved his gun, reminding them he was armed, gesturing for them to pull off their hoods.

The robed man backed into the darkness where the truck lights didn't touch him, an observer of them all, visible only by a single red eye pulsing in the darkness.

"¡Mal ojo! The evil eye," whispered the big man who had helped Justin, crossing himself. "It's the devil."

The taillights disappeared down the arroyo.

"Don't leave me." Justin's plea fell into the great emptiness of desert silence.

He felt as if he were falling, his numb fingers grasping at the arms of the cross, the effort tightening the rope across his throat. Gagging, orgasm shook his body.

He saw himself, as if from far off. The heels of his cowboy boots clicked smartly as he strode through the noisy, smoke-filled casino. He let María stuff the quarters into the slot, their bodies pressed together merged with sweat and the intensity of their desire to win.

He was going to keep his promise. He was going to do big things for her. Red flashing lights suddenly lit up their machine. In a cacophony of horns and bells, quarters fell like silver water, bright as light.

Chapter Thirty-Two

Spy Wednesday

Ahead, the *morada* squatted low and impregnable in a patch of dry weeds and sage-colored chamisa, windowless with but a narrow door in the blank mud surface. On the flat roof was a frame belfry, the bell visible through the lattice. A cross atop it and the Stations of the Cross freshly painted, dressed it up in their humble way for Holy Week. A steady stream of gray smoke poured from a chimney pipe on the roof, filling the air with a sweet, piney fragrance, a carved figure of Jesus naked to the waist dragging a cross marked the entrance.

The day fit Sunny's mood as chilly air drove away the unseasonably warm weather, and dark clouds scudded across the sky. Without its bright sun, the landscape appeared stark and threatening, the thought that the two men who chased Justin might come looking for her never far from her mind.

Ann's surprise invitation to learn the truth about Los Hermanos left her no choice but to tell Molly why, even though it meant bringing up Sumner, Kay Waring and the interview with Raymundo Manzanares in Santa Fe.

A group of women outside the *morada* greeted them, and took the large crockery bowl Ann had brought, adding it to a table loaded with food. "Panoche," Ann said. "Mama's famous recipe. Enough for an army."

Sunny had tasted the slightly sweet pasty pudding, and thought it like eating pureed wheat-bread. But Molly was raving about it, and happily chatting with the women about the other dishes.

Sunny stayed right on Ann's heels, following a path trampled in the weeds to a narrow door in the side of the *morada*. A man stepped out, answering Ann's knock, greeting her.

"Brother de la Luz, this is the friend I spoke to you about.

"No cameras," he said abruptly.

With her assurance, he opened the door wide, welcoming Sunny inside. "This is our chapel," he said proudly.

As he closed the door, the windowless room was plunged into near darkness except for banks of red votive candles that glowed on a tiered altar set against the far wall. The smell of incense and hot wax permeated the air and mingled with the sweet odor of burning pine from the small iron stove in an opposite corner. In the flickering light, she saw the room was empty except for worn, crudely made wooden benches circling the room's perimeter. As her eyes grew accustomed to the dimness, the crucifix with its life-size Christ seemed to fill the room with a breathing presence, suffering and sorrowful. The wood, smooth and real as skin, bled with blood so skillfully rendered it seemed poised to fall afresh from the crown of thorns and the cruel nails in the hands and feet.

In awe, Sunny looked into the round beatific face of her host. "What do you do here?" she asked so softly he had to bend toward her.

"We pray and do penance," he answered simply, but with ardor. "Understand this is an emotional time for us. We come here at the beginning of the week and don't leave again until Easter Sunday."

She could see the chapel was only about half the building's space and wondered what occupied the rest of it? There were definitely muffled voices and sounds of shuffling feet beyond the dividing wall.

He seemed to notice her inquisitive stare. "The procession is about to start and I'm needed," he said abruptly, holding the door open for her to leave.

Outside about thirty people were gathered in small groups. The only child among them was Jimmy Ruiz, wearing a starched white shirt and proudly holding a statue of Jesus almost half his size. His attention was riveted on a man in a suit that Sunny remembered read the Sunday announcements during the Palm Sunday service and seemed to be leading the group today.

"The *Hermano Mayor*," Ann whispered, she and Molly joining her. "Today, Holy Wednesday, is known as Spy Wednesday in this *morada*. We think of Judas, who bargained to become a spy for the Jews, and of his betrayal of Jesus. Father Emilio says we still betray him with our greed and love of money and material things."

She nodded toward a tall wooden cross set in a pile of stones about fifty feet beyond. "That's the *Calvario*. Some of the people make *la procession de los Dolores,* the procession of sorrows, to it. Some will do penance along the way in celebration of God's forgiveness and penitential service.

"Jimmy and Mrs. Ruiz play a big part today." She made a little wave to Mrs. Ruiz who was holding a large image of the Virgin Mary in both arms as she waited at the head of a group of women standing separate from the men.

Ann stopped talking as a man, big and thick bodied, approached. He wore a filet of thorns around his head and circlets of cactus bound his waist, embedded in his bare flesh. He moved to the front of the line and the *Hermano Mayor* gestured toward the ground. The man laid face-down, prostrating himself before the group.

Sunny took hold of Ann's arm, wanting to know what was happening.

"All I know is he is doing penance for some great wrong, Sunny. The *Hermano Mayor* set the punishment, I'm told. The man is a devout Penitente, but he may be expelled."

Noise filled the air before Sunny could ask more. Seven young men dressed only in white cotton pants emerged from the *morada*. Several of them whirled wooden boxes on dowels, their percussive clacking sounding like hail falling on a tin roof. As they passed, Sunny clasped her hands over her ears against the almost deafening sound. Others followed, rattling chains padlocked to their wrists.

Then, a man stepped into the line fingering a small flute, the high shrill notes so melancholy goose bumps rose up and down Sunny's arms and on the back of her neck.

"*El pito,*" Ann yelled above the noise, struggling to make herself heard. "The man is called a *pitero* and is important in all the ritual. The noise makers are called *matracas*. They're usually used only for Good Friday, but the boys wanted the practice. Loud, aren't they?" She laughed, holding hands to ears.

The small crowd began to move forward, chanting in unison, Jimmy Ruiz' voice a clear and steady soprano floating above the others. Molly leaned against Sunny and whispered, "That sounds almost like a Gregorian chant—oh, dear." Molly stiffened, biting her lip as the first person in the line stepped upon the back of the man prostrate on the ground, followed by the others.

The procession reached the *Calvario*. Jimmy and his grandmother carrying their statues came to meet facing each other at the base of the cross, their faces wet with tears. The group drew close around them singing of the Passion, their emotion building in intensity, as Mrs. Ruiz slowly tipped the Holy Virgin toward the *Cristos* held aloft in Jimmy's trembling arms.

As the statues came close together in the symbolic last embrace of Mother and Son, Sunny was moved to tears thinking of her own son, worrying about Justin, feeling for little motherless Jimmy.

Leandro Martinez stood half-way along the path back to the hotel. Ann called to him, "Uncle Leandro. Tell Sunny what you told me once about the Pueblo men and the sun and about the Penitentes and their rituals. She needs to understand our ways."

He laughed, and Sunny thought he should do that more often, it so changed his demeanor.

He obviously liked to tell the story and embellished it with many details, which boiled down to a youthful Leandro and an Indian boy spying on the elders of the great Taos Pueblo as they climbed, backs to the ladder, to the roofs of their high-storied adobe city before dawn. "Tómas, my friend, says they do this every morning to bring up the sun. Without their ritual the sun would be lost to the world. It is the same with us."

He sought her face for some sign she understood his revelation. "We don't only do penance for ourselves, for our own trespasses," he said urgently. "It's for the redemption of the world. Without our suffering mankind might forget. It is a living Eucharist."

Sunny remembered little Jimmy Ruiz' response to what it meant to be a Penitente. "Being Jesus," he said. Sunny appreciated the power of the myth that held these people, even if she could not embrace it.

Chapter Thirty-Three

"Justin's gone?" Ann asked incredulously. "Did you check his room? Did anyone see him? Didn't he tell anyone?"

Gordon Grantwood huffed. "He didn't clean the bathhouse pools. The desk called me in when they couldn't find you," he said pointedly to Ann. "Yesterday and today were supposed to be my day's off, the first I've—"

"I, for one, suggest we celebrate," Leandro snorted, clapping his hands.

"Thank God María's with the Tafóyas," Ann said. "I've got to agree with Uncle Leandro, I'm not sorry to see Justin gone. But María is going to be devastated. They were…" Her face reddened. "Friends. Regardless of our opinion of him."

Sunny held her tongue. There was no need now to say anything about yesterday and her suspicions about Justin, so she was startled and flustered when Gordon looked at her in an accusing manner and said, "You seemed to get along with him pretty good. Maybe you know something we don't."

Leandro loudly interrupted with his own concerns, saving her from having to find an answer. "If you work today, Gordon," Leandro began, "you can be off tomorrow and Friday. But, Ann, that means, you're going to have to come in some, vacation or no vacation. And you're going to have to get that massage therapist who freelances over at that hippie herb store to fill in."

The old man's energy and stamina amazed Sunny as he issued orders like a general in full charge of his troops. His stocky tanned body looked as fit as a man twenty years younger. If Gordon or Ann had ambitions about Ojo Tres, she thought, they might as well forget them unless they were willing to bump off Leandro.

Chapter Thirty-Four

Ann and Molly decided to drive to Eagle Wing for a late lunch, a movie and dinner, since their plans for Thursday were now off. Sunny turned down their invitation.

Dangerous men or no, she was going to have a look at Justin's apartment for signs of a struggle. If so, she'd report it to the law. If it looked like he left on his own, she'd bet her bottom dollar he left some kind of instructions for María to follow him, or at least a note of explanation for his sudden departure. She wanted to find it before anyone else did.

She decided it might not be a bad idea to take her gun with her. Relocking the apartment door, she hurried through the pool area, enjoying the antics of a bevy of splashing children, the sun shining bright now and heating things up again.

She looked up just in time to see Gordon blocking her path. She wasn't in the mood for confrontation, but with the pool on one side and him on the other, she wasn't sure how to avoid it.

Then, from the corner of her eye she saw two boys barreling down the sidewalk straight toward Gordon. Should she warn him? *Oh, too bad. Too late.* They jumped together, belly flopping into the pool, drenching his shirt and pants from shoulder to ankle.

His feet drumming with rage, he screamed, "No running. No running. No diving either, you little brats." He looked ready to plunge in after the pair as they planed water at each other, ignoring him. Heading for Gordon like a Green Bay Packer tackle, a woman shouted, "Don't scream at my boys!"

Sunny darted away, leaving Gordon to fend for himself. She heard the splash and turned in time to see the irate mother push Gordon headlong into the water. Payback, she smiled to herself.

"Oh shit, she's on the move again," Robson Steele said under his breath, hastily pulling his boots back on. *This is a damned pain in the ass!*

Having seen her go in her apartment, he hoped she would stay put for awhile. Yesterday he had to be halfway across Santeria County on urgent business and had no choice but to take a chance that she wouldn't get into any real trouble. So far today she was with her mother.

It looked like she was headed for the parking lot. He exited by the side door at the end of the short hallway where his room was located and into the parking lot after her.

He kept to a fast stroll in case he came up on her suddenly so it didn't look as if he were chasing after her. Better she not see him at all.

He caught sight of her, through the trees, hanging back just in time to see Sunny go to the second room from the end of the bunkhouse. He knew exactly who that room belonged to. He tensed, seeing the screen door standing open against the building and the door to the room slightly ajar.

Suddenly she turned and ran back to the edge of the orchard, searching around and finally finding a short stout branch. She returned to the partially open door and shoved the branch at it, leaping back as it swung wide open. She waited, brandishing the branch above her head like a club. Then advancing slowly, she pushed the door all the way against the wall, making sure no one was standing behind it.

He smiled. *Pretty smart lady.* He moved cautiously up to the next tree to get a better view of her. *My God, I wonder if she knows how to shoot that thing?*

Standing at the doorway in shooting stance with the gun drawn like she saw on TV, Sunny let her eyes search around the stark room. It looked little changed, certainly no one had touched the rumpled sheets and the overflowing trashcan and the dirty dishes. The chairs were upright. If there had been a struggle, it didn't show. She guessed the door had been shut too hastily to catch, and had blown open on its own. She stepped into the room and locked the door.

She noticed little stuff missing, the cards, a pocket-size transistor radio and a jar of loose change. *That's good. That's all stuff he would take with him.* The hooks along the bathroom partition were empty of jeans and shirts. Gone too were the backpack, his running shoes, the Stetson and those gray cowboy boots. She was feeling pretty confident that Justin got out before the men who were looking for him returned.

There was definitely no note for Mária in plain view. Crossing to the bed, she lifted the mattress and found nothing. The coiled springs were the old fashioned kind with no covering and she could see through to the floor under the bed. There was nothing there but an accumulation of dust and part of a broken wine bottle.

She flicked on the switch to the overhead light. Except for a few dead flies there was nothing secreted in the cheap glass fixture. She ran her fingers under the tabletop, finding nothing except old wads of chewing gum. The torn telltale jeans and the pile of dirty clothes had been stuffed into the oven.

The refrigerator was empty except for a tipped over jar of mustard and little hard dried things in a frozen dinner tray. Sunny pulled the single ice cube tray from the small freezer compartment, finding nothing, not even ice. She wrinkled her nose at the smell of garbage and backed away. *Buddy, I don't care if you've written María a Shakespearean sonnet, I'm not going digging through that.*

The medicine cabinet was bare, but she noticed his toothbrush lying on the sink. *Maybe you were in enough of a hurry to overlook something else.* She wasn't sure what she was looking for now, but renewed the search with more interest.

The bathroom sink was just a bowl attached to the wall with no cabinet below. She ran her fingers along the back of the drain pipe and over the surface of the underside of the bowl. The toilet tank lid gave a dull clunk as she removed it. She plunged her hand in and let her fingers explore all around the rusty flush mechanism. Satisfied it was empty, she replaced the lid. She was about to give up. There wasn't anyplace else to look. Suddenly she reached over and slipped the toilet paper off the wooden roller.

"Bingo," she said aloud, giving a little chortle of surprise at a piece of paper wound around the center of the roller and taped into place with Scotch tape. *Good hiding place.* With her fingernail, she edged under the tape, loosening it. From under the paper a small rectangular card fluttered to the floor. She retrieved it.

Justin's face, a younger Justin, stared up at her from a Missouri driver's license. Only it wasn't Justin. It was Billy James Tilton, 16, from Billings, and the identification was probably his social security number. So it wouldn't be difficult to find out more about him. She guessed Billy might be wanted. The license had been issued for three years and was due to be renewed this month. There was something so sad in the young face.

She unfolded the other paper. It had what appeared to be coordinates jotted on it and a rough map. She turned it over and saw there was some other writing in fine neat printing. No time to figure out where Justin had gone and what the markings on the paper meant. But she was sure of one thing, somebody probably wanted this piece of paper. *Badly.*

Her stomach flip-flopped with rising fear. She shoved her gun in her fanny pack and replaced the toilet roll. The longer she stayed, the greater the chance that someone would catch her here. And they might have a bigger gun.

Fumbling, she dropped the piece of paper just as she stepped outside. She scooped it up and jammed it into the back pocket of her jeans.

Just as Sunny came out of Justin's room, Robson Steele turned at a sound behind him, seeing a man in a robe and hood. "What the hell?" The man's quick advance threw him off balance where he was squatting on his haunches behind a tree. He fell hard against the trunk and hit the ground. Swiveling his weight, he grabbed hold of the man's leg, trying to bring him down. In that instant before oblivion, he knew he'd been hit mid-chest, his arms quivering and releasing their hold, an image through a red bloody film of his heart suspended, not beating.

The attacker zapped his mark twice more, before stuffing the stun gun back in his pocket.

The scuffle had been brief, but long enough to let Sunny get out the door and away. He watched her retreating back through the branches. He saw her stuff a paper in her pocket, and was pretty sure it was what he was looking for. He had been all over that place once and was coming back for another go at it. *Now fucking A, how do I get it back?*

In frustration he kicked the inert figure balled near his feet, delivering the punch expertly in the area of the kidneys.

Chapter Thirty-Five

Sunny waited while the hotel kitchen made up a sandwich for her to take back to the apartment to eat later. She wandered into the hallway between the office and the breakfast bar and dropped coins in the vending machine, hoping the Snickers bar hadn't been in there since 1902.

A sudden draft made her turn her head.

"What in the world happened to you?"

"I need help." Robson Steele slid along the wall to support himself, his face pale and gray. He managed to gasp. "My heart's out of rhythm, running a mile a minute." He held a hand clutched to his chest.

Sunny ordered the girl behind the desk to help her. "Grab his key!" She adopted a no-nonsense doctor-tone. "Rob, put your arms around our necks. We need to carry you or you'll never make it."

He was dead weight by the time they got him to his room. "Alright. All together, heave!" They dumped him onto his bed. "Elevate his feet." She tossed the girl a pillow, and put another under his head. "You shouldn't lie flat," she said. His eyes were closed, his skin clammy and cold to her touch, his shirt drenched with sweat.

"We need to get you out of this." A couple of buttons flew as she ripped the shirt open, and together she and the girl pulled it off. She looked around for something warm to put on him and spotted his suitcase open on the fold-down stand by the dresser. She grabbed a sweatshirt, momentarily startled as she gazed down on a 9mm Glock nested in his socks.

She whirled around at his voice, sounding faint and thready, and pulled another shirt over the gun. "Get ice, a big bowl of ice. I'll tell you what to do with it." He fell back against the pillows.

The girl from the desk was rocking back and forth on her feet and looking worriedly over her shoulder. "If you don't need me, I've got to get back to the desk. Mr. Martínez is very mad if we leave the desk."

"Not half as mad as I can get. This man needs a hospital. There's got to be some kind of emergency procedure here, some kind of ambulance. Move your ass and get someone on the phone I can talk to." Sunny barked at the girl, who whirled and ran out of the room.

Sunny was on the verge of asking what the ice was for, when Rob's eyes fluttered open. "The ice," he said, between shallow breaths. "Hurry."

She sped down the hallway and burst through the swinging doors into the kitchen. Without waiting for an invitation, she grabbed a stainless steel mixing bowl off a stack and pulled ice trays from the refrigerator. "A man may be having a heart attack. I need ice!" The chef and his helper chopping and stirring kept cleavers poised like they were entertaining a crazy woman.

Back in the room, she filled the bowl with water, as Rob directed, and set it beside him on the nightstand. As he motioned, she helped him swing his legs over the edge of the bed and moved the table closer to him. He plunged his face down into the water, holding it there for a count of five, then up gulping in air, repeating it several more times. "Drowning reflex," he managed to say, water running onto his shirt. "Old emergency room technique."

He sank back on the pillows trying with the palm of his hand to tap a normal, steady rhythm on this chest. "Shocks heart… normal rhythm… works sometimes… sometimes not." His words came like a bad phone connection. "Like now." He gave a wan smile.

The girl's footsteps sounded loud in the hall, and she appeared in the doorway, saying proudly, "My uncles will take him in their van." She hurried to get out the words, seeing Sunny's look of concern. "My uncles, they're in charge of the volunteer fire department for Ojo Tres. It's quicker than waiting for the Santeria County ambulance all the way from Eagle Wing. Okay?" She didn't wait for approval and hurried away even as more questions bubbled to Sunny's lips.

Opening his eyes, he said. "Look at my chest?"

She composed herself, pulling up his sweatshirt. Not the time for a smart ass comeback. "I'm sorry. What am I supposed to be looking for?"

"Burns, like dots." He held his fingers about three-quarters of an inch apart. "Space between the dots."

"Here," she said, surprised to find exactly what he described in the center of his chest, right at the heart. She drew a circle around them with her fingernail. "What is it?" She tried to concentrate on the spots and not his well-shaped torso, smooth and lightly tanned. He looked like he worked out, a lot. He had a little hair on his chest, gray like his head. Sunny liked a little hair.

"Could you keep looking?"

She flushed with embarrassment until she realized he meant for her to look for more burns like this.

"It's important. How many. Where?"

Sunny nodded and gestured for him to roll onto his side.

He obliged, and Sunny drew back suddenly seeing a holstered gun concealed under his pants leg near the top of his boot.

"See anything?" he asked.

She wondered if he meant burns or the gun, and ran her hand over his shoulders and back as fast as she could. *I don't know anything about this man. Guns like that? Shit, he's no real estate agent. He could be anything. A drug dealer. A hit man. Big fat liar for sure.*

"I don't see anything," she said. Then she spotted it, a pair of perfect burned circles branded right at the base of his skull. "Whoa. Yes. Right here." She touched the place lightly. She found another set of the same marks on the side of his neck.

His words were muffled, but she heard him say, "The son-of-a-bitch zapped my neck and the back of my head after I'm down? Now it's personal"

It was as if he'd got a shot of adrenaline. He rolled to his feet, and for a moment he and Sunny were almost touching.

"I need to level with you," he said, fighting wooziness. Reaching out, he got a grip on her arm, holding on for dear life, his gray eyes searching hers.

She watched the pulse in his neck. It wasn't going boom-pause-boom-pause-boom but boom, boom, boom, boom faster than she could say the number of beats.

She heard voices and heavy footsteps coming down the hall. "I think your drivers are here."

He pulled her ear down close to his mouth. "Watch your back, Sunny. I was waiting for you to come out of that Justin kid's room—" The words came out in short bursts between breaths. "Some guy dressed in a robe and hood, honest to God, zapped me. He used a stun gun," he said pressing two fingers hard and quick into her chest in imitation. "I think he was following you, and I was just in the way."

The two men paused in the doorway like they were interrupting a tryst.

"What are you waiting for?" she greeted them. "This guy needs help fast." On the way to the van she described the stun gun wounds.

An oxygen tank hissed as they opened the valve and put a mask over Rob's face. She wouldn't take odds on his chances.

Sunny ran back into the lobby and thanked the desk clerk for her help. One of the men from the kitchen slipped up behind her holding out a sack at arm length with the sandwich she had ordered and forgotten. "Oh, yeah, right. Say, could you put that in a bigger bag?" Her hands drew the dimensions. Her crazy credentials fully established, he returned with the small sandwich in a full-size brown-paper grocery bag

If the desk clerk wondered why she headed back to Robson Steele's room, she didn't ask. Inside, she noticed for the first time that his window had a clear view to her apartment. How long had he been watching her? And why? Careful not to disturb anything in his suitcase as she searched it, she found nothing of interest but the gun. She put it into the paper bag. *No need to leave this. I might survive a stun gun but not a bullet from this baby.*

She filched the unopened roll of toilet paper from the back of the toilet tank and threw it into the bag. *You won't be needing this anytime soon.* She closed the room and returned to the lobby.

Gordon came rushing up, all agog. "I was in the massage room. I've got evening appointments. I saw the fire department van. What's going on?" Sunny noticed the girl at the desk seemed to be leaving her to deal with Gordon.

"One of the guests seems to be having a heart attack," she said.

"Who?"

"Robson Steele in number 16," the girl said. "I should have paged you." Her eyes were wide, expecting trouble.

"I am in charge tonight—" He seemed to forget the girl and turned to Sunny. "I don't think he's any older than we are. Damn. He'll be all right, won't he?"

"With the medical care available?" She shrugged.

Did you know him well?" he asked Sunny.

She searched his face. *Was he trying to insinuate something?* On the surface, it seemed reasonable interest in a guest. Still, she found her back getting up. "No. I just happened to be in the hotel when he took ill." She certainly wasn't going to share any of her suspicions, or anything she knew, with Gordon.

"Is there someone to notify? Family? An employer?"

She shrugged. "He told me he's in real estate. I don't know what agency." She was instantly sorry she'd said anything.

"Real estate?" Gordon moved toward her, questioning sharply. "Did he say if he was interested in Ojo Tres?"

"For God's sake, Gordon." Sunny was embarrassed to think she had asked Rob the same nosy question. "I don't know anything about him. Now please step back. I hate it when people get up in my face."

"I'm sorry. I have a one-track mind sometimes. The dining room's still open. How about dinner? Amends?" He didn't specify for what.

"Sorry. I'm eating in tonight." She held up the sack and was instantly sorry. *Dinner for twelve, anyone?* His expression was openly curious. *Well, let him wonder.*

About seven, Sunny checked for messages at the hotel after making sure there was a light in Gordon's massage room so she wouldn't have another chance encounter. There were still a few people coming and going from the bathhouse.

Leandro Martínez was behind the desk and looked up at her as she entered. He plucked a note from the cubbyhole above her room number and held it out to her.

She waited to read it, asking first if there was any word on Robson Steele's condition. He shook his head. She sketched the bare bones of what happened, when he asked.

The phone booth was free and Sunny accessed her home voice mail, as instructed. Moira's message was short and intriguing. "Big, big blow up here. Call me in the morning. At Blue's game tonight. Big party afterwards with Max's hockey buddies." *Go Blues!* Sunny fought back a wave of homesickness. She could almost hear the blades on the ice, the smack of the puck, the roar of the fans and the prickly feel on her tongue of an ice cold Bud.

Chapter Thirty-Six

Holy Thursday

Sunny was certain the numbers, N35°48.261 W 106° 11.815, on the piece of paper she found in Justin's room were directions to something, but she couldn't make sense of them or the map, which was nothing more than thin pencil scrawls outlining a spidery trail. Definitely no X marks the spot. On the back were meaningless notations, dates, random names and numbers.

It was the penmanship that intrigued her. Neat, tight, artful, it belonged on a classy hand-addressed invitation. It certainly didn't fit Justin's rough edges. Was it the work of the person Rob said was following her? She got up and pulled the curtains tighter, imagining someone peering through the crack.

Taking the spare roll of toilet paper she lifted from Rob's room, she carefully worked out one end of the tucked-in paper wrapper and slipped the map and Justin's license into the core. Even to her critical eye, once tucked back, the wrapper showed no signs of being disturbed. She pushed it out of sight into the back of the bathroom vanity, and placed their spare roll handy on the back of the toilet tank.

Rob's gun? Everywhere she looked was too obvious—the mattress, the oven, the cabinets, suitcases, nightstand. The old refrigerator! She slipped the heavy gun into a plastic grocery sack Molly had stowed in a drawer and, standing on a chair, reached over and found what she was looking for, the old-fashioned exposed cooling coils which gave her something to hang the bag on totally out-of-sight behind the bulky appliance.

Do I really expect someone to rifle the room? Come after me? Damn straight I do. All this was making her head ache, and she massaged her temples to make it go away, drawing some comfort from the weight of her own gun in the cargo pocket of her sweats.

Where in the heck are Molly and Ann? It's after eleven. They should be here by now. She tried to read, then to keep from pacing, gathered dirty laundry, dumped the remains of her sandwich in the trash and looked in the refrigerator like something might appear that hadn't been there twenty minutes ago. She settled for a glass of orange juice.

She almost dropped the glass at a sudden knock on the door. "Molly?" She swallowed against the tightness in her throat and called again, controlling the tremble in her voice. "Molly? Is that you?" The juice began burning back up her gullet. She closed her hand around the Smith & Wesson 380, checked the clip, and holding it down in front of her chambered a round, holding it down at her side. "Molly, answer me or I'm not opening the door!"

Sunny was completely taken aback. The man's voice was deep and quiet. "Sunny Bay? It's Tony Tsia. Ann's husband. Ann told me you and Molly are visiting. Maybe you remember me?"

She would have recognized him anywhere despite the added pounds the years had brought and the long hair, now gray, and hanging loose to his waist. She opened the door wide, tossing the gun onto the foot of Molly's bed.

"Tony! I hope I'm grown up enough now to call you that. Come in."

In the dim glow of the porch light, he stood with his hands locked in front of him, his shoulders thrown back, the mesmerizing black eyes peering at her with fierce intensity above cheekbones so pronounced they seemed like circles of bone and flesh padded onto his face. It took a moment to realize the look he wore was one of anguish.

"It's about María, Sunny. She's asking for you."

"I don't understand. María's with friends in Angel Fire since yesterday." It was then she saw María in the car. She was sitting hunkered down in the middle of the front seat.

Tony's dark, worried eyes followed her own, then turned back to her. "Sheriff's department picked her up hiding behind the Two Feather Casino over at Eagle Wing and took her to the hospital. She's been through something bad. She won't talk about it. She's pretty banged up. Bruises on her face and back and legs."

"Was she raped?"

He shook his head. "That's some relief." His voice trembled, "I haven't been much of a father lately."

He stopped, a passivity descending on his features as if an unseen hand had passed across it erasing emotion and feeling. "The doctor at the hospital is from our Pueblo. He recognized María and called me. I can't reach Ann. The girl at the hotel said you might know where she is."

Sunny wondered why, given the serious circumstances, he didn't put aside his differences and call Leandro.

"Ann and Molly should be home any minute. Come in and sit down?"

"No. I need to get back." He looked around at the buildings and over his shoulder at the hotel, and there was loathing in his expression as if he couldn't bear to stay in this place any longer than he had to.

"María keeps asking for you. Please."

Oh no, you aren't going to drop María in my lap if that's what you've got in mind. "You need to be here, Tony," Sunny said sharply. This is something you need to explain to Ann. María needs to see you together, like a family."

He finally nodded. She followed him to the car. He stopped in his tracks mid-way.

Leandro was limping toward them from the hotel. He was still several feet away when he boomed, "What brings you here, Tony Tsia?"

Tony bristled at the hostile tone, a look of hatred distorting his face.

What had Leandro done to make Tony hate him so?

She didn't have time to speculate. Ann's Bronco swung around Tony's car, braking noisily, the door slamming behind her. At sight of her mother, María was out of the car. Ann's whole body strained forward to reach her child, running so fast that her arms moved like windmills to keep her balance.

"What's happened? María, what are you doing here? Where are the Tafóyas? Tony…" She pleaded, "What is this about?" She rubbed at the bruises on María's face as if they were erasable, a low keening cry coming from her lips as she pulled her daughter into her embrace. Her face seemed suddenly crumpled and old.

Now that Sunny got a better look at María, she saw the bruises around her mouth and up her cheek, purple as plums. The girl clutched a brown paper bag to her chest for dear life. She looked from one to the other of them like someone watching her house burn to the ground. They were all talking to her at once. She didn't think the girl was processing much of what was happening. Suddenly she pulled away from her mother and threw herself against Sunny.

Ann grudgingly accepted the rebuff, Tony explaining they were here because María asked for Sunny. Ann collapsed against him, Tony holding her tightly around the waist.

Dark circles smudged the skin under María's eyes. She blinked at Sunny, her look dull and uncomprehending at first. Sunny asked again, "María, honey, were you with Justin? Do you know where he is?"

Something moved in the dark eyes then, slumping back against the chair, she clutched more tightly to a sack in her arms.

"Here, take some soda. You need to drink something, María. It will make you feel better."

She didn't pick up the can, but allowed Sunny to bring it to her lips and took a couple of sips before waving it away, croaking out sounds so serrated Sunny could barely make sense of the words at first. "You helped him— Those men."

"Do you mean the men who were chasing Justin? The ones who came to his room while I was there?"

The girl nodded. Then once again her chin drooped toward her chest.

"Did they hurt Justin?" Sunny gently cupped María's chin so she looked at her. "We need to help him." The girl's eyes grew blank and distant.

"Did those men do this to you?" She gently touched the red abraded skin around María's wrists.

"He did it." The whispered words seemed pulled from the girl's throat.

"Who is he, María?"

"The devil. It was the devil." The small slender hands knotted and unknotted.

"María." Sunny tried not to sound disbelieving or impatient. "What do you mean? I don't understand."

The small hoarse voice insisted. "He had a red eye. *Mal ojo! Mal ojo*, the evil eye," the girl insisted. "Little Nicky, like that." She struggled with the words, and her eyes came up hopefully to Sunny's.

"Like in the movie, María?" *She isn't making any sense.*

The girl rocked her head up and down, and her eyes took on some of their normal shine as they held unflinching on Sunny's own as if willing her to understand.

"Okay, María. Let me try to remember that movie. Adam Sandler plays Nicky. One of the devil's sons, right?" The girl grew animated, twisting her face to one side in imitation of the actor and bugging her eyes at her soda as if she was going to make it fly into the air.

Sunny hesitated, unsure how far to take this. She needed facts, not imagination. "Nicky does that thing about releasing the power, and every time he does, his eyes turn real burning red? Is that what you mean happened for real, María?"

The nod was vigorous, her hand trembling as she brought it up to the side of one eye and with her forefinger tapped against her thumb in a steady blinking motion. "Like this," she gasped.

"I don't understand the blinking eye part," Sunny said feeling frustrated. She was getting nowhere and maybe doing more harm than good.

María's hopeful face grew grim and helpless once again. Tears welled in her eyes and spilled down her cheeks and onto her arms. "It's my fault. It's my fault." She sobbed, her face buried in her hands.

"None of this is your fault, María." But the girl no longer seemed present.

Sunny asked gently, hoping yet to break through, "What's in your sack, María?"

The girl shook her head and pulled it tighter to her like a child resisting relinquishing a toy. "I want to go home," she repeated.

There was nothing supernatural about the bruises and scrapes and being dumped out at a casino. The kid needed sleep and food, professional help.

It was pointless to ask anything else, but she had to try once more. "María, please, was Justin with you? Do you know what's happened to him?"

Blanching pale as paper, María froze. Not looking at Sunny, she clutched the sack to her chest. "I want to go home."

She had tried and failed. Sunny wondered what the Santeria County Sheriff's Office was doing about all this. Not much. A sixteen-year-old girl running away with a boyfriend got into more than she bargained for. Sad, but not the stuff of manhunts.

Should she tell Sergeant Ortega about the men following Justin, Robson Steele and the man in the hood? She smarted just imagining the tall cop's reaction to the devil with the blinking eye.

Chapter Thirty-Seven

Sunny slept in, waking when Molly returned from Ann's house where she was taking a shift watching over María, fearing the girl might take off again to find Justin.

Molly reported that Ann and Tony had talked for much of the night, and she got the impression that a lot of the anger at each other had gone like smoke in the wind.

"Here's your clean laundry," Molly said, putting a stack of folded clothes at the foot of the bed.

"Hot dog. I was down to Big Electric Blue."

Molly laughed. It was their code word for nothing left to wear, a joke about Molly's most infamous fashion pick for Sunny, a brilliant blue warm-up suit that could be seen a block away, and the cause of a never-to-be-forgotten teenage tsunami.

"It's marked me." Sunny giggled, as she chose her favorite dun-colored tee shirt, khaki cargo pants and faded brown anorak. She was beginning to feel like a sitting duck in these four walls, waiting for whoever was following her to come looking for the things she'd hidden. She felt safer out in the open, dressed for action.

She slipped her gun into her camera case, slinging it over her shoulder, wondering about Moira's message to call. Was it possible that was only last night? So much had happened. She checked the time. It was already late in the morning in St. Louis.

"Big, blow-up. Big!" Moira said without preamble as she picked up Sunny's call. "Sumner and Kay Waring had it out. Mr. B even used the F-word. He was on the intercom with me when she went bursting into his office, so I heard it all."

Did this mean the interview with Manzanares was off? Trying to get a word in edgewise when Moira was wound up was like trying to break through bumper cars at the amusement park.

"Moira," she shouted over the torrent of words, "Just give me the time, not how to build the clock."

"You're going to beg me for details, Sunny Bay," Moira threatened.

"Is the interview on or off, please?"

Sunny heard her sigh. "Sumner advises you to call Manzanares and level with him about who you are and who the client is. The letter of agreement obligates us to do the job, regardless of this blow up, unless Kay or Manzanares calls it off. Leave it up to him to see you or not."

"And if my call gets back to Kay, then what? Tell me the rest of what you heard."

When Moira finished a blow-by-blow, word-by-word, Sunny realized she had forgotten her father started his career working for Killian Drummond, the largest public relations firm in town at the time. She had not known Kay Waring was Tom Killian's daughter.

According to Moira, Sumner shouted at Kay, "Your father pulled off a cover-up to protect your brother, Jack. Or have you forgotten that? Jack engineered phony signatures on petitions. Not me. But blood's thicker than water. I was the account supervisor on the project. Somebody's head had to roll, so I got fired under a fucking cloud, to keep the client from filing charges against the firm."

Kay played a trump card. "You don't think you stand a chance getting this big bond issue campaign you're so hot for if I disclose that piece of toilet paper hanging to your shoe, do you?"

And he said, "Thirty years building my reputation should stand for something. You start one of your whisper campaigns about me and I'll take out a full-page ad, tell the truth about the whole thing, name names like your brother's and your sainted father's. Something I should have done years ago."

"Go ahead." Kay Waring had laughed. "A lot of the right people will think thou protest too much. Either way, I win. I'm out of here, but your whelp had better not screw up this assignment with Raymundo, or I'll find a way to bring her down too."

When Moira told her that, she knew she wasn't going to call Raymundo Manzanares. Kay would find a way to call foul.

Chapter Thirty-Eight

The letters that had been waiting in her mailbox were burning a hole in her pocket.

Sunny didn't recognize the handwriting on the top envelope. It was blood red, greeting-card size, with no return address. She turned it over and held it to the light, then lost interest in it as her heart skipped a beat, and she felt giddy for a moment. The other letter was from Doug.

She stepped out on the veranda, looking for a quiet spot to read it. Across the way, Robson Steele was banging hard on her apartment door. *Oh shit. He's figured out I took his gun. I can't face that right now.* Part of her felt guilty; she should walk over and tell him she was glad he survived and just get him his damn gun. But all she could think about was the letter from Doug.

She scurried back into the lobby to take the back way out of the hotel. A cleaning cart momentarily blocked the hallway. Without a pause, she burst through the door to the kitchen, knowing it had an outside entrance. The same two men who had been there when she commandeered the ice looked up from their cooking pots. One fluttered his hand as if he was trying to bar her way, and the other pressed up against the stove front and gave her a wide berth.

She took the same road she had walked yesterday with Molly and Ann, moving at a slow trot, whistling Grace Slick's 'Somebody to Love,'" feeling its edge of recklessness and total defiant freedom matching her mood.

As she neared the *morada*, she was amazed to see a crowd of people, with more trudging in from the highway. Suddenly, a familiar voice called, "*Hola!* Sunny!

She broke into a smile. It was Jimmy Ruiz.

Jimmy grabbed her arm, examining the healing area of her burn. "Me too," he said excitedly, pulling up his shirt. Sunny ran her fingers over the pink spots, the skin drawn a bit around each one, but otherwise looking well on the mend.

"Man, I wouldn't have believed you could heal like this that first day I saw you. We were lucky!" She shaded her eyes and looked toward the crowds. "What's going on?"

"Pilgrims walking to Chimayó, to the Santuario. It's a holy place," he said solemnly. "They're stopping here for Stations of the Cross, and to rest. And to use those," he said, pointing out two outhouses off to the back of the *morada* where long lines formed at the outside toilets.

"The ladies serve refreshments too," he said, indicating a table filled with orange slices and cookies and five-gallon coolers of water.

Father Emilio caught sight of them and waved. He looked like a rancher in a plaid shirt and jeans. "Why is he dressed in regular clothes?" she asked.

"He comes to worship and make penance with us every year. Today," Jimmy said proudly, "he doesn't come as a priest. Today, he comes as a Penitente. You can come too," Jimmy was saying. "It's alright."

She leaned down level with the boy. "Jimmy, thank you. But I need to go."

Seeing his disappointment, she pulled the GPS receiver from her pants pocket. "Here, look at this. It's a global positioning system." She pointed to the sky explaining the satellite. Together they watched the small screen. She let him punch buttons, and using the *morada* as the starting point, they walked a short distance watching fine lines develop a map of their path.

"Wow! Way cool! Can I come with you? If you go up that road there are old mines and stuff. Please, can I come with you? I've never been to the mines. Grandma won't—" He stopped, realizing he had said too much.

"Not on your life, Jimmy Ruiz. You aren't going to get me in trouble with your grandmother."

He grinned. Suddenly Sunny wanted a photo of this small boy to remember him by. "Is it okay if I take your picture?"

Standing beside one of the white painted crosses against the stark desert background she saw more in the image than a small boy in jeans and sneakers. He was the dark, fierce, and proud blood of the Penitentes.

She used the digital camera, so he'd be able to see the results. Scarcely containing himself until she snapped it, he was fascinated by his picture viewed in the small screen. She let him take a photo of her, but resisted his pleas to join him at the cookie table, and headed away toward the base of the mesa.

Sunny wiped sweat from her face when she reached the top, but was pleased that the altitude no longer left her breathless. Clouds had gathered again, gusts of wind chilling her bare arms. Untying her jacket from her waist, she slipped it on, trying to figure out what had been going on.

The lip of the mesa was torn away, tire tracks leading off from it. Probably a big make out place for teenagers. She looked back down the steep incline and decided she wouldn't like to be along for the ride.

She headed for an outcropping of rocks, shaded by bushy piñon trees, and found a place to sit.

Doug's message was brief. At first she thought it was a joke.

I took the Thos. Moser chest of drawers. I'm buying a house. Getting married, Sunny. It happened so quickly. Wouldn't take back the chest, except Penny insisted. Matches her suite. Isn't that a coincidence?

Now even the memory of that glorious day in Maine, when they'd visited the Thos. Moser workshop and bought the piece, was tainted. She shook with anger, furious at herself for not taking back her key, getting madder by the moment thinking about Doug being in her house, dragging off her furniture for Ms. Knockers. *Anymore surprises, asshole?*

She ripped open the other letter. A too-cute replica of an embossed penny headed the notepaper followed by a "for your thoughts!" message. Two small clippings fluttered to the ground. Sunny picked them up. Ads cut from a magazine for breast augmentation and exercisers promising to increase size. Tears stung her eyes reading the single line of type above Penny Cregan's name: *Heard you could use these.*

He had talked about her to Penny. Talked about her body! Told her intimate things. The enormity of Doug's betrayal swept over her. Her hurt bore down like physical pressure around her heart and she ran blindly from it.

She ran until she could run no more. Panting and exhausted, she turned, looking in every direction. The mesa spread out like a table around her without visible landmarks in any direction, its monotony and soundlessness painfully lonely. The clouds were gone, the sun blazing straight overhead, washing out shadows. She had come a long way. But from where?

Sunny pulled out the GPS receiver. A zigzag map-line marked her path. According to the readout, she was more than a mile from the point she'd emerged onto the mesa.

The fluttering of something white caused her to look up, something moving over there beyond the clump of cactus and the dense green needles of piñon trees just beyond her. As she approached, black and white magpies suddenly swooped out of the trees, their startled chattering breaking the silence.

She still couldn't make out what was moving. She reached into her camera bag. With the reassurance of her gun in her hand as a precaution, she tiptoed closer to the brushy screen and pulled the branches aside.

She shrank back, hands over her mouth, tears beginning to roll down her cheeks. "Oh my god, no. No! No! Please, God. Please!" The shirt covering the boy's groin whipped in the wind. She stumbled forward, her eyes locked on the body hanging on the cross. For a moment Michael's face swam before her eyes, and she felt the familiar terror that never leaves you that something will happen to your child, something horrible at the hands of an unseen monster.

"Who did this to you?" she cried over and over in grief and rage. She forced herself close, gagging at the smell of his putrefying flesh, gasping in horror at the violence done to him. The familiar blond head was sagging forward and seemed to look down at her. She saw deep tears in the skin around the eyes, one open and blue dulled to near white, one missing from the socket. She remembered the magpies, drawing her arms in close around her chest. Patches of cactus thorns embedded in his flesh shone silvery in the bright sun.

Circling behind the cross, she saw short regular cuts in the flesh of his lower back, and she thought about what Kay told her about the marks on Raymundo Manzanares. She stared at the trails of black dried blood from the wounds across his shoulders and followed them down the rough wood to the pile of whips and cactus and glass and clothes at the base of the cross. The bloody rites and murderous crucifixion inflicted by the Brotherhood was shockingly real now.

She reached out and touched Justin's blood, the wood warm to her fingers. The cleaned up figure of the crucified Christ rendered in oil and metal and stone didn't come close to this.

"They won't get by with this." She spoke aloud to Justin, trusting he would hear her somehow. She pulled out a roll of film, her fingers fumbling it open, before remembering her 35mm Nikon didn't have a battery. She dropped the useless box, kicking it away angrily. She was stuck with the limits of the cheapie digital camera.

Cursing and all thumbs, she punched at unfamiliar buttons, couldn't remember where to zoom the lens, how to adjust for brightness. The height of the cross and the angle of the sun made it difficult to see the playback screen. Swept by waves of fresh grief, she forced herself to breathe, to calm down, to concentrate objectively on the legend Justin's corpse told. She worked feverishly, unsure the camera was recording well, but covering every detail.

Calmer now, she began to ask questions. Did María witness this? Did she see Justin murdered before her eyes? If so, why is she still alive? Leandro! It must be Leandro! He would spare María, for all his talk. Mrs. Ruiz' words echoed through her head. *Leandro is evil incarnate.* The carnage before her was evil.

She remembered the old man's response to Justin's disappearance. Did he already know the boy wasn't coming back? Leandro's physical limitations made it impossible for him to act alone. Who were the others? Was one of them the man in the robe and hood? Who was the devil with the blinking red eye? She had to talk to María again.

Suddenly, she was listening hard, realizing the sound she had been hearing at the edge of her brain was the steady hum of a motor. There was no doubt, it was coming her way. Panic seized her. She scanned the mesa, seeing nothing, but knew sounds were deceiving in this thin air. It could be far away or it could suddenly rise out of a dip or wash and be almost on top of her before she knew it. She dropped the camera in her bag, slipping the strap over her head, trying to decide which way to run.

The clump of piñon with the magpies was too close.

The pitch of the engine changed as it downshifted, louder and much closer now. She had no choice. Thirty feet away, at the top of a gentle grade, was another clump of piñon. From here it looked too thin to shield her, but it was all there was. Scrambling and slipping, she climbed. Reaching the stunted trees, she hunkered down behind the bushy branches.

With fingers numb with fear she unzipped the anorak's collar and fumbled out the concealed hood, putting on the jacket to cover her bare arms and pulling the hood over her bright hair. She tightened the drawstring around her face, leaving only breathing room and a small area to look out. Clawing with her bare hands, she pulled dry needles from under the piñon and scooped pitiful handfuls of sandy, rocky soil, building a barrier in front of her. Sun glinted off glass.

She dropped flat to the ground, pulling herself into a tight ball just as a pickup truck bounced into sight and pulled to a stop in front of the cross. Two men jumped out of the bed of the truck. They were the same ones who had come to Justin's door.

The doors to the truck's cab opened and two more men emerged. Through the low branches she squinted to see, afraid they might somehow sense her looking at them if she kept her eyes wide open.

Her body went icy and numb. The taller of these last men was wearing a long dark robe and hood, and seemed to be looking right at her hiding place as he swept the area with his eyes. She held her breath until he slammed his door and walked around the truck to join the others.

The men talked and laughed among themselves as they unloaded tools, their voices reaching her, but her mind couldn't seem to sort out the words.

They approached the cross, whooping at the stench of the body. Suddenly, the man who had been driving ran toward the first group of trees she'd considered for a hiding place, pulling down his pants and squatting behind it. His bowels squirted onto the rocks. The other men made catcalls and rude sounds, calling him chicken-livered, while they laid a tarp on the ground, leaned a ladder against the timber and set to work. The man in the hood rested against the truck body watching, a shotgun held loosely at his side.

Justin's body fell with a soft thump onto the tarp. Sunny bit down hard on her finger to keep from crying out. The man who cut him down stepped from the ladder, taking a long drag from a cigarette that dangled from his lips.

Together the men raked and rolled the clothes and bloody pieces of cactus and glass and whips and threw it all in with the body. Working quickly, they loosened the cross and worked it out of the ground, filled the hole and raked and scattered rocks, obliterating any evidence of what had happened here.

The buckle of the camera bag was pressing into the soft curve of her belly. *Don't move! Don't make a sound. Lie still.* Out of the wind and with the sun on her back, she was suffocating in the jacket and hood. *How long are they going to be there? How long can I lie here?*

She licked her lips, her tongue feeling thick and dry, and tried not to think about the water bottle in her bag. She longed to straighten her aching legs cramped in a tight fetal position against the rocky ground. She stared at the truck. *No matter what, lie still.* Her gun was useless. To reach for it meant death. She had no doubt. So she didn't move.

They sang in cadence as they heaved the heavy timber onto the truck. It shifted from the weight, then settled low on the tires. The tarp with Justin's remains and the other tools were tossed into the truck bed. The two men she recognized climbed into the back. One sat on the cross while the other balanced in a sitting position on the edge of the truck bed as they prepared to leave, their faces fully visible.

Sunny inched her fingers to her camera, then was unable to control their trembling as a cold sweat washed over her, emitting a fume like spoiling meat and metal, a sweat so strong she knew instinctively that it was the smell of fear. Tears ran into the edge of the hood, soaking it, and as if paralyzed, she didn't move to wipe them. *Justin, baby, I couldn't. I'm so sorry.*

She watched the men get ready to leave, when something caught the eye of the robed man. He adjusted his hood trying to see. The empty film box she had dropped and forgotten scooted a couple of feet along the ground blown by the wind.

He made a lunge, grabbed it, crushing it in his hand. His head, seeming all the more terrible for its black hood, swiveled slowly as he scrutinized the area. He picked up the shotgun and threw the bolt, motioning to the men, showing them the yellow film box. They fanned out, one climbing up the incline toward her

She lay still as death, not breathing. Breathing would make sound, so she would not breathe. He stopped so close she felt the spray of his urine as he took a leak. She heard him zip, turn back

212

downhill, yell "*Nada*." Her ears were ringing. She tried to fight back the blackness closing over her.

The gunning engine, as the truck roared away, jerked her back to consciousness. She could not have blacked out more than a few moments. The hooded man rode standing on the running board, still looking back for a sign that anyone was about.

As soon as the truck was out of sight, Sunny rolled over to sit up, vomit spilling hot down her shirt front. She dug out the bottled water, washed the bitter taste out of her mouth and tried to clean her shirt before gulping down what was left of the water. *Get up! Get out of here. They could come back.* She rubbed her cramped legs and struggled to her feet, steadying herself as the blood rushed into her limbs.

Retrieving the GPS receiver, she marked her coordinates and an icon for the spot where she'd found Justin. There might be nothing left of his body or the cross, but she had photos and the location.

If she could retrace her trail, she could soon be back where there were people. She took off running. It proved a false start that showed on the screen in her hand as a thin line diverging at a sharp angle from the map line. She quickly doubled back, walking this time until she could get her bearings and the spidery outline of her progress began to parallel the path she had taken to get here.

She labored for breath, stopping every few minutes to listen, imagining the sound of a motor, the men waiting in ambush. She forced herself to keep running, fighting fatigue, stumbling as she tried to keep her eye on the receiver, afraid she would lose her way.

Each clump of cactus and pile of rocks she passed looked the same as all the rest. Then, she came upon her own footprints in some loose sandy soil. Suddenly the topography began to look familiar. She yelped with joy. Maybe fifty feet ahead was the outcropping of rocks where she had stopped to read her letters. She made for it on a dead run.

This time she knew it was no quirk of imagination. The sound of the motor was real, and it was close. Too terrified to look back, she sprinted, legs pumping until her sides cramped, squeezing off her air. Somehow she kept moving, half walking, half running, chest heaving.

As she looked back, dust rose up in clouds as the truck sped along the trail she had come, careening around vegetation and rocks, gears grinding through washes. It was gaining on her.

Remembering the shotgun the robed man carried, she tried not to run in a straight line so she would be harder to hit. *Or is that only on TV?* But then she forgot everything and just ran, catching her second wind. With a last burst of speed she was over the lip of the mesa.

She hit the steep incline too fast, stumbling, rolling head over heels in a cascade of small boulders. Pummeled, terrified she would hit her head or break a bone, she clutched at the sparse vegetation along the way, her fingers finally grasping firmly onto a large round weed. It slowed her enough so she was able to gain her balance and rise to her feet.

Like a giant crab, she moved onto the steep roadbed bouncing on her downhill leg as her uphill leg and arm and hand worked to guide and balance her descent. Halfway down, she reached the huge wash she had gone around on the uphill journey. If the truck followed her, it could traverse the chasm faster than she could on foot and catch up with her.

She dropped over the lip of the cut, sliding part of the way on her rear end, then climbing diagonally up the steep grade on the other side. She looked back. The truck was poised at the top of the mesa, the engine gunning but not moving.

Not waiting to see if the men were coming, she ran with precarious speed, knowing it was her only chance. With both arms winging out, her body rising and falling like a surfer riding waves, she reached the base of the hill.

Looking up, she saw the hooded man watching her, standing tall and rigid atop the mesa, the skirt of his robe blowing around his legs.

The sounds of the mournful flutelike *pito* reached her, rising high over the barren landscape. Were the men who killed Justin part of the people she saw ahead of her moving from Holy Cross to Holy Cross, reaffirming the meaning of each station along the way? These people with a little boy she liked and a priest of her own faith? She didn't know. She just didn't know.

She had never felt more alone or more terrified. The killers had seen her and knew who she was and what she knew. She didn't have any room to make a mistake now if she was going to get out of this alive.

Chapter Thirty-Nine

Sunny melded into the sizable crowd now milling around the *morada*, welcoming the noise and chatter. She couldn't be sure the men weren't following her on foot. She kept her head down, looking out the side of her eyes as best she could to see if anyone seemed to be following her. Once he removed his hood, the tall man could be anyone.

Right now she had one objective and took her place in line for the outhouse. If she didn't pee soon, she was going to be disgraced

The woman ahead of her bobbed up and down with urgency, her enormous hips rocking like a small boat in the wake of a ship. She seemed to know most of the crowd and laughed loudly, drawing attention as she called to people moving by.

Sunny ducked her head and tried to look inconspicuous, but the woman turned and looked down at her, speaking in heavily Spanish accented English like they were old friends. "My God, kid. You got some sunburn." She pressed her fingers into Sunny's upper arm, leaving white prints in her reddened skin. "You better put something on that. Or it's going to peel, you know."

Her skin felt hot and tight and was beginning to sting furiously. "First things first." Sunny grimaced. "Look, you're next," she said, diverting the woman's attention away from her.

"Not a minute too soon!" She laughed as the wooden door slammed behind her.

To Sunny's surprise the woman was waiting for her when she emerged. "My name's Annabella." She offered Sunny a wet paper towel for her hands, slices of fresh orange wrapped in tin foil and a cup of water.

"Thanks. My name's—" She hesitated, and then said, "I'm Molly." She felt silly lying to this woman, but she was in paranoia mode. She ate the orange slices and gulped down the water gratefully.

"Hey, you going our way, come with us." The woman's good nature was irresistible. They followed the path worn in the field by so many feet, joining six other women who were friends of Annabella. Sunny worked her way into the middle of the convoy, grateful for the cover.

"Where are all these people coming from?" Sunny asked.

"We're all from Taos," they said at once. "But people come from all over New Mexico, Colorado, Texas lots of other states too," Annabella told her, gesturing broadly like she was pulling people from all over the world. "They predict 40,000 this year at Chimayó. You better come with us. You rub all over with the holy dirt from the Santuario and cure that sunburn."

Sunny saw the chimney of Ann's house just above the rise.

"Thanks for the offer Annabella. This is where I'm going. Girls, have a blast!"

She trotted away from the group, stiffness overtaking her tired limbs. For a moment as she moved with the women she felt safe and protected. Now the street where Ann's house stood looked empty and sinister. She hid behind a tall pole fence, trying to work up courage to step out into plain view, imagining a truck roaring out of hiding, men with shotguns going door to door.

She didn't dare risk going back to the apartment. Ann's was the only other place she could go. She had to get help, take her evidence to the law.

What if Leandro is responsible for what happened to Justin? Could she really count on Ann? These people always have their guard up, protecting secrets. One minute they pull you in, the next they push you away. Would anyone believe her?

She clutched her camera bag with its precious cargo of photographs. Without those, there wasn't a chance in hell anyone would believe her now that Justin's body had been taken away.

She counted three houses and a trailer between her and Ann's house. Squeezing her eyes shut for a moment, she prayed, then stepped into the open, crossing the street and loping through the back yards. With trembling fingers she unhooked the gate in Ann's patio wall and stepped inside.

Chapter Forty

The man guzzled his beer, trying to think. He needed to get all of it straight in his head, what he was going to tell Jimmy Dodson, and what he wasn't. He held the cold bottle to his temple with one hand and cradled his head with the other.

Things had gotten out of hand. Now, to top it off, there was this bitch and her photographs.

A rush of blood burned his face, and he struggled to rein it in. Rage made him make mistakes, and he couldn't afford anymore. He'd gone overboard with Justin. He'd have to be a bit more subtle about the girl.

He opened another beer. He was parked right out in the sun and it was hot in the cab of the truck, as he waited for Jimmy behind the boarded up motel a mile out of Ojo Tres.

One thing sure, he wasn't telling Jimmy about the tape he transferred from his video camera. He had Jimmy's hired thugs dead to rights, photos of them all with the body, and Leandro Martínez' niece to boot.

That video tape was his insurance policy. My goddam ace in the hole if that smart lawyer tries some legal maneuver to screw me out of the Springs on this land deal. Those Mexicans, he told himself, were Jimmy's doing. He sent them to get back the drugs from Justin. He was counting on holding Jimmy's involvement with them over the lawyer's head, if worst came to worst. Complicity? Conspiracy? Whatever the hell you call it.

Where is that little fucker, anyway? And what was the business he couldn't tell me about that brings him to the Springs today?

Chapter Forty-One

This was turning into the worst day of Jimmy Dodson's life.

He sat stunned, absolutely stunned in the guest chair across from Leandro Martínez, who sat behind his big desk paring his fingernails with a pocket knife and enjoying his lawyer's discomfort.

When Leandro summoned him to meet with him, he'd already gotten the word *sub rosa* from his wife's brother that Leandro wanted to sell Ojo Tres now, quick, a preemptive strike.

Leandro had no idea Jimmy's brother-in-law owned the land company that controlled the listing agreement on Ojo Tres. They'd been stringing Leandro along with all the money he would get for the place, and setting up false offers, stalling until the Easter drug shipment would give them the money to buy it through a straw party. This was why Jimmy loved being a lawyer. There were so many ways to screw people, make a big profit, and cover the money trail.

Jimmy took in the man lounging against the wall to one side of Leandro, the pressed blue jeans, the buttery leather boots, the bolo tie at the neck of the silk shirt.

Introduced as a lawyer, he peered at Jimmy through small round glasses. Chinaman eyes, Jimmy thought, like so many of the Pueblo people. "Ah, yes, Daniel Catanach," he said, shaking his hand. He'd been all over the papers and on TV, protecting the tribes from a revenue-sharing lawsuit on their slot-machine profits brought by the states' attorney general.

What the hell is he doing here? Jimmy ran his fingers under his collar.

He knew Tony Tsia, standing stiffly, hands resting on the back of a straight chair. When they met in his office, Tony wanted to sue Leandro, or kill him if he wasn't legally successful. His being here told Jimmy something important had changed.

But it was the small old man in the corner that held his attention. He had known even before the introduction that this was Tómas Acoma. His presence more than the others rocked Jimmy off his feet as he looked into the old face, feeling a little like a hare facing down a rattlesnake. Under other circumstances he might have been amused to find the same kind of shrewdness in the hard, wizened face as he saw in his own.

But right now he wasn't amused as he listened to the old man outline his offer to Leandro, telling it all in impeccable English tinged only slightly with the flatter rhythms of his native Tewa. Twice he lifted the sheaf of legal documents he held in his hand in a kind of emphasis, but never once referred to them or the lawyer.

When the old man finished, they all seemed to be waiting for Jimmy's reply.

Jimmy tipped the chair back on its hind legs and folded his hands over his stomach, a gesture he'd seen his father use a hundred times. "Well, now—" His voice didn't have quite the sententiousness he was striving for, so he started again after clearing his throat. "I can't possibly allow my client to sign those." He gave a dismissive gesture toward the papers the old Indian held in his hand.

"You don't get it. You're here, Jimmy my boy, to be a rubber stamp," Leandro cut in. "I'm not asking your advice. I just need to sign the papers in front of my own counsel to make it all proper and legal. Those are words you Dodson's know little about."

"This is absolutely fucking ridiculous, Leandro." Jimmy felt a trickle of cold sweat running under his shirt. He might get away double crossing the Doofus... but not this new bunch who wanted Ojo Tres, or else.

"This is blackmail, extortion! Do you understand if you sign that shit document you turn over all the land you own, this hotel and everything in it to Ann and Tony Tsia and their heirs? And that you are relinquishing the mining and water rights to the Pueblo? You're buying their silence for something that happened sixty years ago and nobody cares a fuck about."

Jimmy stabbed his finger at the Pueblo lawyer. "I don't care what kind of hot shot you are; you couldn't win a clay pot from Leandro Martínez in a court of law with that old tale about the Indian boys."

"We're set to subpoena your records on this matter." The voice was smooth and low. "I understand from Mr. Martínez that you threatened him recently and claim to have physical evidence, old trial records, et cetera. Mr. Acoma has a considerable civil claim here, if not a criminal one. I think you pointed that out to Mr. Martínez yourself."

"You told them that?" Jimmy turned astonished eyes on Leandro. "My God, you're a senile old fool," he spat with disgust.

Daniel Catanach went on as if he hadn't been interrupted. "If you don't cooperate, I won't have any trouble getting a judge to sign a search warrant for your office and home on the basis of suppressed evidence which you claim to be in your possession.

"We've already taken all the preliminary steps to sue. But all that can go away, Mr. Dodson, with Mr. Acoma's offer to Mr. Martínez. We've agreed Mr. Martínez will be paid substantial installments from the profits of the established business as well as any commercial endeavors from the mines or water. It isn't extortion. Mr. Acoma wishes to right an old injustice for his son, his family and the People.

Mr. Martínez has come around to believing his freedom and half a loaf is better than none."

"And it's better than being turned into a snake, eh Tómas?"

"You remember well, Leandro."

For a moment in this room, they were boys again, Tómas pinning Leandro to the ground, sure he was trying to pull a fast one on him over the Jake and the sale of the stolen goods. Pointing into Leandro's eyes, he moved one sinewy arm in the smooth wave-like motions of a serpent, the Pueblo people's warning to punish a treacherous friend by turning him into a living snake crawling on its belly for eternity.

The two men looked at each other with great respect without saying more. No one else in the room understood. But they did. And that's all that mattered.

Spluttering and threatening, Jimmy watched Leandro sign the papers with a flourish and push them toward him to witness. He swatted them aside like he was killing flies.

"This is stupid, Leandro. Really stupid! I'm not signing anything. If any of you think this is a done deal, you're dead wrong. What you've just signed constitutes a sale, asshole! Don't forget you've got a listing contract, and that's binding. You haven't had the last word by a long shot."

He turned to Tony Tsia. "I wouldn't pop the champagne just yet. You're all going to hear from Jimmy Dodson."

He stomped out of the office. He was late to meet the Doofus. He'd set the meeting thinking he had good news. Now what was he going to do? The idiot was already a lit sack of Roman candles. No telling what he'll do when he finds out he's been cheated of his birthright once more by his Uncle Leandro.

Jimmy's mind searched like a dropped cat for a place to land. To hell with meeting Antonio Martínez, he had bigger fish to fry.

Chapter Forty-Two

"Mom," Sunny called softly. "Mom, help me." She entered the patio at Ann's house. Molly, drying her hair with a towel, dropped it, catching Sunny as she collapsed into her arms, sobbing and shaking.

She hadn't called her Mom since she was twelve, and clung to Molly, while she spilled out her story between sobs. She spared no detail about Justin or the killers, about how she'd fooled the two thugs, about the man in the hood and robe, about him following her and nearly killing Robson Steele, about the hooded man watching her from the top of the mesa.

Molly pressed a tissue to her nose, and only then did Sunny stand on her own. "I can still wipe my own nose." They both gave a shaky laugh.

Sunny was first to see Ann standing in the doorway with her arm around María, who was wrapped in an old quilt and still holding the sack clutched to her chest. Both had been awakened from naps by Sunny's sobbing and heard everything.

"What are we going to do, Ann?" Molly pleaded. "The killers know Sunny saw them. We can't go back to the apartment. The law is going to need to talk to Sunny. But we don't want to endanger you."

"You're staying here, right here, goodness yes." Ann gave Molly a hug. "We'll all be safe together until we can figure out what's best to do."

"You don't understand, Ann. You may want us to go when I tell you my suspicions. Justin was beaten with whips, scourged and—" She paused, tamping down panic as images came at her in flashes, finally able to speak. "Justin had those marks, the *sello*, the seal of the Brotherhood cut in his back. They crucified him, for God's sake. Justin was crucified on a cross. This was done by Penitentes," she said.

Before Ann could answer, María broke away and ran to Sunny, holding the sack out to her. She already guessed what it contained. She pulled Justin's cowboy boots from the bag.

Ann let out a gasp. "María, are those Justin's? I don't understand." When she had been María's age a crucifixion went awry and the Brotherhood brought Raul Esteban's shoes to his mother's doorstep. Still she shook her head side to side in vehement denial. "This isn't the work of the Brotherhood. It makes no sense. There is some other answer."

With Sunny's arms around her, María's story came rushing out, the chase, her hiding, being found, tied up and gagged, everything she'd witnessed, the man handing her the boots, seeing Justin not yet dead, crying out as they drove away. Her last words were only a faint whisper.

Afraid the girl would lapse back into silence, Sunny held her at arm's length, urging her to describe everything she could remember about the men.

"They wore hoods. When the bad man made them take them off, I was too afraid. The devil said, if I looked, he'd do the same as Justin to me. I couldn't look!"

"It's okay." She smoothed María's hair back. "I was scared too. I couldn't risk taking pictures of those men when I thought I had the chance. We can't change it. Okay? It's called self- preservation. It's human. What we can do now is make those men pay for what they did to Justin."

After a few moments, María stopped snuffling and blew her nose. Her voice, tiny and flat, trembled as she spoke. Her general description of three of the men, matched Sunny's own. The fourth man, who gave her the boots, hadn't been part of the crew Sunny saw when they took Justin's body away.

They had identical impressions of the tall height and slender build of the man in the robe and hood, but María hung steadfastly to his being the devil, a devil with a blinking red eye. "*Mal ojo*," she insisted.

"That is a dangerous accusation, María," Ann said sharply, telling how an innocent woman was dragged from her bed and murdered near San Juan for the same charge.

"I know what I saw, Mama." Her voice took on more spirit. "He made me stand with those men under the cross, in the bright lights from the trucks." She started to weep again, her face in her hands. "The man in the robe stood in the dark, his red eye, glowing, watching us."

Even with the warm sun on her she drew the quilt tightly around herself. "I was afraid he'd take us to Hell with him."

At this she burst into fresh tears. "I deserve to go to Hell! It's my fault." She looked from one to the other of them expecting no absolution. "I pretended to be pregnant. It's a lie. It's an awful lie. I got him killed."

"Don't say such a terrible thing. You were foolish, but you're just a child, María," Ann said, rubbing her daughter's arms and kissing her hair. "You aren't the only one to make a mistake over love. And you won't be the last."

"You're mother is right, María. Justin was killed because he stole from bad men." The girl looked momentarily comforted.

"I'm sorry—" Sunny got to her feet, walked away, then turned back to the girl. "I have to ask this."

The girl didn't look away.

"You knew about the methamphetamine?"

She nodded. "Justin was going to sell it to get money for us. She told them about the abduction from the barn and their escape from the truck.

"There's no way to ask this but plain out. Why do you think they didn't kill you?"

Maria shrugged, eyes brimming again.

Ann stood, uncertainty playing across her face. "I know what you're driving at, Sunny, even if María doesn't. You think Uncle Leandro was involved because María was spared."

"It makes sense, Ann, where nothing much else does. You're the one who said he'd kill Justin if he didn't keep away from María. That has to come out when I go to the law. Are you prepared for that?"

"Leandro would never have perpetrated this charade, never put blame on the Brotherhood."

"You think what they did to Justin was a 'charade'?"

"The Penitentes do not go around crucifying people. The ritual of reenacted crucifixion is rare, an honor earned by a devout person. They would never do this to an outsider. We have our share of bad apples like everyone else, but this was some kind of madman, a sick rage against Justin. This person wanted to make it look like Los Hermanos did it."

"He wore a Penitente robe and hood."

"Pretending to be a Penitente! The men haven't worn robes in our *morada* since the forties. The robe you describe may not even look like our robes did." Ann paused seeming to weigh something. "Excuse me. I'll prove it to you."

She returned with a battered white hatbox. These are old snapshots that belonged to my father," Ann said, sorting quickly. She held up a photo. "This should convince you. This is what our robes looked like." She handed the old black and white photograph to Sunny—three young men arranged like stair steps.

Leandro, the smallest had the same combative stance as he did today. The slender youth in the middle, Ann's father Leon, wore white pants gathered at the waist by a cord, a hood pushed back off his face. The third man was tall and wore a long dark robe and cowl that hooded his features.

Goose bumps erupted on Sunny's arms even before María let out a soft cry of fear. "That's the man who killed Justin."

"Don't be silly, María. That's your Uncle Antonio. He's dead." She ran a finger lovingly over his image, saying proudly, "He was the youngest *Sangrador* to every serve our *morada*."

"Ann, your uncle could be a body-double, and the robe and hood look exactly like what I saw."

"What we saw," María chimed in, something of the old María returning.

Ann took the picture, dropped it back in the box and slammed the lid down. "Stop it. You're both overwrought."

"I've got no choice, Ann," Sunny said, tired of arguing. "I've got to get my photos to the sheriff. I've got to try to make him listen. Whether you think so or not, it would help to have that picture of your uncle. And I've got to tell him about the threats you said Leandro made. I'm sorry."

"What threats?" No one had heard Tony come in, and they turned their startled faces to him.

Chapter Forty-Three

"Mrs. Ruiz and Jimmy will be here any moment," Opal said, pulling a plate of food from the refrigerator. Antonio plucked a chicken leg from the plate, tore into it, as he followed her.

"Can't you get rid of them?" He hadn't been here five minutes. He was hot and dirty and wanted a shower. Fucking Dodson stood him up. He planned to wait here, then drive to the pay phone to call him. The lawyer better have a good excuse.

Opal punched up the pillows on the cot in the storage room, next to the bathroom. There was no window, only a door leading onto the back porch, with a heavy table resting against it. "You can eat and rest in here. I'll do what I can to hurry." She's bringing Jimmy, so lock the door."

"This had better not take long," he said, a dark expression crossing his face.

"It's Adeline's regular treatment day. She broke her shoulder last year when she ran off down the same arroyo that almost got me. She's still got a lot of pain in—"

"Oh yeah, which arroyo is that?" he asked, not wanting to hear about Mrs. Ruiz' aches and pains.

"You know the one, between here and Eagle Wing, just before you get to the bridge. Some call it *Quebrada Seca... Dry Gulch.*"

He snorted. "That's pretty funny, isn't it? She breaks a bone—" He raised his voice for attention as his mother kept glancing over her shoulder listening for the front door to open. "You know? *Quebrado?* That's slang for a break, a kind of lucky break. Oh hell, forget it. You haven't got time for me. Give me my plate, I'm hungry."

"Lock this behind me," Opal said. She shut the door to the room and listened for the key to turn. Satisfied, she crossed the room just as her mynah bird began hopping to-and-fro on his swing calling, "Come in, come in."

She spotted Antonio's jacket slung across her easy chair in front of the television. She snatched it up, looking for a place to hide it. A videotape, along with his cigarettes and lighter, were under it. *Oh no.* He would be climbing the walls without his smokes. She started back to the storage room, but the front door was already opening. No time. She dropped the smoking materials into her apron pocket and laid the tape under a couple of rental tapes by the TV set, pushing the jacket out of sight under the chair cushion.

"Hello, Opal," Adeline Ruiz called. She gave a shooing motion at Jimmy's back, reminding him to remove his ball- cap and greet Opal politely. She launched into a soliloquy of her pain.

"Let's get started then." Opal said, nervously hurrying Mrs. Ruiz to her bedroom.

Behind the curtain, she heard Mrs. Ruiz' shoes clunk loudly as they dropped to the floor, the rustling of her clothes as she removed them. Opal handed through a sheet, keeping her eyes on Jimmy who was busy talking to the bird.

"You can give him some of those pieces of grapes on that plate by the cage," Opal said. "But watch your fingers. Tristan isn't very careful. Maybe he doesn't see so good. He's getting old like me. Are you going to be alright out here by yourself?"

"Don't get into Opal's things, Jimmy," Mrs. Ruiz called in a firm voice from the bed.

The curtain dropped, his grandmother giving Opal directions to massage just so, just there.

Jimmy finished giving all the grapes to the bird. Almost by mutual consent the boy and the bird tired of each other when the fruit was gone. He wandered around the room. With nothing else to do, he went into the bathroom and relieved himself, spending some minutes washing his hands and letting the soap float in the water.

For a moment he thought he heard noises coming from beyond the wall and put his ear against the rough surface to listen. It was definitely something. He hurriedly dried his hands and flipped off the light to the bathroom. Looking toward where Opal and his grandmother were, he waited a couple of seconds, then went to the door where he'd heard the noises and turned the door handle to the room slowly. He found it locked, and no matter how hard he listened, there was no more noise, but he had the sense of something poised behind the door ready to spring at him. A shiver went up his back, and he scurried back into the main room.

"May I watch television if I keep it low?" he called and jumped into the cushioned chair, pulling up his feet and holding his ankles with his circled hands.

He waited, but no one said "no." He hit the remote and watched the snowy figures doing a cooking demonstration. Changing channels, he could find nothing interesting. He stood and looked at the videos. "Mush," he said aloud, reading the titles. The other tape had no label, but he shoved it into the VCR and adjusted the remote.

The boy's screams rent the small building. "Grandma! Grandma!"

The two women surrounded him, staring at images on the small screen. It was over in seconds, and Mrs. Ruiz fumbled with the remote until Jimmy grabbed it and the tape began once more. Scarcely believing their eyes, they recognized María Martínez, and two men they knew who once attended their church with a couple of others they had never seen standing under a tall cross. But it was the anguish of the crucified man, bloodied and lacerated, his mouth contorting in soundless cries that filled the room with horror.

"Shut it off," Mrs. Ruiz commanded. "What is this? Opal, where did this come from?"

Opal felt a loud buzzing in her head, thoughts spinning through her mind like comets.

"Try to remember who was here. Who might have left this awful thing," Mrs. Ruiz demanded, drawing Jimmy close and murmuring consolations to him as he clung to her.

Opal stood as if rooted to the floor looking at the blank screen. She forced herself not to look toward the locked room. There had to be a logical explanation for Antonio to have this. If only she'd given him time to speak of it. "I can think of no one, Adeline."

"I'm sorry, Opal, I'm taking this to the sheriff," Mrs. Ruiz was saying firmly. "This is murder, perverted murder, not our religion. I can't believe my eyes. María Martínez? That poor boy who works at the Springs." Suddenly her eyes grew wide and she shook Opal by the shoulder.

"Leandro. Leandro Martínez!" Both women looked at each other with a sudden chill of shared realization. "Didn't I tell you? Ann was overheard at the bathhouse saying if that Anglo kid didn't stop bothering María that Leandro would kill him. My niece, Rosita, heard that with her own ears." She crossed herself.

Opal seized on the possibility. Of course, this was Leandro's doing. Antonio must have found the tape and was going to the law. That's why he was in such a state. *But Adeline is handling this now. Better it come from her.* Otherwise there might be questions she and Antonio would not want to answer.

Chapter Forty-Four

"Go around. Go around me," Mrs. Ruiz shouted to the rear view mirror where she saw a truck hanging almost on her bumper. She pulled her car over as far as it would go on the narrow pavement and slowed to let the other vehicle pass. "Stay buckled up!" she screamed at Jimmy, who had snapped off his seat belt and was on his knees looking back over the front seat at the oncoming driver.

Mrs. Ruiz clutched the steering wheel in both hands, first accelerating, then tapping the brake, fast, slow, fast, slow. Her head barely rose high enough to see over the wheel to the road beyond, even seated on a cushion. The ten-year-old Lincoln Town Car might be a luxury she couldn't afford, but after the accident, she was through with models like her old car that had folded up on her like a tin can.

They passed a group of pilgrims walking along the road, Jimmy signed the cross and waved wildly, pressing his face against the glass. The group waved back, holding up a statue of the Virgin. The truck dropped back at the first sight of the pilgrims, and Mrs. Ruiz gave a sigh of relief.

She looked at her grandson taking everything in. So much curiosity. She would give him one more minute. Then he had to sit down. The arroyo was coming up just around the bend. Her hands closed tighter on the steering wheel. She could still feel the sensations, losing control of the car on a patch of ice and plummeting down over the bank. It happened last December, and there were still no barricades, even though she had written letters to county and state officials.

"Grandma," Jimmy screamed. "The truck! He's going to ram us!"

Mrs. Ruiz' arm swung out instinctively against Jimmy's back, holding him tight just as the truck's bumper hit the rear of the big car with a thud. Jimmy, grasping the seat back, held on for dear life, then turned and slipped from her grasp to settle into the seat. He grabbed the seat belt, clicking it in place around him just as the truck hit again.

"Grandma, that man is wearing a hood over his face," he cried, trembling with fear and hunkering down as he saw his grandmother's face pale as death as she pumped the brakes and struggled to hold the car on the road. Her eyes searched the rear view, watching the truck begin to pull closer again, but unable to make out the man, seeing only that the people on the road a moment ago were now out of sight.

"Jimmy," she said, her voice as stern and calm as if they had been in the classroom. "Put that video inside your shirt. No matter what happens to me, you are to hold on to that tape. Get it to Sergeant Ortega." Her voice was suddenly hoarse. "Jimmy, I love you. I love you with all my heart. *Nino, mi corazon!* You must always be a good boy and remember everything I've taught you."

Even when God took his mama to heaven, Grandmama had always been there, small and strong and reliable. He wanted to tell Grandma he loved her too, but his lips seemed frozen in his face as he tried to move them.

The truck slammed harder this time, sending the Town Car into a long swerve toward the edge of the arroyo. Mrs. Ruiz fought the wheel, but it spun in her hands, and she rode the brake as the car edged over the lip of the arroyo, bumping and sliding downward. With all the strength in her frail body, she forced her hands against the center of the steering column, the huge horn wailing like a banshee.

Chapter Forty-Five

Antonio stopped the truck and stuffed the black hood that hid his face into his pocket. He could already see people up on the road running toward them. *Goddamn that fucking horn! It must be stuck. They can probably hear that all the way to Eagle Wing.* He grabbed a dirty canvas cap from the glove compartment, pulled it down on his head and slipped on the oversize sunglasses that hid his eyes and brows. The disguise was the best he could do under the circumstances.

He ran and slid down the steep incline toward the car. He had to get that tape before anyone got here. *It's still my ace in the hole. As long as I have that, nobody is going to go against me or else I'm taking them into the hole with me.*

The old lady was muffled in the air bag that rose like dough around her. As he opened the door, she gave a loan moan. Panicked, Antonio jammed the heel of his hand against the side of her neck and twisted her head hard against it, the imagined snap like an explosion in his head. He felt momentarily queasy as her head lolled toward him like a rag doll.

He slipped his hands in past her waist, searching for the videotape on the seat beside her. He moved her feet, seeing nothing on the floor. He found her purse, but no tape. *Where the hell is it?*

He ran around to the other side of the car. He could see the boy inside all but hidden in the cushioning airbag, still and unmoving.

Antonio pulled at the door but found it stuck tight resting against brush and boulders. *Shit! Shit!* He ran back to the driver's side and climbed into the back seat, leaning up over the front to search the boy.

A face suddenly mashed up against the glass peering at him, then another and another. His heart pounded in his chest as he realized the people walking on the road had arrived, five of them.

"We need to get help," he screamed, climbing out of the car.

The first woman to arrive gave up in dismay, tapping her cell phone against the heel of her hand when it signaled it was out of range. "No damn good here," he told her as two of the women urged him to drive for help. He tossed them the keys and said he would stay to help get the boy out of the car.

The two men swung into action with Antonio, and the three of them cautiously rolled the car past the rock that mashed against the door. Antonio released the trunk and, under pretense of looking for the tire iron to use as a pry bar, made a quick search for the videotape.

"Hurry it up. It's right there. Give it to me!" a voice said excitedly from behind him. Big and burly, the man set to forcing the door open to get to the child. The woman with the cell phone climbed into the back seat murmuring assurances as she gently felt for a pulse on either victim.

"I can't tell," she said, shaking her head. "I'm not a nurse. I can't tell."

"What happened?" they asked Antonio.

"I don't know. She was driving erratically in front of me, then all of a sudden she seemed to lose control. Maybe she was on some kind of medication, or had a heart attack," he offered trying to sound serious and sad.

The door came open with a loud wrenching scrape of metal on metal, and Antonio rushed over. "We need to get this kid out of here. There could be a fire." He let his voice rise with urgency and command. He was certain the tape was somewhere in the front seat or the glove compartment.

"There's no danger of fire. There's no gas leaking," one of the men said, bending down to look under the car. "These babies are really built." He slapped the car's roof, "And the old lady must not have been going very fast when she went over the top. The car looks like it just kind of slid down, till it hit the boulder. I think the airbags may have hurt them both more than the impact."

"Don't move the boy. We shouldn't move the boy until the ambulance gets here. That's what they always tell you. Remember that TV show, *911*? I distinctly remember you aren't to move a victim if you don't know what you're doing."

"That's ridiculous," he snapped. "He may need CPR. He could smother in that airbag. Let's move him."

The woman still sitting in the back seat glared up at him, guarding the boy like a bulldog, the statue of the Virgin Mary she had been carrying propped beside her, the useless cell phone still clutched in one hand. The other hand was on the boy's shoulder as if daring Antonio to try to touch him.

Barely able to control his temper, he was trying to figure out how to dislodge her without raising suspicion when the ambulance roared up, the siren giving a kind of burp as it came to a halt. *Christ, I've never known an emergency vehicle to arrive in this county that damn quickly. I'll never get that tape now.*

Paramedics made their way down the steep hill with stretchers and equipment. The women who had driven his truck were right behind the medical team, flushed with excitement and trumpeting the obvious, "We did it. We found help."

The group pressing around the car began talking all at once. Antonio inched his way back up the hill. *Fuck the tape for now.* He had to get away before anyone from the sheriff's department arrived to question witnesses. He had acted in anger again. *Jimmy Dodson would really shit his pants if he knew about this.*

The keys dangled in the ignition of the truck. He eased into it and took it out of gear, letting it roll silently from the scene. At a safe distance he started the engine. Even if people remembered him or the truck, it wouldn't make him a suspect. Good Samaritans often didn't stick around for praise. He smiled at his own joke.

Odds were good, that even if the videotape were found, no one would have any reason to play it now that the busybody was dead. And he was pretty sure the kid was a goner too. Only his mother knew why Mrs. Ruiz was on her way to Eagle Wing. *That might be a problem.*

Antonio swung into the casino parking lot. He left the borrowed truck in the usual place and picked up his own car. There was still a chance he could retrieve the tape if he hung around Eagle Wing, the tow lot, the morgue at the hospital.

Chapter Forty-Six

Tony Tsia pulled past the two Santeria County Sheriff's Department cars in the parking lot to let Sunny off. He had insisted, and she had reluctantly agreed to go in alone. They would wait around the corner at a McDonalds. "You're Anglo. We'll just prejudice your case."

That sucks. She took in the stark new building, its cinderblock and concrete adobe a curious mix of government austerity and patronage excess. It had cheap frames in the windows and doors, but an ornate fountain with a large bronze plaque and splashing water dedicated to a dead sheriff.

The deputy on the desk behind the glass partition that separated the waiting room from the offices beyond was fresh faced and pretty and filled out the brown and tan uniform with one of those thin-waisted, voluptuous bodies the Old Master's liked to paint. Only there was nothing feminine about the way her hand rested on her holstered gun or her stride as she swung off down the hall calling over her shoulder to Sunny, "The sheriff is out in the field. Sergeant Ortega is on duty, but he's with someone. I'll see if he can see you when he's free."

Sergeant Ortega. Even with the photographs and eye witness testimony to back her up, she was getting a case of cold feet imagining his scrutiny.

When the young woman returned, she was smiling all over herself and buzzed Sunny through the door. "You did say your name is Sunny Bay, didn't you?"

"Yes, that's right." *One guess what that grin's all about?*

"Last door right."

Sergeant Ortega stood when she entered, his big frame seeming to suck up all the light in the small office. The room was crowded with files and boxes, and the man leaning against the only filing cabinet had obviously vacated the visitor chair for her.

He spoke immediately before she had a chance to react. "Pretty good for an amateur, but I found my gun in the second place I looked. I figured you for one of those movie types who hides everything in the toilet tank. I guess I was lucky you didn't put it in the box of Fruit Loops," he said, dangling the 9mm for her to see.

Well, aren't we hale and hearty again and full of ourselves.

"Sergeant Ortega, doesn't that constitute B&E?" she said, remembering the lingo Max used for breaking and entering when thieves had invaded her house.

The chair resisted with a loud squeak under the weight of the lawman as he sat down. "Please take a seat, Ms. Bay. Mr. Steele isn't bringing any charges against you for removing his gun and holding it hostage without his knowledge. And I'm not accepting any complaint from you about the manner in which he took back his property. Are we clear?"

"Perfectly." She regarded Rob with accusing eyes, "How did you get in my apartment?"

"Professional secret," he said curtly, seeming slightly uncomfortable. "I saw the paperwork for carrying the gun on the airplane. What the Sgt. and I are interested in is why you came here thinking you'd need a gun?"

She flushed with embarrassment. *If you saw that stuff, you saw my panties and private things, Mr. Snoop.* "That's really my own business," she said, turning to Sergeant Ortega, "isn't it?"

"It depends," he said, seeming to be waiting for her to answer Rob's questions.

"I brought it for protection. I didn't know what I might be facing here in New Mexico."

Sunny was already digging her gun permit out of her billfold and handed it across the desk. He looked at it and handed it back.

"So you were carrying the gun concealed? Do you have it now?"

"I understood concealed carry is legal in New Mexico." She brought her camera bag up on the desk and started unzipping it to produce the gun. The lawman's big hand closed over hers.

"Ms. Bay, please hand me the case."

He brought out the gun, the small 380 dwarfed in his grip as he dropped the clip and handed it to her. She slipped it into her jacket pocket, and he left the gun lying on the desk just out of her reach.

"Ms. Bay, let me go over a few things that are bothering me." He handed her a piece of paper. "We were keeping an eye on this young man."

It was Justin's face with the name Billy James Tilton under it, the same name on the driver's license she'd found in his room. She skimmed the list of offenses, mostly petty, but saw that Billy James had spent nine months in a county jail for possession of methamphetamine and that he was wanted for questioning in a suspicious death involving a man in a meth making operation in Missouri.

"You don't think I'm involved in drugs?" She hoped she sounded as outraged as she felt. This wasn't going like she thought it would at all. She had come for help. Come to do her civic duty to report a crime. And here she was practically being accused.

"The fact is, Ms. Bay, Mr. Steele followed you to the suspect's room. And while he was watching you, and trying to decide what to do, someone almost killed him with a stun gun. Now that person, who was wearing—" Sergeant Ortega looked uncomfortably at Robson Steele. "According to Steele here, he was wearing a long dark robe and a black hood. He was following you. Or maybe, just maybe, he was a lookout for you and attacked Steele to let you get away."

He rolled the chair back as far as it would go and stretched his legs, his hands in his lap, looking at her with those black hawk-like eyes accented by winged brows, knit together now in a horrific scowl. "Then you help Mr. Steele get medical help, but you steal his gun."

"I thought it was better for me to take it than for the person that tried to kill him. For Pete's sake, I didn't do anything wrong."

"Well, let me tell you how much trouble you could be in, Ms. Bay. Mr. Steele is Agent Steele. Drug Enforcement Agency. DEA."

"I know what it is," she said more defensively than she meant to and looked at Rob, her eyes seething, then back at Ortega. "Pardon me, but he told me he's a real estate agent. I figured that was fishy when he told me he was following me, and watching my apartment." She turned on Steele. "Real estate agents don't usually make their sales with 9mms nor have guns strapped to their legs. I saw the other gun when you had me checking out your chest."

Ortega's usually impassive face was in danger of cracking a big smile when she swung back to him. "Maybe if Agent Steele had been honest with me, I could have helped him out. As it was, I suspected him of being a bad guy." She continued as if Rob had left the room.

Sergeant Ortega rolled his eyes. She knew he was upset because he began talking in rapid Spanish, then stopped and drew in a deep breath. She didn't quite get all the words he strung together, but the gist was clear that she was to totally butt out. "I thought I made it clear that you were to leave the crime fighting to us. Civilians have a way of getting in the way," he finished forcefully.

Rob, who had remained absolutely silent, suddenly blurted out, "You make it sound like I'm some kind of voyeur. I wasn't watching you. I was babysitting you."

"You were what?"

He turned to Ortega. "It's a long story, but I want to get this clear. My boss is an Army buddy of a friend of Sunny's in St. Louis. She was upset and afraid, told this guy's wife she thought she might be in danger. I was already staking out the Springs watching this Justin and keeping an eye on anything that looked like drug movement, when I get assigned to keep an eye on Nancy Drew here."

"By whom?" she said with disbelief, ignoring his jab at her.

"Max something?"

"Max Metzger asked you to watch out for me?" A lump rose in her throat, and she couldn't speak for a long moment thinking of Max and Moira looking out for her. Then, she glared up at Robson Steele. "Well, I'll tell him you did a lousy job of it, Agent Steele. You let Justin get murdered. And me? I came close. And it's still not over."

Sunny felt suddenly weak as her words tumbled one over the other. She couldn't even fully enjoy the shock on their faces as she told them everything that happened. The thugs who followed Justin, María's tale, finding the crucified body on the mesa, the men chasing her, Leandro's threats, the man in the robe and hood with the blinking red eye. "I can prove there was a murder," she said, reaching for her camera bag.

Sgt. Ortega let her remove the camera and GPS unit from her bag unchallenged. She ran through the photos on the tiny screen, saying apologetically, "I had to shoot up, almost into the overhead sun. Some are kind of blurry and overlit. I wasn't familiar with this camera." Their lack of enthusiasm underscored her doubts.

When she showed the photo of Ann's uncle, Robson Steele grabbed it, studied it and agreed that someone dressed like that was what he glimpsed when he was attacked.

"I think it may be the work of the Penitentes," Sunny finished breathlessly, some of her confidence returning.

Sergeant Ortega looked askance at her for a long moment.

He jabbed a finger at Ann's Uncle Antonio. "First off, no *morada* in this county uses robes like this anymore, and I know them all. Such garments haven't been used since way back."

He continued. "We'll have prints made from your digital camera. On first blush," he said pointing, the cross looks new, authentic, and there aren't many carvers doing this kind of work. We'll probably be able to pinpoint its origin. It's a start, but we need to find the actual cross for compelling evidence."

She could scarcely bear to look again at the next photo, when he turned it toward her, the one of the cuts along Justin's spine. "It's impossible to know without an autopsy, but *Sangradors* are skillful. They make cuts deep enough to scar, but not to destroy muscles in the back. These appear crude and haphazard, deep," he finished, "to produce maximum pain."

He continued through each photo pointing out details, not trying to convince her one way or another, but helping her understand that the photos were helpful but that they needed investigating and Justin's body to be able to prove anything.

"We don't even have a crime scene," he began, pointing out the nondescript scenery in the background.

"Yes, we do," Sunny began excitedly. She held up the GPS unit. "I have the coordinates of just where the cross stood," she said triumphantly. She brought up the screen mapping her route. "Sergeant Ortega, those men were in a hurry. There's bound to be something, some kind of evidence they left behind."

He spoke into an intercom then to Sunny. "Would you loan that to us long enough for us to get it recorded?"

"Of course. There's something else." She turned to Rob. "You know while I was in Justin's room? I found something he had hidden." She stopped short as both men closed in at the same time staring down at her.

"Found what?" Rob asked first.

"I found Justin's driver's license with his real name on it and a piece of paper with coordinates, a kind of map and other notations."

"That's not possible," Robson Steele said. "I searched that place thoroughly." He looked at Ortega, his face flushed.

"It was in the toilet paper core. And that's where I hid it in our apartment."

"Oh, for christsakes." He moaned as Ortega broke out in a loud laugh.

They moved her to a small conference room, and for the next hour Sunny went over every detail, answering questions for the record for Sergeant Ortega. She even recalled Justin's coordinates, winning an "'Atta' girl!" from Rob. Her temples ached from the florescent light that buzzed like a hive of angry bees overhead as she looked at a book of photos. She finally came across the two thugs who had come to Justin's room and had been on the mesa. The identification mobilized Robson Steele, and he disappeared into another office for a long time.

The deputy was dispatched to McDonald's to bring back Tony and María. María sat between Tony and Sunny wrapped in her quilt, clutching the cowboy boots as a child might a doll. This time she told her story into a tape recorder for Sergeant Ortega. Toward the end of it she shook as if from an inner cold, her eyes dry, her expression empty as she spoke of the robed man with the eye of the devil, the *mal ojo*. Ortega's jaw worked in and out, but he didn't interrupt her. Nor did he take the boots from her.

When Robson Steele came back into the room he sat and made sure he had their attention. "Now this is what we're going to do."

Chapter Forty-Seven

Jimmy Ruiz sat huddled against Sunny, his right arm and left wrist in casts, headed back to Ojo Tres. Robson Steele was driving them. Tony and Maria were in the car ahead, two Santeria County Sheriff's Department deputies leading the convoy.

María looked out the window from the back seat of her father's car, giving them a little wave. Jimmy edged closer to Sunny.

They were all baffled at Jimmy's reaction of fear and anger toward María at the hospital, the two had always been close. He screamed when he saw her, fighting and incoherent. María had been removed quickly.

Sunny ached for the girl, first Justin, now this. If there was any good, it seemed to be María's growing acceptance of her father and an obvious reconciliation between Ann and Tony.

Robson Steele slowed the vehicle as they passed the place where Jimmy and his grandmother plunged off the road.

Passing pilgrims heading for Chimayó had erected a small cross to mark the spot of the accident, the ground strewn with offerings of plastic flowers and the dried blooms of *chamisa,* candles sputtering in the breeze. Jimmy kept looking back as long as he could see the memorial, but didn't speak. Sunny dropped a kiss on the boy's head.

Sunny adjusted the paper bag near her feet. Sergeant Ortega's deputy had turned over Mrs. Ruiz' purse, a videotape they found

Jimmy clutching to his chest and some car insurance information from the glove compartment. *Death comes and suddenly nothing's so important anymore.* She would be glad to hand these reminders of the tragedy over to Father Emilio, who would be handling arrangements for Jimmy and for Mrs. Ruiz.

"Don't forget, we have to stop at the church," she reminded Rob. It was the first time she had spoken to him since leaving Eagle Wing. He nodded, but didn't answer her, his steely silence certainly living up to his name.

Before the call about the accident intruded, they were locked in bitter protest over his plan to put her and Molly on a plane that night for St. Louis. She had battled and won over Rob's vehement objections when Tony offered to bring some strapping young men from the pueblo to move them from the apartment to Ann's house, and provide round-the-clock security. She had to take care of business in Santa Fe, and then they could go home.

Their angry words replayed in her head.

"No, I don't understand," he shouted her down.

"It's my job. Unless the client cancels, I go."

"Then to hell with you if you won't listen to reason."

"If those killers have any sense at all, they'll realize I've taken my evidence to the authorities and be long gone."

"You think you're dealing with an intelligent group of coordinated criminal minds, Sunny? Don't bet on it. Somebody likes to hurt people just for the hell of it. Think about the way the murder was done, leaving the body exposed, coming back to dump it. That was worse than stupidity. That's an irrational, pathological anger at work. So all we can do is try to remove the logical targets. You, primarily."

"You're still angry with me."

He took his eyes off the road, looked at her. "Not angry, anxious and worried."

"Sergeant Ortega seems okay with my decision."

She couldn't be sure if his reply was a snort or profanity muttered under his breath, but she gathered it was the latter because he looked quickly down at Jimmy and seemed relieved that the boy had fallen asleep.

"Ortega's got thousands of people pouring into this county. And if that isn't enough, the department's got its hands full with this suspected movement of drugs. All he did is fit you into that, which is pretty damn white of him considering what a pain in the ass you are."

Sunny considered not bringing his lapse of political correctness to his attention. But then she couldn't help herself.

"Goddamn it," he responded, reddening at her criticism and so agitated he had to jerk the van back to keep from running across the center line. "Don't you get it yet? You'll be driving to Santa Fe entirely on your own." His words fell as clipped and hollow as an axe hitting a log.

"Sergeant Ortega said—"

"He said he'll let his people know. And he will. It only works if some emergency doesn't come up that takes them off their designated patrol routes. I don't have to remind you how desolate some of that road is. It's too loose, Sunny."

She was tired of arguing and looked out the window, her thoughts racing with the events of the last few days like the crazy mixed-up sequence of a dream.

When they reached Ojo Tres and pulled up to the church, Sunny carefully eased the sleeping boy's head to rest on Rob's shoulder. "I'll be quick." She climbed out of the van, taking the paper bag she was to leave with Father Emilio.

A man wielding a broom moved along the wide steps outside the vestibule. He nodded at Sunny, then continued sweeping.

"I have a package for Father," Sunny said.

"He won't be back until time for Mass. Tonight. Around eight."

"May I leave this in his office?"

He laid aside his broom with reluctance, took out a large key, beckoned her to follow.

The minute she walked into Father Emilio's office and saw his computer, it sparked a sudden idea. She plopped the sack on the desk, throwing a quick thank you over her shoulder to the man.

"You look like the Cheshire Cat," Rob said, when she climbed into the van.

"It's one of those convoluted chain things, the computer, finding people on the internet—" She waved away the words. "Never mind. Remember the old photo of the hooded man? María Martínez and I both thought it was the man we saw, and even you agreed it resembled the person who attacked you. However the Antonio in the photo is dead. But he had a son, also named Antonio Martínez, who no one has heard about or seen since he was a child. What if he's come back?"

"And you think our hooded man is this Antonio," Rob said, looking pointedly at his watch. "I'm to meet Ortega after I drop you off. Talk while I drive."

She pointed the way to Ann's house. "Ann and Mrs. Ruiz both say Leandro virtually stole the Springs from his older brothers while they were off fighting the war. I think deep down Ann resents it. So, why wouldn't it make Antonio's son angry? Revengeful, maybe even pathological? Sounds like the killer you described to me."

Her eyes moved like a laser beam probing the side of his face as she waited expectantly for his answer.

"If my aunt had whiskers she'd be my uncle." He rubbed his nose, as if wrestling with how to put his opinion more diplomatically, then sighed, resigned to failure. "Look, your logic is as full of holes as Swiss cheese. If Antonio the Younger resembles his father so much, why wouldn't Leandro Martínez or Mrs. Ruiz recognize him? And don't tell me it's because he wears a hood all the time."

She stuck her tongue out, giving him a raspberry. "He's disguised maybe, other than the hood, I mean."

"Okay, for the moment suppose that's so. But from what you tell me, Leandro Martínez would be the logical victim. But that's not the case, is it? Justin James doesn't fit your theory, and his death is what we're investigating."

Before she could think of a counter to his argument, she waved him to a stop at Ann's house, just as his radio squawked. Rob picked it up, listening intently. "Okay," he answered. "Good job on short notice." He shot a glance at Sunny. "Can't talk now."

When he put down the receiver he said tersely, "We had people on the mesa this afternoon investigating Justin's death. I thought you'd want to know that he isn't being forgotten."

He put both hands up like a wall, seeing questions forming on her lips. He reached across her to open the latch on her door, rousing Jimmy. "Sunny, you know I can't say anything about an investigation. So don't ask," he said, pulling the mantle of authority around him.

"Can't you at least tell me if you've found Justin?" She sounded genuinely bereaved.

He hesitated, then shook his head, "No, Sunny, not yet."

"But you're going to keep looking?" It seemed more a statement of faith than a question.

He nodded, reaching over to pat her shoulder.

She unbuckled Jimmy's seat belt and her own. "Will I see you again?" she asked.

"No. When you step out of this vehicle you're on your own, Sunny, unless you've given up on this dumb idea of driving by yourself to Santa Fe tomorrow."

Chapter Forty-Eight

Why had he been so harsh? In his rear view mirror Sunny looked so alone, so vulnerable. Robson Steele fought the urge to turn the van around. No, we'll just end up in an argument. He didn't have the heart to be charming. There was still a big hole in that organ five months after Helen's death. The cancer had taken a long time to kill her, and he knew he wasn't ready to entertain ideas of someone else. Not even someone as pretty, smart, courageous and entertaining as Sunny Bay.

But when the message he'd wanted to hear finally came, it was hard not share it with her. Hell, it had been hard to keep from grabbing her and dancing in the street.

No one believed he would get the sheriff, King Harvell, to turn over the investigation into Justin's death to the New Mexico State Police Tactical Response Team, but he had. Super professionals, the team had no turf wars, and the briefing went smooth as silk, everyone on the same page. He took an imaginary bow. Within two hours of his call, the team was ready to roll. They slipped in undercover to scour the mesa with National Forest Service crews and a couple of DEA agents under the guise of posting signs restricting campfires.

More than anything, he wanted to tell Sunny the team had used the coordinates she turned up in Justin's room. They led to an uncharted mine, turned into a huge drug making lab, and the dumping place for Justin's body. His remains and evidence of both the murder and the drug activity were on the way to labs in Albuquerque and Santa Fe.

It was no surprise that the methamphetamine operation was temporarily shut down, all hands needed to move product. It was a big operation, proof that a lot of drugs were on the move. How the drugs were to be moved remained the question in everyone's mind.

He couldn't tell Sunny any of this, and he wouldn't if he could. If she knew she had been right, it might encourage her to pursue her latest hunch, despite Ortega's explicit warnings. She was like a dog with a bone once she got an idea, like this long lost son theory. But, given her batting average, he decided to share it with Manny Ortega.

Chapter Forty-Nine

The minute he saw María Martínez and that Sunny person and Tony Tsia climbing out of a black Jeep Cherokee following some big Santeria County copper into the hospital, he gave up on getting the tape back. He drove away from Eagle Wing fast, hatching scenarios to cover his tracks. Suddenly the conversation he overheard between his mother and Mrs. Ruiz popped into his head. They suspected Leandro as soon as they saw the tape. Leandro, of course!

He chewed on the inside of his cheek, a scheme taking shape. It would work if he could get his mother to cooperate.

Antonio was hurrying so hard that his tall frame hunched forward, making it seem his head was walking ahead of himself.

Opal looked up as if his presence was the stirring of a strong wind. She pulled his cigarettes and lighter from her apron pocket and gave them to him without speaking. She had remained sitting in the orchard ever since Mrs. Ruiz and Jimmy left, and she had discovered the door to the infirmary pried open and Antonio gone.

He lit up, taking deep agitated draws one after the other, taking note of her stony silence. *Got a little attitude, have we? Which button should I push today?* He followed her line of vision, watching the sheets and towels she had hung to dry on the rope line by the back porch rise and fall clean and white like sails at sea. Her washing filled him with bitter resentment for all the times he'd been sent home from school because his father sent him in dirty clothes.

He reminded her about being teased and jeered, called names. *Poor little Antonio.* At last, her hand reached out and stroked his arm. He hid his smile. A mother's love is good, a mother's guilt is more useful.

He was impatient to launch the plan that had come to him as he drove back from Eagle Wing.

"Ma, I'm sorry I left like that, but I didn't know what else to do. After the boy stopped screaming, I heard what you and Mrs. Ruiz said about Leandro. You were right. I have proof Leandro was responsible for that terrible thing you saw on the video. That's why I was so upset that I couldn't talk to you. I was afraid to go to the sheriff without your approval, given our situation." He pressed his fingers to his lips and dropped his eyes to keep her from reading any of the emotions flooding through him.

"Oh, Antonio. I knew it. I knew it in my mind." She gave a sigh of relief, standing to embrace him.

"I didn't dare come out of your storage room. There would have been too many questions."

"You did right, son. Adeline is a good woman, but she tells everybody's business to anyone who—"

He waved aside further words. "I decided to follow Mrs. Ruiz when I heard her go to her car. I thought I could intercept her on the road. After all, she knows me by sight, even if she doesn't connect us." He was having a hard time keeping his hands still. "I had to tell her what I knew about Leandro so she could make a stronger case with the sheriff, but still keep my name out of it."

"Ma, listen to me. By the time I caught up to her, there had been a terrible accident. They didn't survive. They're dead, both of them."

Antonio found it easy to turn on tears, and he let them flow down his cheeks, explaining how someone rammed Mrs. Ruiz' car causing it to plunge over the arroyo. He held Opal's arms to calm her, shaking her slightly.

"Now this is important, Ma. I saw Leandro Martínez driving away as I was pulling up. Are you listening? It was Leandro that rammed their car."

"Jimmy and Adeline?" Antonio's words seeming to register only a little at a time, like seeping water. "Oh, please, dear God, why little Jimmy?"

A worm of jealously curled in Antonio's chest. He lit a cigarette and blew the smoke up in the air impatiently. He had to get her mind back on the task at hand. "Ma, listen to me. It was Leandro's doing. It's up to us to make sure Leandro doesn't go unpunished for this terrible murder."

Opal sat very still. "You said you want me to do something?"

He began speaking intently, as if his words could mold the matter of her brain as his hands might putty. "This is what I want you to do, Ma. Listen carefully. Call the sheriff. Tell him Mrs. Ruiz was here, and she talked about having evidence that Leandro killed that boy who worked for him at the Springs, the one that disappeared this week. Tell him she talked to you about it."

"Wouldn't the Sheriff think it odd if I called him with that information just now?"

Antonio was shaking his head. "It's got to be now. Otherwise, Leandro will come up with something if we wait."

She looked at him uncertainly, but didn't argue.

"Now this is important. Tell the sheriff she had proof, that she had the crime on videotape. Tell him she said she didn't know what to do with it. You can say you told her she had better go to the sheriff about it. And that's where she was headed this afternoon, with the tape in hand. You can even say you saw it."

SHIRLEY GIEBEL

"But what if he asks questions about what was on the tape?"

Oh, for christsake. You saw it *in her hand*. You saw her holding it *in her hand*. Don't say that you *played* it. That gets too complicated. Tell the sheriff Leandro must have found out, and may have had something to do with Mrs. Ruiz' accident.

She was backing away from him. "I can't do this."

"Don't tell me you're still scared of the old bastard? I know for a fact that Leandro was in Eagle Wing this afternoon, because I saw him there. Ma, he can't prove he didn't do this. He had the motive and the opportunity and no witnesses to say otherwise. Isn't that some kind of sweet irony after what he did to you and Pa?"

She pressed her temples. "You shouldn't ask this of me, Antonio. It's only going to bring something bad down on both of us."

"I thought you loved me. I thought you wanted revenge on that spiteful toad for cheating me of my birthright. I won't let you abandon me all over again." He slapped her hard.

He saw fear move across the landscape of her broad face. She reared back, still as death, only the whites of her eyes visible in their sockets.

Antonio shouted. "Ma! Ma!" He began shaking her. "Ma, we got no time for one of your spells. Come out of it."

Opal's eyes slowly focused, touched the side of her face where he had slapped her. Her long pause made him hold his breath, releasing it only when she said, "I'll call."

He rewarded her with his smile. "You're cold," he said, taking hold of her arms, feeling goose bumps roughening her bare flesh. He arranged his jacket around her shoulders and helped her to her feet.

"I knew I could count on you, Ma." But he followed her into the kitchen and stood over her until she put through her call to the sheriff.

258

Chapter Fifty

"Goddamn it, Ortega, what else can go wrong?" Sheriff King Harvell could count ten people he knew who got killed on their last day on the job or their careers blew up in their face just as retirement was within their grasp. Well, it wasn't going to happen to him.

"You're on top of that stuff up at Ojo Tres. I want you to answer this one. Opal, that healer woman up there, the one with no last name, just called. It involves Leandro Martínez." He slowed down and repeated exactly what Opal had said to him on the phone.

"Did she say Mrs. Ruiz and Jimmy were both killed in the accident?"

"Didn't I just say that?"

"You did, but they weren't. The boy had a couple of broken bones. That's all."

"Well, she obviously heard the story wrong from someone else, maybe the radio or TV. Those bums never get anything right."

"Maybe. I don't think anyone's had time to print or air it yet. It's probably not important. Just kind of curious is all," he finished, thinking out loud.

"This woman says there's an incriminating videotape? Know anything about a tape being found in that accident?"

Sergeant Ortega wasn't sure what his answer would bring. At the moment, Harvell's face was set into that griped look they all knew so well, like he was pissing a peach pit. "Yeah. The boy had a videotape tucked under his shirt. The report of the deputy on the scene said it was sent back to Ojo Tres this afternoon with the rest of the personal belongings of the victims, sir."

"Well, can you put your hands on it now?"

"My guess is that the personal effects will be with Father Emilio."

"Well, that should be easy. Just call up the priest and check it out, then get your butt up there and retrieve it. You'll need to question Martínez. Just you treat him the way I always have." Harvell jabbed a warning forefinger in the air. "Understand?"

Ortega's dark eyebrows came together fleetingly, but he mustered a smile. "Got it, Chief." Manuel Ortega understood Martínez got preferential treatment from Harvell for unnamed favors.

It bothered him more that after all the years Harvell had been sheriff, he still didn't know finding the parish priest in Santeria County on Holy Thursday might mean covering back roads through half a dozen towns.

The priest would be performing four Masses today spread over more than fifty miles of narrow paved and dirt roads in the ten villages in his parish. The last Mass was at 8:00 tonight in Ojo Tres along with the ritual of the Washing of the Feet and the long rosary prayers of Los Hermanos that followed. That's if there were no extras like baptisms, weddings, or an overload of confessions to hear. Somewhere in between the man is supposed to keep track of a videotape?

"Overtime is authorized." Harvell turned and spun out the revolving door and headed home before anything else could come up.

Overtime pay or not, where was he going to find the time, Ortega wondered? Sheriff Harvell made no bones about riding out his term in office. That meant handle your assignments and bother me at your own risk and only if I need to make a decision. Manny blew out a long breath. The lieutenant was out on disability, and besides himself, that left only the Under Sheriff and ten deputies, two cadets fresh out of the Academy and half a dozen volunteer Reserve Deputies. They were all in the field on alert on this drug movement and trying to keep the roads clear and pilgrims moving safely along the roadways. That's why he was surprised to see just the person he wanted to talk with come down the hall.

"Tobin, you handled that accident out on 102, didn't you?"

The deputy, small and thin with a boyish face looked like he might be a few years away from his first shave. He finished pouring himself a cup of coffee and nodded. "Why?"

"See anything suspicious or out-of-the-ordinary?"

"Like what? Everything's in my report." Ortega sensed a slight defensiveness in his answer.

"Probably nothing. But something's come in that Sheriff Harvell asked me to look at about the videotape found on the boy. It's alleged to have a connection to a disappearance up at Ojo Tres. There probably is no connection, but it would help me if you could just run over what you found."

Tobin rattled off facts like he was reading directly from the report he'd turned in, concluding that the victim of small build and seventy-five years of age, according to her driver's license, allegedly met her death as a result of the impact of the airbag.

"What about the autopsy?"

The young deputy stirred his coffee. "Well, you know about the cutbacks. This death looked pretty straight forward." The man looked uncomfortable. "Harvell sent down word to the coroner not to bother, just fill out the certificate from the report we turned in."

"What's your opinion?"

The man hesitated. "Look, I'm not going against Harvell."

"I just asked your take on things you saw. Give me a lead if you think there's one, and I'll keep you out of it, if that's the way you want it."

"Okay. The paramedic pointed out some bruising on the side of the old woman's neck. We got some pictures. But everything points to the airbag. Besides what else could it be?"

"Who got there first? I heard there were several people."

"Five, well six, to be exact. The real witness to the accident was a guy in a pickup truck who was behind the old lady and saw it go off the road. He was in the car trying to help the victims when the others got there. He said the old lady was driving all over the road and ran off."

"He was in the car? What did he say to you? Were you suspicious of him?"

The wary look came back into Tobin's eyes. "He loaned his truck to two of the women to go for help, then when help got there, he just disappeared before we got on the scene. We didn't talk to him. We don't even know who he is."

"What about a description?"

"We got plenty of those, five different ones, to be exact. The witnesses only agree that it was a he and that he was tall."

"Why do you think he left like that?"

"Well, one witness was adamant that the guy was feeling over the victims for valuables, not trying to help them. He got angry when she wouldn't let him move the boy. Maybe he did swipe something and wanted to get out before it was discovered," Tobin offered.

"Was anything missing?"

"Who knows? The lady's purse was on the front seat, and her billfold was in it, still had money inside. She was wearing a heavy gold ring with a small stone of some kind. Nothing appeared missing."

"Your report said the videotape was found tucked under the boy's shirt when they lifted him away from the airbag. Didn't that strike you as strange? Was it a rental or what?"

"Tell you the truth, Sarge, we didn't pay much attention. Maybe it was X-rated, and he was keeping it from Grandma. Who knows? The kid was unconscious and nobody was thinking about anything but getting him to the hospital."

"You get a name on this witness? Or a good description of the guy's truck? You said a couple of the witnesses drove it."

"Nah, you know women." He blushed suddenly at Ortega's stern look. "I mean, hey, Sarge, don't bust my balls. You ever know a woman to come out and say a vehicle they saw was a specific make, model, year and color?"

"Not many men do that either," Ortega said, but he was reminded of the nondescript unrecognized truck in the area a few days ago that Jimmy had seen. While he was in Ojo Tres he would ask the boy what he remembered before the accident, unless he was too traumatized.

"And this witness," Ortega asked again, looking at the name on Tobin's report, "any idea where to find this Rose Archuleta to question her again?"

The deputy shook his head ruefully before he spoke, "She's on her way to Chimayó. They didn't know where they'd spend the night." His cheeks burned bright cherry red as he waited for the reprimand he was sure would follow.

When Ortega didn't say anything, Tobin raised his eyes gratefully and started talking breathlessly. "Jeez, Sarge, you been out in the last few hours. People are pouring in from everywhere. If you want my opinion..." He was feeling the glow now of the Sergeant's attention. "No drug runners are going to risk hauling drugs over these roads. Too damned slow. Too much chance of being stuck in a traffic jam. We got too much law out there. Tribal police, city police, highway patrol, and most of our department. Drug runners aren't dumb. They're not going to take it right under our noses. Mark my words, there just ain't going to be no drug shipment through this county right now."

"Thank you, Tobin. I'll be sure to pass that along to the sheriff and the DEA," he said evenly.

Tobin wasn't sure how to take the remark. He pulled himself up to his full height and pushed his empty cup through the opening in the trashcan. "That all, Sarge?"

"What about the car? Anything inconsistent there?"

"I reported rear bumper damage. I thought that was kind of funny. All the damage from the accident was to the front end and the passenger door when the car hit a big boulder. Otherwise the car was a cream-puff, didn't have a dent on it."

"Do me a favor, Tobin. Go take another look at the car. See if you can make out if the bumper damage looks new. Maybe this guy in the truck rear-ended the old lady, and she lost control. And find out what Leandro Martínez drives. I'll check back with you later."

"Yes, sir," Tobin said, relieved to have an excuse to leave. "And Sarge, I'll take a shot at trying to find that witness."

Ortega nodded and picked up the phone to call Harvell.

He heard the TV in the background as the sheriff called for his wife to shut the damn thing down. "Yeah. Why aren't you on your way to Ojo Tres?"

"I am." He explained his suspicions and waited for Harvell to process them.

"I'm ahead of you, Ortega." He growled. "I called the coroner and rescinded my order as soon as I got that call this afternoon about the videotape." He started to hang up, then said loudly, "Ortega. You still there?"

"Yeah, Chief."

"Tell me, what would you have done if I wouldn't allow the autopsy?"

"You're still the sheriff, sir. I count on that."

264

Harvell rarely laughed, but when he did it seemed to come from the bottom of his soles and up through the belly. "Goddamn, Ortega, you're a fucking politician."

Ortega eyed the thin slices of turkey on whole wheat with lettuce and pretend mayonnaise. His wife did her best to keep him on a low-fat diet. She remained unmoved when he predicted that one of these days the lard-laced staples of his childhood would reemerge as healthy food, then what would she say?

He polished an apple on his shirt before biting into it. Nothing like the apples from the orchards of this valley stretching out for miles between the river and the highway, he thought, feeling a sense of contentment. He dropped the core in his lunch bag, waited to pull back onto the road until a couple of big semis barreling down on him passed by, both legitimate over-the-road truck companies, he noted.

He weighed Tobin's theory that no drugs were likely to be moved under their noses against Robson Steele's belief that something was going down during Holy Week. Tobin was wrong, he felt it in his bones.

Ortega slowed so he didn't miss the cutoff, a shortcut to the Springs on one of the back roads to Chimayó. Dust danced up behind him on the hard packed dirt road, illuminated and ghostlike in the bright slanting rays of late afternoon sun.

As he came over a hill he saw a band of young men walking along the road and quickly counted twelve. They were walking fast and wearing green windbreakers, all carrying dark green backpacks. The one in the lead carried a wooden cross. *Must be students or some kind of team—maybe from the Junior College at Chamacita. But they're sure taking the long way around to Chimayó.*

He pulled abreast of the youth with the cross, keeping the motor running as he rolled down his window. Smiling, he called, "It's going to be dark before you get to Chimayó. Everything okay?"

He waved at Ortega, kept his distance from the car.

"Yeah, we got a late start. But we're prepared for walking out here at night." One of the group set down his backpack and pointed to strips of fluorescent tape along the sleeves of his jacket. He pirouetted like a model, more bright tape strips and lettering across his back proclaiming *Campo Santo—Camp of the Saint—Youth for Christ.*

Ortega nodded, still smiling as if they had answered his question. "You some kind of church group?"

"Like the name says," the group's leader answered, trying to hold on to the smile on his face.

Ortega did the same. "*Campo Santo,* Camp of the Saint, huh? Nice name." A little tingle ran up his neck. This band isn't local, Ortega concluded. It would be disrespectful. Around here *Campo Santo* is what the Penitentes call the symbolic Calvary in processions from the *morada.* It isn't something you can exactly translate.

"Where you from?" He tempered his suspicions, remembering there was a cemetery named *Campo Santo* over in Rio Arriba county, a common enough name for burial grounds, though he couldn't imagine any connection with a youth group.

The youth seemed somewhat flustered, and an older man stepped forward. "We're from out of state. What's with the third degree? You got some problem with us, officer?"

He could sense the group pulling closer. He was out- numbered twelve to one and didn't like the odds. "There's no problem. I just like to know about folks. I plan to get to the *Santuario* myself tomorrow." He pointed at the sky. "Well, I wouldn't lose any more time."

Ortega put the patrol car in gear and pulled away slowly, touching the brim of his hat and keeping his face friendly as he scrutinized the faces of the rest of the group. He recognized none of them as locals. What did seem familiar was the collective wariness and the hard eyes turned on him calculating their next move. He accelerated, seeing the last two of the group in the rearview mirror watching to see that he kept going.

"Angelic." He held the radio transmitter to his mouth. "I thought you might be on duty by now." Angelic Flores had been the best dispatcher the department ever had before she had been forced to take retirement to care for an ailing husband. She was filling in on reserve status for this busy week while her daughter took over for her at home. "Ang, patch me through to Tobin please."

Tobin came on flustered and apologetic. "I haven't had time to look at the car, Sarge. I'm…"

"Tobin," Ortega interrupted, "never mind. All these pilgrims you're seeing, notice any of them wearing green jackets and carrying green backpacks?"

Tobin laughed. "Sarge, you seeing little green men, or what?"

"Damn it, I'm serious. Have you?" Ortega filled him in on the bunch he had just encountered. "It may be nothing. But there was definitely something suspicious about them. If it's what I'm thinking, this may be just the break we need. So tell me what you've seen."

"Oh hell. I'm not sure. Let me think."

"Tobin, when you get through thinking, call it in to Angelic. Right now I'm going to get her in touch with everybody we've got out and ask them if they've seen groups who look anything like this." He knew he could count on her to pick up on any variations and ask the right questions. Unlike Tobin, nothing got by her.

She agreed to radio him as soon as she had the information and to find out what she could about any organization called *Campo Santo*. "And Angelic, no little green men jokes, understand?"

"Please." She gave a good-natured groan as she signed off.

Chapter Fifty-One

"You don't have to identify the source. I know it was Opal who called you. That old cunt hates my guts," Leandro said, making papers jump as he hammered his fist on his desk after Ortega explained the call made to Sheriff Harvell implicating him in the deaths of Justin James and Mrs. Ruiz. "Hell, why isn't Harvell here himself? He knows me, can vouch for me, or didn't he give you the word before you came up here throwing around accusations?"

"Sheriff Harvell regrets he was unable to come," Ortega said evenly, "and no one is accusing you. It's routine. We have to follow up on complaints. That way no one can question the sheriff's impartiality."

"Well, this is nothing but pure damn spite from a bitter old woman." Leandro propped a foot on the desk between them, staring at Ortega over a scuffed boot.

"Spite over what, sir? It may be relevant if it motivated this accusation against you," Ortega said.

"It's ancient history, and personal, Sergeant."

"Tell me anyway." Ortega leaned, avoiding the boot, to stare directly at Leandro.

Leandro swung his foot back to the floor and leaned toward the younger man, meeting the black eyes.

"Oh, goddam it, the old witch was married to my brother Antonio."

"Go on," Ortega encouraged.

"Talk about water over the dam," Leandro grumbled. "The bitch deserted him and their baby for a singing career that flopped. She came here years ago looking for them, all remorseful, with no money and no where to go. She hung around here with some fanciful idea I'd get her son back for her."

"Did you?" This time it was Rob asking the question. Leandro shot him a glance, seeming to take note of him for the first time since they'd been introduced. The joint interview was Ortega's idea, since he and Rob were both in Ojo Tres, and he was hoping Rob might catch something he wouldn't.

"No, Agent Steele. I didn't even try, and she hates me for that. Don't ask me why she's waited until now to get back at me."

He wanted to press Leandro about young Antonio Martínez, but Ortega was signaling that he needed to wrap this up.

"I'm sure we'll clear it up quickly." He flipped open his notebook, jotting notes. "Tell me about Justin James. What was your relationship?"

"To be honest, it was hostile. A good worker once you got him going, but one of those guys you got to ride all the time. He was always watching the clock, grabbing a smoke, taking a piss, or complaining because I'd hired him as a wrangler and turned him into a pool boy. Which was kind of true. But around here you do whatever job needs doing, depending on the season."

Ortega fidgeted, "What about your background check?"

"I didn't do any. Who's got time? Guys like Justin drift in and out. Six months is about as long as they stay. I've never had any trouble keeping anyone in line." He lifted his bulky shoulders like a boxer and jabbed an imaginary punch.

A dark look crossed Leandro's face, his baleful glare at Ortega laying bare a menace he made no attempt to cloak. "You've probably heard I threatened to kill him, if he didn't leave my niece alone."

"Did you, Mr. Martínez?"

"No." The tone was so flat, it wasn't denial so much as regret at not having carried out his threat. "Then this week he doesn't show up. Except for making us shorthanded, I didn't shed any tears."

Ortega paused, scribbling notes, delaying. Rob knew the signs. He called it a dry well interview, one you couldn't get a handle on and wasn't likely to turn up anything new. Still, he plodded on.

"Sir, if you had made good on your threat, tell me how you planned to kill Justin."

"Well, hell, I didn't give it much real thought. I was just hoping to throw a scare into him. That's one of the frustrations of being old and lame." He laughed, patting the top of his bandy legs, skillfully reminding them how absurd Opal's accusation was. He could think about it all he wanted, but he couldn't do it.

"You could hire the job done, Mr. Martínez. Did you?"

"Why would I risk that? Anyone dumb enough to kill for you is too dumb to keep a secret. Besides, Harvell checked the kid out as a favor to me, and was taking care of the problem. He said to sit tight because the DEA—" He paused pointing to Rob. "Had the kid under surveillance to see if he could lead you to some supposed drug activity. By then, Justin seemed to be avoiding María, so I agreed. It was just a matter of time before Harvell would have arrested his sorry ass even if he'd had to make up something."

Rob spoke up, "Unfortunately, Mr. Martínez, the surveillance failed. So we're left with the fact that you threatened his life and he disappeared." *Murdered, dumped and found on your property, I might add.* "That makes you a person of interest."

"I have no knowledge of Justin James since he was on the job here. I had nothing to do with his disappearance or anything that may have happened to him. That's the truth, and you can take my word for it," Leandro said, with the air of a man who was used to that happening. "Are we done?"

"Not quite. The Toyota SUV parked in the hotel lot is the only vehicle registered to you. Do you drive anything else?"

"No, it's equipped for my specific handicap. Can't drive anything else."

Ortega made a notation. He'd already checked the SUV's front bumper, and found it as unblemished as the day it was driven off the lot.

"Did you drive to Eagle Wing at any time today?"

"Are you investigating Mrs. Ruiz' death as an accident or something more?" he asked, seeming to leap to the proper conclusion about Ortega's meaning.

"Just answer the question, please."

"As a matter of fact, I drove over to pick up supplies and stopped for a late lunch at Los Vaqueros over on west Santa Fe Road near the junction with 102. Why?"

He gave Ortega the names of people at the places he'd shopped, and the approximate times.

"One very quick question, sir," Rob said. "Your nephew, your brother's son was named after his father?" Getting Leandro's nod, he asked "Are you in contact?"

"Antonio and I were estranged. Never knew the kid. Don't have any idea if he's alive or dead." The implication was that he didn't care.

"Thank you for your time." Ortega and Rob stood and shook hands with Leandro.

"Am I in the clear?"

"You've been very direct. It's still an open investigation. You'll hear from us."

Leandro watched the lawmen talk a minute in the parking lot, then drive off in separate vehicles. He wondered if he'd made the right decision not to tell them he'd met with Jimmy Dodson at the restaurant.

He wasn't sure what he was going to do about this latest offer. Six million bucks! It burned like a fever in his brain.

Jimmy Dodson promised him he could legally quash the deal with the Indian. He assured him the Pueblo lawyer wouldn't find enough evidence for a case even if he got a subpoena to shine a light up his tight Dodson ass, as he put it.

According to Jimmy, the new buyers had muscle and more cash than God, and wanted to expand their business into New Mexico permanently. They called themselves *Campo Santo.*

Chapter Fifty-Two

Father Emilio hurried from the sanctuary after hearing confessions, the church humming with people greeting one another and filling the pews for Mass. "I only have a few minutes," he apologized to Sergeant Ortega. "I know you understand that this is Holy Week."

"We wouldn't be here if this wasn't important, Father." The priest introduced himself and shook hands with Rob. "The videotape from Mrs. Ruiz' belongings is there on the desk," the priest said, donning a robe from a small closet and securing it with a cord around his waist. He slipped a crucifix over his head, "The tape has no label. You're free to use my equipment, if you need to view it here."

"Father, if you can have someone fill in for you for a few minutes, it would be appreciated. I would like you to see the tape with us."

Father Emilio knew Ortega was well aware substitution was often a necessity when he was delayed because of bad roads or parishioners' needs. He sighed, stepped to the sanctuary door, beckoning a small man in a black suit.

The man peered at the visitors around the Priest's shoulder, taking in Rob's yellow block-lettered DEA windbreaker and Ortega's uniform, his face full of distrust.

Manny Ortega knew the look well. Even after all these years his badge still marked him as an outsider in many of the Penitente communities. He thought of his four brothers, his small mouth pursing with irony. They were all in their respective *moradas* at this very moment. During Holy Week he felt like an outsider even in his own family.

The Priest assured his stand-in every thing was all right, closing the door. He pointed with his finger to the clock on the wall, "We need to get started."

Sergeant Ortega filled the priest in on the details they had so far of the murder of Justin James by crucifixion, made to appear a rite of the Penitentes.

"This is terrible. Murder through some sick mockery of our Christian beliefs and traditions? How can I help?"

"María Martínez gave testimony that her captor made her and the men who carried out the crucifixion stand under the cross, and remove the hoods they were wearing. The girl insists this hooded man stood in the dark, the rest of them illuminated by truck lights. She said it was the devil, that he had the *mal ojo*, which she described as a blinking red eye."

He turned to Rob. "The minute Agent Steele and I heard about the video tape, we thought her 'blinking eye' might be the red on-light of a video camera."

"And you are hoping I will recognize someone," the Priest said.

Ortega nodded. He held little hope for fingerprint evidence but put on a glove to handle the tape, pushed it into the machine and pressed play.

In the sanctuary beyond the office a resounding hymn of the crucified Redeemer rose in the dolorous voice of the faithful, but it couldn't insulate the perversion before their eyes. No one moved or made a sound or looked at one another as the grainy images flickered soundlessly onto the small screen.

A faceless tableau of hooded men emerged with María posed in front of them at the foot of the cross bearing the still living mutilated boy, his mouth moving in screams of agony.

The girl stared straight into the lens, arms straight at her sides, rigid as stone, terror gluing the skin of her face to the bone. Slowly each man removed his hood in unison, as if at some command, to stare full face into the camera.

Father Emilio drew in breath sharply. "Could you back up and freeze just on the faces of the men, please."

The tape wavered, then tracked, as Ortega rewound, then found the frame. The faces were as plain as if they stood in the room.

The priest bowed his head, drawing into himself, as if struggling with what to do.

"Father," Ortega urged, his fists clenching and unclenching, betraying the calm professional tone of his voice. "If you can identify these men, we need to know now."

Father Emilio regained his composure and pointed to the two men Ortega couldn't identify. "Richard and Joseph Terrazas. They once belonged to our church and the local *morada*. I haven't seen either of them here in well over a year, until yesterday." He tapped the screen at the bigger of the two. "Richard is a wood carver. He asked to do penance at Spy Wednesday service. He was covered in cactus, and people stepped on his back. Not nearly enough penance for this awful thing he has done," the priest said bitterly.

Father Emilio was already moving to his desk. He copied from a directory and handed over the paper with the men's names and addresses to Ortega. "The other brother, Joseph, is completely out of your jurisdiction. You'll see by the address that he lives over by Taos. He's a bad apple—drugs, gambling, always running with a rough crowd. My guess is that he's the reason Richard is involved in this."

"We all make our choices, Father."

"Then may God speed you in yours, Sergeant."

His mind was already racing ahead, cutting through red tape, getting the arrest of the brothers underway.

"If that's all, officer, I have a Mass to serve."

Ortega snapped his fingers, remembering something he wanted to ask, "Father, one more moment, please? You help your parishioners with the internet. Any chance Opal asked you to help her locate her son? And if so, did you have success?"

"This is turning into a fishing expedition, Sergeant Ortega," Father Emilio snapped, "and it's close to violating my parishioner's confidentiality. I must trust you have a good reason."

He turned back to the desk, searched for a moment, drew out a single piece of paper and handed it to Ortega. "These are the hits for the name Antonio Martínez in the Bay area, where Opal said to check. I suppose there's no harm in giving this to you, but I'm curious why you're asking?"

"Opal inserted herself into this investigation, Father. She called Sheriff Harvell to accuse Leandro Martínez in the deaths of the boy and Mrs. Ruiz. There seems to be bad blood between the two. Do you know anything about that?"

The priest's forehead knitted in deep furrows, when he looked up at Ortega. "I've overstepped giving you the information I have, but the confessional? That remains sacred. But I can tell you that Opal's call to the sheriff is not something she would have done on her own. I know this woman. Someone put her up to that. I'd stake my life on it."

"But who? Why?" The question seemed to hang in empty air as the priest swished through the door to the sanctuary.

"What's your take on the tape?" Rob asked, as they stepped outside. "An insurance policy to keep anyone from talking? Or a warning about what happens if you try to run off with the booty? Somebody's got to be missing that tape real bad."

"It's a windfall for us. First we get a positive ID from Sunny on our drug runners, and now these two guys' mugs turn up on the tape, so we also get them for murder."

Ortega checked the time. "It's not too late. I'm going to take a run over to talk to Opal. You'll be in Eagle Wing before me, it's better you handle the chain of evidence with the tape."

Rob agreed, put his hand on Ortega's shoulder, stopping him. "I've been doing some thinking about the robe and hood this guy wears. I think it's more than keeping him from being recognized. He thinks that get-up makes him powerful, the avenging angel we saw him playing out on that tape of the murder. I hate to say Sunny may be right, but when you get down to it, the best suspect for this damned mishmash of a case is Opal's phantom son. Think you can get anything out of her?"

Ortega snorted. "I'm going to give it a try. Just don't give me any more supernatural avenging angels crap," he said, giving Rob a good natured punch to the shoulder.

Chapter Fifty-Three

Sunny came running into the church yard. "Tony Tsia said he saw your cars here. I was hoping to catch you." She patted her chest, panting for breath. "There's something important I need to tell you. Something Jimmy Ruiz told me."

"Get in the van," Rob said, flipping on the dome light. "I need to take care of paper work, chain of evidence, for this." He held up the evidence bag with the videotape.

"What's that?" she asked, settling in the back, the two men in front.

"Need to know only," Ortega said sharply, then softened his tone. "How is Jimmy doing?"

"His Uncle Jesus had to come to pick him up. It's María. He seems terrified to be near her."

Rob and Manny exchanged glances.

"Come on guys. Why the look? It might help María, if there's an explanation."

Rob got a nod from Manny, gave Sunny an abbreviated version of the tape, debunking the devil's blinking red eye.

"Of course, why didn't I think of that?" She bumped her forehead with the heel of her hand.

"This all makes sense. Mrs. Ruiz and Jimmy were at Opal's when he found and played that videotape. He thinks María was in on killing Justin. Poor kid. Did you identify any of the men on the tape?"

"Two local guys, and your two thugs. At least one of them feels remorse." Rob repeated what Father Emilio told of the big man who wore cactus and let people step on him.

Sunny's eyes grew large. "I saw that. Ann invited us to the ceremony. I know exactly who you mean. I'll never forget it. How could he think that exonerates him from what he did to Justin? If I could get my hands on him, I'd…"

"Calm down Sunny. What did Jimmy tell you?" Rob asked.

"Mrs. Ruiz saw the tape and was driving it to the sheriff. On the way, a truck kept bumping their car until it went over the arroyo. Jimmy says it was no accident. The man was trying to hurt them. Just before it happened, Mrs. Ruiz told him to put the tape under his shirt, and no matter what, to give it to you." She nodded at Ortega.

"Did he get a look at him?" Ortega said excitedly.

"Jimmy got a good look, only the man wore a hood covering his face. It must be the same man that's come after all of us. Now, this makes my skin crawl," she said, a shiver passing through her. "He's sure the man was hiding at Opal's place and followed them."

Ortega raised his eyebrows. "The first person at the scene of the accident was a man in a truck. Why does Jimmy think—?"

"He says he heard noises in Opal's storage room. He tried the door. It was locked, but he felt a presence behind it, certain someone was in there."

"The phantom son," Rob and Manny said in unison, laughing.

"Laugh all you want," Sunny said, sounding hurt. "But I bet you find Antonio Martínez is the hooded man."

"We're laughing from frustration," Ortega admitted. "Everybody's got a little piece, but nothing fits into solid evidence. Father Emilio did an internet search for Opal to find her son. He came up with this." He pulled the list from his pocket.

Sunny peered over Ortega's arm, pointing to the entry *Antonio K. Martínez* at a San Francisco address. "I'll bet it's that one. The *K* could stand for Klafsky."

"I don't understand."

"It's another one of my theories," she warned. "Just don't laugh." She gave a boiled down version of Garcella Klafsky's career and disappearance, and finding the opera star's rare recording among Opal's things. She recounted Ann's history of her Uncle Antonio's marriage to an opera star, how she deserted her infant son, and finished with her certainty that Opal was an alias. "The parallels are too striking to dismiss. I know it's bizarre, but I think she's Garcella Klafsky."

Ortega and Rob shot each other another look. The basic facts fit Leandro's. Ortega groaned with exasperation. "We don't need any more complications in this case."

"There's something else," Sunny said, biting her lip. "Why would someone transfer the photos of Justin's murderers onto something as cumbersome and easily destroyed as full-size VHS tape? Why not a micro-size cassette or a CD?"

"Is this twenty questions?" Rob asked, rolling his shoulders to relieve his fatigue. "Tell us. Why?"

"To make CDs and minis requires kind of pricey new hardware and software. So, I'm guessing our guy's using an older video camera that's only capable of recording into a VCR. And that blinking recording light isn't usual either. A good camera store might be able to dig up a brand and model number. Catch someone with that kind of camera? Isn't that at least circumstantial evidence?"

"I thought I'd better drive you home before you uttered another theory and Manny exploded," Rob said. He was suddenly serious.

"Sunny, dammit, you be careful tomorrow. I'll do what I can to keep in touch."

He pulled up in front of Ann's house for the second time and pulled out a pen and scribbled a number on a pad. "If you get into trouble, try me at this number." His jaw was set, but there was softness in the gray eyes as they came up to meet hers." He tore off the paper and handed it to her. "If you don't get me the first time, keep trying."

He walked her to the door, patted her arm awkwardly, then jammed both hands in the pockets of his windbreaker. She gave a stiff little wave, held up the slip of paper, thanked him, then shoved it in her pocket and slipped into the house.

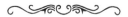

Less than five minutes later, there was a knock at the door. *Rob again?* Sunny raced to answer.

It was Gordon Grantwood, all Harrison Ford attitude in a black turtle neck sweater, a denim jacket carried over one shoulder. "You've moved. Ann said you're staying with her now. I guess you forgot to check your messages. I just found this in your mailbox. It's from yesterday. No trouble," he said before she could thank him.

He handed her a pink phone message slip, his eyes darted around taking in as much as possible through the partially opened door.

Raymundo Manzanares had stepped up the time of their meeting tomorrow to 11:15. She quickly read the directions to his studio, the message taker's script as small and neat as a CPA's, and found nothing new. There was no indication of the time the message came in, or who had recorded it.

Gordon looked at it, shook his head, huffed something about lots of people filling in right now who don't know what they were doing.

"I can't thank you enough, Gordon. You've just saved my derriere. If I'd shown up late, our firm would be in real trouble."

"At least you say thanks. That's more than I get from anyone else around here," he said, feet crunching gravel as he walked to his car.

Chapter Fifty-Four

Good Friday

The floorboards over Opal's head had squeaked relentlessly through the night. Each time his footsteps came into her bedroom, she stopped breathing in the little cellar under her closet, her heart beating as if it would burst from her chest.

It had been hours since she heard any movement, but in her mind's eye she saw Antonio sitting like a cat at a mouse hole, quiet, listening, waiting for her to betray her hiding place.

His ranting still echoed in her ears.

"You told him. You betrayed me! First you deserted me. Now, you betray me." Glass shattered. Furniture hurtled across the room. The birdcage crashed to the floor, the mynah bird squawking and thrashing, running its repertoire of familiar words. The stomping of a boot, then silence.

"Tristan," Opal murmured softly, hugging her breast and rocking with grief. "Tristan, my baby."

She hadn't betrayed Antonio. Sergeant Ortega had come, looking at everything as he asked his questions. He had run the beam of his big flashlight in the store room, his fingers finding the jimmied door. He wanted to know about her son. Did she find him? Was he here in Ojo Tres? He wasn't wanted for anything, just questions, information. The lawman told her about a man wearing a Penitente hood and robe, involved in a killing, maybe responsible for Adeline and Jimmy's accident. Did she know of such a man? Did she know how the tape Mrs. Ruiz was taking to the sheriff came to be in her house? What did she have against Leandro Martínez? Was calling Sheriff Harvell her own idea? She told him nothing.

She knew Antonio would know about Sergeant Ortega's visit. When he came to ask what she had told the lawman, she wanted him to believe she was gone.

She scribbled a note telling Antonio she was off to deliver the Sanchez baby and propped it against a jelly jar on the kitchen table where he was sure to see it. There were many, many Sanchez families, he wouldn't know where to begin looking for her. Going into her bedroom, she slid back the closet door and lifted the floorboard to which she had glued some old pairs of shoes and a box or two to disguise it from anyone who looked inside.

She let herself down into the cramped narrow hole she dug to protect herself from Leandro, should he come to beat her again. She was afraid she had grown too large for the space. She pushed hard against the rocks lining the pit, molding herself, scraping skin, finding herself just able to sit by drawing her knees tightly to her chest. Replacing the cover, her fingers found the beads of her crucifix in the deep darkness and she prayed.

Hours passed. She was sure Antonio was gone. She was numb and wet, stinking of urine. A new fear crept into her mind. Her body might not move at all, and she was trapped. Nearly suffocating on panic, she pushed against the flooring, lifting it enough to slide open the closet door a crack.

She clawed her way out of the hole, struggling to bring circulation into her numb legs. The odors of herbs and oils told her most of her medications lay in ruined heaps.

She knew what she had to do.

Not daring to turn on lights, she made her way in the darkness, stumbling against the overturned birdcage. Patting her hands against the floor, she moved them in widening arcs until her fingers closed over Tristan's stiff body. She picked him up, smoothing the satiny feathers and holding him to her breast. She found the phone and dialed. Her voice was barely a whisper, and she had to repeat. "Father Emilio. It's Opal. Please help me. My life is in danger. I think others are in danger too. There are things I must tell you."

Chapter Fifty-Five

The rising sun flooded onto the highway between gaps in the deep canyon walls as Sunny pushed the rental car as fast as she dared over blind hills and around curves. Inspirational as the light itself was the sight of pilgrims heading for Chimayó, their breath hanging in the frosty air as they talked and sang.

What Rob said about being entirely on her own weighed heavily and, as a precaution, she left Ojo Tres before anyone who had seen that telephone message would expect her to be on the road. It was 7:20 when she crossed the Santeria County line, having seen only one of Ortega's people. She couldn't be sure if the deputy was acknowledging her or just being friendly when he waved back. The trip so far was mercifully uneventful, the tires zinging and thumping on the narrow pavement like a metronome counting off the miles.

By the time traffic began to pick up, she had reached the interstate and pulled off at a truck-stop café just out of Santa Fe, with a cluster of gas stations, tourist shops and strip mall nearby. She had time on her hands and bought a battery for her camera, then decided a big breakfast was just what she needed.

The restaurant was busy, the counter and booths jammed with truckers and tourists and a group of local residents, all of them senior citizens who, judging by the sound of their joshing and good natured arguments, were retired from everything but strong opinions.

She was getting stomach butterflies thinking about the morning ahead, and lost her appetite, settling for coffee.

"You a nun or going to a funeral?" the waitress asked. Her smile took any rudeness out of the question.

Sunny looked blankly at her a moment. "Oh, I get it." She self-consciously patted the heavy silver cross that lay suspended against her black knit top, the midi-skirt and black boots—her version of what a *People* magazine photojournalist would wear. "Just going to a job I'm praying will be over in a hurry."

The girl laughed, put down the coffee, tore off Sunny's check and laid it under the saucer.

Outside, Sunny filled the car with gas and checked the fluid levels. Dipping the window washer up and down in the reservoir of fluid, she grabbed a handful of paper towels and went to work on the windshield. *If I fail to see someone following me, it isn't because my windows aren't clean.* She had meant to make a little joke with herself, but only succeeded in bringing back a pall of worry and looked around carefully at every car in the lot. No one seemed in the least interested in her, and she pulled away as a driver behind honked impatiently for the pump.

A strange looking rock formation straight ahead caught her eye. She pulled over to get a better look. The sign said Camel Rock, and indeed, a long thick neck of brown sandstone rose from a hump of rock-strewn dirt with a flat rock atop it that looked uncannily camel-like. A photographic crew was unloading and setting up cameras. Sunny rolled down her window and the nearest photographer strolled over. An assortment of oriental carpets, kilims, and dhurries spilled rich brilliant colors down a portion of the grade and over rocks where three people were busy arranging them.

"An advertising piece for one of the galleries over on Canyon Road," he said in answer to Sunny's question. "Hey, move that camel statue and the samovar about a foot to the east," he called to one of the assistants. "You with a studio from around here?" he asked, pointing to the Nikon she had around her neck. "I'm from St. Louis. I'm here to do a little publicity photography for a client." She grimaced, "The client from Hell."

"I thought I had all of those. Hey, hey, hey, where you going with that?" He gave Sunny a hopeless shrug. "New guy, first shoot. Got to go." He looked truly sorry, and her ego felt buoyed by the open admiration in his eyes.

"Go, go," she said, smiling. "Been there."

"Card?" he asked. They exchanged quickly. One of those modern rituals that never amounts to anything, but Sunny guessed it was something akin to a lady's hanky tucked in a manly tunic in a bygone era. Moira was all for inventing business cards activated with super glue that only came unstuck when the guy actually got around to making the callback.

The soaring roof line of the Santa Fe Opera came into view, appearing like a space ship or some enormous ark suspended on the high desert hillside. Molly had urged her to be sure to stop by if she had time. It would be easier to take a few minutes, then explain why she hadn't. She had to admit the place looked interesting.

She parked and walked down to a terrazzo terrace that overlooked the great hall with its sweeping golden-wood roof. Its open-air sides were protected from chilly breezes by a series of battened wind baffles rising like sails of Chinese junks anchored in harbor. The back of the stage was open, and Sunny caught her breath at the panorama of piñon-dotted hills and purple-hued mountains. It would, she thought, be a spectacular setting for Manzanares' opera about the Penitentes. But then, so would St. Louis.

She realized the stop had taken more time than she thought. *Molly, you and your opera. Now I've got only twenty minutes.*

She dug out the telephone message with instructions to Manzanares' place and studied it quickly, trying to get her bearings.

A sudden chill gripped her. For the first time she noticed the neat tight script looked like the same writing on the map with the coordinates she'd found secreted in the toilet roll in Justin's apartment.

Surely her cell phone would work in Santa Fe. She found Rob's number, punched it in. "Come on, come on," she spoke as the phone kept ringing, flipped to voice mail.

"The hidden map and coordinates I found in Justin's room were written by someone who works the desk at Ojo Tres. I'm sure of it. I'll call back later."

She pressed the star key and tossed her cell phone into her handbag, immediately wishing she hadn't been so impulsive. He might think the message just a contrivance to contact him. And to tell the truth, she couldn't be absolutely sure about the notes without comparing the two pieces of paper side-by-side. *Why do I always jump to conclusions?*

She almost missed her turnoff.

Chapter Fifty-Six

Ahead, a tall adobe wall curved around marking the perimeter of the Waring property, the house number set in ornate tiles. She shouldered her camera bag, crossed over a plank bridge and onto a walkway of black sea-stones leading to a tall, museum-quality carved gate. She unlatched it and slipped inside. Tender green shoots and just-budding trees gave a suitable frame of welcome to the house. She was learning to love these mud buildings, their perfectly proportioned contours seemingly shaped by hand in sweeping caresses.

A table, with the remains of breakfast for two, set before an elaborate outdoor fireplace, soaring upward in the form of a thick sculpted tree trunk.

"You came, and right on time."

Sunny whirled at the familiar voice behind her, her mouth dropping.

Kay Waring moved toward her, and Sunny stepped back, keeping her at bay like she might a snake. "What the hell— What kind of game are you playing? Is Raymundo Manzanares even here?" Sunny blurted.

"Oh, he's here all right." Choosing the question she wanted to answer. Kay beckoned Sunny to the patio wall. "Come take a look for yourself."

Below them in a second courtyard, a man, tall and dark, naked to the waist, waved at them. Then, shouldering a wood beam, he disappeared through an open overhead door the size of a small airplane hanger in the exposed front wall of a two-story addition tucked into the hillside and connected to the main house. The whine of an electric saw cut through the stillness, sending the smell of burning wood into the air.

"He's a real hottie, isn't he?" Kay shouted over it.

"Goddamn it Kay Waring, if you're here, you sure as hell don't need me," she shouted over the sound of the machinery, following Kay down a flight of stone steps.

She spoke over her shoulder. "I wanted to see if you'd break our agreement, because I wouldn't pay one red cent if you did."

Sunny thundered after her, ready with a retort, but instead her heart skipped a beat as they reached the bottom. Shoved under an overhang in the wall, she found herself face to face with a leering skeletal face of a figure of Death. The seated carving was bolted to a platform of poles laced together with wide leather straps on a crude cart with large wooden wheels.

"Scary even if it is just wood, isn't it?" Kay shouted, pointing to the figure, formed of jointed blocks of wood with twig protrusions suggesting ribs. Death sat slightly forward, a small bow in its hands drawing a bead with an arrow aimed directly at them. "It's from Raymundo's *morada,* and it's very old."

The figure hit a nerve, reminding her of her brush with real death, putrid and cruel. She took refuge in shaking anger to blot out unexpected feelings of fear. "Don't change the subject."

Kay turned and said something, but the loud unrelenting hum of the saw, intensifying as they neared the doorway, drowned out her words. Sunny pushed forward right at Kay's heels.

"I thought Mr. Hottie Penitente refused to see you," she screamed, as Kay turned back to her, the power plug to the saw dangling in her hands. Too late to retract her words, they seemed all the more amplified in the sudden silence.

Sunny heard an embarrassed cough inside the studio. How could she possibly suffer through an introduction now? Kay was grinning wickedly, enjoying every minute.

"If you must have answers, Raymundo came to his senses that he needed me. Homer went to Europe on business, and I came to Santa Fe. I hope you'll also believe my threats to Sumner were very real. I expect some decent publicity out of you at the very least."

She hated Kay Waring. She hated this place. She hated this whole situation, but she was stuck with it. She pulled out her Nikon, checking the light meter, adjusting settings.

"Raymundo is dying to meet you. You're in luck. You'll be able to get some great photos. A woodcarver who used to live in Ray's village is here today. Raymundo's such a stickler for authenticity, and only this man does work in the style of the old *moradas*. Ray's been trying for two months to get him to construct the crucifix for the last act. Wait until you see his work. It's almost worth all the noise."

Raymundo stepped from the shadow of the studio. "I'll only be a minute, *amigo,* while I talk to these lovely ladies."

No doubt about it, Raymundo Manzanares was a hunk. But his most attractive feature was an energy that seemed to sweep ahead of him and wrap itself around her. It was open and warm and genuine. "Sunny Bay, that you think me a 'hottie', did you say, makes my day."

"Yes, well, there's definitely a compliment in there somewhere." She felt flustered, glad to be able to pull her professional cloak about her. "I need to get started." She clicked off half a dozen shots of him. "I'm a little concerned about the light in the studio," she said, peering behind him. "It looks a bit dim in there."

"Oh, it's just a matter of your eyes adjusting from this bright sunlight. Come. See for yourself," he encouraged.

She stepped into the room, his arm lightly guiding her. The other man, with his back to them, lifted his powerful arms, swinging a long-handled adz, sending a chip of wood flying from the heavy timber stretched the length of the long workbench. The carver, wiping away sweat, laid the tool down. Watching him fit the cross-arm into the notch, her head began buzzing, and she felt her body resisting as they approached. The cross took human form, prostrate, like a man in adoration, that she couldn't blink away, Raymundo's words seeming to echo from a tunnel.

"There aren't three woodcarvers left in the whole state who do the kind of work this man does. But if I call Richard an artist, he'll want to charge me more." He was laughing, jesting, trying to make her at ease.

The man turned at their approach. Suddenly everything else in the room seemed to disappear, images of Justin's crucified body flooding her brain. She reeled backward on trembling legs, a scream escaping as she recognized one of Justin's killers—the big man who lay prostrate in a wreath of cactus at the *morada*, doing penance as worshippers stepped on him.

Chapter Fifty-Seven

The man was finishing his coffee and donut in the shop across from the Arizona and New Mexico Land and Mine Consultants office building just as the Santa Fe Police broke down the front door and went in, guns drawn. *Go down the hall, boys, just like the tipster said, last office on the right. Keep those guns up. See that thing sprawled on the desk? That's what's left of Ed Martin's head. Somebody quick, bag the bowling trophy, the one with blood and brains sticking to it. Guess what? That's the weapon used to beat the bloody truth out of the dickhead, his lies about Ojo Tres, Jimmy Dodson's double cross with Leandro and this bunch called Campo Santo.*

He stood with the other gawkers at the restaurant window as medics rolled the body out in its zippered cocoon and slid it into an ambulance. ""Hey, Mr. Tall-and-Built-Like-a-Door, do you mind?" The frizzy blond head of the waitress poked around his arm, looking up at him. "You're blocking my view."

He moved aside, letting her shoulder in front of him. "That guy... that guy they're taking out of there?" she said loudly, so nobody missed it. "That's got to be Ed Martin. He was just in here a little while ago. His brother-in-law's that guy running for Congress. Jimmy Dodson." She puffed up with importance as everyone listened to her. "He just got through telling me he was in to do a little paper work on a big land deal. Nobody else there, closed for Good Friday, you know. I'm the last person he talked to. Except the killer. Ain't that something? Look, I got goose bumps."

The man smiled at the little prickles of skin on the woman's bony upper arm.

The waitress stepped back, mashing down on the top of his foot. "Didn't you hear me excuse myself?" The halfway apology hung in the air as she went to catch the phone. He squelched the rage rising up in him. He couldn't afford to do anything to be remembered. Ignoring the pain in his foot, he forced a smile. "Hey, I walk on them myself, no problem."

He left exact change to pay his bill and a better than average, but not generous tip. "Sorry about your loss." He nodded across the street. She adopted a sorrowful look as if she was bereaved family and came out from behind the counter to return to the window.

He waited. Everyone's attention turned once again to the crime scene, police roping it off with yellow tape, a TV camera crew already catching the action. He retrieved his gym bag from his booth and sauntered back toward the rest room where he slipped through a door marked Employees Only and into the alley. He hopped over a low chain-link fence and made his way down a short street between Don Gaspar and Galisteo Road where he had parked his car in the lot of a business with a sign on the door announcing it was closed until Monday.

He turned left on San Francisco heading for the highway. He had plenty of time if nothing went wrong. Near the Santa Fe Opera he pulled off onto the shoulder, watching the road. He propped open his car hood and turned on the flashers. If the highway patrol stopped, he could always say he was waiting for Triple A.

Studying his reflection in the rearview mirror, he was satisfied the oversize pair of sunglasses and floppy-brimmed cotton hat pulled low on his head was a sufficient disguise. He toyed with donning the hood and robe to scare the bejesus out of her. Like it had scared poor old Ed Martin. Too bad it was covered with wet blood. Still, it was tempting, just to see her face. Just for the fun of it.

He didn't have long to wait. He saw her car coming from the opposite direction across the divided highway and watched her slow, hunting for her turnoff. He gave a snorting gleeful laugh, seeing the flash of bright blonde hair. Right on time for your appointment. He settled down to wait. From this vantage point she would have to pass by him on her way back to Ojo Tres. Sunny Bay was never going to testify to what she'd seen on the mesa.

Funny, he couldn't remember why that was important. His head was aching bad. When he felt like this, it seemed he had a big black hole in his mind sucking away his thoughts. He felt for his pills, popped one and sat back, breathing slowly.

Oh, yes, it was coming back to him. Sunny Bay is a snoopy girl. His plans to overtake her on the drive to Santa Fe got changed. Unexpected, big distractions, like Sergeant Ortega stopping by his mother's house, and having to do something about Jimmy's double cross and putting the screws to old Ed Martin.

He swallowed another pill. In the close air of the car's interior, he remembered his mother's voice calling out silly things, meaningless words, and he remembered shutting her up. Had he hurt her? He couldn't remember. The medication wasn't taking hold. The thought of his mother brought bitterness and rage. If he killed her, she deserved it. She left him, she left him alone, a little defenseless child at the mercy of his father, the first Antonio Martínez.

Chapter Fifty-Eight

Ortega caught the noon news on TV. The murder of Ed Martin, brother-in-law of Santa Fe lawyer and political candidate Jimmy Dodson slain in his real estate office, led the broadcast. "Police confirm that Dodson, who is expected to announce his candidacy for the U.S. Senate, and his wife, a silent partner in her brother's land office, appear to be missing. They are wanted for questioning," the reporter intoned meaningfully, then added, "to see if they can shed some light on this tragic event."

"Isn't that the Jimmy Dodson you asked me to check out?" asked Angelic Flores, popping the top on a can of Diet Pepsi and offering Ortega a sip as she sat in the lunchroom with him.

"Yeah. Find any connection between him and this *Campo Santo?*"

"Your little green men?" she asked mischievously. "Well, maybe this is a possibility. Dodson has been trying to unload the old family homestead, pretty well run down now, that sits on five acres or more. It's overgrown with cottonwoods and brush cause there's a creek runs through, making it hard to see from the road. It's posted, but every year the pilgrims trespass and get in there to camp and every year Dodson files a complaint to have them moved, but not this year. This year he came in for a permit for some religious group to camp there. Want to bet that's related?"

"When you coming back to work dispatch full-time?" he asked, grinning, tapping her shoulder affectionately.

He hurried down the hall, hoping to quickly clear an accumulation of paperwork before heading back out into the field and checking out the Dodson property. The radio squawked endlessly. Reports of traffic jams on all the tributary roads leading into the Santuario de Chimayó. Fender benders. Complaints of teenagers littering and dropping water bombs. Someone upending a portable toilet while occupied. A stolen baby stroller. An altercation between camera-toting tourists and some of the locals. A man in a wheelchair struck by a motorcycle and needing an ambulance. The annual headache.

He tried first to reach Rob Steele to let him know about Dodson's property. As he let the phone ring, his eyes fell on a message note taped to his desk. Call Father Emilio. It was marked Urgent, the time just before 6:30 that morning. Tobin took the message and didn't give it to him. Unfortunately Tobin was thinking again.

Rob came on the line to Ortega's agitated "Stupid bastard." He apologized. "Not you, Rob. Somebody screwed up bad, an urgent message from Father Emilio mishandled. Let me think. What was I calling you about? Oh, yeah—" He filled him in on the Santa Fe murder and the Dodson property. Before he could get the address out of his mouth, Rob cut in.

"Ortega, you're not going to like this any better than any of the rest of us on the task force, but we've been told to stand down on this."

Angelica stood at the door, waving a message. It had to be from Harvell; it was their signal. "Hold on, Rob." The message essentially told him to do exactly what Rob just said. "I don't get it. Why? Right when we've got the chance to nip a narcotics ring in the bud."

"You on a land line? Secure?"

"Yes."

"The FBI didn't know *Campo Santo* was in New Mexico until you set the wheels in motion last night asking for information. They suspect it of running a drug pipeline from Mexico to California and points east by drawing in a lot of smaller drug operations, especially in their new specialty—meth. You still there?"

"Just taking it all in. Sounds like mergers and acquisitions have hit the drug world."

"The agent-in-charge calls it a cartel in religious skirts. That's the kicker. *Campo Santo* is organized as a church with all the protection that affords. It's relatively new, but already getting big, entrenched in five states. It appears law abiding, runs seemingly legitimate operations, mostly private religious training camps for boys in remote areas where there isn't much oversight, like Ojo Tres. FBI thinks the organization could be something bigger. The FBI hopes to catch them with the drugs, get solid indictments here as a legitimate reason to go after them everywhere. The FBI's calling the shots from here on in."

"Which means?"

"Which means we can make arrests as long as we don't go onto the Dodson property to do it. The FBI has it under surveillance."

"Anything else?"

Rob passed along Sunny's suspicions about the handwriting on the telephone message and the map notes she found in Justin's room. Ortega groused. "She's always got these intriguing ideas, but I need hard evidence. Get both pieces of paper from her, pronto, so an expert can compare them. If she's right, they're evidence."

"Any word from the crime lab on Justin?"

"Not yet. You making progress?"

"No sign of the woodcarver or his brother. The interview with Opal went about how I expected. No answers. Not enough of anything for a search warrant on hearsay from little Jimmy. Damn this is frustrating."

"Let me know what's on Father Emilio's mind if you catch up with him."

Ortega shouted down the hall when he hung up with Rob to check with Angelica again, only to find the priest still couldn't be reached.

Some grinding deep in his gut told him the Priest's call was the break they needed. *Damn you, Tobin.*

Chapter Fifty-Nine

Elaine Martin Dodson left the keys hanging in the ignition of the Lincoln Navigator. Before getting out, she checked her new short hairdo in the mirror, liking the auburn bangs and green contacts. She scarcely recognized herself but the change made her look ten years younger. Shutting the door, she took off the rubber gloves, shoving them into her purse.

Walking without hurry, carrying a shopping bag, she moved between cars on the mall parking lot until she reached a small nondescript gray Kia. It belonged to a James Dawson who'd agreed to thirty-six months of payments when he purchased it. He breezed through the credit check, which he'd been building in Dawson's name for three years. "Why do we have to be poor to hide, Jimmy?" she complained, getting in, slamming the door. "I loved that Lincoln."

"How do you think I feel giving up my Mercedes?" he snapped, thinking of his baby left with keys in the ignition in one of El Paso's least desirable neighborhoods. It no doubt made its way to a chop shop hours ago.

Tears threatened Elaine's new shade of mascara. "Poor brother, Ed. If only we could have warned him."

"If only." He squeezed her hand. *There isn't much room in a lifeboat. Always remember that, Jimmy.* He could almost hear his father's knowing laughter whenever he said that.

Jimmy knew the jig was up when the two armed thugs from Campo Santo, who he'd hired to help the Doofus with Justin, came looking for him. He'd been warned to deliver Leandro's signature deeding the Ojo Tres property to the cartel, or else. He failed. He was sure the Doofus had killed Ed, and was probably headed for him next. He had only one choice—disappear for good.

Mr. and Mrs. Dawson sailed down the interstate in their Kia for their new life in Alpine, Texas, the car's trunk full of her jewelry, new passports, clothes, two Forrest Moses paintings and a load of cash Jimmy Dodson kept in a storage locker for just such a turn of events.

Chapter Sixty

Richard Terrazas recognized Sunny as one of the Anglos who was at the *morada*. One look at the horror on her face was certainty enough that, somehow, she knew about the dead boy and his part in his death. He moved across the studio floor like a charging bull.

His sudden move drove Sunny's adrenaline through the roof as she mistook his intent as an attack on her. She grabbed a piece of wood from the floor, swinging it like a bat. It took her a second to realize he was running past her, not at her, headed for his pickup truck parked down the hill.

Her legs carried her on a dead run after him, feeling as if they belonged to someone else, the wood scrap raised to do battle, her heart pounding. The truck door swung open, and he was inside, just as she swung the length of wood shattering the window, the weapon flying from her hands, palms stinging from the force of the blow.

The truck exhaust puffed dark, oily smoke as it shot forward. It stayed in her sight long enough to get the license plate number. She mumbled it over and over, running back to where Raymundo and Kay stood dumbfounded, commandeering the telephone near the entrance to the studio.

With hands shaking so hard she almost dropped the receiver, she dialed 911, responding to the quiet competence of the dispatcher, calming her, taking information.

"You're doing fine, stay with me now. Do you know which direction he headed?"

"I don't know the direction," she stammered. "But I know he didn't take the road to the interstate." She thought about the roads she noticed on her way meandering off into the hills. "He turned in the direction of those mountains back of the Opera house."

"Can you do one more thing, please?" Sunny asked. "Alert Sergeant Ortega at the Santeria County Sheriff's office. He's already looking for this man for a murder committed there."

Raymundo pushed past Kay to confront Sunny. "Richard is my friend. Please explain what just happened."

Before she could get out a word, they heard sirens. One police car raced along the road on the distant ridge above them, headed toward the hills. Another eased itself up the drive, two officers from the Santa Fe Police Department getting out with guns drawn.

"The man is gone! We're okay." Sunny shouted. "I'm the one who called."

The officers' questioning was thorough—how Sunny knew the suspect, why he was wanted by the law in Santeria County, his involvement in the murder, detail after detail. They questioned Raymundo and Kay, nailing down a time frame, establishing the unlikelihood the woodcarver could have anything to do with the murder that morning of a Santa Fe real estate agent.

As the officers drove away, Sunny knew she couldn't stay here; she couldn't go through with the interview and photography. She girded herself for a fight with Kay as she begged off, surprised when Raymundo agreed immediately, signally Kay to silence.

"You poor girl, of course we understand." His face reflected genuine concern. "We can only imagine the horror of finding the crucified body of your friend."

He pulled up a chair for her. Sunny allowed him to help her sit, gratefully accepting the cold bottle of water he offered.

He sat too, his knees almost touching hers, his hand on her shoulder. "You know… you experienced this terrible thing, and so did my mother. Did you know that? Only it was my father who died," he said gently. "When you told the policeman your story… Tell me about that poor girl you said Richard gave the dead boy's boots to. How old is she? Is she going to be all right?"

"She is only sixteen." Sunny said. "I can't imagine she'll ever be able to forget." *Will I?*

"Ah, the girl needs help. She shouldn't keep it bottled up," he said, his eyes as liquid as melted chocolate. "Allow me." He moved to a small chest, pulling out a worn album, turning to a photograph of a young girl, her head turned shyly to one side. "This is my mother. She was only a year older than the other girl when her lover was murdered." His voice broke. "Sadly, she never recovered."

He handed her a second photo of an old woman dressed in black, pressing a man's worn shoes to her chest. The face faintly resembled the photo of the young girl, but the innocence was long gone.

"This is my mother as she was until the end of her life. I can't look at her without sorrow," he said softly. "It's her story I'm telling. Her justice I seek."

Sunny touched the old face in the photo. His sincerity reached her as Kay's bluster would not. But even a tender trap, is still a trap. If only there was some way to end this amicably.

"Before this thing this morning—" He took the photo, looked at it a long time, tucked it into the album. "I was going to suggest you focus on this character, based on my mother at the end of her life, for your article." He looked at her shyly.

"She is the most difficult of my characters to cast. She embodies so much tragedy. The voice is crucial. I envision it as almost otherworldly. We have to attract the right singer, and there are so few—"

Kay's voice interceded sharply, so sharply Raymundo stood, stepping back. "You are being your most unreasonable self again

Raymundo. Your sainted mother be damned. The singers you think would do are dead, or out of the ballpark for regional opera."

"Sunny doesn't need to hear our disagreement right now," he answered, sounding whipped down by what was evidently only one more version of an ongoing argument. "I just thought it was a good angle for the article, if Sunny would rethink her decision. We could reschedule."

Kay protested angrily. "There isn't time." She whirled on Sunny. "Sumner contributed a brilliant media plan. I've counted on you for photos and this background article." Her eyes narrowed viciously.

Sunny ached to go. Her mind raced through the dilemma like a rat through a maze trying to find a way out so everyone could win. What flew into her mind was crazy.

The crazy thought rattled around in her cranium so she scarcely heeded Kay's haranguing until she said, "Either you come through like you agreed or I'll—"

"What if I could give you something better? Something spectacular!" Sunny knew full well the pitfalls in her proposal, the odds that she could bring this off zero to none.

But Mrs. Ruiz' words came back to her. *She sings like a bird. She knows all the operas. You should hear her. She gets in these wistful moods and sings as if she's in another world.* The same excitement ran up her spine as it had when she listened to the old recording, the voice of the Prairie Nightingale winging in effortless, dazzling coloratura to the highest notes of Mozart's "Queen of the Night". Manzanares wants otherworldly? Oh yes, indeed.

"Does Garcella Klafsky mean anything to either of you?"

"If you mean do I know who she was? Certainly, I know. But get to the point."

"I've found her, Kay. She's alive." Sunny turned to Raymundo. "Garcella looks as tragic as the photo of your mother, and I'm told she still sings. I heard the recording of her performance at the Met. It is the voice you envision, Raymundo."

Sunny was in full public relations pitch. "Beside the voice, this woman was married to a Penitente and suffered because of it. If you could get her for this opera in any capacity, think what a stir it would create?"

Kay rose to the bait, head high as if basking in the applause of millions. She deflated fast. "What's this coup to cost me?"

"Kay," Raymundo interceded. "I want to hear this voice. I want to at least meet this woman. I'm intrigued," he pleaded, catching Sunny's excitement.

Kay ignored him, her own eyes locked on Sunny. "What's the deal?"

"Just this, Kay. I give you Garcella's current identity, where she can be found and the names of a couple of people who might be helpful in gaining you an audience." She kept her fingers crossed behind her. Father Emilio and Ann would need a lot of convincing.

"The rest is up to you."

Kay thought about it for a long moment. "Go on."

"In exchange, I get two letters right now from you, witnessed by Raymundo. The first letter exonerates Sumner of anything to do with those bogus petitions so long ago or anything else you may think you have on him because of it. You also agree to release me from this leg of the assignment with promise to recompense all time and expenses."

She was wondering how much farther she could take this. She mentally crossed her fingers. "In the second letter, you recommend our firm. Make it a real love letter Kay. I'll be parsing every word."

"I'll be damned if I will do that."

"Kay," Raymundo began. "Do it. We've nothing to lose and everything to gain."

"You'd better deliver." Kay turned on her heel toward a small office at the side of the room, then turned back. "What about my photographs?"

Sunny laughed inwardly, remembering the chance meeting with the photographer at Camel Rock and dug out his card, handing it to Kay, praising him as the best in Santa Fe.

"Let him know I sent you. Now, let's get to those letters."

Chapter Sixty-One

Now what? First there were the patrol cars screaming over the hill scaring the piss out of him. Now Sunny turned not toward Ojo Tres, but into Santa Fe. He jumped out and slammed down the open hood, then slid under the wheel. The car lurched and bounced as he forced it into the rough trough between the divided highways and barreled up the other side to follow her car.

As he closed the distance, he picked her out. She had her arm resting on the frame of her opened window, her blond hair blowing wildly in the warm wind, as easy to follow as a flag. Staying close, hidden behind a floppy pulled down hat and sunglasses, he followed as she took Alameda and turned abruptly into a strip shopping mall and headed for a clothing store. The shop was too small to follow her inside, so he settled back to wait.

He almost missed her when she came out, mistaking her first for a young boy. Her hair was tucked up under a ball cap and she had changed clothes, the jeans and bright plaid shirt camouflaging her slender body. She carried three or four shopping bags. How did women do it? She hadn't been in the store more than forty-five minutes, and she'd practically bought it out.

He started the car, ready to back out, when a car pulled up behind him, blocking his way. He looked frantically trying to spot Sunny. By the time he got to the exit, she was gone.

Which way? Traffic was heavy, and she seemed to have been swallowed up by it. He hammered impatiently on the steering wheel, trying to catch a break in the flow. Finally he blasted his horn, keeping it smashed down with his hand, and screeching his tires, pushed into the busy street as horns blared, and headed for the highway. He was betting that she was headed back to the Springs. A sense of depression hit him, a sickening feeling that she had eluded him, as he wove in and out changing lanes.

It was just past the spot along the highway where he had waited for her when he caught sight of her car up ahead. Locking her in view, he settled into a steady pace keeping a couple of cars between them, amusing himself thinking how he was going to make Sunny pay.

Traffic moved at about the same speed, and before he knew it he was jammed in a kind of convoy with cars tight on every side. Suddenly the cars in front of him slowed as a U-Haul truck lurched onto the highway, the stream of cars at his left boxing him in and keeping him from passing. Angrily grabbing off his sunglasses, he threw on his blinker trying to ease his car into the fast moving traffic. Horns blasted and no one budged, one driver deliberately closing any possible opening.

He pushed the accelerator to the floor, almost clipping the fender of the car ahead of him as he pulled onto the shoulder, kicking up a cloud of dust. He sped along it until he could pull ahead of the U-Haul trailer. When he was finally able to get clear, Sunny's car had vanished.

Then he remembered the restaurant and gas stations near the intersection. She must have pulled off while he was trying to get around the trailer. If she didn't pass by in a reasonable time he would have to come up with another plan, try to catch her on the lonely high road. But for now, all he could do was wait.

Chapter Sixty-Two

For a few carefree moments—clothes shopping and driving with her hair in the wind—Sunny forgot all the terrible things that had happened. But as she thought about the lonely road back to Ojo Tres, her muscles grew so tense her hands cramped on the steering wheel, her breathing quick and ragged.

Flashes of the woodcarver, the hooded man and Justin's ravaged body began bouncing like a game of bumper pool in her head. *Whoa! Stress syndrome? I absolutely refuse.* Grab a Coke, she counseled herself. Get your head together. Take a pee, for Pete's sake.

She flipped on the turn light and whipped off the highway heading for the restaurant where she'd had breakfast. 'Taking hold of herself,' as her grandmother always put it, seemed to help, her breathing becoming steady and the anxious feeling dissipating as she climbed out of the car into bright sunlight under a dome of azure blue sky. She walked into the restaurant, nearly empty in the mid-afternoon lull, her waitress of the morning already gone for the day. At the counter she ordered a Coke to go and headed for the rest room.

She didn't believe in thunderbolts, but there was no denying that the idea hit her like a dart hurled from heaven as she stepped up to pay for her drink and a pack of gum. Of course, it was the perfect solution. She waited impatiently to get a stack of change, hurried to the pay phone and dialed the hotel at Ojo Tres. Ann said Molly would be keeping her company all day while she covered desk duty. *Please be there.*

"I'm so glad you called, Sunny. We were just talking about you. How did your interview go?" Molly asked, when she came on the line.

"Molly, listen carefully." Who knew more about opera than Molly? Who cared more about Opera Theatre than Molly? Molly had the Irish gift of persuasion, and if anyone could get Opal to at least listen to Raymundo Manzanares it was Molly.

Now she just had to convince her. The stacks of quarters melted into the slot of the pay phone, but when they were gone Sunny turned aside, a satisfied grin on her face. Molly would do it. Buoyed with success, she felt as if several loads had been lifted from her shoulders.

She felt downright giddy as she pulled back onto the highway toward Ojo Tres.

Chapter Sixty-Three

Federal search warrants were issued, and the Santeria Area Task Force led by the Federal Bureau of Investigation moved into place outside the old Dodson place by mid-afternoon where *Campo Santo* drug carriers were camped.

Vacations for task force member agencies were cancelled, and every available person pulled in who could be spared while still keeping order and safety for the nearly 40,000 people moving through the area.

An earlier plan for a raid on Saturday morning when many of the pilgrims would be gone had to be scratched as the situation escalated with more and more movement at the campground. Lawmen, dressed to blend in with the pilgrims and community services along the wayside, were on a high state of alert and trying to hide their nervousness.

Robson Steele got his car as close as possible, then caught a ride on a flatbed truck with a crew delivering portable toilets, recognizing the "workers" as other members of the task force. He helped unload, then slipped in with the stream of pilgrims. He found Manny Ortega and joined him at a roadside stand with volunteers from the local fire department handing out orange slices and cups of water.

"Look, but don't stare," Ortega said, nodding at the old Dodson property across the way, marked with No Trespassing signs on what was left of fence posts. Through the overgrown grove of cottonwood trees and brush on the other side of the road Rob caught glimpses of bright yellow.

"Here comes another one." Ortega nudged his elbow as an erstwhile school bus slowed to make the turn into the weedy driveway where two wooden carpenter horses blocked its way.

The lettering on the side of the yellow bus read Antioch Baptist Church. "I'll say this for them," Ortega said in an aside to Rob, "they're ecumenical. I've seen at least two other denominations since I've been here. We've got a line on two of the buses. They were reported stolen up in Colorado last night. We're checking now and expect the rest of the buses to be either stolen or the regular driver bribed to 'borrow' the bus and return it before it's missed Sunday morning."

The bus driver gave three short beeps of the horn that brought two men from behind the screen of brush and trees. The guards scrutinized the crowd and the stands along the roadside. Seeming satisfied that no one was paying particular attention to them, they moved the barrier, and the empty bus lumbered through. The men set the horses across the drive once more and disappeared up the gravel road after the bus.

"Pretty damn clever, isn't it?" Ortega said as he sliced another bunch of oranges to add to the heap of wedges in front of him.

"Yeah. Nobody's going to stop a church bus to search it for drugs," Rob said. He took a piece of orange and sucked on it, stripping out the pulp with his teeth and tossing the peel in a basket. "The surveillance agents count about one-hundred and fifty men, drug mules, camped just over the hill in the middle of that property. Not all are wearing those green jackets, but all of them have backpacks. The FBI thinks they've been walking in here for a week dumping their goods and going back for more. That's probably why we didn't see more of them at one time."

Ortega wiped the sticky juice from his hands and washed the knife. "The latest word from command is that two, maybe three more buses are expected. Then they think this bunch is going to load up the drugs and their people and slip those innocent looking buses right by all our checkpoints. The Feebs don't want to move in until the bad guys are on board. Fish in a barrel, someone said." Ortega fingered the big gun concealed under a sweatshirt.

"Nervous?"

"Yeah. Nobody knows for sure what kind of firepower they may have. There are more of them than us. And with this crowd, anything can happen."

Rob had no words of consolation. He was worried himself; he had been on raids like this a dozen times and seen a lot of things go wrong.

"Any other progress?"

"Your girlfriend Sunny." Ortega laughed, pretending to fend off Rob's dirty scowl. He told him about her emergency call after her encounter with the woodcarver who'd been in on killing Justin. "Richard Terrazas was picked up an hour ago. Maybe I should fire Tobin and hire her."

"Any word when she's headed back to Ojo Tres?" Rob had been hoping she would call.

Ortega shook his head, then asked, "Any hits on those Antonio Martínez leads?"

"The Martínez in San Francisco, the one Sunny picked out, looks promising."

Ortega burst out laughing.

"We ran the California division of motor vehicles. The DMV photo is four years old. This guy has black hair, kind of a modified Elvis Presley pompadour with sideburns and a trimmed beard, and wears tinted glasses. A shave and a haircut and a pair of contacts and his own mother wouldn't recognize him."

"Has he got a sheet?" Ortega asked.

"Not even a speeding ticket, as far as we can tell. He was honorably discharged from the Navy at the end of his hitch. His Navy photo was also inconclusive. File suffered moisture damage and a rusty paper clip obliterated some of the features.

"I take it he doesn't resemble the Martínez clan?"

"No, definitely not. We ran the two other Antonio's on the list that were in the right age range and got DMV photos. I had to be in Ojo Tres this morning. I showed the three photos to Leandro and Ann. Nothing. No familial resemblance, and no one looking like any of the photos at the hotel or in town."

"Any luck with San Francisco?"

"Yes and no," Rob said. "Only the Martínez Sunny picked can't be located. He hasn't lived at the address listed in some time, according to the neighbors. More interesting, and a hell of a lot more frustrating, there's no trace of any taxes, payroll, nothing recent under Martínez' Social Security number. Last job was for a security outfit over in Oakland. Records show he got laid off, but he may have been close to getting fired. There were a couple of warnings in his file about anger issues. Then nothing. Whoever this Martínez is, he's dropped from sight."

"We can't seem to catch a break, can we? I missed connections with Father Emilio again, literally," Ortega said, as he shook his head worriedly. "Phone broke up when they patched him through. Ongoing problem on phone lines up here. Dispatch is still trying."

The two stood disconsolately, silently mulling over their next moves. Rob's cell phone vibrated against his leg. He dropped down on one knee out of sight of the men across the road to take the call. He was almost out of range and had to keep shifting and turning his direction to keep the connection. "You're sure. Absolutely sure?"

He looked up at Ortega, and the big man leaned down to hear him. "The two ringleaders at Justin's murder? Guess what? My men just spotted them in a car over on 503. It looked like those two were tailing some guy. Only the weird thing is the guy they're tailing seems to be in hot pursuit of another car. They couldn't be sure if a teenage boy or a small woman is driving that car. But the vehicle's description fits what Sunny is driving."

"But why would she be off on 503 heading for County 98?" Ortega asked. "That takes her straight into Chimayó, and it's way out of her way."

Why indeed, but they both had the uneasy feeling that it was her. It was the very thing they had tried to prevent by trying to convince her not to go to Santa Fe.

"What are you going to do?"

"She's not task force business," Rob said harshly through tight lips, distress hollowing out his cheeks. "She's on her own."

"Yeah, but those two thugs are very much Task Force business. We know they're neck-deep in this drug operation. We need to pick them up. Keep them away from here if nothing else." He put his hand on Rob's shoulder. "Go," Ortega encouraged. "I'll radio it in. You're going to need backup."

Seeing the relief on Rob's face, Manny Ortega wondered if his friend would ever admit to himself that it was more Sunny's welfare that had him in high gear than the prospect of nailing the drug runners. He definitely cared what happened to that girl. It was written all over him, from the grin to the bounce in his step as he sprinted down the road to his car.

Amor de lejos es pa los pendejos, his grandmother used to say. Love at a distance is for fools.

Chapter Sixty-Four

Sunny slipped her hand in the shopping bag on the seat beside her, pulling a corner of the garment out to look at it once more. The hooded black cashmere poncho shot through with subtle bursts of magenta in its weave was for Moira. *You're going to love this, kiddo. Who would have thought I'd find anything like this in that hole-in-the-wall shop?*

Her foot came up to the brake as flashing red lights ahead caught her eye, and she shoved the poncho back into its bag. Sitting forward to get a better look ahead, she could see ambulances and fire trucks. It looked like a bad accident, a big truck and several cars involved. Traffic was stalled for a half mile.

Uncomfortable at being hemmed in, Sunny waited for a momentary break in traffic and switched into the lane where cars still moved, if only at a snail's pace. Any movement was better than being at a dead stall in this mess. Suddenly the lane was blocked by highway patrol cars, a row of orange traffic cones funneling her toward the intersection where the highway veered sharp right.

"No, no, no! Damn, I can't go that way," Sunny spoke out loud. No matter what, she needed to keep away from this intersection. According to the signs a half-mile back, it would end up putting her on the road to Chimayó.

She tried to pull over, to squeeze through the barrier, but another car angled in behind her, boxing her in. She glared angrily at the driver and shouted something it was probably better he couldn't hear. Then she saw it was the same idiot who had been on her tail since right after she left the restaurant.

He stayed doggedly behind her, crowding up to keep cars from coming between them. At first she thought maybe he was flirting. Then she worried he was some kind of nut she'd offended someway, and he was exhibiting road rage.

A knot of uniformed officers, arms moving like pinwheels, herded reluctant vehicles off the main highway. Frustrated, Sunny let down her window. Maybe if the patrolman knew her predicament he would allow her to go through. As she rolled close, she put on her most distressed face, pointing urgently to let him know she wanted to veer left. He pointed, exaggerating the motion to go right, getting red in the face and shouting for her to move it.

She screamed through her lowered window, "I don't know the road. I'll end up getting lost for sure."

Her words were lost in the blast of horns. He motioned her on in no uncertain terms.

The narrow pavement ran like a black ribbon between two deep ditches, with no shoulder to pull off on to get her bearings. She rolled up her window, feeling a chill beginning to creep into the air.

A car in the line behind her pulled out into the oncoming lane just enough for the driver to check what was going on up ahead. Sunny caught her breath. Behind the wheel, reflected in her side mirror, was the man with the Pancho Villa moustache and eyes hard as flint that had looked her up and down at Justin's apartment, and cut him from the cross.

Instinctively, she pulled the ball cap down tighter on her head, tucking up a wisp of escaping hair, her heart beginning to beat like a trip hammer.

She had to believe it was no coincidence they were on the same road. They were after her.

She fumbled for her cell phone, punching in numbers and getting them wrong, then slowly and deliberately punching in Rob's number. A no service message flashed. She threw the phone down, trying not to panic.

She looked for road signs and saw only sporadic hand-lettered signs with arrows to guide the walkers on the way to the Santuario de Chimayó. It suddenly occurred to her that maybe that was her best chance after all. She had been trying to avoid all that traffic around the shrine, but at least at Chimayó there would be people, lots of people, and even if these men followed her there, she had a better chance to lose them. Maybe she could seek sanctuary inside the church.

The car with the two men moved up, aggressively passing a slow moving truck, then forced an opening to slip back into line two cars back.

She lifted her eyes to check her rearview. The man who had been following behind her was still practically locked to her bumper. He seemed suddenly harmless compared to the other two.

"Okay, geeky guy," she said, like speaking to an old friend, "stay on my tail now, honey. Stay right on my tail. You're all that's between me and the bad guys." Sunny stepped on the gas, and the car shot along the narrow road. She was glad to see the geek kept right after her.

Little Miss Nosey looked right at me and didn't recognize me in the hat and sunglasses. This is going to be easier than I thought. A new plan began to form in his head, a much better plan. She was heading for Chimayó. At some point she would be stalled in traffic all alone in her car.

With growing excitement, he visualized himself tapping on her window. He knew he had a way with women, he would explain he was following her to protect her. He would pretend to be worried about her, convince her things could get rough for a woman alone with all these Penitentes running around spiked up on religious fervor.

He imagined the trust in her eyes, unlocking the door, inviting him into the car, glad to see him. She was such a little thing. He let his hand slip to his calf, feeling the hasp under the material of his pants. The knife was ready and waiting. All he had to do was slip the long blade in flat, sideways between the ribs, and twist. It was the twist that would do the trick. He shuddered with the wetness between his legs.

But no, no, no. He shook his head, as if ridding his mind of all thoughts of the plan. I'd have to abandon my car. It can be traced to me. I'm an asshole. I don't deserve to have things go right. Better I pass her now. Get there before she does. Get rid of this disguise, and she won't recognize me.

His life depended on silencing her, making sure she didn't testify to what she'd seen of Justin's little punishment.

He smiled as her signal light began blinking. She slowed to make the sharp turn. *Now, now!* Laying on the horn and gunning his motor, he pulled into the lane of oncoming traffic. Flashing his high beams in warning, the car heading directly for him began braking and pulling to its right, gravel spraying from its tires as it smoked along the edge of the asphalt. Abreast of Sunny's car, he saw her look wildly toward him, swerving to the right, creating a narrow chute that he shot through and sped away.

Adrenaline pumping with the close call, he laughed. "See you in Chimayó!"

In his rearview, he saw she still hugged the edge of the pavement as a car further back in the line followed him into the passing lane. "You drunk, buddy? You aren't going to make it."

Mesmerized, he imagined the straining motor of the other car, the driver pushing the accelerator to the floorboard, the screams of the motorists in the other cars.

His head swung forward, eyes on the oncoming car as it yawed and burned rubber, clinging to the edge of the pavement, the passing car slipping back into its lane just in time to avoid a crash.

Letting out pent-up breath, he did a double take, recognition coming like a punch in the gut as he suddenly realized who was driving the car. From hunter to hunted. Cold sweat began trickling out of his armpits, soaking his shirt. The two thugs from *Campo Santo* were after him. They must not have seen the girl.

How could they identify him? His car? He'd been so careful. Unless—Jimmy Dodson! The asshole gave him up. It had to be. The last conversation he'd had with Jimmy he as good as told him.

"I warned you not to screw with these guys. They play for keeps. They're real pissed off at you... tell me you've made some incriminating videotape, you stupid bastard."

"But they don't know who I am, unless you tell them, Jimmy. You're my lawyer. You can't tell them."

"Not unless it gets down to a choice of you or me."

His mind circled through his dilemma like a buzz saw. Maybe if he delivered the girl's body these thugs would forgive the videotape.

He found an empty driveway and parked the car under a tree. Running on foot, he was soon lost in the mash of pilgrims moving toward the shrine. He was the hunter once more.

"I think that son-of-a-bitch made us, Raul." The short man known as Pepe spoke to his companion, peering ahead to catch sight of the other car.

"You think the lawyer tipped him?" Raul bit a corner of the moustache that drooped over his lip.

"I don't know." Pepe moved his hands nervously in his lap. "Want to know what I think? I think the best thing we can do is get back to California. Get this mess behind us."

"You got dog shit for brains?" Raul glared at him. "We go back to California when they tell us to go back to California. Stop worrying. The money we're piping out of here will lose a lot of evidence, including a certain videotape. Right now we've got a job to do. We've got to get this guy. Nobody can control him. He's nuts! We got to stop him. And then we make sure the little *chocha* with the big blue eyes don't live to testify to what she saw."

"Yeah, I guess," Pepe said glumly. "We should never have gone along with him. I tried to tell you—"

Raul pounded the steering wheel. "He had our balls to the wall. He had the stuff. The kid was stealing. He wanted the little *zorrero* dead. Orders were to keep him happy. So, don't bring that up again."

Pepe braced himself against the door and the dashboard as his partner pulled the car into the narrow lane to pass. "Jesus, *amigo*! This narrow two-lane crap is a goddamn deathtrap. Makes me miss the fucking freeways, I can tell you that."

Raul laughed, tailgating the car ahead. "Now watch this. Every time I pull out that kid ahead pulls like a chicken to the right. Roll down your window." He blasted his horn coming alongside the car, and Raul screamed "Want to race?" The other driver seemed frozen, looking straight ahead, both hands clutching the wheel. "What, no *cojones, el pollo*?"

"There's a truck coming." Pepe cringed in his seat until the car was safely in its own lane. He wiped sweat from above his lip.

"Keep your pants dry, we're around him." Raul rubbed his hand over his moustache. "Can you believe that? That Anglo kid got no balls. That one never even looked at me." He gave a long, low whistle as they rounded a curve with bumper-to-bumper traffic ahead. "That ought to make you feel at home if you're missing the freeway."

"Very funny," Pepe said. "Hey, slow down. See what I see, *amigo*? There! That's his car. You think he went in that house?"

"Nope. I think he's on foot now."

"Maybe that's smart, leaving the car back here. This is like driving in a parking lot."

"We'll get closer. Park somewhere so we can stand on the roof and maybe spot the guy. As tall as he is he'll stand out, right?"

They're gone. They're really gone. The two thugs had looked right at her, screamed something, but didn't seem to recognize her. Unable to believe her good fortune, she slowed and let a stream of cars pull around. Maybe they weren't chasing her after all. Or, maybe they recognized her and were toying with her, waiting for a better to time to go in for the kill.

Making little headway in the stalled traffic, she suddenly felt trapped. She needed to get out of this car.

A man and woman were headed her way on foot, struggling to carry a large statue between them. She reasoned that they were going to a car nearby. Sliding down her passenger-side window she called, "Hello. Do you have any idea where I might park?"

The two looked at each other. "You can have our place, if please, you help us haul this?"

"You got it," Sunny said, leaping out and opening the trunk. Together the couple hoisted the load and set it inside. "Where you folks from?"

"Laguna Pueblo," the man answered. "We brought many family crucifixes and a statue of the Virgin to be blessed. We have many uncles, many aunts, all of them ailing. We filled little bags with holy dirt from the Santuario to take to each of them. It has much healing power. Much power."

He helped his wife into the back seat of the car. She seemed too shy to speak and merely smiled at Sunny. Her husband said something to the drivers of the two cars behind them and began pushing his hands with a backward motion until they backed up, making a space. He motioned Sunny to back up and jumped into the front seat beside her. She followed his direction and turned down a steep dirt lane, past a field, continuing toward a compound of houses.

"The dirt from the Santuario really works?" Sunny asked, hoping she didn't sound skeptical.

"My wife," the man spoke proudly, "was born with a hole in her spine. Her parents walked all the way from the Pueblo to bring her here when she was a tiny infant, to rub her back and legs with the holy dirt. They prayed, and every year they make the pilgrimage. Today she walks with me, a wife and mother. Yes, Miss, the dirt is miraculous. Ever since the Santuario de Chimayó came to be."

Sunny listened to his simple story of how a crucifix was buried at the church and how it disappeared and reappeared in a hole where the shrine was eventually built. She couldn't doubt the sincerity of these people. But how could a handful of dirt cure what surely must have been a diagnosis, or misdiagnosis, of spina bifida?

"There, at the first truck. Let me out." He directed Sunny to back around in the small gravel lot where there were at least ten other vehicles. She helped him lift the bag from the trunk and carefully load the precious cargo onto the truck bed. He removed a hand-lettered sign from the window of his truck and told her to put it on her dashboard where it could be seen. "This is my cousin's property. The sign will let him know you are to park in my place."

"Thank you. You're lifesavers." As they pulled away, she tried to imagine what it must be like to be one of the pilgrims who walked all night under the stars to get to this holy place, to believe in anything so completely.

Sunny sat a moment trying to think what to do next. Anyone who had seen her in the car would recognize her if they spotted her again in her ball cap and bright plaid shirt. She needed to be able to change her appearance.

She retrieved the black top she'd worn that morning, somewhat wrinkled and smelling slightly of dried sweat. It would have to do. Digging in her purse, she found her hinged hair grabber. She gathered her hair, smoothing and rolling it into a bun, securing it with the clip. She ripped open the shopping bag on the front seat. *Moira, sorry, but I need to borrow the poncho.*

Chapter Sixty-Five

Good Friday

Silver crucifixes tied to a fence reflected back the afternoon sun as Sunny approached the little wooden church. Rivers of walkers flowed down from the roadsides leading to the area like tributaries feeding the gathering sea of worshippers.

Plunging forward, she was squashed and pummeled in the crowd, not sure which way to go, as she worked her way through queues of people waiting everywhere for food and drink, for toilets, for a chance to go into the sanctuary.

She skirted around a row of small shops doing a brisk business in religious artifacts, crossed a foot bridge over a fast flowing brook, and stopped to look around. Next to her, three women draped rosaries on a tall cross they had leaned against a wall, lighting small votive candles beside photos of the ill and newspaper clippings of the dead. Tired and spent, the women took up vigil, patiently waiting their turn to visit the shrine.

Everywhere she heard talk of *el Pozito*, the little well of holy dirt in the floor of a small chamber at the back of the church where believers sought cures and miracles.

In the waiting throng were those in wheelchairs or carried in the arms or on the back of relatives, those lugging wooden crosses on stooped shoulders and a few ending the last few hundred feet of their journey on their knees. Sunny moved cautiously, her eyes darting first to this group, then to that one for a glimpse of the two thugs or even the Geek in the white hat and sunglasses, before they saw her.

Suddenly directly behind her she felt movement, but before she could turn, a hand clamped on her shoulder.

"Sunny! It is you. I thought so!"

"Gordon? What are you doing here?"

"It's my day off, remember? I didn't want to miss this. Isn't this something?" he said, gazing around at the crowd. "But what are you doing here? Weren't you going to Santa Fe?"

She squinted into the sun to look up at him. "I got finished early. Thought I'd get some of the miracle dirt. I mean, what could it hurt?"

"I wasn't sure it was you. You look so... well, elegant with your hair up." He reddened and quickly added, "I'm screwing this up, aren't I?" He gave her a rueful smile.

Today, away from the Springs, Gordon seemed an entirely different person, carefree and playful rather than badgering and annoying. She hadn't forgiven him. Still, there could be little harm in saying what she was really feeling, "Gordon, I must say it's nice to see a familiar face." *And maybe with a big tall guy like you in tow, I won't be such an easy target.*

"I was thinking the same thing. Come with me. You can't come to Chimayó without eating at Léona's. You simply have to try the Ice Cream Burrito. My treat."

Sunny laughed. "Without hot sauce, I hope."

"Definitely," he said, describing ice cream in a chocolate tortilla with plenty of whipped cream. Gordon already had her arm tucked in close to him and was pulling her along.

He ordered at the window, bringing their treats to where Sunny found a place on a low wall to sit. Judging by the full tables, it was a popular place.

Ortega put on the lights and the siren and laid on the speed. Headquarters agreed under the circumstances that he had to get to Chimayó. Sunny was in more danger than she knew. She would think she could trust this man. Manny felt a little sick at his stomach that he had been so blind.

When Father Emilio had at last been reached, he repeated everything Opal told him with his characteristic attention to every detail.

"If she'd just told me that when I questioned her last night," Ortega railed.

"Manny, he's her son. You have children; what would you have done?" the priest responded. "Anyway, when she spoke to you, she couldn't yet face the truth. But, she knows now he would have killed her, if he had found her, believing she'd betrayed him to you. And she's sure he killed Mrs. Ruiz, God rest her soul. While he was ransacking her house, he threatened to kill others. The one she heard him shout most was that girl from St. Louis, Sunny. You need to warn her. The man is a psychopath. He's very sick."

Thinking about the blatant masquerade, Ortega suddenly felt less certain of his ability to do this job. *I shouldn't have taken him at face value. I should have checked him out.* He cursed the traffic, almost impenetrable even with the siren and red lights flashing as he pushed toward Chimayó. *Please don't let me be too late.*

Sunny was feeling relaxed with the sun warm on her back, when Gordon spoke.

"You interested in seeing what all the fuss is about?" He motioned toward the church.

"Looks like a long wait," she said, eyeing the line of people waiting to get in. She thought of the reverence of the couple who'd given her the parking space. "But, hey, anything that inspires that much faith and draws this many people must be remarkable. Let's go."

"Guess what? I know someone here. We can avoid the crowd. My friend guards the back entrance that isn't open to the public."

"That doesn't seem right, Gordon. Some of these people have been waiting for hours."

"Relax. It's okay, believe me. Hey, don't look now," he said, his body taking on the stance of a bulldog protecting his territory.

"What is it?" She looked cautiously over her shoulder.

"It's Robson Steele. I really don't like that guy. It's just a gut feeling. You said he's in real estate, Sunny, but I don't think he's who he says he is. He's always skulking around. Know what I mean?" Gordon slipped on sunglasses that hid his eyes, but gave back her own image in the reflection.

She didn't want to explain starting the real estate rumor, or about Rob being Agent Robson Steele. She felt herself beginning to squirm. What if Rob was looking for her? *Duh, he doesn't know I'm here.*

"I think we should at least speak," she said, calling Rob's name. She waved her arm frantically, but he turned without seeing her, walking uphill toward his van. Suddenly her cell phone rang. She was so startled she dropped her purse. Before she could retrieve her phone, it stopped ringing. She punched in his number and got the no service message. When she looked up, Rob had disappeared.

"How about we get that holy dirt first, huh?" Gordon drew his mouth down in mock resignation. "Then we can look for Rob, if you must." He smiled down at her.

He led her deftly through the thickening crowd, keeping her attention with a running line of patter. Suddenly Sunny froze. The two men who had been following her were standing on the roof of a car looking over the crowd. The fat one with the moustache pointed excitedly in their direction and was already climbing down off the car.

Gordon's height was suddenly a liability. Standing a head taller than most of the crowd, they would be easy to follow. Sunny didn't wait. "There's Rob," she lied. Gordon swung around, trying to see where she was pointing. She pulled her hand from his grip and, bending down out of sight, pushed deeper into the crowd away from him. Trying not to attract attention, she hid behind a group of burly men long enough to pull out the hooded poncho, slipping it over her head, covering her body and her shoulder bag. She was sweaty, the wool prickling her skin, but she had no choice. She fumbled, managing to pull the hood up around her hair and face before standing up.

Keeping her head lowered, she scanned the milling crowd. She forced herself to focus, and quickly spotted Gordon not more than twenty feet to her left. He was calling her name, looking for her. She felt suddenly guilty about leaving him so abruptly without a word of explanation. Those men might take it out on Gordon just because he had been with her. She owed him a warning and took a step forward to rejoin him.

As he slowly swung his head her way scanning the crowd, there was something sinisterly familiar about his tall thin frame. For a moment she couldn't seem to get her breath. *Stop it! You can't keep flashing back every time the least thing reminds you of what happened.*

The inner counselor calmed her enough that she could think clearly once more. Gordon was just trying to help. But she was sure those two thugs would be keeping Gordon in view, hoping to get to her. She just had to keep as far away from Gordon as possible and apologize later for deserting him.

Oh my god, he's coming right this way. She took refuge beside a family, and as Gordon walked by not four feet away, she was leaning down to make over the couple's small child. "What a beautiful little girl you are," Sunny said. "How old are you?" The child held up four fingers. "What is this?" she asked, pointing to the palm leaves fashioned into a cross the child held in her small chubby hand. Only the dark luminous eyes answered as she held it closer to Sunny for her to see.

"She got that Palm Sunday, and she hasn't let go of it yet." Her mother laughed. "We've come to light candles in the church today. She's very excited."

"And what's your name?" Sunny asked, wondering how much longer she could go on talking to the child before the parents yanked her away from the strange woman.

"María Anna Medina," the child spoke clearly. "And I'm going to have a little sister."

Sunny noticed that the blessed event was clearly going to be soon and congratulated the parents. Slowly standing, she smiled and turned aside, searching once more for Gordon's location. He was nowhere to be seen.

Panicked, Sunny whirled, looking in every direction. The crowd suddenly pressed back on itself to part a way for a phalanx of men carrying a huge cross toward the church. "What is it?" Sunny asked a stranger by her side.

"The reenactment of the crucifix coming back to Chimayó from Santa Cruz," the man whispered with awe in his voice. "The original crucifix of Our Lord of Esquipulas now hangs over the altar there in the Santuario."

The rest of the man's explanation was lost to her as her attention zoomed away from the pageant and fixed on Gordon on the other side of the divide. And not just Gordon, but the two men beside him. He seemed locked in a battle of words with the two thugs. Her lips moved as if in prayer. *My God. Help me.* This time she could not stop the images. She saw the three men before her exactly as they were that day on the mesa below Justin's crucified body. There was no doubt in her mind this time. Gordon's tall form morphed with the tall man in the black hood and robe burned in her memory. With certainty came cold fear.

"Pardon?" She realized the man who was explaining the pageant was looking at her strangely and thought she must have spoken something aloud.

"Would you mind standing just there a moment?" she asked. "It's my boyfriend. We're having a little quarrel, and I don't want him to see me right this minute." She fixed him with her pleading blue eyes and brightest smile. The man was probably in his early sixties with a shock of white hair, but clearly enjoying the diversion of being pulled into the middle of a romance.

"*Si.* Okay. Tell me what we do."

"Look carefully to your right without staring. See the tall man in the dark shirt right over there?"

"*Si*, I see him."

"He went off with those two friends of his and left me all alone."

"*¡Santo Dios!* Those two are ugly. You're very *bonita*."

Sunny giggled. "Tell me what he's doing now."

"Looks like he's going to get help finding you. He's sent his friends in opposite directions, and he's headed this way."

"Thanks. I need to teach him a lesson. Could you walk just a little way with me? Put your arm around my waist like we're together? Then, when I'm in the clear, I'll just slip away."

He drew himself up proudly with her tucked under his wing. Wrapped in the poncho, she walked right by Gordon and the men unnoticed.

She steered her protector in the direction she had last seen Rob, hoping to find him, until she saw Gordon heading the same way.

How about the back way into the church? Surely Gordon would consider that the last place she would go.

"Thank you," she whispered, gently pulling away as they melded into the crowd. He squeezed her hand. "*Por nada.* It's nothing." Then unexpectedly he called after her "*Vaya con Dios.* Go with God."

At the edge of the parking lot she slipped through one of the long lines of people waiting to get in the portable toilets. She found a short path that led directly down to the church, the area all but deserted. Sunny slid along the wall, the adobe as thick as a fortress, guessing that just beyond her fingertips was the altar of the nave. But it was impenetrable. There was no door. Gordon had lied. She knew why. A dead witness is a good witness.

She turned to run. Like a long shadow swallowing her, he was there, pulling her to him, nearly knocking her off her feet.

"Let me go!" she screamed, writhing in his arms. "Help me somebody! Help me!"

In one swift movement he brought the heel of his hand up hard under her chin. Blood spurted from her lips as her teeth sunk into her tongue, silencing her as she struggled with the intense pain.

"Shut up. I gave you fair warning to keep your fucking nose out of things that didn't concern you."

She saw the knife, blade flat in his right hand, not comprehending what it was at first until she felt the punch drive against her ribcage, knocking her sideways, his arm around her all that kept her from falling down. The knife fell from his grasp and landed at her feet.

Hysterical laughter welled up in her. He'd hit her shoulder bag under the poncho. *Moira's poncho!* He had put a hole in Moira's poncho. It was all she could grasp for the moment. "Damn you. You've ruined it!"

With all the force she could muster she tromped the heel of her boot into his arch. His arms loosened momentarily, and she drove her elbow back into his midsection, feeling the jar in her body like driving her fist into a stone wall. He shifted backward, struggling for balance. She let the dead weight of her body drop toward the ground, slipping from his grasp. With what was left of her strength, she wrenched away, and scrambling to her feet, she sprinted out into the open, running hard toward the parking lot. She screamed again for help, her injured tongue seeming not to work, her words coming in hissed lisps.

Suddenly a familiar voice was calling out her mother's name. "Molly. Is that you kid?" It was the enormous hips planted in the path that she recognized first. Annabella, who had befriended her outside the *morada* at Ojo Tres in what seemed a thousand years ago, stood arms akimbo, anger contorting her round face as she confronted Gordon. "What you think you doing to my friend?" Her body was a pillar of defiance, chin thrust forward, hands on hips, head and shoulders rocking like a metronome with her words.

"Annabella, stay away. He'll hurt you," Sunny implored, forcing herself to speak clearly.

"Him and who else?" she said, spitting on her hands and rolling them into fists as she let out a sharp whistle between her teeth. Almost instantly five other women deserted the lines to the toilets and, screaming like banshees, raced to their friend's aid. Others seeing the melee began walking down the short incline to see what was going on.

Watching the woman warily, Gordon reached down and retrieved his fallen weapon.

"Take a hike." Annabella thumbed her challenge at Gordon.

His face suffused with anger, Gordon moved aggressively on her. His long leg kicked from the side, as he spun to gain momentum, catching the big woman in the side of the face, knocking her down. The crack of bone hung in the air. The crowd pulled back in shock, uncertain what to do.

Grabbing Sunny by the hair and getting a grip under her arm, he swung her to her feet.

There was a collective outflow of breath from the group. "He's got a knife."

Fighting Gordon's grasp, Sunny looked back, seeing Annabella lying still on the ground, her friends gathered in a helpless circle around her.

"I'll kill you if you've hurt her." Sunny forced the words, shoving aside the pain it took to speak. "I know who you are. I know all about you. I've got pictures of you and your buddies on the mesa taking Justin off the cross," she lied, willing to say anything to gain time. "I've taken everything to the authorities, told them everything. The law is looking for you right now." She was talking as loud as she could as he dragged her along, and people were beginning to look and edge toward them.

"Stay out of it!" Gordon yelled at a couple of men who seemed to want to intervene. "This is between me and my wife." They shrugged, backed away.

"Shut up, bitch. Or do you want me to shut your mouth for you again," he threatened.

Weakening in his steely grasp, all she had left to defend herself were words, true or not, lies or educated guesses, anything to keep him diverted. "It's over Gordon, or should I say Antonio Martínez? Those coordinates I found in Justin's room and the telephone message you brought me last night? Sergeant Ortega says you wrote them both."

When he didn't deny it, she pressed on. What did she have to lose if there was even a sliver of a chance she could convince him he would gain nothing by killing her? "Those coordinates? That's how they found Justin's body." She mentally crossed her fingers, hoping he didn't know one way or the other. "Your DNA is all over the body. My testimony would only be a drop in the bucket to that. The guy who made the cross..." She choked. "The woodcarver. They got him too, and he's singing like a canary."

There was confusion in his face. "Ann has a photograph of your father in that Penitente robe and hood. I guessed right away that it was you dressing up, pretending to be something you aren't."

He leapt, closing the distance between them, howling. "You know nothing about me or my father. He was a great man. He was a *Sangrador*."

"Only you aren't skillful like your father, Antonio, Jr. You cut the seal of obligation in Justin's back." Sunny spit away blood oozing from her tongue, struggling to form words as it grew numb in her mouth. "The cuts you made were sloppy. You did it for torture, not religion."

She was running out of things to say. *Think! Think!*

The people in the crowd closest to them were listening now and began circling them, forcing her and Gordon into a tiny arena. Hissing like a cornered animal, he brandished his knife at the circle, the men staying back out of striking distance of his long arms.

Oh god, yes. How could she forget? The videotape. "There's the videotape, Mr. Director." She saw something flicker in his eyes. She panted for breath. "Tell me, everybody." She motioned with her hands as if gathering the people around. "What kind of fool makes a videotape of a murder he's committed? A fool's Fool, wouldn't you say?"

There was a murmur from the crowd. He kept the knife flat, aimed at about the level of her throat, as she danced like a boxer in the tight circle bobbing and weaving with her head.

It felt like standing on a ledge, her knees almost ready to collapse under her, but she couldn't stop. If she got him angry enough, distracted enough, maybe someone could bring him down. There was only one lie left, a lie that would tell the tale. "I know your mother deserted you, Antonio, left you alone with your father. But it gets worse, Antonio. She's done it again. You know who gave you up to the law? Your own mother. Just like that." Sunny snapped her fingers, nothing more than a pathetic gesture as they slid by each other because of the sweat in her hands. But the point was made.

"No, no, no! You lying bitch!"

Screams went up from the crowd as they fought to get out of the way. Gordon drove forward, then crashed to the ground, the knife clattering harmlessly out of his reach. For a moment Sunny was unable to fathom the arms and legs writhing in front of her until she heard Rob shout, "Cuff him!" and saw him roll to his knees, three uniformed officers holding Gordon firmly.

She saw Sergeant Ortega running toward them, the lights of his patrol car still circling behind, his face pale with fright until he saw her.

"Hey, glad to see you finally joined the party." Rob grinned up at him. "How about a hand here."

Deputies began dispersing the gawkers, taking notes from those who had been closest to the action. A siren sounded close, and an ambulance made its way slowly through the crowd toward the back of the church where Annabella had fallen.

"Sunny?" Rob put a supporting arm around her awkwardly. "How bad are you hurt? Do you need the ambulance?" She stuck out her tongue for him to see, hoping fervently that the end wouldn't fall off. "For you, that's a serious wound," he said, with a straight face.

Chapter Sixty-Six

Easter Sunday

Rob handed her the newspaper and a dozen foil-wrapped Easter eggs in a tiny basket, then walked to the window looking out with his back to her. Sunny cranked up the hospital bed. It wasn't the Easter morning she had expected.

Right under the Eagle Wing Courier banner was a three-line headline:

Federal, State, Local Agencies Raid Dodson Property Arrests, Confiscation of Drugs, Other Evidence in Criminal Probe.

Law enforcement officers raided the Dodson property at 29415 Don Gaspar Road Good Friday afternoon confiscating drugs and rounding up 147 suspects and other evidence in a criminal investigation.

More than 75 officers with local, state and federal agencies carried out the raid at about 5:30 Friday afternoon and served federal search warrants on the suspected traffickers. Unofficial sources estimate the street value of the confiscated drugs at more than eight million dollars. Gunfire heard by bystanders was unconfirmed and there are no reports of injury or death connected to the operation.

The raid was led by the Federal Bureau of Investigation and also involved officers with the federal Drug Enforcement Administration (DEA), Santeria County Sheriff's Office, New Mexico State Highway Patrol, tribal officers and Eagle Wing police. It was the result of an ongoing drug and criminal investigation that has been conducted through the Santeria Area Task Force.

Authorities are being tightlipped about the investigation, and have not disclosed names of specific suspects or evidence that was seized. Arrests were made but criminal charges have not been issued as a result of the raid at this time, The Eagle Wing Courier was told.

Sunny folded the paper. "Pretty sketchy. What else can you tell me?"

"Not much, Sunny. These things move slowly. Things don't get tied up in a neat package at the end like we get used to on TV or in the movies." He walked over to the bed, pulled up a chair and took her hand.

"Am I going to have to come back to testify?"

"I don't know yet, Sunny." He hoped for her sake she was through here. He didn't like the paleness of her face or the hollowness in her eyes when she stared off into space, which she did frequently.

"Might as well get it all over at once." He took the paper, folding it back and pointing to three obscure paragraphs.

Body Discovered by Forest Service at Ojo Tres. A National Forest Service crew discovered an unidentified body this week on a mesa above the Ojo Tres Mineral Springs as they were posting signs in the area restricting campfires.

Santeria County Sheriff King Harvell said officers are investigating the death as suspicious because the cause of death is undetermined. The victim is an Anglo male believed to be in his late teens or early twenties. An autopsy is scheduled, but it may take weeks to obtain results, according to the Office of the Medical Investigator in Santa Fe where the body was taken.

Sheriff Harvell would not comment on reports of a connection between the dead man and the recent unexplained disappearance of an employee at Ojo Tres. He has asked anyone with information about the victim to call Crime Stoppers or the Sheriff's Office at 367-7415.

"This is bullshit," Sunny fumed. "All of you know perfectly well that it is Justin and what happened to him. Why aren't you saying?"

"Truth?"

"Please."

"Justin's death, the drug lab and the people behind it are all part of a larger investigation that extends to California and elsewhere. I can't tell you anything else because it's need-to-know only."

Sunny tore out the page with the story about Justin, folded it and laid it aside. "You know I told Gordon that Justin's body had been found, that his DNA was on it. I was only guessing, telling him anything to keep buying time."

Sunny grew quiet trying to put the thoughts of those moments of the standoff with Gordon out of her mind. "I can't get used to calling Gordon, Antonio Martínez, so I'll just keep calling him Gordon. Please tell me there will be justice, finally, for Justin. Please tell me he'll be charged, and those other murderers will be tried and punished."

"They found the Penitente robe and hood in the trunk of Gordon's abandoned car. There was old blood and evidence of fresh blood on it. He may have killed a land agent in Santa Fe before he followed you to Chimayó. A waitress identified him, putting him at the scene. All I can promise is that we are doing everything in our power to put him away."

"You have notified Justin's family?"

"Yes. Sergeant Ortega took care of that himself."

"I intend to stop by his hometown to talk to his mother on my way home."

"You're driving?" he asked with surprise.

"I've decided I need to decompress. I hate flying, if you must know. I like the open road, and the rental car company agreed to let me make the one-way drop. New Mexico does something to you. I feel a little like Alice coming out of the rabbit hole. It is going to take me a few days to get back to real life."

"When are you leaving?"

"Molly is staying in Ojo Tres for awhile. She and Ann are bringing the car and my belongings to Santa Fe today. The white coats promise to release me by noon."

Sunny let her fingers trail along the little hairs on his arm, not looking at him. He had scarcely left her bedside since they admitted her for injuries and exhaustion.

"Sunny," he began, a faint color spreading over his face. "You know I have feelings for you, damn it."

"I know." She squeezed his hand. Despite Moira's usually correct opinion that men always say I think and never I feel," Rob surprised her by opening up about his personal life.

"I'm still not completely over my wife." He turned his head, struggling to find the words to continue. The gray eyes came up and held hers as if hoping for her understanding. "I just feel like I'm too old a cowboy to start another campfire."

"I know." Her thoughts wandered.

He touched her hand, getting her attention. "So will you say yes?"

"I'm sorry, say yes to what?"

"I said, I get to St. Louis once in a while. May I call you?"

"Call me, huh? You're going to call me?" She began to laugh wildly to his chagrin, unable to tell him the joke she shared with Moira. She finally managed, "Let me give you my card. If you'll just hand me my purse, bottom drawer of the nightstand." Waving off his question as to what was so damn funny, she dug out a business card and handed it to him.

Taking it as if he expected it to explode in his hand, he waited for her to stop grinning. When she didn't oblige, he took out his billfold and shoved the card into a plastic sleeve. "I'll call. I'll look you up, I promise."

Sunny held his image in the light of her incredible blue eyes and placed a silent bet with Moira.

Chapter Sixty-Seven

Epilogue—June, 2002

Sunny decided not to leave her seat for the intermission. Her son, Michael, home for a long weekend was looking handsome in his dark suit, but bored.

"You look like you could use a Coke. Aren't you enjoying this after all your mother and grandmother went through?"

"Hey, it's opera, Mom. I obviously didn't inherit the Bay arts genes. Mind?" he asked, standing.

"Run along." She shooed him.

Opera Theatre of St. Louis won out for the world premiere of Manzanares' work and the return of the long-lost diva. During the first intermission, Sumner and Molly were mingling with the glitterati and holding hands like honeymooners, and she soon lost track of them. Kay Waring was in her element, chatting up the cadre of out-of-town critics, dropping "adventurous" or "risk-taking" opera every chance she got.

As the hall emptied for second intermission, the departure of so many warm bodies all at once seemed to lower the temperature of the intimate Loretto Hilton theatre, and Sunny rubbed her bare arms to chase away the chill. Staying seated gave her the chance to come to terms with the set.

At the end of the second act a chorus of Penitente men had lifted the tall wooden crucifix into place to the eerie accompaniment of the flute-like pito. For a moment she had been unable to breathe. She knew from Molly that the last act would recreate the crucifixion of the young hero guilty only of illicit love, and she wasn't entirely sure of its effect on her even after these many months since the events of last Easter. To clear her mind she thumbed the program, amazed at Opal's photo, transformed once again into Garcella Klafsky. She would sing the finale. Sunny refused any credit for finding her and avoided coming to the theatre during rehearsal, opting instead for reviews from Molly. "Her voice doesn't have quite the technical range it once did," Molly explained. "But wait until you hear. Her voice is more stunning now because she sings some inner tragedy that's almost painful to hear, so much emotion."

Sunny tried not to think that Opal was singing solely for the money to help in Gordon's defense. But she had to admit she would do the same for her son, do anything for Michael.

She felt movement at her side and was amused.

"You're back? I half expected you to skip the rest."

The hand that reached for hers was not Michael's.

"You didn't tell me you had such a brilliant son. Your friend Max dropped me off and introduced me to Michael. He insisted I take his seat."

"Well, this is a surprise. What are you doing in St. Louis?"

"An assignment I took so I could see you, Sunny," Rob said, looking at her as if he had missed her a lot.

He was a little grayer than when she'd seen him last. She leaned toward him, but just out of kissing range. "Nice to see you too, cowboy."

"I've kept your card." He opened his billfold and pulled it out. "I called, but there was no answer. So I called Max, and— I promised I'd look you up, remember?"

Now she owed Moira twenty bucks.

CPSIA information can be obtained
at www.ICGtesting.com
Printed in the USA
FFHW020639160119
50158974-55070FF